THE HUNT

A Thrill of the Hunt Anthology

L.E. Perez
Kelly Abell
T.M. Witko
Susan Burdorf
J. Nicole Parkins
Laura Stapleton
L. Marshall James
Kristin Durfee
Miranda Nading
A.L. Awtrey

2

Table of Contents

Foreword

This time around I have the pleasure of writing the foreword for this wonderful anthology series. I am honored and beyond excited to speak a bit about it.

Thrill of the Hunt started as a thought and a hope that other authors would feel like I did and want to contribute a story for the reader but also for each other.

This second incarnation, titled **The Hunt**, is a blessing. Not just because it is another Thrill of the Hunt anthology but because even more writers answered the call this time around. This anthology is almost twice the size of the first and features ten authors in total. Amazing!

What's in it for them? Not what you would think. Exposure certainly and branching out into new genres and connecting with the readers of other authors, but also a chance to give back. All eBook proceeds will be donated to *St Jude's Children's Research Hospital*. Beyond that it is an opportunity for us to tell our stories and more than anything that is what every writer wants.

In that vein, the length of this book resulted in me cutting out the work of another author that I had planned on inserting. Snippets really of thrills and chills, 100 word shorts. I will include some here.

Buyer Beware

"She bought the place sight-unseen," my sister explained. "The agent said it was cheap because the previous owners had disappeared a year prior leaving everything behind, stressing the police had investigated and determined there was no foul play."

"When my sister said that," she continued, "I got a bad feeling, and said so, but she isn't one to listen to 'bad feelings'."

Now I wish I had. Lying bound and gagged under the closet floor I couldn't make a sound to tell her, or the cop she was talking to, that I was there and dying next to several corpses.

The Electrocutioner's Key

He owned the property, lived alone, and spoke to no one. So, had the trust fund that paid the taxes not been pilfered by the accountant no one would have known that Buchinsky had died.

The city wouldn't have auctioned the property. The new owners wouldn't have requested a survey. The surveyor wouldn't have run into the barn in a sudden thunderstorm. The petrified body of Buchinsky wouldn't have been found in the antique electric chair.

But if the key to the cellar hadn't been labeled, the bones from practicing his suicide on unsuspecting vagrants wouldn't have been discovered.

Melanie Greenwood-author, supporter, and avid reader

       My hope is that Melanie will contribute a longer story for the next incarnation. I'm sorry, didn't I mention? I'm hoping for a Thrill of the Hunt 3 (TOTH3)

       So, what are you waiting for? Turn the page, start reading and lose yourself in our stories. And, if you think about us at all, realize that reviews are extremely important for exposure so please leave a review. Even a few words help.

L.E. Perez, Author
Publisher @ Palmas Publishing
www.palmaspress.com

10

L.E. Perez

When They Call

By

L.E. Perez

L.E. Perez

Samantha Barry was clinically dead at the scene of a horrible motorcycle accident, when they called.

When she opened her eyes a week later, Sam quickly realized she wasn't alone. The idea of an afterlife was not something she had ever given a thought to but something or someone had hitched a ride back with her. As if that wasn't enough, she awoke to the sound of children crying. The crying didn't just haunt her, it hurt, whether she was awake or asleep.

Sam was losing her mind, at least that's what everyone thought, but she knew better. The children were calling her for a reason and she was dead set on finding out what she had tapped in to when she died.

What she discovers is beyond her comprehension and sets her on a path back to the night she died. If only she hadn't answered when they called.

L.E. Perez

Acknowledgements

A very special thank you to all of the authors participating in this second incarnation of the Thrill of the Hunt Anthology-The Hunt.

You have all inspired me to be a better writer and a better person. And, through it, have helped me achieve a dream, Palmas Publishing.

Special thank you as always to my partner in life for over 26 years. I can't do this without you.

I am grateful that through this minor endeavor we are able to donate all proceeds of e-book sales to St. Jude's Children's Research Hospital.

On to Book 3!

L.E. Perez

Prologue

Her life started the day she died.

Samantha Barry always enjoyed her ride home. There was nothing better in her opinion than riding her motorcycle at night when there were fewer cars on the road.

She'd worked the late shift and the highway after midnight felt serene with just a random vehicle here or there. The sting of the wind on her face always made her smile behind her kerchief. It was such a bright night, the moon lit up the pavement much better than the infrequent lamp posts lining the edge of the road.

She took a moment to breathe in the night air and revel in the freedom that riding her bike gave her and stole a glance at the moon. The sound of screeching tires snapped her eyes back to the road but it was too late.

The indescribable sound of the vehicles impacting one another was immediately drowned out by the cacophony of grinding metal and breaking glass. Only the explosion of the motorcycle's gas tank managed to muffle the sound.

Sam got a final glimpse of the moon as it welcomed her to its heights before the bone breaking smash onto the concrete and the skid into the jersey wall that finally stopped her forward momentum.

She never stood a chance.

****

Sounds filtered in brokenly. Hushed voices.
Beep...beep...hiss.
More voices, clearer now.
Beep...beep, beep...hiss.

Children...children's cries filled her senses as they ripped through her. She could feel their fear, their pain.

Beep...beep...hiss.

What were the sounds? Who were the children?

Sam struggled to open her eyes wanting to know but the glimmer of light in the darkness faded as quickly as it came and she succumbed to its blessed peace.

****

When Sam finally opened her eyes a week after the accident she couldn't move. Pain filled her consciousness as awareness filtered in. She stared at the ceiling panels trying to figure out where she was.

A hospital'

She was in a hospital. Wait, how did she know that?

'I told you.'

Confused, Sam tried to move her head but was greeted with a stabbing pain radiating from the base of her skull to her forehead.

'Stop! You need to relax'

A tear leaked from the corner of her eye. The pain was unbearable. The beeping sound in the room increased with every breath she took.

'I told you, relax, you're-'

She ignored the blinding pain and tried to move her head looking for the source of the voice.

'Samantha'

Panic was beginning to set in as she tried desperately to understand. Sam tried to call out but the tube down her throat prevented it.

The beeping was faster now as the sound of children crying grew louder in her head. The children cried for her, they needed her, she needed to get to them. But who were they?

'Just breathe, slowly, it'll be alright, I-"

The machine shifted from a beep to a shrill alarm as Sam went into cardiac arrest, the solitary voice echoing in her head.

-promise.'

L.E. Perez

Chapter One

"Are you sure you want to do this?"

Samantha Barry grabbed her beat up leather jacket and gave her mom a peck on the cheek.

"Yes I'm sure." Shrugging into it she picked up her pack. "I won't be gone long."

Biting her lower lip, Madeline Barry watched as her daughter finished lashing her pack to the back of her motorcycle. She hated seeing her leave. Her plan to travel down to Florida on a motorcycle terrified her.

Madeline had watched her daughter die twice less than a year ago after being hit by a drunk driver. The doctors had been amazed at her recovery, calling it nothing short of miraculous. The broken bones had healed after numerous surgeries and though the burns and road rash along one side of her body had resisted grafting, Sam wore her scars and limp with pride.

Madeline's concern was the head injury. The motorcycle helmet Sam had been wearing that night had absolutely saved her life. Unfortunately, the headaches and visions Sam now suffered from were something she had kept from her doctors, but she couldn't hide them from her mother.

Sam finished up and shivered in the cool air before she caught her mother watching her.

'She's worried about you.'

She gritted her teeth at the sudden pain in her head and gave her mother a hug.

"I promise I'll be back soon. Two weeks, tops."

She carefully threw one leg over the bike and settled in. Sam took a deep breath and set about the controlling the fear that threatened to overwhelm her whenever she got on her new bike. This one was nothing like the one she used to own. That one had been a crazy fast Ducati. This one was a comfortable cruiser, customized just for her.

Her injuries had been severe enough that her doctor had warned against riding again but she'd thrown every expectation out the window and written her own course.

Running a hand through her hair she smoothed it back before putting her helmet on. Her thick dark hair was kept at shoulder length now. After the accident, any vanity she'd had had been tossed out along with any peace she hoped to have.

The morning was cool but it promised to warm up as the day progressed and with her ride south, she knew she would be happy about the shorter hair in the warmer states. Pulling her gloves on she took a satisfying breath. She felt content and in control for the first time in almost a year

Sam started up her bike and reveled in the feel of it. The low rumble was soothing, like a lullaby for her soul. She caught her mother's eye and threw her a smile.

"Love you Mom."

"I love you too. Please call when you stop and don't forget to take a break if your leg-"

"Mom...I know, I won't push." Sam didn't have a choice about stopping but she wanted to put as many miles behind her as she could.

Without another word she pulled out of the driveway and headed out to face a destiny that had tortured her for over a year. With any luck, she would find some answers too.

****

'You need to pull over.'

"I'm fine." Sam could taste the lie on her tongue. Her right leg was throbbing, from her hip all the way to her ankle and her head felt like it was about to split.

24

When They Call
'There's no need to hurt yourself.'

She drove another 14 miles before she found a truck stop to pull into. She'd only been able to travel about one hundred miles.

'You're never going to make it this way Sam.'

She ignored the words and parked her bike. It took her a moment to maneuver the bike into the parking spot and by the time she got off she had to catch herself as her leg started to give out.

"Dammit." Reaching into her pack she pulled out the collapsible cane she kept on hand. There were adjustments she'd had to make over the past year and this one bothered her the most. She could tolerate the cries of the children that haunted her dreams better than she could her inability to be who she was before the accident.

Standing tall, she walked as well as she could, ignoring the sympathetic stares she got. Only one person didn't stare at her, which surprised her. The little girl pulled away from her mother and took her hand.

"I'm sorry miss."

"What?" Sam looked at the little girl in confusion.

"They don't mean to hurt you. They need you." The girl's whispered voice sent a chill up her spine.

"Emily! Leave the lady alone." The frazzled woman at the counter pulled the little girl away from Sam and yanked her toward the exit. "Go on now!"

Sam looked at her hand and at the little girl who had held it.

A slight cough snapped her out of her reverie.

"Ma'am?" The hostess stood there patiently.

"Yes, I'm sorry. One please." She let herself be seated before she let herself think about what had just happened.

"The children know."

Sam gritted her teeth determined not to answer.

"Let them guide you. Let me"

"Haven't I?"

"I sorry ma'am, haven't you what?" The waitress looked at her expectantly.

"Nothing I'm sorry, I'll have a cup of coffee and... She quickly perused the menu, "a western omelet please, light on the cheese."

"Sure, anything else?"

"No thanks." Sam watched as the waitress placed the order but not before looking back at her a time or two.

Sighing she pulled out her phone and texted her mother to let her know she was all right.

Digging around in her satchel she pulled out her notebook and skimmed through the observations she'd made in the past year. The children's cries had haunted her throughout most of her recovery. Sometimes they were just whimpers, barely heard for months at a time, but at other times the sound threatened to drive her mad.

She had tried to understand not just the children's cries but also the voice she had been hearing since she woke up after the accident. She couldn't tell if it was male or female or even if it was real or not.

Her mother knew there was more going on than she had let on but she couldn't really speak to anyone about this, not yet.

Sam couldn't stop the chuckle that escaped her. People get locked up for less.

Stretching out her leg she raised it and let it rest on her cane. It took the edge off while she looked at her notebook. Through her journaling, observations and research, she had been driven to go to Florida. And not just anywhere in Florida either, a little town called Cassadaga.

It didn't make any sense to her and much as she tried to understand what the cries meant, she couldn't. She hoped someone there would.

'We'll figure it out when we get there'

Squeezing her eyes tightly at the sudden pain the voice caused she took a shallow breath. That was the other problem. The voice.

I'm not a problem. I've always been here

"Yeah," she muttered. "Says you."

The slight cough made her look up and she looked sheepishly at the waitress who had once again caught her talking to herself.

"Miss?"

"Sorry." She moved her notebook so the girl could set her cup down and pour out her coffee, purposefully avoiding the odd looks she gave her. "Thank you."

Without another word she read through her notes and the information she had been able to find.

Her 'ability' as it were, was not unique. There were a lot of documented instances of people who had been clinically dead reporting hearing voices, though they were considered as being from the other side. She didn't necessarily believe in life after death and all that but there was definitely something going on that she couldn't quantify.

In another life she had been a police officer. That was before the accident. At twenty-four she was effectively retired from duty, on an extended medical leave of absence. She hated it. Her whole life all she wanted was to be a police officer and for all of that to end so abruptly…

"Gah!"

Sam shook her head and tried to distract herself. She pulled up the web on her phone and looked up her destination again. Cassadaga, Florida or as it was otherwise known, the Spiritualist Capital of the World. If any place would have answers for her it was there.

'Tomorrow'

She ignored the words and smiled up at the waitress as she set her plate down.

"Thank you." She tore into her food realizing only then that she had completely forgotten to eat earlier.

By the time she got settled back on the bike almost an hour later, her leg had stopped throbbing and she felt sated. She was still a bit apprehensive about where she was headed but she needed answers. By her calculation she would be pulling into Cassadaga safely sometime-

'Tomorrow morning'

"Oh shut up." She muttered.

Chapter Two

A flat tire slowed her down right outside of Savannah so by the time she pulled up outside the Cassadaga Hotel it was time to check in. She looked like crap and felt little better. Her head felt like it was splitting inside her helmet as she yanked it off, sweat flying everywhere. Her body hadn't fared much better. She had pushed herself and her stumble when she got off her bike reflected the level of her exhaustion.

"Whoa there." The hand that grabbed her by the elbow was dark and calloused and belonged to the middle aged man who had gotten out of his car next to her.

"Sorry." Sam shrugged off his help and grabbed the cane for support.

"Hey...just trying to help." He leaned against the driver side door and watched as she struggled with her pack.

Unbidden tears pricked at her eyes as she fought against a broken strap, her hands cramping and so slick with sweat she couldn't get a good grip.

"Do you need some help lady?"

"No."

'Yes'

Pain tore through her head and the added combination of heat and exhaustion overwhelmed her as she collapsed into the man who offered to help.

"Holy…" Matthew Pence caught her as she fell and swept her up in his arms. Even with leathers on she was light as a feather.

"Gabe! Gabriel!!" He rushed into the lobby and called out for the front desk manager before laying her down on the couch.

"Dammit Matt what the hell are you-" Gabriel Evers stopped cold when he stepped out of his office. "Who is that?"

"Hell if I know?" Matt looked down at the woman who was just beginning to stir. "Reservation?"

"There's a Sam Barry coming in today but I thought that was a guy. Shit."

He waited as the young woman opened her eyes.

"Miss? Are you okay?" He kept his deep voice gentle.

Sam took a deep breath. "I think so." She had definitely pushed herself to hard.

She found the other man and smiled at him. "Thank you."

"My pleasure little lady. You were looking a little green around the gills, I'm glad I stayed out there."

"Me too." With a tentative smile she swung her legs onto the floor and sat up. "It was a long ride."

'Yes it was'

"Hmmm." Gabe slapped the side of his jeans and extended a gloved hand. "I'm Gabe, Gabe Evers, and this is Matthew Pence. This is my hotel. And you are?"

"Sam," her lips quirked at his raised eyebrows, 'sorry, Samantha Barry."

"Our mysterious reservation."

"Mysterious?" Sam gratefully accepted the cup of cold water Matthew gave her and took a sip before looking back up at him.

"Mysterious. We don't usually have folks traipsing through here in the middle of August. You may not have noticed but it's hot as blazes out there." Pulling off his gloves he wiped the sweat off his forehead.

She took another sip of the cold water. "Oh, I noticed. A little too well I'm afraid. I'm sorry I showed up this way but would you mind if we continue this conversation a little later? I think some rest is in order." She moved to stand but was pushed back down.

"Let me go get your stuff first." Matthew didn't wait for her acknowledgement.

"Is he always like that?"

"No, but I think he likes you." Gabe tried not to notice the way she brushed the hair out of her eyes. She was breathtakingly pretty. He wondered about the scar on one side of her face that did nothing to detract from her beauty.

"So, what brings you to Cassadaga? Psychics, séances?"

I like him

Sam bit her lip.

"Research...I'm looking into something."

"Oh?" Gabe looked up her reservation and keyed the key card for her room. "Here you go, three nights correct?"

"Possibly more if that's okay?" She got up unsteadily and signed the paperwork he presented. She really had pushed herself. All she wanted was to take a hot bath, grab a bite to eat and get a good night's sleep.

"Here you go Miss." Grateful, Sam watched as Matthew brought in her pack and handed her the cane. "Thought you might be wanting this. Bad leg?"

"You could say that."

Sam grabbed the pack and slung it across her shoulder. "Thanks for your help."

Grabbing her cane, she turned back to Gabe. "Elevator?"

"Sorry no," He couldn't help but glance at the cane. "Listen, I can switch you to a room on the first floor."

Sam turned away. "No. No thank you."

31

Both men watched as she limped away and waited until they heard her footfalls on the far stairs.

Matthew let out a long whistle.

"Well...she's not from around here, that's for sure."

"Hmm." Gabe looked down at the address on her registration. "Alexandria, Virginia. Wonder why she's here?"

"If anyone can find out, you can Gabe."

"I don't do that anymore Matt."

"Uh huh...Oh, here." Matt pulled a crumpled letter out of his back pocket. "Miriam wants a word with you."

"She could've called." Miriam West ran the diner down the street among other things.

"You know she's old school, likes writing notes."

"Damn." Gabe glared at him as he left. Tossing the letter on the front desk he went back to his newspaper. It didn't take long before curiosity got the better of him and he pulled out Sam's information again.

"What are you doing in Cassadaga Samantha Barry?"

Chapter Three

Sam threw herself onto the bed the minute she walked into her hotel room. What the hell was she doing here? She rolled over onto her back and groaned. The cries had started again just as she crossed into Florida and it was costing her to stay focused.

'Sleep'

"Stop it!" Grabbing her head, she couldn't stop the tears. The pain was unbearable of late and the temptation to abuse the pain meds she had was something she had to fight more and more.

Her hands shook as she wiped away her tears. She had driven all this way because she couldn't take it anymore. She had set up an appointment for a reading tomorrow so she could begin to figure everything out and hopefully control the voice and the cries.

Pulling her bag over she took out her toiletries and fresh clothes. The wonderful smells from the hotel restaurant were making her stomach rumble and all she wanted for the evening was to freshen up and get something to eat.

****

Gabe knocked on the door and waited. The sound of the shower running made him smile but he quickly stopped himself. Miriam's note had been more for his guest than him. Apparently she had an appointment the next day with Miriam herself for a reading and now he had questions.

He'd done his best to tame his curiosity but it had gotten the better of him and now here he was.

Hand raised to knock again he took a step back when the door swung open.

Water dripped on the floor as a very wet and frazzled Samantha Barry answered the door.

With a nervous swallow, he watched as she fought to keep the large towel wrapped around her.

"Yes?"

It took him a moment to realize he was staring, "I... There is a message for you from Ms. Miriam about your appointment tomorrow."

Sam smiled at his stutter and tilted her head for him to continue.

"Uhm...I left the letter at the front desk." Idiot, he thought. He was so intent on questioning her he forgot to bring the reason he was there.

"I'll be down in about fifteen minutes."

"Sure, sure." He cursed at himself when she closed the door.

What the hell had he been thinking? Closing his eyes, he could still see her standing there. There were more scars evident on the exposed parts of her body but just like the one on her face they did not detract from the beauty he had just been exposed to. The confidant way she had stared him down even as she tried to hold the towel around her had made him feel something he hadn't felt in some time. Desire.

****

Sam chuckled to herself as she closed the door. It had been a long time since anyone had looked at her like that. It had taken time but she wasn't ashamed of her scars and if he could look at her like that...

'You need to stay focused'

She ignored the familiar stab of pain and got dressed. It wasn't until she headed down that the cries started again.

"Why Cassadaga? Couldn't you see someone up north?"

Sam stopped in her tracks as Gabe blurted out the accusing question. Ignoring him she held out her hand and waited for him to hand her the note.

"What, no answer?"

Her head was already pounding and now she was furious. Who the hell was this stranger to tell her what she needed. He hadn't lived her life for the past year.

"I'm not sure what you're talking about."

"That note in your hand is from one of the most well-known spiritualists in the country. She doesn't do readings for just anyone."

Sam ignored him as she read the note and breathed a sigh of relief. When she heard who the note was from she had feared that her trip would be for nothing.

"Well?" Gabe was on a roll and he had no idea why.

Furious Sam shook her head. "You don't understand; no one could help me. All they wanted was my money." Her voice rose with every breath. "I need the crying to stop. I need this voice in my head to stop!"

'Breathe'

"Shut up! God…" She fell against him as pain ripped through her skull. It was getting worse and unless she was able to stop it or control it somehow she knew she would not survive it.

Gabe fought his instincts against self-preservation and held her tight his cheek resting against her head.

Her pain became his and as he felt her relax against him he clenched his teeth against the wave of pain he absorbed from her. It almost knocked him to his knees.

"I'm sorry." He whispered absently.

35

Sam felt the pain melt away and looked up at him in astonishment.

"How?" She felt euphoric without the pain. "How did you do that?" Her words were a whisper. For the first time since waking up after the accident Sam felt like herself again. She had no idea how he had done it but somehow he had taken on her pain.

The deep lines etched on his face eased as he released his hold on her.

"Sorry." His tone was gruff and as he took a step back from her, Sam could only stare.

Sam watched as he walked behind the counter and grabbed a bottle of water from the mini-fridge. Without another glance at her he downed it in two swallows.

"Please." She didn't know what else to say.

"I'm one of Cassadaga's oddities, an empath and psychic."

"You're not an oddity." Swallowing thickly, she tried to process what had happened but it just confused her and made her just a bit angry.

"You understand don't you? You know what's happening to me. What did happen to me after the accident."

Her impassioned and accusatory words struck him. Coming back around the counter he took her by the hand and led her to the couch. She needed whatever answers he could give her.

"The voice, the one in your head, it's a part of you now." Before she could object he continued.

"You died didn't you?"

Sam's breath caught in her chest. How could he know that?

"Don't say it." He said. "I can see the answer in your face. It doesn't happen to everyone, but some who die and 'cross over' for lack of a better term touch something on the other side and when you come back, something is woken up. That voice you hear is you, just a different version of you, more in tune. I like to think of it as your inner self."

"So I'm talking to myself?" Her words dripped with sarcasm. He was so serious about what he was saying. Disbelief drove her to her feet.

"Why the pain, the headaches?" She could just feel the ache starting again.

"You're fighting it. Just let it be."

"But-"

"The crying is something different." He struggled to find the words to explain and started pacing. "The crying, is it constant, at least since your...uhm...accident?"

'Let him help'

Teeth clenched she let herself hear it without fighting it. Nope, still hurt.

'Just listen to him'

"Sam... Samantha." Gabe was forced to shake her by the shoulder when she froze in front of him.

"What happened?"

Sam dropped onto the couch and buried her head in her hands. "This is all too crazy."

He pulled up a chair and faced her. "It may well be but you came here for a reason. I may not be in the business anymore but let me help. What have you got to lose?"

Sam felt physically and emotionally drained. The cries started affecting her physically just a few weeks ago. Whenever the cries intensified she suffered severe vertigo and nausea. Before that it was more a nuisance than anything else. Research had led her to several psychics, one of them had led her here.

"How?" She looked at him with tortured eyes. "How can you help?"

"Let me go with you." Her surprised look spurred him to continue. "The voice is a positive, whether you believe right now or not. The cries though...I'm not too sure. I've never heard of anyone experiencing both. One or the other, yeah, but both..."

"So what happens to the folks who hear the cries?" She could sense his hesitation and it sent a chill up her spine.

"They don't last a year."

Chapter Four

Sam stared at the ceiling of her hotel room trying to process all of the information that Gabe had been able to provide.

According to him, the folks they had record of who had been afflicted with the cries had all either died under mysterious circumstances or committed suicide. The only survivor that he knew of personally was Miriam West herself. Miriam had been sixteen when she was struck by lightning and had been dead for over three minutes before she was brought back but not without something hitching a ride.

Miriam's family had tried to commit her after a failed suicide attempt shortly thereafter.

She'd never told anyone in her family what was going on and had just run away from her home in Jacksonville eventually ending up in Cassadaga.

The story according to Gabe was that she had fought whatever had hitched a ride and won.

Gabe promised to go with her to see Miriam.

Before getting her something to eat and walking her back to her room he had made a point of taking her hand again, effectively easing the pain that kept her up most nights.

She couldn't sleep though. The analytical side of her wanted to dismiss it all as bull, but she knew. In the deep recesses of her soul she knew she was on the losing side of this battle if she didn't accept help.

'It's about time'

"Oh shut up." She muttered.

Rolling over she reached for her journal. She didn't know what would happen tomorrow but she knew enough to trust her instincts so she started writing.

Dear Mom...

****

Gabe looked down at his hands and flexed them. He had forgotten how good it felt to help someone. Unfortunately, he had also forgotten how much it could hurt to absorb someone else's pain.

The wave of pain he had taken in from her had scared him. He never believed it was possible to be in control of so much pain and the thought that Sam had been managing it for almost a year blew his mind.

He smiled at the thought of her. She was tough and different from anyone he had met since the discovery of his powers and his move to Cassadaga.

Sam had surprised him with her openness once he had explained what he knew. And while he still couldn't quite picture her as a police officer he understood the impact of the accident on her. She was looking for answers but she was also looking for purpose, something he understood all too well.

The most astonishing thing to him had been the extent of her injuries. It shouldn't have been possible for anyone to survive an accident like that. But she had, with terrifying consequences. The fact that she had brought the cries back with her scared him. But she had an inner ally that she was only now beginning to accept.

He truly hoped Miriam would be able to help her.

Before saying goodnight he'd asked her if he could hold her hand and when she had allowed him to he had made a point of absorbing as much of her pain as he could. Her gratitude had shown on her face when they had finally parted ways.

Something about her had touched him. As an empath he was able to get a read on people but with her there was a significant difference. There was a light in her that shone through the pain. It was a light he had heard about but never touched until now. She was special but what would happen when the cries got louder, what would happen when they called?

L.E. Perez

Chapter Five

What should have been a good night's sleep, was anything but.

The cries haunted Sam throughout the night, mingling with whispered voices similar to when she had woken after her accident. They didn't sound very much like children anymore.

By the time she was able to drag her tired broken body out of bed it was already after nine.

'Wakey, wakey'

The pain that hit with those words was bearable now but the sound of the cries was non-stop now playing like a bad song. Try as she might, she couldn't drown them out and as soon as she thought that she might be feeling sick, she was, barely making it into the bathroom to get rid of what remained of last night's meal.

"Ugh…" She rinsed out her mouth and brushed her teeth. The throwing up was new. She felt more unsteady than usual. Things felt different. She felt different.

She glanced at herself in in the mirror. She still hadn't regained all of the weight she'd lost during her recovery but she hadn't lost any of her spark. Each scar on her body told the story of the accident. The road rash scars, the burn scars, the surgical scars. They were all healed. She hoped this Miriam West could heal the rest of her.

****

"Yo Gabe!" Matthew knocked on the front counter and went around to the closed door when he didn't get an answer.

Knocking briskly, "Gabe?" It wasn't like his friend to not be up and about.

The Gabe that answered the door was someone he barely recognized.

"Damn boy, you look like crap."

Matt's laughter echoed in Gabe's head. He felt like he had a hangover and apparently he looked like he did too.

"Shut up Matt and make me a cup of coffee." He headed back into his small apartment to change. Last night had been rough. His empathic abilities fed off him so the more he used them the more he needed to replenish himself and he hadn't. Sometime in the night he had drunk a half gallon of orange juice and he still felt awful, the vestiges of Sam's pain mixed in with his exhaustion.

Matt peppered him with questions as soon as he came back out.

"So, what's up with the mystery lady? What did Miriam have to say? Did she tell you anything about that limp of hers? Why is she here?"

Ignoring him he drank some of the coffee Matt had made. "Yuck!" Awful as usual.

"Look, we talked okay? And yes I'm going to try and help her out but anything else you'll have to find out from her."

"Aww, come on G-"

"No." He looked at his watch. "She should be down in a few, leave her alone okay?" His tone softened when he referred to her.

Matt took notice of how he referred to her and gave his friend a broad smile. Gabe liked her and that was good enough for him.

"No problem, scout's honor." Hand raised in a three finger salute he brought it down quickly when he heard the voice of the lady in question.

****

"Hello?" She tapped the bell on the counter and took a step back when Matt appeared instead of Gabe.

"Hey there little lady, feeling better?"

"Yes, thank you, is Gabe in?" She tried to peek around him with no success.

"He is. He's getting respectable." Matt came around the desk and offered his arm. "Shall we wait?"

Sam gave him a small laugh. The cries were intense now almost like they knew she was trying to find answers. Foregoing the cane, she relied on his arm to escort her to the couch.

They sat for just ten minutes before Gabe rushed out.

"Hey, sorry I'm late."

"You're not, I'm just anxious. I couldn't stay in the room any longer."

"Well, Miriam should be in. Your appointment isn't for another hour but I'm sure she wouldn't mind seeing you earlier."

"I was hoping you'd say that."

She clenched her teeth as she stood. The cries felt like frantic fingernails on a chalkboard now.

"You okay?" Gabe couldn't hide his concern, not giving a damn that Matt was there to witness it.

Sam shook her head. "No, it's getting worse. What if...?

"Nope, no what ifs. Think positive remember?"

They both smiled knowingly at one another oblivious to the fact that they weren't alone.

"Well, you two run along then. I've got the hotel covered till you get back." It wasn't the first time he'd covered for Gabe but he had been surprised to get a call so late last night. Regardless, he would be here when they got back with a heck of a lot more questions.

Chapter Six

YOU NEED TO ANSWER WHEN THEY CALL

The sign outside Miriam West's home didn't make any sense to Sam but it obviously meant something to the woman she was about to see considering its prominence in front of her home.

The brightly colored cottage was located just a few hundred feet from the diner she ran. There was all manner of talismans located on the property but what stood out the most was definitely the sign.

Gabe never got a chance to ring the doorbell before the door was whipped open. The woman who greeted them smiled knowingly before waving them in.

"Come in, come in. Hello Gabriel you're looking well."

"Hey Miriam, this is Sam."

"Yes, yes, I know, Samantha Barry. Your email was a bit cryptic but the referral was sound." She pushed them both toward the flowered couch against the far wall.

"Sit, sit. I'll get us some tea and we can talk a bit."

Sam watched her leave and couldn't suppress a shiver.

'Get out'

"What's wrong?" Gabe saw the change in her as soon as she sat down.

'Get out now'

Fingers pressed against her temples Sam rocked back and forth as the pain intensified. The cries were drowning out any sound and she could only stare at him.

"Sam…?"

47

L.E. Perez

"We have to get out." She lurched to her feet and headed for the door on shaky legs.

Tearing the door open she walked as quickly as she could back toward the hotel. She caught some of Gabe's apology to Miriam but she didn't care. She needed to get away from there as soon as possible. She'd almost made it to the door when Gabe caught up.

"What the hell was that about?" He grabbed her roughly by the shoulders and forced him to look at him. She was white as a sheet.

He looked up and down the street and made a decision. Taking her by the elbow he steered her toward his car. Getting her settled, he jogged around to the driver's side and got in.

"Where are we going?" Her voice was laced with pain.

"Anywhere but here." Putting the car into gear, he drove. Straight out of town and down the road. He drove for ten minutes before pulling over.

When she reached over and grabbed his hand, he knew that the pain had become unbearable and he allowed her to share it with him.

It was a few minutes before either of them could speak.

"She can't help me." Sam's voice was hoarse. She didn't know what had happened but when she stepped into that house it had all clicked.

"What do you mean, I thought-"

"We thought wrong." She didn't know how to explain what she knew. Not just what she suspected, but what she knew with absolute truth.

He had no response to that so he let her continue.

She took a deep shaky breath. The ringing cries in her head had enveloped her when she walked in that

48

house. They were there as well and what she had finally figured out was that there was a very good reason Miriam was the only one known to survive the cries. She fed them.

When they called, she fed them. The voice in her head was exactly what Gabe had said, a gift. But even it had been fooled initially until the moment Sam had walked into that woman's house.

"She survived those cries by giving them others, people like me looking for help. That's why she's so 'well renowned' and so selective."

Gabe had to laugh. "You're crazy."

"Am I? It got worse the closer I got and when I went in there my little subconscious friend spoke to me quite clearly. It said get out. The moment I acknowledged it the cries got worse. I don't even know how to explain what I felt in there Gabe...I... I felt like I was dying."

Gabe tried to process what she was saying. It was crazy, right? There was no way it could be true, and yet...Miriam's history was shrouded in wild stories. It was hard to know what was true or not. Add in the fact that Miriam was the one who had encouraged him not to use his abilities when they would obviously help those suffering like Sam was. Was it possible?

"You don't believe me." She said flatly. "You know what, I don't care. Take me back. I need to get the hell away from here."

His touch was already wearing off and the proximity to Cassadaga was not making her condition any better. On the contrary, she felt worse than she had ever felt, even after the accident.

'Let him help'

"You can't leave until you get your answers." He was trying to understand and her inner voice's warning was doing more to convince him.

49

'Together, you can do it together.'

Sam closed her eyes against the dull ache. This couldn't be real.

'You can't let her continue to hurt people'

"I don't care. It hurts too much." Her words directed internally and externally.

"Dammit Sam let me help. If what you believe is true…"

Sam took a deep breath. He was right. She couldn't let what she believed to be happening to continue.

"We need to confront her. I need to confront her but…I'm going to need your help."

Gabe knew exactly what she meant and he promised to be there every step of the way. Cassadaga was his home and he refused to let anyone take away from all the good it's done.

Chapter Seven

Gabe had given Miriam a call apologizing for their abrupt departure and had arranged for another meeting later that afternoon.

By the time they were on their way, Matt had been enlisted to help as well. He knew a lot more about Miriam's history and had told them what he knew including some of the rumors that had circulated in the past about her.

"The cries are going to be intense, you know that." Gabe was worried and scared.

"I know. I'm trusting you and that little nagging voice to keep me tethered. I'm guessing that she overcomes folks when they succumb to the cries. I'm not about to do that." Now that she knew what she was facing, she felt better. Win or lose, the cries would end today.

'You may lose'

"And I may not." Gabe's puzzled look made her laugh. "Sorry, talking to myself remember?"

He shook his head; she was entirely to calm about it all.

"I'm not you know...calm that is." Sam touched his arm and smiled. "See, I'm finally listening."

"I see that."

"It's my only advantage."

"Not your only one." He extended a hand which she took gratefully and squeezed as the cries picked up again.

"No, not my only one." She grabbed her cane and headed for the door. "We really need to talk after this if-"

"No, no ifs remember? Think positive"

****

51

Miriam West lit her candles and waited. Samantha Barry had become known to her almost a year ago when the cries had started again. The cries and voices gave her no option. Samantha Barry had to give herself to them.

"You have to answer when they call, you have to answer when they call. Oh my, my, you have to answer when they call." Her singsong was familiar to anyone who visited the diner. Only she had ever understood the meaning and only she ever would.

****

Sam rang the doorbell and held her breath. She understood the sign outside Miriam's house now. She had to answer, but with what? She smiled when Gabe gave her hand a squeeze. Miriam had seemed surprised that Gabe would be accompanying her again but had taken it in stride.

The door swept open.

"Samantha my dear, are you feeling better?"

Gabe had apparently told the woman that she was on some medication that wasn't agreeing with her. She still didn't know how she felt about that but at least he had told Miriam something plausible.

"Yes, yes I am. I'm sorry about what happened earlier." Sam let herself be led in and shuddered internally when the woman took her by the hand.

"No worries dear. Why don't we have some tea and then we can do that reading you came all this way for." She stopped at the door to the kitchen. "Would you like some tea as well Gabriel?"

"Yes ma'am, thank you."

As soon as she left the room Sam let out the breath she had been holding. Being in this house was

52

overwhelming, the cries seemed to increase exponentially. Gabe took her hand for a moment to ease her torment.

"Thank you." She whispered.

"Here we go." Miriam put the tray down and grabbed her cup. "So, are you fully recovered from your accident dear?"

Surprised at the immediate change in direction, Sam reached absently for her cup and took a sip.

'Don't'

She immediately stopped and tried to catch Gabe's eye. He stopped before drinking anything.

Sam put her cup down and smiled at the woman sitting across from her. She ignored the bead of sweat that ran down her face.

Miriam West assessed the young woman in front of her. She had taken a sip which should be enough for her purposes but Gabriel had not. They knew. They knew about the cries. Eyes narrowed, she pasted a smile on her face.

"So, are you ready for your reading dear?"

"Actually would you mind very much if I asked you some questions?" Sam felt herself weave in her seat. There had been something in the tea.

Miriam stood up and glanced at the door. When the two locks fell in place she smiled brightly at them.

"What do you want to know?"

Sam closed her eyes as the words washed the cries over her.

"Sam... Sam!" Gabe grabbed her by the hand trying to ward off what was happening to her.

'Open your eyes!'

Her eyes snapped open in time to see Miriam smash her cane into the back of Gabe's head. She glared at Miriam even as the cries intensified.

"You should have come sooner dear. I might have been able to help you."

Miriam's laughter echoed in her head mixing with the cries. Sam pushed herself off the couch and caught herself as her head spun.

"You really should have just drunk the tea dear it would have made everything so much easier."

Sam's head was spinning. When Miriam grabbed her by the hand her mind exploded. The cries became screams.

'Fight Sam, fight!

"Let me go!"

Miriam's hysterical laughter echoed in her head.

She swung at the older woman and was rewarded with a palm to the chest that robbed her of breath.

"You need to answer when they call, didn't you know?"

"What do they want?" She screamed.

"They want a soul dear. They've always wanted a soul. I made a deal with them so I make sure to answer when they call. You all always find your way to me so I give them you."

Miriam pulled her over to the table covered in candles. "Ready for your reading dear?"

Sam's wobbly legs were barely holding her up and Gabe was just beginning to stir. She felt herself weakening as Miriam spoke in a language she didn't recognize and poured hot wax into Sam's palm.

'Samantha!'

Sam yanked her hand back and flung the candles on the table at their mistress. The tablecloth and her clothing catching fire. Miriam's screams drowned out the cries in her head. Stumbling over a fallen chair she reached Gabe and fell to her knees.

"Gabe...Gabriel..." Coughing she looked back at the spreading fire. Miriam had fallen by table and was still rolling trying to put out her clothes. Black dots marked her vision as cries called to them both. They were calling.

'NO... Sam eyes open.'

"I can't anymore..." Her strength was abandoning her. "I'm tired"

'Sam! You can't give in or she wins. You can't...'

"Sam?" Gabe groaned as he rubbed the back of his head.

Smoke...

"SAM!" He found her lying unconscious next to him. The room was full of smoke, flames across the room flared from a body by the table. Miriam.

"Dammit Sam." He couldn't tell if she was breathing. Throwing her over his shoulder in a fireman's carry he tried the front door but it locked. Without a thought he kicked at the door until it gave.

He could hear the fire truck in the distance but his focus lay in front of him.

"Dammit Sam." He started CPR when he realized she wasn't breathing.

"Don't die on me Sam, please don't die on me."

L.E. Perez

Chapter Eight

'Samantha...Sam'

Sam opened her eyes and looked around the room. Hospital again.

"Ugh"

"Sam?" Gabe scrambled out of the chair he had fallen asleep in.

"Water, please." Her throat felt raw. She sipped from the straw he put in her mouth and gave him a small smile. "Thanks."

"How are you feeling?"

"I don't know," she whispered. "How am I supposed to be feeling?"

"You were dosed with Rohypnol, suffered smoke inhalation and scared the crap out of me when you stopped breathing."

"Oh, sorry. Miriam?"

"Dead...the cries?"

Sam thought about it.

'They're gone. They needed to be freed. She had corrupted them.'

"Gone" Her tone was wistful. Her body felt like it had been through the wringer but she had survived. "Guess I'll be going home soon."

"Yeah." Gabe patted her hand and scratched absently at the stitches on the back of his head. Things were going to be ugly for a while at home and he didn't care. All he wanted was for Sam to stay.

'He wants you to stay.'

Sam smiled. "I know."

"You know what?"

"Nothing, nothing...do you mind if I stay for a while? I could use a vacation."

He smiled and gave her a tender kiss.

"We both can."

About the Author

L.E. Perez, also known as Laura E Perez, lives in Orlando, Florida and writes the stories that need to be written, be they romance, thriller, suspense, urban fantasy, or paranormal. When she first proposed this anthology she didn't think she would get a response. Well, she did and with its second incarnation, she hopes to find newer audiences for all of the authors who are participating.

Check out her website at: www.leperez.com

You can follow her on Facebook:
www.facebook.com/lepereznovelreads
Twitter: www.twitter.com/honorcpt
Instagram: www.instagram.com/leperezauthor
Wattpad: www.wattpad.com/lauraperez127
Goodreads:
https://www.goodreads.com/author/show/6879107.L_E_Pe
rez

L.E. Perez

60

Kelly Abell
Text Copyright © 2016 Kelly Abell

Monster in the Woods

While attempting to escape a wicked summer lightning storm in the Appalachian Mountains, seventeen-year-old Graham Sawyer stumbles on an abandoned hunting cabin. But nothing could have prepared him for what's inside. His first instinct is to back out the way he came, try to forget he ever found the place. But he hesitates. And it's that hesitation that changes his life forever.

Running on adrenaline and survival instinct, he's forced to make decisions he's never dreamed of. A monster roams this forest, torturing the innocent. Question is, can Graham turn the tables, changing the hunter into the hunted? All he knows for sure is what he can't handle with his wits, he'll trust to his bow and arrows.

Who's the monster now?

Kelly Abell

Monster in the Woods

BY

Kelly Abell

Acknowledgements

A project like this does not come together without the work of many people. I'd like to thank all the authors in this anthology. You've all been a joy to work with.

Thanks to Lisa Guertin for being such a loyal and accurate proof reader. Your help is so appreciated as always.

I'd also like to thank the staff of Adventures Archery in Riverview, FL for the information about bows, arrows and the lessons on how to shoot accurately. I think I've found a new hobby.

For my husband of 30+ years thanks for always supporting my writing. Much love to you, my dear.

To my readers...without you, I couldn't do what I love. Thank you from the bottom of my heart. Enjoy Monster in the Woods.

Graham wrapped his thin foam pillow over his head and around his ears to shut out the sound. His mother and her boyfriend of the week were going at it in her bedroom down the hall. Even though his room was located on the opposite end of the trailer, the paper-thin walls did nothing to prevent the noises of their love making from reaching his ears. He seriously needed to invest in some industrial-strength earplugs. The kind those guys wore on the gun range. He could use his phone, but falling asleep to music always gave him nightmares.

His mother's surprised expression had greeted him when he came home just after sunset. She and *Roy,* the man who sat pawing her on the sofa, had just finished a pizza, leaving him none of course. The empty box and beer cans littered the cheap coffee table.

"I didn't think you'd be home tonight," his mother said in her raspy smoker's voice. He'd never noticed before just how old she looked, but in the harsh florescent light of the overhead ceiling fan, her face appeared tired and worn, her dull black hair streaked with gray. Heavy makeup on her face and around her eyes settled into the wrinkles, only further emphasizing them instead of covering them up. She looked closer to fifty than thirty-eight years old, which she'd just turned on her last birthday. Life as a waitress at a bar could wear you down, he guessed. How men still found her attractive puzzled him. But, apparently, they did because the evidence sat on the couch, a large meaty hand resting on his mother's thigh.

He'd shrugged, not acknowledging the bald, overweight man wearing nothing but his boxers.

"Hadn't planned on it. It's going to storm." Opening the fridge, he pulled out a soda and the package of bologna. After making a sandwich and grabbing the stale chips off the

69

counter, he'd retreated to his room to watch TV. Thank God for satellite television, the one thing his mother managed to always pay for on time. He'd watched his favorite survival shows until he'd fallen asleep only to wake up to the symphony of grunts, moans, and shouts of ecstasy coming from the other end of the trailer.

Thunder rumbled across the nighttime sky and lightning flashed through the slits in the window blinds. If he hadn't smelled the storm coming, he wouldn't be here cocooned in his pillow. Instead, he'd be camping under the stars in the national forest surrounding the trailer his mother managed to rent from Neal, the guy who owned the bar where she worked.

Graham liked Neal. He'd gotten Graham interested in survival skills. A former marine, Neal shared his battle stories with him while he ate a grilled cheese after school in the bar. The closest thing to a father Graham ever had, Neal taught him how to camp in the woods with only a knife and a bow. He'd been hooked on learning to survive in the wild from the first time he snared a rabbit, skinned it, and cooked it over an open fire he'd started with dried moss and a flint stone.

To Graham's way of thinking, a real man did those things. The fact he'd been too thin to play football, too short for basketball, or too scrawny to wrestle didn't bother him. Surviving a week in the woods with only wits and a few essential items tested the fortitude of a man, and he'd done it. Many times. After graduation, he wanted to audition for one of the survival shows he watched on TV. Especially the ones who paid serious money if you lasted the entire time. Afterward, he'd use his good grades and go to college. Get a degree in something useful which would take him far away from this God-forsaken mobile home in the backwoods of Kentucky.

In a few months, he'd turn eighteen and he could do whatever he wanted. His mother didn't much care, though. He'd been on his own most of his entire life. Neal thought him crazy for wanting to do one of those shows. He thought he should go on to college. There'd be plenty of time after he graduated. But Graham had a plan for his future. He had no doubt, once he auditioned, the producers would be so blown away by his skills at such a young age they'd scramble over each other to have him on their shows.

He sighed, pulling the pillow tighter around his ears. *Christ, how long can two people have sex?* He rolled over, marveling at his mother's stamina. From the looks of Roy, he doubted he'd be able to keep up. He prayed the guy didn't have a heart attack.

****

Graham woke to the watery light of morning. He glanced at his clock which blinked 12:00 AM. *Damn, we lost power again.* Nothing new, considering the power lines leading out to this desolate land were ancient. Graham and his mother were lucky to have any power at all during the hottest months of the summer. Every storm that rolled through knocked down the powerlines, and the crews were unable to reach them for days. Neal had even bought them a generator to keep the air conditioning running, but his mother always forgot to buy gas for it while in town. This forced Graham to spend most of his summers in the woods. The moss-covered ground remained cool under the shade of the oaks, maples, and evergreens, which beat sweating to death in the oven of a trailer he lived in.

He rose, grabbing a change of clothes from the tiny dresser built into his closet. He hustled to the bathroom just outside his mother's bedroom door. He didn't feel the least

71

bit sorry about waking them at the crack of dawn with the noisy shower. After all, they'd kept him up until the wee hours of morning with their racket.

He showered, shaved, and brushed his teeth. He pulled on a pair of faded blue jeans, a white T-shirt, followed by a light-cotton, long sleeve, button-down shirt. He rolled up his sleeves, thinking about the 90 degree heat forecast for the week. Unusually hot for June, which would explain the rash of thunderstorms. Some had been violently strong with torrents of rain lasting for hours. No worries, though. He had a favorite cave he crawled into when he felt a storm coming.

He took a last glance in the mirror, running fingers through his damp, light-brown hair. His pale-blue eyes were bloodshot, a result of his lack of sleep. He really needed a haircut, but it would have to wait until pay day. His part-time job working for Neal didn't start for a week yet. The good man always gave him a week after school let out for the summer to take an extended camping trip before he settled into his job as a back bar attendant at the Smokin' Dawg.

On his way out of the bathroom, he grabbed a few toiletries to ease his camping trip. Nothing felt better than a good tooth brushing after a day or two in the wild. He'd have to get used to chewing roots, though. Those shows would never allow him to take a toothbrush and toothpaste with him. In his bedroom, he packed what he would need for seven days in his backpack. Neal had taught him how to fold his clothes military style so they would fit in the smallest space possible. On top of the clothes, he tossed in what he'd grabbed from the bathroom, his Bowie knife, and several pairs of socks. Not feeling like roughing it too much, he grabbed the roll of duct tape from his nightstand and tossed it into the pack as well.

Graham left his room. He sat in one of the worn out recliners, tying his boots. His mother emerged from her bedroom, makeup smeared under her eyes, hair a rat's nest of tangles.

"You're off, then?" She reached into the cabinet for the coffee canister.

"Yep. Be home in a week."

"I wish you wouldn't do these camping trips, Graham. I'm afraid you're gonna get eaten by a bear or somethin'."

He snorted. "You don't give me a minute's thought. You've got your latest *flavor of the week* to keep you company."

"Shut up. Roy'll hear you."

"Anyone in Grady's Lake who doesn't know you're the town slut by now must be deaf, dumb, and blind, or new. Where'd this guy come from? Just passin' through?"

She reached him in three strides and slapped him across the face. "I may not be no pillar of society, but I am still your mother, and you will not speak to me that way."

Graham rubbed his cheek involuntarily. Her treatment of him no longer hurt his feelings. It just pissed him off. He picked up his pack, grabbed his bow along with an extra quiver of arrows, and wrenched open the door. He glanced over his shoulder at her. "One of these days, one of these men you bring home is gonna kill you, Mama. Neal, although God only knows why, would marry you and take care of you. Why don't you let him?"

Her hand moved to rest at her throat. Yeah, she remembered the night Graham had come home to find Arthur, a man she'd picked up at the bar, on top of her, his hands wrapped around her neck squeezing the life out of her. Had Graham not come home when he did, she'd be dead. He'd shot the man between the shoulder blades with an arrow without a moment's hesitation. The sheriff hadn't arrested him after his mother begged him not to. Being one of her previous lovers, he'd agreed. They threw Arthur in the county lock up for attempted murder, and, as far as Graham knew, he remained there.

When his mother didn't respond, he exited the trailer, slamming the loosely bolted screen door behind him.

****

Graham rode his bike down the dirt road from the trailer the five miles it took to get to the edge of the national forest. It never ceased to amaze him how many trees managed to crowd themselves into the acreage in the woods. The sun barely trickled through the thick canopy of leaves, and the branches nearly intertwined where they hung over the deeply potholed road.

He turned off onto a narrower path covered with pine needles. He slid to a stop at the entrance of one of the many popular hiking trails. Dismounting his bike, he chained it to a post left for hikers and filled in the log. He'd stay on the trail for about two miles then wander off to see what he could see. In his mind, only sissies took the trail. A true woodsman could survive anywhere.

A week ago, he'd found an old logging road he wanted to follow to see where it ended up. The logging trucks no longer rumbled through these woods, but the men who worked the old camps had left a number of interesting things behind. He'd follow the road for a while, work his way to the lake, catch a few fish for dinner, then take them to his cave. Satisfied with the plan, he hitched his pack onto his shoulder and started off.

He reached the lake about two hours later, dropping his pack on the sandy soil. He breathed in deeply, the odor of summer after a hard rain filling his nostrils, the heat of the sun warming his shoulders. His leg muscles burned from the

74

uphill hike on the logging road. He looked forward to a relaxing two hours of fishing, but he may not get it. Thunder rumbled across the sky as steely storm clouds gathered in the distance. The storm he'd sensed this morning had moved in faster than he'd anticipated. He surely wouldn't want to be anywhere near the lake when it broke. He calculated the distance to the cave and concluded he had about an hour to catch his dinner.

Reaching into his pack, he removed a small tin box. Opening it, he uncoiled a length of fishing line and removed three fish hooks he'd carved from a deer bone he'd found in the woods. He figured either a cougar or the pack of wild dogs he'd spotted in the past few weeks had themselves a good meal. There'd been nothing left but hide and bone.

Gathering some sticks, he formed a frame, securing the ends of the sticks with thin strips of bark. Flipping over a rotting log on the bank, he gathered a handful of grubs, skewering them onto the fish hooks. He carried his entire invention to the shallow edge of the lake. He could already spot several trout and a few bass lazily cruising through the reeds. He removed his boots and socks, rolled up his jeans, and stepped into the cool water. The slimly bottom oozed through his toes as he slogged into the thickest part of the reeds. Firmly staking his frame into the ground, he hung three lines with the baited hooks onto the top stick. Satisfied, he returned to the bank to wait.

Graham glanced at the brooding clouds gathering over the tops of the mountains. He didn't like the greenish tinge at the edge of the front nor the bright splashes of light dancing behind it like flashbulbs popping in an old Hollywood movie. He eyed the frame of sticks carefully, hoping he wouldn't go hungry tonight. As if summoning the fish by sheer will, the sturdy sticks jerked once then twice followed by the splashing of a fish tail.

75

"Gotcha." He said, hurrying toward the water.

Two large trout struggled caught by the juicy grubs on the hook. Grinning, for it never ceased to amaze him how well some of his contraptions worked, he unhooked the fish, cleaned them, and wrapped them in brown paper. Slipping his package into the front pocket of his backpack, he washed the mud from his feet and hands, pulled on his boots and trudged in the direction of the cave just as the first fat drops of rain splashed onto his head.

His instinctive sense of direction guided him while he hiked through the dense vegetation, the strong wind whipping at his hair and clothes. Occasionally, Graham would glance up at the dark greenish clouds, judging the distance of the worst of the storm. Bolts of lightning danced across the sky, followed by a deafening crack of thunder. *God must've gotten a strike.*

The memory of his grandmother sharp in his mind, he recalled how she'd ease his tension during many Kentucky thunderstorms by telling him God bowled with the angels. He missed her. The weekends spent at his Meemaw's were the best times of his short life. When she died, he grieved terribly. The only one who'd ever really given him the time of day had departed, dying from cancer at the young age of sixty. She'd smoked like a chimney all her life, and it eventually caught up with her. Now, all he had were his occasional weekends with Neal in the woods to remind him someone really did give a shit about him.

Lightning struck a lone tree nearby so hard pieces splintered off like shrapnel. He jumped, the sharp odor of ozone filling his nostrils. "Shit."

He needed to find shelter soon. He must find something closer than the cave. Getting his bearings, he headed toward a place where he knew he'd be safe. Cursing himself for not gauging the approach of the storm more accurately, he trudged through the now pouring rain toward an abandoned ranger's cabin just east of the caves. If he hustled, he'd reach shelter before the brunt of the storm reached him.

Impossible to run full-out with sheets of rain surrounding him, he increased his pace, once or twice getting slapped across the face with a sapling branch writhing in the increasing gale-force winds. The hair on his arms raised, followed by a tingling sensation.

"Uh oh," he breathed, immediately crouching on the balls of his feet and making himself into as small a target as possible. He recognized the imminent strike of lightning.

Within seconds, a bolt struck the ground mere yards away. Dirt and debris sprayed upward, raining down on his head and shoulders, a zing of electricity zipping through his body.

Okay, this is getting serious. Graham paused for only a moment to get his bearings. The ranger's cabin couldn't be more than a half mile deeper into the forest. It sat at the end of one of the old abandoned logging roads, but he approached from the opposite direction. He hacked his way through a thicket of undergrowth and stepped into an overgrown field behind the dilapidated old cabin. Never had he been more grateful to see shelter. Another loud crack of thunder hastened his pace.

He tried the door and found it padlocked from the outside. *Odd. Why wouldn't it be locked on the inside?*

Glancing around the yard in front of the cabin, he found a heavy rock. It took two hard smacks before the padlock broke open. He removed it and threw it into the yard. A bolt of lightning struck nearby, so close he felt the ground tremble. Wasting no more time, he stepped into the darkened cabin and pushed the door shut behind him.

He placed his pack and bow on the floor, turning slowly, allowing his eyes to adjust to the gloom. He stumbled against the door, shock reverberating through his body. He sucked in a breath. He spun around to his pack, unzipping the front pocket and rooting for his flashlight. He clicked it on and turned slowly on his heel. "Holy shit. What the hell is going on in here?"

"Mm. Mm."

Before him, staked to the floor like an animal skin laid out to dry, lay a woman. A naked woman. He shone the flashlight at her face, and she jerked away, vocalizing what would have been a scream had she been able to open her mouth. He lowered the flashlight to keep it from shining directly in her eyes, but studied the blood and bruising on her face. Her nose and jaw appeared to be broken with one eye swollen shut. Bruises covered her entire body, both her ankles and wrists were manacled, fastened to chains bolted to the floor. Her right ankle had swollen to the point the skin nearly covered the metal digging into her flesh.

He moved toward the door. He had no clue what he'd just stumbled on, but he wanted no part of it. *This is some bad shit here. Storm or no storm, I'm leaving.*

He had his hand on the door, ready to jerk it open when she moaned. He rotated slowly and faced her again, shining the flashlight just above her head. One crystal-blue eye met his gaze. Never had he seen one glance filled with so much emotion. Pain, agony, desperation all rolled into one expression. She moved him beyond words. No decent man could run away and leave her to whatever monster had done this to her.

Wait. Whoever did this could return at any moment. He needed to get her out of here, but how? The storm had reached near hurricane strength, lightning bounced all over the place, and, from the looks of her feet, he'd have to carry her. His mind spun with the myriad problems he'd have trying to save her.

She grunted.

He moved to her side, kneeling next to her. "It's okay. I'll get you out of this. I don't know how, yet, but give me a minute to think."

Her nakedness unnerved him, so he glanced around the cabin for her clothes or a blanket—anything he could cover her with. Despite the heat of summer, the cabin remained damp and cool. He noticed a moth-eaten blanket draped across a sagging sofa. He grabbed it and covered her. The tension around her eye softened.

"Mm, mm," she grunted.

"Can you move your jaw? Speak at all?"

She shook her head, wincing.

"Okay. Let's do this," he suggested, observing that even the smallest motion of her head caused her tremendous pain. "Give me one grunt for no and two grunts for yes."

She nodded, relief evident in her one good eye. She attempted a smile, but after the first twitch of her busted lip, moaned instead.

"Is the man who did this to you coming back soon?"

She grunted once, then quickly followed with two grunts.

Graham stared at her, confused. She shrugged.

"You don't know?"

She nodded.

"Hmm. All right. Well, let's see if I can find a key for these manacles around here somewhere."

"Mm."

He glanced at her. She looked in the direction of the door, then raised her eye upward.

He followed her gaze and saw a large key hanging from a hook by the door. It just couldn't be so easy, could it?

79

He scrambled for the key. Starting with her feet, he unlocked the first manacle on the left ankle. She groaned in relief.

"This next one isn't going to feel so good. Hang in there for me, okay?"

She closed her eye and nodded, a small tear leaked down the side of her cheek.

What kind of evil sadistic bastard does this to a woman? His stomach churned when he took a closer look at her ankle. He had no medical degree, but clearly she had a broken bone or a bad sprain.

"Ready?"

She nodded, her eyes still closed.

He unlocked the iron cuff, easing it off her foot as gently as he could. The skin turned a bright shade of pink as the blood rushed into her toes. She uttered another closed-mouth scream.

"I'm so sorry. I know it must hurt, but it had to come off. It's cutting off your circulation."

She nodded, tears oozing out of both her eyes.

He wanted to throw up. Quickly, he unlocked her wrists. "Can you even sit up?" Scooting around behind her, he lifted her by the shoulders, breathing a sigh of relief when she didn't scream.

"I'm going to pick you up and put you on the sofa. Then I'm going to look for some clothes to put on you. If I can't find anything, you can wear some of mine. I've got sweatpants and a T-shirt I think will fit. They'll be too big, but as long as they don't fall off, we should be okay. On the count of three. One...two...three...." He lifted her body, which weighed hardly anything. Her blonde hair hung over his arm, oily, damp, and stringy. How long had she been here?

Gently he placed her on the couch then went to retrieve his pack. Best not to waste time looking for clothes around the cabin when he had some readily available. He removed the gray sweats and T-shirt and helped her dress, discouraged by how weak she seemed.

"How long have you been here?"

She grunted three times.

"You don't know? Damn. Do you know the man who took you?"

One grunt.

"Never seen him before?"

One grunt.

"Are you from Grady's Lake?"

She grunted twice this time.

"I don't know your name, so I'm just going to call you June, since it's the month we're in."

June nodded.

Once he had her dressed, he looked around the cabin for some fresh water. The pump at the sink appeared rusted closed. He pulled out a plastic water bottle from his supply. It just happened he had a straw. He offered it to her, carefully slipping the straw through her swollen, bloody lips. She attempted to draw water through the cheerfully green-striped plastic but couldn't. Her hand gently touched her jaw, and she shook her head.

"Damn. We'll have to figure out something, but we need to get out of here first. Did the man keeping you here have some kind of transportation?"

She grunted twice.

"It'd have to be a four-wheeled drive to come in on the logging road. How long has he been gone do you think? And do you know where he went?"

She closed the fingers together on one hand like she held a pencil. She wiggled her hand.

"No, I don't think I have anything to write…wait. I do have a pen and a pad of paper. Hold on. He rummaged in his pack and came up with a pen. He couldn't find the pad, so he grabbed a roll of paper towels on the only table in the room. Jerking one off, he held it to her with the pen.

She smoothed it onto her thigh and wrote in very shaky script, *Gone maybe an hour. Said he'd return soon. Don't know what soon means. Guessing, of course.*

Graham nodded. "He could be back any minute. Did he ever leave you for long periods of time before?"

She nodded.

The pen scratched across the paper towel. *Mean. He'll kill us if he finds us.*

"Great," he said, his tone sarcastic. "What's your name?"

She scribbled. *Ann.*

They were going to have to venture out into the storm whether he wanted to or not.

Thunder rattled overhead, but the noise mixed with another rumble. The sound of an approaching truck engine. They were out of time.

"Climb aboard. Can you hold the strap of my pack?"

She nodded.

He turned, kneeling in front her facing the door. She wrapped her arms around his neck, and he carefully locked her legs around his waist. He stuffed the roll of paper towels and the pen into his pack, along with the extra quiver of arrows not attached to his bow. He handed it to her. He hurried to the door, opened it, careful not to bump her damaged ankle.

This is going to be impossible.

Headlights bounced along the rutted road as the truck grew closer. Graham suddenly remembered he'd left his flashlight on the floor of the cabin.

82

"Damn it," he cursed, returning through the doorway. He needed his flashlight, if not for the beam, as a weapon.

Ann grunted her panic, bucking on his back to get him to hurry.

"I know, I know, but I've got to have the flashlight." He bent to retrieve it, and her weight shifted, nearly causing him to tumble over.

"Is there another way out of this place?"

She grunted once.

"Of course not."

The sound of the truck engine grew much closer. The storm had darkened the sky, but he'd surely see them if they left now. Graham's mind whirred. He'd have to stand and fight. "I'm going to put you on the couch. Be still. Hopefully, he won't notice you're not there and I can knock him out."

She screamed through her closed lips, violently shaking her head. "Mm-mm. Mm-mm…."

"Calm down. I'm going to be behind the door, and I'm going to club him over the head with the flashlight. Trust me, it'll take down a grizzly. Then we'll leave. If we try to go now, he might have a gun."

He dumped her unceremoniously on the sofa, but they were out of time. The truck had skidded to a stop just outside the cabin. Graham covered her with the moldy blanket, for all the good it would do. Her good eye pleaded with him. "It's going to be okay. I won't let him hurt you anymore." He stepped away just as boots stomped up the steps.

He scrambled to stand in the space behind the door when it swung open.

A massive bald man stomped over the threshold, into the room. Three times Graham's size, the guy wore jeans, a wife-beater, and thick-soled hiking boots. A flash of

83

lightning illuminated the entire cabin for a brief second, revealing the empty manacles lying askew on the bloodstained hardwood floor.

"What the hell?" the man roared. He glanced wildly around the cabin. "Who's been in here, bitch?"

Graham prayed she'd stay still on the couch.

"Where the hell are you?"

Wait…I know that voice.

She whimpered from her under the blanket, a soft sound. The guy's head jerked to the left.

Shit, he heard her.

The brute stomped to the sofa and yanked the blanket away. "How did you get free?"

Recognition flashed in Graham's mind. *No freakin' way. It can't be.*

Despite his short stature, Graham carried a lot of solid muscle. Years of hiking, rock climbing, and training to survive in the wild had developed his upper body strength. He put all of his power behind the swing of the heavy Maglite. He connected with the base of the man's skull. The guy didn't even scream. He just crumpled like clothes falling off a hanger and hit the floor with a thud. Graham turned on the beam. Strands of dull-blond hair and blood stuck to the edge of the lens, making a weird shadow on his victim's head.

Stepping over him, he leaned down and lifted Ann straight from the sofa, slinging her over his shoulder in a fireman's carry. She grunted in pain, but he didn't stop. The man on the floor groaned and began to stir. They had to get out of here now. He remembered the truck. Where were the damn keys?

"Hang on," he told Ann, kneeling to fish around in the man's pockets. He found the keys, breathing a sigh of relief.

84

He grabbed his pack then shoved the flashlight into it. Securing Ann firmly onto his shoulders, he snatched his bow and arrows. He stepped around the man, reaching for the door to open it wider.

Just as he moved forward, a beefy hand shot out and clasped around his ankle, jerking his foot out from under him. He went down hard, his elbows slamming painfully into the hard floor. Ann landed on top of him, screaming and writhing. Breath whooshed from his lungs. His flashlight skittered across the floor out of reach. Graham, gasping for air, rolled her away, at the same time taking a heavy boot and kicking at the man's face. The older man dodged the boot then caught sight of his opponent. Recognition dawned in the man's eyes.

"Well, well, well. Look who we have here. If it ain't Trashy Tracey's boy."

His grip tightened painfully on Graham's ankle. Graham tried to think, regaining oxygen to his brain with short, shallow pants. Too close to shoot the bow, but he could swing the sturdy piece of wood like a club.

"You trying to steal my woman, boy? You think you're man enough?" He yanked Graham closer. "I believe it's high time I taught you a lesson, ain't it? I think I owe you for the last time you shot me."

"Shut up, Arthur," Graham growled. "How did you get outta jail?"

The man laughed. "Good behavior."

"Well, that ain't what's going on here. I'm takin' this girl and makin' sure you go right back to jail, you sleazy son of a bitch."

"Oh ya are, are ya? You and who's army?"

Graham winced as the man's fingers squeezed his ankle with bone-crushing force. "I don't need an army," he said through clenched teeth, and at the same time, swung the

85

recurve bow in an arc, crashing it down on the man's wrist. The hand-carved oak connected with skin and bone. Graham thought he heard a crack. Maybe Arthur's wrist, maybe the bow. He prayed for the former.

Arthur yelped, releasing his hold. Taking advantage of his freedom, Graham scrambled to his feet, out of reach. He swung the bow a second time, this time catching Arthur under the chin, snapping his head back. The older man hit the floor but bounced up.

He rubbed his chin, his lips splitting his face with an evil grin. "So…you think you're man enough to take me on, do ya?" Arthur got first to one knee then to his feet. He shook his head from side to side.

Graham had stunned him. He just needed to finish the job and incapacitate him completely. *Damn he's a big sucker.* Neal's words floated into his mind. *The bigger they are, the harder they fall. Use the man's weight against him.* Graham, smaller and lither, maintained eye contact with Arthur, heart pounding, adrenaline coursing through his veins. He waited.

As expected, Arthur charged, slipping slightly on the rain-soaked cabin floor. He roared, "I'll teach you a lesson you'll never forget, boy."

Ann screamed from the floor nearby. Graham let him come. Just as Arthur reached him, he leapt out of the way, grabbing the big man's belt from behind and throwing his entire body weight into Arthur's forward momentum. They flew through the still open cabin door, tumbling onto the wet decking outside. Graham's head bounced off the corner of the handrail post, shooting bolts of pain through his skull, but his opponent hit it head on.

He shoved the man's face into the wood with the entire weight of his body, then popped up, stomping on Arthur's neck. He steadied himself against the post, stars

86

swimming before his eyes, bile rising in his throat. He swallowed hard, fighting the pain and nausea. He spotted the Maglite and shoved himself off Arthur's body.

But the big man remained conscious. His foot shot out, tripping Graham as he tried to scoot into the cabin. A meaty hand grabbed the same ankle he'd held before and twisted. Pain seared as the tendons stretched. He went down on one knee, but, if he stretched, he could just reach the Maglite. He shot his hand toward his prize, closing his grip around it just as Arthur yanked.

Arthur's other huge fist slammed Graham in the kidneys. The breath whooshed out of him, his vision blurring. He could not let this ogre get the best of him. Ann's life, and his own, depended on it. Summoning what strength he had left, he rolled, ignoring the screaming pain in his ankle as he did so. He pulled all the power he could from his abs, rose, and swung the Maglite, connecting with Arthur's jaw. Blood and teeth sprayed Graham. He didn't stop to think, he just bashed the man over the head again.

Arthur collapsed on top of him, releasing his ankle as he did so. Blood from the heavy man's wounds, dribbled onto Graham's face enhancing his nausea. The putrid smell from body odor and rotting teeth didn't help either.

It took him several minutes to wiggle out from under him. He checked to see if he'd killed the bastard. He punched the button on the Maglite and watched for the rise and fall of Arthur's chest. Not dead…yet.

Graham rose to his feet, his injured ankle stabbing him with bright bolts of pain.

"I sure hope he didn't make me lame, too. That'll be a bitch."

He tested his weight, and the ankle held. It hurt, but he could still walk on it. *Thank God.*

87

He limped into the cabin and grabbed a dirty rag he spotted lying on the table. He found his pack and took out a bottle of water. He soaked the cloth, wiping the blood from his face. Then he cleaned off the flashlight. Ann leaned over the couch, tears flowing from both eyes. She raised her eyebrows, giving him a tentative thumbs up.

"He's down. But probably not for long." Graham turned to the man lying prostrate on the porch of the cabin, then glanced at the manacles bolted to the floor. He lifted one of Arthur's beefy arms and pulled. "Damn, he's heavier than a two-ton grizzly. And just as ugly."

It took him several minutes, but he finally dragged Arthur to the spot on the floor Ann vacated shortly before. To Graham, it felt like days had passed. He wanted a beer and a soft bed, but he could forget both for quite a while.

He clamped the manacles onto Arthur's thick wrists, pleased when the metal pinched his skin, drawing blood. The man didn't flinch.

"He's still out cold, thank God." Graham moved to his feet and chained his ankles. "There. It oughta hold him till I can return."

"Hmm?"

He glanced at Ann. "I need to get you to a hospital then I'm coming to deal with this mother— I mean, um, asshole."

Ann's expression changed from curiosity to concern. She shook her head. "Mm mmm."

"He can't just stay here chained to the floor, although it's what he deserves. I've gotta deal with him." Graham had no idea what he intended to do, but he had quite a bit of time to think it through.

He gathered everything from the mud-streaked floor but his bow and arrows. Spying the keys in a puddle under the wooden table, he crouched to retrieve them. He carried his stuff to the vehicle then returned, swiping the rain out of his eyes and smoothing his hair back away from his face.

Arthur moaned.

"He's coming around. Let me get you to the truck." He glanced down at his dripping clothes. "Sorry I'm so wet. I'll try to get ya there quick. Lock the doors till I come for ya."

He carried her out into the deluge of rain. She buried her head into the crook of his neck. He felt the warmth of her breath against his skin. A wave of rage coursed through him. The poor girl may never be the same again. He didn't blame her if she never trusted another man her whole life.

He placed her in the front seat of the cab. "Lock the doors." He closed the door and waited to hear the click of the lock.

He had one more thing to do before they left. Re-entering the cabin he reached for his bow.

Arthur moaned, opening his eyes. He spotted Graham with the bow and tried to rise. The chains yanked him firmly into place.

"What the—" He jerked on the chains. "What have you done, boy?" he bellowed. "Turn me loose, right now!"

Graham crouched, ignoring the pain in his ankle. "I'll be back soon enough," he said, his voice cold as steel. "Then you and me are gonna have a discussion about the kind a man who beats up on women. I think you might be a changed man, when I've said my peace."

"You little shit," Arthur yelled, yanking at the chains again.

Graham nocked an arrow in his bow. "I think you might just be strong enough to yank those bolts free, if you worked at it hard enough. I believe I need to make sure you stay put."

He drew the bow to his anchor point, his middle finger touching the corner of his mouth. "By the way, do you know how many pounds of pressure a good re-curve bow has? I carved this one and strung it myself." He flexed his fingers on the grip of the bow. "Feels real nice in my hand. And you know what else?"

He released the arrow. It penetrated straight through Arthur's wet sleeve, pinning his right forearm to the cabin floor. The man screamed in agony. He writhed on the floor, his wet, stringy hair slapping his face. His eyes widened with terror as Graham slipped another arrow from his quiver and placed it on the bow.

"No! Don't!" Arthur cried.

Graham drew the bow string. "I never miss."

He released the second arrow, pinning Arthur's left arm to the floor as well. A loud crack of thunder drowned out the big man's yell.

Though Graham wanted to stay and do the same thing to Arthur's legs, he needed to get moving. The rain may have washed out the logging road, and he needed to get Ann to the hospital.

"You hang out right there. Don't go nowhere, hear? We'll have our little chat once I return."

Arthur panted from his prison on the floor. "Oh you bet we'll talk," he growled through clenched teeth, what few he had left. "I'm gonna kill you, you son of a bitch."

Graham smiled. "We'll just see about that."

He slung the bow over his shoulder, tossed the keys in the air and caught them in his palm. "See you soon."

****

Graham tossed his bow in the bed of the truck and climbed into the driver's seat. He started the engine and cranked up the heater. Ann needed to be kept warm. Maybe he should go to the cabin and get the blanket.

No. He'd better get them out of the woods before the stream running north of the cabin became a full-blown river. It crossed the logging road about a mile downhill from where they were, and if it flooded, they'd be stuck.

"Hang on, I'll get you to a hospital as soon as I can. Buckle up. This probably ain't gonna be no comfy ride."

Ann tugged at the seat belt but didn't have the strength to pull it across her body. Graham reached over and buckled it for her. Then he adjusted the fan on the heater. They were both soaked through, and Ann had to be suffering from shock. He needed to get her warm.

He turned the vehicle around in the cabin's small yard and headed toward the logging road, the windshield wipers slapping a rhythmic beat against the rain still pounding outside.

****

After carefully negotiating miles of muddy terrain, Graham made it onto the main highway leading into Grady's Lake. He picked up speed, glancing at Ann. Her head leaned against the headrest, eyes closed. The tight lines around her mouth pinched in pain. Even in the darkened daylight, he could tell her skin had the deathly pallor of someone gravely injured. He hoped she didn't have internal injuries of some kind.

Dirty bastard. How could anyone treat a woman…no…a girl so cruel. She can't be no older than me.

Anger spread throughout his entire being, penetrating every cell down to the nucleus. He remembered the look of sheer terror in his mother's eyes when he'd caught Arthur choking the life out of her. He should have

91

killed the sleaze-bag then, but his mother begged him not to. Why women protected people who hurt them baffled him. Why would she even defend the man who'd nearly put her in a grave and would have, had it not been for her only son coming home early. He shook his head. *Boggles the mind.*

A soft snore roused him. He glanced at Ann. Her mouth hung open slightly so she could breathe, her nose so bent and crooked, he didn't know if she'd ever look normal again. Glad she'd dozed off, he took the opportunity to carry out his plan before she could protest.

Graham sighed. His lower body hurt where Arthur had kidney punched him, but he'd survive. He'd been through worse than this. Guilt settled in on him, and he pushed away his complaints. How could he complain when, next to him, sat a woman who'd been through hell. Purpling bruises covered most of her face, along with deep violet finger marks on her arms. How she'd endured the torture he couldn't fathom, but he'd avenge her. By God, he would. Both Ann and his mother, and any other woman who'd had the misfortune to run into Arthur Bingham.

The Smokin' Dawg loomed through the curtain of steady rain on the right side of the road. Graham pulled the truck around to the rear. At two o'clock in the afternoon, most of the lunch crowd had gone and only a few regulars' cars remained in the gravel lot.

Ann stirred as the engine cut off. She lifted her head, her one good eye widening. She shrugged her shoulders in a why gesture.

"I need to see someone for a minute. I won't be long I promise. Lock the doors if you're scared. I'll be right back."

He slipped out of the driver's seat and closed the door. He heard the snick of the locks popping into place. *Poor kid. She's terrified.*

92

He pulled open a screen and banged on the solid metal door built into the red brick building. He waited while he heard the clicks of deadbolts being unlocked.

The door swung outward and a tall, burly man with biceps the size of tree trunks stepped outside. Long, salt-and-pepper hair hung past his shoulder blades in a tail. No beard allowed a person to see the sharp features of his face. He stared at Graham, brown eyes wide.

"What're you doin' here? I though you was campin'. Looks like you been swimmin'."

"Hey, Neal. Yeah, but I ran into some trouble and I need your help."

The bar owner narrowed his eyes. "If that ripped shirt and bloody lip are any indication, looks like bad trouble. What's going on?"

"Come here." Graham gestured toward the truck. He saw Ann's eye widen in horror.

He motioned for her to unlock the truck, and he opened the passenger door. "It's okay, Ann. This is a good friend of mine. His name's Neal. My mom works for him. He's a nice guy, really."

"Holy mother of God, what happened to her?" Neal said as he leaned around the truck door and caught sight of Ann's condition. "Why the hell you'd bring her here? She needs the hospital, boy."

"I know, but I can't take her there."

Neal grabbed Graham's arm and yanked him away from the truck and out of earshot for Ann.

"You didn't do this to her did you?" He barked the question, his tone sharp.

"God no, man. What do you take me for? I'd never hurt a woman. I found her like this in the old rangers cabin up on the ridge."

"Jesus. Do you know who hurt her?"

93

"Yep, and that's why I need your help."

Neal stared at Graham. "Who was it? Someone we know?"

"Arthur Bingham," Graham stated, flatly.

Shock filled Neal's expression. "He's in jail."

"Not no more, he's not. I don't know who the hell let the monster out, but they did. I've got him chained up same as he had her when I found her, but I don't want him to get away. I gotta get to the cabin." Graham wrapped a hand around Neal's arm. "Please get her to the hospital for me, okay?"

Neal nodded. "What's your plan?"

"Best you don't know any more than you already do. Say you found her left in this truck on your parking lot. I'm sure the truck's stolen."

The older man's gaze never left Graham's face. "Call the sheriff, boy. This ain't for you to handle."

"I will. I just gotta make sure he don't get away." Guilt stabbed at his soul for lying to the only man who'd ever loved him, but he had no choice. He trotted to the pickup, pulled out his bow, then leaned in the driver's side to get his pack.

"Neal's gonna get you to the hospital. I'll try to come see you when I can. Take good care of yourself and don't let what happened to you ruin your life. Okay?"

Tears leaked down Ann's cheeks. She nodded, touching the four fingers of her right hand to her lips and drawing them away in a "thank you" gesture.

"I don't know what you're sayin'," Graham told her. "But you take care."

He stuck his arm through both the bow and the pack's strap, slinging both onto his shoulder. He held the quiver of arrows in his hand as glanced at Neal.

94

"Graham, I don't know what you're planning, but it can't be good. Don't do this. Let me lock up and come with you."

Graham waved at the only dad he'd ever known. He couldn't draw anyone else into this plan. Things would move quickly once Ann could speak and began to relay her story. He had to get to the cabin and make sure nothing remained of Arthur for them to find. Ever.

****

It took longer than Graham thought it would to reach the cabin again. Watery sunbeams filtered through the trees to the west, attempting to chase away the last of the dreary clouds. The storms had moved on to terrorize some other town, but mud remained, slowing his progress tremendously.

During the return trip to the cabin, his anger boiled. No man on the face to this earth had a right to treat any woman the way Arthur had treated his mother and Ann. He didn't even know the girl, but he felt a responsibility toward her. Someone had to make this monster pay, and he knew just how to do it. He would strike the fear of God into Arthur and maybe the fear of the devil, too. For this man would end his day in hell.

With every step, Graham convinced himself of the righteousness of his mission. He could outright kill the man, and he'd be totally justified to do so, in his opinion. But he had a heart. He'd give Arthur the chance the bastard hadn't given Ann or his mother. He deemed it more than fair. Right?

Drawing an arrow in his bow, he stepped onto the cabin porch. With a heavy boot he kicked open the door. Arthur remained right where Graham had left him, chained

95

to the floor. Blood had pooled under both arms where the arrows penetrated, and his face looked a bit peaked, but the old codger still had plenty of fight and hate left in him.

"You let me the hell up from here, boy. I'm going to kick your scrawny ass from here to China." Arthur struggled against his restraints then bellowed in pain. "You get these goddamned arrows out of my arms right now!"

Graham pulled up the only chair in the room and sat down. "I can. But I think the arrow's gonna do a lot more damage comin' out than it did goin' in. You might want to leave 'em be."

Graham pulled a pair of aluminum cutters out of his pack. "I'll cut them away from the floor for you, though." He started to rise then sat down. "Before I do though, you and me are gonna reach an understandin'."

"I ain't got to do nothin'. You let me up from here and we'll see what's what."

Graham watched the man from his perch on the chair. Arthur's pulse throbbed in the temple of his reddened face. His hate-filled gaze skewered Graham. *Oh, you think you hate me now.... Just wait.*

"Let me ask you a question, Arthur." He didn't wait for a response. "Why do you think you need to hurt women the way you do? Is it because you got a little dick and have to prove you're a man by smackin' around women?" He took one of his arrows and poked the older man in the crotch, hard.

Arthur yelped. "You little sack of shit. I'm gonna kill you."

"Really? 'Cause it looks like to me you're not in a position to do much killin'."

"You let me up from here and fight like a man. Any chicken shit can torture a man chained to the floor."

Graham poked him in the crotch again with the arrow, pleased by Arthur's shriek of pain. "True." Graham stood and straddled the large man. He sat down hard on Arthur's chest, feeling even more satisfied at the whoosh of air escaping through his ugly mouth. "And I'm going to, after we reach an agreement."

He stuck the point directly under Arthur's chin, the razor-sharp edges of the projectile drawing blood. He smiled at the man's clear distress.

"I could shove this arrow right through your throat. It wouldn't kill you, but it sure would hurt like hell." Graham pressed the tip deeper into his prisoner's skin.

Arthur struggled against the chains, eyes widening. The first sign of fear crept into his expression.

Graham pushed a little harder, slicing a hole with the sharp razor edges of the broadhead. "The edges of this tip are sharp as a razor you shave with. The good news is you probably wouldn't even feel it go in, they're so sharp. The bad news? It might not stop bleeding." He yanked away the shaft, leaving four symmetrical cuts in Arthurs' neck.

The older man gasped.

Graham stood, carefully wiping the tip of the arrow on his pants and leaving a brownish-red streak. "Ya know, Arthur. It's a good thing for you I don't have the stomach for torture. I find it not as much of a challenge. So, here's what we're gonna do."

Graham placed the shaft in his quiver and retrieved his flashlight out of his pack. He tapped it in the palm of his hand. "First I'm going to break your jaw. I see a slight bruise there from where I tried before, but you must have bones as hard as a fossil. So this might take a coupla swings. You might lose a few more teeth, but from the looks of 'em you weren't gonna have 'em too long anyway."

97

Kelly Abell

Without warning Graham leaned over his quarry and swung the flashlight, connecting it with the right side of Arthur's face. The man's head whipped to the side, a strangled scream escaping from his throat. When he faced Graham again, the boy saw much more than a hint of fear in those bloodshot brown eyes.

Good. Now I'm getting through to him. Wow, I can't believe how good this feels. It's like I'm some avenging angel, righting the wrongs of the world.

"You deserve to suffer way more than this," Graham told the man as he raised the flashlight again.

Arthur shook his head violently. "No, don't."

Graham swung a second time. This time he heard bone crack.

"There we go. I think that did the trick."

Tears leaked out of Arthur's eyes.

"Did it feel this good to you when you hit Ann? Or choked the life-giving air out of my mom? 'Cause I'm gonna tell you, this is a rush." Graham stepped to the wall where he'd hung the keys to the chains.

"Here's how this is gonna work, Arthur. I'm going to let you go. I'm even going to give you a fifteen-minute head start before I come after you. If you make it out of the forest before I find you, you get to live. If I find you first, you die. Sound like a fair deal to you?"

Arthur glared at him, no longer able to speak with his broken jaw.

"A simple nod will seal the agreement."

Arthur nodded.

"Then we have an accord." Graham laughed. "I heard that on a pirate movie once. Thought is sounded cool. Never thought I'd ever use a fancy word like accord, but it sorta fits." He unlocked one of Arthur's legs. The man struck out at him, his boot just missing Grahams forehead.

98

"Whoa there. Is that the way you want to play this, big man?"

Graham picked up his bow and nocked the arrow. He aimed for Arthur's knee.

"Mm mmm," Arthur exclaimed.

Graham lowered the bow. "Yeah, it might make it too easy to find you if I shoot you in the leg. Okay, you win this round. But you try anything funky again, and the deal is off. I'll just shoot you right through the heart."

Using the cutters, Graham cut the arrow shafts from the tip, allowing Arthur to lift his arms from the floor. The man moaned.

"Yeah, it's gotta hurt like a sonofabitch." He unlocked the cuffs of both hands, stepping away quickly. He tossed the key at Arthur. "You open the last manacle."

Graham retrieved the bow and drew the string, aiming at Arthur's head. "Once you're unlocked, get a move on. Time's a tickin'. It'll be dark soon, and I don't think you want to be out there when a pack of wild dogs starts huntin' for their supper."

Arthur paused, glancing up at his captor, eyebrows raised.

"Oh…you didn't know about them dogs cause you been away in jail. I forgot. Yeah, I ran into 'em about a month ago. Nasty bastards. About six of 'em. They've formed themselves a right vicious pack. Love the smell of blood, too."

Arthur muttered the word, "Crazy."

"What'd you say? You think I'm crazy. Me? After what you did to Ann…to my mother, and you call me crazy? Get the hell out of this cabin. Your time starts now."

Graham held the arrow on the man as he rose painfully to his feet, cradling his arms. "Get!"

Arthur stumbled out of the house followed by the sound of Graham's laughter.

True to his word, Graham waited fifteen minutes. As he did, he stared at the blood stains surrounding the manacles on the floor. Most belonged to Ann, and it infuriated him all over again. Thoughts of his poor misguided mother entered his mind. He'd often wondered what life would have been like had she not chosen the path she had and dragged him along for the ride. He might have had a decent dad, a real house with a fireplace to read by, brothers and sisters. But, his life had other plans.

Neal had taught him the necessities of surviving in the wild, and though he chose to cheat…a lot…he could do it. He might have to for a very long time after this. Not a stupid man, the sheriff would put two and two together soon enough, but he'd have a helluva time finding any evidence if Graham did his job right. Once he'd taken care of Arthur, he'd return and burn the cabin. Then he'd stay hidden till things cooled off. *Odds are nobody will even miss the bastard.*

Time to go. He grabbed his pack, bow, and arrows and headed out the door. At first, he had no trouble following the trail. Blood droplets stained the ground and the surrounding plants. *He's headed for the river. Smart, but not smart enough. I'll circle around him and drive him deeper into the forest.*

Within minutes, Graham caught up to Arthur, disappointed he hadn't been more of a challenge. Dusk fell, and the shadows deepened on the ground, taking on a sepia hue. He'd roamed the woods at night. There'd be a full moon tonight, so he'd have no trouble keeping sight of Arthur. He guessed the man would try to hole up for the night, but Graham had other ideas.

He stopped, ears tuned for noises. Several yards ahead a branch snapped, then another. He traveled left and spotted Arthur working his way through a tough thicket of bushes. Just to keep things interesting, Graham shot an arrow. It sank into a tree trunk less than a foot from the older man. He squeaked in alarm.

"Gotcha, Arthur. You're going to have to move a lot faster and a lot quieter if you're going to avoid me. You're making this way too easy."

Arthur's head swiveled, trying to locate Graham's position. He ducked behind a low-growing blackberry bush, grabbing a few berries and popping them in his mouth. It reminded him he hadn't eaten since breakfast. He reached into his pack and pulled out an energy bar. *Yes, I'm cheating. But I can't cook my fish till this is over.*

As he munched, he moved a few yards north of his position, making more noise than necessary so Arthur would be driven in the direction he wanted. He retrieved his arrow as he walked past the tree.

An hour passed, and the sun blazed the horizon with streaks of orange and pink. Graham marveled over the simplicity and beauty of nature. If only man were as simple. In the distance, a howl rose out of the darkening forest. *Ah, there they are.* He smiled, increasing his pace.

Panic must have taken over Arthur for he crashed through the brush and charged forward at breakneck speed. *He's going to kill himself before I get the chance.*

Graham spotted him in a clearing dead ahead. "Time to end this," he muttered. "I'm hungry, and so are those dogs."

Arthur spun around in circles in the darkening forest, clearly seeking a hiding place, but not coming up with anything. Graham stepped out of the tree line, arrow nocked.

"Boy, you really suck at this, Arthur. You coulda made it to the river by now, and down to the main road if you were any good at this. But as it is, looks like I win."

Arthur faced him, eyes wide. He grunted, held up his hands palm out. His jaw resembled a small eggplant both in shape and color. Both eyes were surrounded by dark puffy circles. Graham smiled, satisfied the man must be in major pain.

"A deal's a deal, man. I've given you more opportunity than you gave my mom and Ann. You know?" Graham slowly nocked an arrow into his bow. "I'll give you one last chance. You got five seconds." He drew the string to his chin. "Five…four…."

Arthur took off running deeper into the woods, in the direction where Graham heard the howling dogs.

He raised his voice. "Three…two…. Ready or not, here I come."

He trotted off in Arthur's direction. Within minutes, he'd caught up to the man perched atop a large tree root, surrounded by a pack of drooling canines, throats rumbling with vicious growls. Arthur's wordless screams could be heard above the din of snarling. Graham almost felt sorry the man. He noticed a stain on the front of his pants. He'd probably pee himself too if he were surrounded by five slobbering ferocious beasts.

Not wanting to attract the attention of the pack, he stood quietly at the edge of the area. Arthur scrambled farther up the tree as the animals closed in. The alpha dog snapped at the man's foot. Graham caught his quarry's expression as Arthur pointed for him to shoot the dogs. Graham shook his head.

A second dog charged, grabbing the edge of Arthur's jeans in his teeth, yanking hard. Arthur lost his balance, screamed, tumbling from the tree root. He didn't even hit the ground before the animals pounced. Snarls and ripping fabric filled Graham's ears. He winced as the older man tried to scream through his broken jaw. The sight of the pack tearing their prey apart sickened Graham. He aimed his arrow at Arthur's chest and released. The arrow found its mark, killing the man instantly.

His job complete, Graham retreated through the trees and hustled to the cabin, not wanting to draw the pack's attention. Reaching the building, he ran up the stairs, slamming the door behind him. He'd ride out the night in the cabin and head up to his cave tomorrow where he planned to spend two weeks instead of one. Neal would understand.

He started a fire with shaking hands in the small fireplace then lit the kerosene lantern. He shivered. Never had he seen anything like those dogs ripping Arthur's carcass to pieces. He couldn't think of a more fitting way for a monster to die.

He removed the wrapped fish from his pack. Taking it to the sink, he unwrapped the trout, fileted the white meat. He found an old iron skillet and a trivet to place in the fire. Soon the fish sizzled in the hot pan. As he cooked, he reflected on the hunt and the subsequent kill. Not quite as challenging as he'd anticipated but satisfying enough. He'd rid the world of one very dangerous predator.

Relaxing on the sofa, he took a bite of the flaky trout. He toasted himself with a bottle of water. Pride surged through him. *Who said I'd never amount to nothing? Man, that was a kick. I could get used to this saving-the-world shit.*

Not only had he saved Ann from a terrifying fate, but avenged his poor mother as well. Should he feel guilty? By eliminating one monster in the woods, had he created another? He smiled, took another bite of fish. *Yeah, that's exactly what I done. And, I'm okay with it.*

103

Kelly Abell

About the Author

Kelly is the author of thirteen novels and other published works. She writes young adult thrillers as well as adult romance, romantic suspense and paranormal romance. Her aim is to write about gripping characters in tense situations that keep a reader turning the pages. She also spends a great deal of time helping other writers through her Writing Tips on her website and as a the Vice President of the Paranormal Romance Guild and a member of the Florida Writer's Association.

When not writing, Kelly enjoys spending time with her husband of 30+ years and her two adult children, when they find the time. She lives in Florida and enjoys all that living in the sunshine state brings, boating, fishing, beaches, theme parks, and more. Her favorite pass time is reading (what a surprise!) She likes Thrillers, Romantic Suspense, and Romantic Comedy.

You can connect with Kelly at the following sites:
Facebook:
https://www.facebook.com/KellyAbellAuthor/
Twitter: www.twitter.com/kellyabellbooks
Website: www.kellyabell.com

Kelly Abell

Horror in Grieselton

In the small town of Grieselton, Georgia an evil has just been unleashed, only no one realizes it... yet! That's where Dr. Samantha Mathewson comes in. When her patient, Brody Fisher, tells her of an evil presence that whispers to him, telling him to do bad things, she thinks he's delusional, and considers hospitalization or at the very least a change in his medication. She will find out soon enough just how wrong she is! Will it be too late to save her patient and herself or will she become the victim of a terrible horror that will haunt her once peaceful town.

T. M. Witko

Horror in Grieselton

By

T.M. Witko

T. M. Witko

ACKNOWLEDGEMENT

I'd like to thank my friends and family for all of their support and encouragement. To Laura Perez for making this book possible and allowing me to delve into the darker side of myself on this one. To Select-O-Grafix for making such an amazing cover. To all of the participating authors in The Thrill of the Hunt 2, I can't wait for people to read all your amazing stories! To Amanda Rash who copy edited this story on such short notice, thank you girl, you're the best! And finally to all the suspense & thriller junkies out there, I hope you like what we've done in this anthology!

T. M. Witko

Chapter One

Samantha Mathewson woke up early Saturday morning to the sound of Delilah barking incessantly. Delilah was her pride and joy. A beautiful black Chihuahua she had rescued as a puppy. Anyone who could harm an innocent animal always made her blood boil. She rolled over with a sigh and looked into the huge brown eyes of her dog.

"Would it kill you to let me sleep in a bit?"

Delilah wagged her backside excitedly which Samantha took as a yes, it would kill her to let her sleep in. She stretched and yawed simultaneously and then slowly allowed her feet to touch the ground. As if on cue Delilah drug her slippers to her human, one at a time. Samantha smiled and patted her on the head.

"Thanks pretty girl."

Delilah barked before darting out of the room. Samantha yawned once more as she rolled her shoulders and snatched her velour robe off the hook behind her door. Slipping it on she slowly started making her way down the hallway, only to have Delilah skid into her. Apparently Samantha was taking too long.

"Hold on, geez, I really need to teach you, patience."

Moments later she was outside the house waiting for Delilah to take care of her business. She tightened her robe as the cool September breeze blew by her. The weather was definitely starting to change. The air smelled different as the leaves started to wither around her. She smiled as Delilah pounced into a small pile of leaves that had formed underneath the large Beech tree.

"Come on girl, let's get breakfast."

115

At the word breakfast, Delilah popped her head out of the leaves, her ears perked up and her tail began to wag. Whoever said that dogs didn't understand the meaning of words surely hadn't ever lived with one. Delilah bounded forth and actually passed Samantha, sliding onto the linoleum floor causing Samantha to laugh riotously.

"Don't you ever learn?" she said, patting the dog on the head.

Samantha went about her morning routine of feeding Delilah and drinking a full cup of coffee before showering. She was planning on going into town. She didn't need anything in particular she simply wanted to get out of the house. So after she had changed into her jeans and sweater she headed out.

The town of Grieselton was formed centuries ago by a group of Dutch immigrants who had set up a colony in the area. At the time it was mostly all wooded terrain. The colonist cleared the trees and set up homes in the area. It was originally named Bosville due to the forest that surrounded the town. Now, rumor had it that one day a young man wandered into the woods and came upon the devil who invaded the young boy, causing him to kill himself. An old seer amongst the colonist said it was the work of a demon in the woods. The town council forbade anyone going out there and soon the legend of a creature so evil it could make you take your own life was formed. It didn't take long for the town to acquire the nickname of Griezel Town which in Dutch, loosely meant, town filled with horror. Over the years it simply became known as Grieselton.

Grieselton was a small town of just under 5000 people, most of which were related in some way. Samantha was a transplant from Atlanta. After her marriage ended two years ago she wanted a change of pace but she loved Georgia and didn't want to leave the state. She had passed through

Grieselton on the way to the Chattahoochee National Forest one day and thought it was a perfect place to relocate. They had a small clinic that served the area and she was hired on as their clinical psychologist. For the most part her clientele was fairly typical, housewives in unhappy marriages, adolescents rebelling against their parents and on a few occasions the severely mentally ill. It was nothing like what she saw in her practice in the city which she found quite comforting.

"Morning, Dr. Mathewson," old man, Grimes said as she exited her vehicle.

"Oh, it's just Samantha, Jerry," she reacted with a smile.

He grinned a toothless grin and nodded. "You going in to see her?"

Samantha scrunched her brows slightly. "Who?"

"Madame Ophelia, of course," he said, motioning his head at the store she had parked in front of.

Samantha chortled and shook her head. "Oh, no, I'm not. Just parking here if that's okay."

He nodded. "She's real good Dr. Mathewson. You'd be surprised how accurate she can be."

"I'm sure she's wonderful," she replied with a smile.

He gave her a quick wave and began walking towards the local diner down the street called, The Shack. Samantha glanced over at the shop in question. Eye See You was spelled out with an actual eye, then a letter C, followed by a capital U. She had never been in there and often wondered what it would be like. Ophelia was the town's fortune teller. She read palms, tea leaves, the wind, you name it, and she could read your future in it. Samantha didn't believe in any of that but she didn't fault those who did.

"Would you like to come in," a crackling voice said, causing Samantha to jump.

117

"No, ma'am, I'm fine. Thank you."

Madame Ophelia watched her for a long moment, studying her which left Samantha quite uncomfortable. Samantha stared at her. She had only seen her once or twice and that was always at a distance. Today she was wearing what appeared to be two dresses that were overlapping one another. Her wrinkled skin bore the remnants of her many years of life and Samantha guessed that she must be at least in her mid to late 70's. She had soft brown eyes that reflected an almost sadness in them. Ophelia cocked her head slightly and then looked up to the sky.

"You be careful now, you hear me. I sense something in the air."

Ophelia removed the scarf she wore atop her head and Samantha realized that her hair was completed shaved off. She immediately began to wonder if maybe she had cancer in the past because most of the older African American women she had known in Atlanta would not have shaved their heads otherwise. She was squinting into the sky, her hand on her head, which she was rubbing lightly. Samantha glanced up as well but didn't see anything but clear blue skies.

"Something is coming."

Samantha turned back to the old woman who was now staring at her with a seriousness that startled her. Her brown eyes suddenly looked as black as coal. Ophelia could feel something, something she hadn't felt in quite some time. And the girl before her, she had an unusual aura around her. Ophelia reached her hand out to her, grasping her fingers around Samantha's wrist. Samantha took in a sharp breath as Ophelia's body shuddered almost violently. Samantha immediately jerked her hand away, watching as Ophelia's eyes became soft and caring again.

"We all gots to be ready for it, understand?"

118

"Umm, sure okay, well, have a ... great day, ma'am," Samantha said quickly as she scooted passed the old woman.

Samantha couldn't get away quick enough. That was the strangest thing she had ever witnessed and she had seen some strange things in her life. She walked briskly passed a couple of stores and nearly knocked a young child over as she and her mother were exiting Grieselton Thrift. Samantha felt horrified as she recognized them immediately.

"Oh my gosh, I'm sorry," Samantha stuttered a quick apology.

"It's alright, Dr. Mathewson. Are you alright?" Martha Towers asked.

"Yeah," Samantha responded, not correcting the Dr. this time. She glanced over her shoulder and saw that Ophelia was no longer outside of her shop.

"Oh, don't mind Ophelia. She means no harm," Martha indicated, seeing where the good doctor was looking. "Let me guess, theirs an evil coming?" Martha inquired with a jubilant chuckle.

Samantha gave a small smile as she turned back to her. "Yes, something like that."

"She's always predicting our demise," Martha added as she placed her hand on her daughter's shoulder. "We still on for Wednesday?"

Samantha glanced around to see if anyone could hear them and then smiled. "Yes, that shouldn't be a problem."

"That medicine you put her on seems to be really helping."

"That's good to hear, Mrs. Towers."

Samantha was not a prescribing psychologist but worked closely with the providers at her clinic. They would often defer to her on medication recommendations for her clients. Simple things like anti-depressants or anxiety meds she was comfortable sharing her input on, it was the harder

119

ailments that she withdrew from. Most of her clients however, saw her as the one prescribing the medication instead of the practitioner in the clinic. After two years, she stopped correcting people. She heard a throat clearing and realized that she must have zoned out. She offered Mrs. Towers a smile.

"I better be going now."

"Sure thing," she said with a wave.

Samantha made a hasty exit yet again. Who knew that going into town could be so stressful. The only thing she found that she missed about the city was the anonymity of her and her clients. It was rare that she ran into anyone she worked with when she was living in Atlanta but here in small town USA it happened more than she was comfortable with. She'd had people in the grocery store stop her to talk about treatment or approach her table in the diner to set up an appointment. At first the idea of the loss of their confidentiality terrified her but then she realized that it was their confidentiality to break not hers. If they wanted the town to know they were in therapy it was their choice.

"The usual?" Mary asked as Samantha stepped into the diner.

"Am I that predictable?"

Mary smiled. "People have their habits. The usual?" she asked again.

Samantha nodded. Mary grinned and walked away to get Samantha's BLT with a side of potato salad and sweet tea to drink. Samantha took a seat in the booth by the window. She enjoyed this particular spot as she could see everything going on outside. People watching was one of her favorite pasttimes. There were not a lot of folks wandering the streets this afternoon and she wondered if perhaps there was some kind of event going on that she hadn't heard about.

"Here ya go, Dr. Mathewson," Mary said as she set her sweet tea on the table.

"You know you can call me Samantha. I'm not on the clock," she added with a grin.

"I know." Mary winked and started to walk away.

"Hey Mary."

"Yes, Dr. Mathewson?'

"Do you know what's going in that vacant shop over there? I just noticed that the 'for sale' sign was gone."

"I think I heard that it's going to be some kind of coffee shop," she replied with a shrug.

"Really? Oh that will be nice."

Mary nodded and headed over to the front door to welcome another patron that had just entered. Samantha took a sip of her sweet tea looking at the empty storefront. It would be nice to sit in a coffee shop again. That was something else she missed about Atlanta. By the time Samantha had finished her meal and gone to the grocery store she was exhausted. She stumbled into her home and dropped the groceries on the countertop as Delilah barked persistently around her.

"Hold on, oh patient one."

Samantha walked her bouncing dog to the door to let her out. She never went on a leash because she would never stray too far from home but Samantha always waited for her none the less. As she looked above into the sky she saw that there were storm clouds building just to the east of her home. The loud cackle of thunder clapped in the sky causing Delilah to run back to her owner.

"Huh, maybe Ophelia was right. A storm is definitely coming."

T. M. Witko

122

Chapter Two

The weekend had flown by. A storm had indeed passed through Grieselton, dropping more rain than the town could handle so there was flooding everywhere for a most of Sunday. By Monday it had cleared up considerably but it was still a bit sloshy outside. Samantha trekked through the parking lot, avoiding the small puddles of water still present, as she made her way inside the clinic.

"Morning, Dr. Mathewson."

"Morning, Carol."

"Did you get any flooding out by your place?"

"Yes, Delilah was driving me crazy because all her 'spots' were under water or to wet for her delicate features," Samantha said with a chuckle.

"I can see her doing that."

Both women laughed as they talked about the antics of Delilah before Samantha needed to get into her office and get logged onto her computer. She had six people scheduled, all follow ups. Not too difficult. As she scrolled through her clients for the week she stopped at the name of her last client on Thursday. Brody Fisher. She hadn't seen Brody in about six weeks, not since she had him hospitalized. The receptionist must have scheduled the appointment. She quickly logged into the Electronic Health Record, or EHR as everyone in the clinic called it, to pull up Brody's discharge summary. She quickly scanned to the last page.

"Schizoaffective Disorder," she read aloud.

That was the diagnosis that Samantha had given him. She looked at the treatment recommendation and saw they were requesting that he be seen twice a week. She let out a frustrated sigh and ran her hand through her hair. Therapy with patients like this tended to be difficult. Most had trouble comprehending the magnitude of their disorder or simply didn't trust the therapeutic process. Hopefully Brody would be open to it. She continued to read, noting that they wanted him to continue his medication regimen as well which included Risperidone, Sertraline and Trazadone. That she knew the clinic could manage.

"I wonder how he's doing?" she pondered briefly before she prepared herself for her first client.

The day was exceedingly slow. One of the side effects of all the rain was that most of Samantha's clients didn't show up so she had a lot of down time to read. Oh she'd like one to believe she was catching up on the latest research but she wasn't. She was perusing through the latest issue of Travel magazine, starring at the beautiful pictures of Jamaica, a place she had always wanted to visit. When it was time to leave for the night, she gathered her belongings and logged out of all her systems before locking up her office. As she turned around she walked right into a wall of flesh.

"Dr. Mathewson."

Samantha sucked in a breath startled by the appearance of Brody Fisher. "Brody, you scared me."

He offered her a cryptic smile. "You all alone?"

"No, well, the clinic is closed. Let me walk you outside. Unless you need to visit right now?"

He didn't move at first and his eyes twitched slightly. "When do I see you?"

"Umm, 4:00 on Thursday," she said directing him towards the exit. "Is that time okay?"

"I got something real important to tell you, Dr. Mathewson."

She stopped walking. "Is it something we need to talk about right now? Are you feeling like you may hurt yourself?"

124

His head tilted to the side slightly and then he grinned again. "I already did."

He then showed her his arms which bore several superficial cuts on them.

"You gonna send me back?"

"Brody, come with me to my office. Let's talk."

He nodded as she led him back to her office and unlocked the door. She moved aside so he could step inside first and then closed the door behind them. Brody took a seat in his normal spot, nearest the door. Samantha offered him a small smile before taking a seat at her desk and picking up her phone.

"Hey Carol, Brody Fisher just got here. I'm going to visit with him for a few minutes. Can you stick around a little bit longer?"

"Sure, Dr. Mathewson. Just buzz me when you're done."

"Thanks Carol." She hung up and once again smiled at Brody. "Can you tell me what happened, Brody?"

He twitched slightly. "I don't like the medicine."

"Okay, well, we can look into maybe a different one. I'd like you to continue taking it for now. Would you be willing to do that?"

He nodded and scratched behind his ear, closing his eyes. He looked better than he did before he was admitted six weeks ago. Back then he hadn't changed clothes or showered in days and was hearing voices. He became highly paranoid and thought his grandmother was trying to poison him. When he started to have thoughts on how he would kill her, hospitalization was in order to ensure her safety and get him on the right medication.

"I did a bad thing, Dr. Mathewson."

She sat up straight and uncrossed her legs. "What bad thing?"

He looked down and ran his fingers along the cuts on his forearms but didn't say anything else. Samantha watched him carefully trying to give him a chance to clarify what he had said. He continued to be silent as his fingers traced along the marks he had inflicted on himself. She waited a little longer and decided a change of tactics was in order.

"May I see your cuts, Brody?"

He sighed and nodded. Samantha moved her chair forward and reached for his wrist to turn his arm gently. She noted approximately 30 fresh cuts, all appeared shallow. They were nothing like what he had done in the past. She released his wrist and offered him a comforting smile, hoping to ease him into talking.

"Is this the bad thing you did, Brody?"

He shook his head. "I'm not supposed to talk about it."

"But if we don't talk about it then I can't help you figure out what to do, right?"

His brows scrunched together in confusion and his eye twitched slightly. He ran his hand through his hair, looking suddenly very lost and afraid. Something had clearly happened in the short time from his release just three days ago to today. But what? That's what Samantha needed to find out.

"Brody," she said, touching his shoulder lightly. "You know I only want to help you."

"You'll send me away again," he said a little more forcefully, moving so that her hand dropped away from him.

"Not necessarily, Brody. If you can tell me what had happened then I'm sure we can figure out a plan for how best to handle it."

"I can't say what I did or something ... bad's gonna happen."

126

She sat up completely. This was not working. She hated to actually have to probe for answers because it felt very leading to her. She preferred to let her clients tell her what they were comfortable sharing but in this case she could see it wasn't working and she needed to know if he had harmed anyone.

"Did you do anything to anyone? Your grandmom?"

He shook his head vehemently.

"You said you didn't like the medicine they were giving you. Is it not working okay?"

He shrugged at this question.

"Brody, are you hearing any voices or seeing anything others don't see?"

He looked up at her and nodded just slightly.

"One or both, Brody?'

He looked around nervously and then leaned towards her slightly. "I keep seeing … something." He turned his head carefully as if inspecting the room. "It's scary and it keeps telling me stuff."

"What kind of stuff is it telling you?"

"It whispers to me all the time. It tells me to hurt myself." He looked down at his arm. "It wanted me to cut deeper but I didn't."

"That's very good, Brody. Is the voice telling you anything else?"

He shook his head and then leaned even closer to her, close enough that Samantha felt a bit uncomfortable. "I'm afraid it's going to make me do something I don't want to do."

"Like what?" she replied with a slight edge in her voice.

His eyes blinked shut. He squeezed them tighter as his brow furrowed in distress. A moment later they reopened and he smirked. Samantha found that strange and out of

127

character. It definitely wasn't the appropriate response. He then sat up completely and chuckled lightly. Samantha was not laughing. She was seriously considering re-hospitalizing him but she couldn't do that without more information.

"I was just kidding, Dr. Mathewson."

Samantha frowned. "Brody, this is not something to kid about. If the medication isn't helping. If you're thinking about hurting yourself or others, well, then we need to do something about that. Change your medication or go back to hospital if necessary."

"I'm fine," he replied with a sigh. "I'm sorry. I shouldn't have done that."

"No, you shouldn't have."

He looked at the clock and then back at her. "I'll see you on Thursday night, right? That's when my appointment is, isn't it?"

She breathed out deeply and nodded before standing up. "Yes, I'll see you on Thursday night but Brody, if anything should come up between now and then will you please come see me. I want to help you."

He gave her a small smile. "I know you do Dr. Mathewson but nothing is gonna fix what's wrong with me."

She touched his shoulder and shook her head. "I don't believe that Brody. If you and I work together and we get your medication right, then you can have a happy and fulfilling life. You have to trust me on that, okay?"

"I almost believe you Dr. Mathewson," he said as he exited her office.

She watched as he walked down the long hallway to the exit. He was shaking his head and she could hear sound coming from him so she suspected that he was talking to whoever had frightened him. She wasn't sure what to do about the situation. He had not said anything that would require hospitalization but she was concerned that he was still seeing things and as evident by his behavior just now, interacting with them as well. She waited until he had exited the building before turning back around to go enter her office.

"I'll check on him this week," she said to herself.

As she went to her desk to log back on her computer the hair on the back of her neck prickled. She turned to see if anyone was there and out of the corner of her eye she thought she saw a figure by her window. She started to approach it, thinking it must be Brody but when she got there, no one was visible.

"That's so strange."

"Something is coming and we all gots to be ready for it."

Samantha heard Ophelia's words and admitted that it creeped her out a bit but then laughed at herself for getting spooked so easily. She stepped up to her desk and turned her computer back on. She would need to chart this encounter before she left, just in case something happened with Brody before she saw him again.

T. M. Witko

Chapter Three

Samantha spent an hour at the office before she was able to leave. She headed home with her head filled with so many unanswered questions. By the time she walked into her house Delilah was beside herself with unbridled energy. She jumped around her excitedly until Samantha picked up the wiggling dog and brought her close to her chest while simultaneously dropping her keys and phone on the table. She walked to the backdoor and set her down, then watched as Delilah darted out quickly.

"Sorry girl, I know I was late."

Samantha closed her eyes momentarily as she rolled her shoulders, trying to wrap her head around all that transpired with Brody. She was trying to work through her concerns about his well-being and whether he was a threat or not. The lines were very clear in her profession and if he didn't make an actual threat to anyone she couldn't re-admit him without his consent. She had spoken to Brody's grandmother before she left the office but she had indicated that Brody seemed to be doing well and that she had no concerns. Delilah's barking and then growl startled Samantha out of her thoughts.

"Hey, what's the matter girl?" Samantha said looking up.

She heard a mumbling that as strange as it sounded, appeared to be coming from the wind. She looked down at Delilah who was launching herself forward and barking at an area on the tree line, she was clearly riled up and felt some kind of danger was present. There was a whirl of wind as the leaves blew up from the ground and the nearly bare branches began swinging, hitting against one another, almost violently.

"Delilah, come girl, get away from there."

Samantha cautiously walked towards her dog who was nipping at the air, growling. As she kneeled down to grab her, Delilah launched forward as if she were chasing something and then stopped abruptly right before the trees. She suddenly whimpered and cowered on the ground. Samantha leapt towards her, snatching her frightened dog in her arms. Her short fur was sticking straight up and was ice cold. She wrapped her underneath her jacket and pressed her against her chest, trying to warm her up.

"Is there somebody there?"

"You will die," a voice whispered in the wind.

Samantha felt a cold chill wash over her body and she swore that a dark figure lurked within the tree line. She couldn't make out what it was exactly, only that it was wearing some kind of hood and that there was blackness where a face should be. She gasped as she turned and started running back to her home. She heard what she could only describe as laughter as the wind started swirling violently around her. She reached for the handle on the door and drew her hand back. It was freezing. She quickly pulled her sleeve over her hand and opened the door, sneaking one last glance over her shoulder. The wind died and everything was as it had been.

"What the hell is going on?"

She quickly set Delilah down and watched her stumble on shaky legs to her pillow bed and plop down on it. Samantha grabbed the throw blanket on the couch as she picked up her phone and then carefully wrapped Delilah in the blanket to warm her up. She took a seat on the floor next to her and gently stroked the dogs head.

"It's okay, baby, mama's got you." She pressed the three buttons on her phone and waited for someone to answer.

"911, what's your emergency."

"I think there's someone in the woods behind my house. Can you send someone to check?"

"Did you see someone ma'am?"

"I … I don't know, I think I saw a man out there but I can't be certain. Please, can someone come check for me?'

"Yes, ma'am, are you at 419 Sycamore Place?"

"Yes."

"A unit has been dispatched. Please stay in the house until they arrive."

"Oh trust me, I'm not going back out there."

The operator stayed on the phone until the squad car arrived and then hung up. Samantha rose from her seated position hearing Delilah whimper as she walked towards the door. She got to the front of her house just as the officer knocked. She breathed in deeply, suddenly feeling very foolish for calling the police for what was likely her imagination getting the better of her. She hesitantly opened the door.

"Dr. Mathewson, is everything alright?" an officer by the name of Reed Hudson asked.

"I'm … I swear, I thought I saw something out back in the woods and I could, I don't know … hear someone talking to me out there. And, well, Delilah was acting crazy, like something was there too. I know it's probably dumb but could you go check to make sure no one's out there?"

"Sure thing," Officer Hudson replied as he motioned to his partner who immediately started walking towards the rear of the house.

Samantha watched from her kitchen window as the two officers pulled out their flashlights and aimed the beam of light at the wooded area behind her home. Each one had their other hand on their holster, prepared if necessary to draw their weapon. Samantha glanced back at her poor

Delilah. She was still shivering but her skin was no longer cold. She was merely trembling out of fear. Samantha turned back to the window and watched until the officers were exiting the woods. Each man shoved their flashlight into their belt as they walked towards the house.

"Anything?" she asked as she stepped out the back door.

"Nope, nothing but little critters roaming about. Maybe that's what you heard," Officer Jones inquired.

Samantha shook her head. "It wasn't 'critters' I heard." She looked back towards the wooded area and crossed her arms around herself.

"If you hear or see anything else just give us a call, Dr. Mathewson," Officer Hudson said kindly as he handed her a business card. "We'll come out again if need be."

She gave him a weak smile. "Thank you, Reed."

He smiled and gave her a slight nod before turning around. She could see they were talking to each other and could only imagine what they thought. The local shrink hearing and seeing things that aren't there. She wondered how long it would be until everyone in town was talking about it. She sighed and walked back inside. She tried to pick up Delilah but she cried as if she were in pain so she set her back down.

"What's the matter, baby?"

Delilah looked up to her with sad and desperate eyes. She sat down beside her and rested her hand on her dogs back which seemed to stop the whimpering. Samantha leaned her head back and closed her eyes. The long day already had the makings of an even longer night. If Delilah wasn't better by morning she would need to cancel her morning clients so that she could take her to the vet. All the pressure of the day made her feel exhausted and as uncomfortable as it was sitting on the floor she found herself asleep.

KNOCK, KNOCK, KNOCK

Samantha blinked her eyes open and immediately turned towards the clock on the wall. It was nearly midnight. She looked back at Delilah who was still shivering. She sighed as she stood up, once again hearing her whimper. Samantha hurried to the door, wondering if the police were back, she reasoned that was the only logical explanation for someone knocking on her door at midnight.

"Ophelia," she gasped in shock. "What are you doing here?"

Ophelia pushed passed her. "I've come to help ya."

"With what?"

"That demon of course."

"Demon, what… Ophelia what are you talking about?"

Ophelia didn't reply, she simply walked through the living room towards the kitchen, stopping in front of Delilah who weakly raised her head. Ophelia sat down in front of her, crossing her legs as she brought out a little leather pouch. She undid the string and slipped her fingers inside it, pulling out what appeared to be mud on the pad of her finger and offered it to Delilah who quickly sniffed it and then pulled her head back.

"It may not smell the best but it will make ya feel better," she said, looking into Delilah's eyes.

Delilah stared at her for a long moment. Ophelia nodded her head slightly and the small dog sniffed again. This time she licked the substance on her finger. Samantha watched in apt fascination. Delilah was a moody little dog and tended to only take food from Samantha. She liked the vet well enough and tolerated the kennel but to actually eat something from someone she didn't know was unheard of.

"Come on girl, eat it up," Ophelia asked sweetly.

"What is that anyway?"

Ophelia continued to watch Delilah. "It's medicine."

"What's wrong with her?" Samantha asked, kneeling down next to Delilah.

Ophelia looked at her with kindness in her eyes. "Dogs can see and hear things that humans often cannot. She saw the demon. It touched her. Without medicine she will die."

"Die … what," Samantha scrunched her eyes shut. This was all too surreal for her and couldn't possibly be true.

"You don't believe me and that's okay."

"It's all so farfetched. Demons, really?"

"Do you believe in Angels?"

"I don't know, sure I guess."

"You cannot have one without the other."

Samantha sighed and then smiled as Delilah stood up. She went over to Ophelia and licked her face profusely and then leapt into Samantha's lap. She grinned and pulled her dog up, squeezing her happily. She then looked at Ophelia who had risen to her feet. Samantha rose as well, still holding Delilah, who appeared for all intents and purposes to be cured from whatever was ailing her before.

"So, you are saying a demon touched Delilah? Why?"

"Perhaps it was after you and she intervened."

Samantha closed her eyes and held Delilah even closer. "Why would a demon be after me?"

"Why indeed."

Samantha sighed and glanced out her back window. "Do you think it's still out there?"

Ophelia nodded. "Yes it is. Now you must stay in here."

136

Before Samantha could question why, Ophelia was out the door. The old woman walked to the tree line and unsnapped a satchel that had been tied to her belt. She pulled out something but from where Samantha was watching she couldn't tell what it was. Samantha cracked the window so that she could hear what was going on. Ophelia began speaking in another language. A language that Samantha couldn't identify. The whirlwind that had happened earlier spun up again, swirling around Ophelia. She continued to speak, getting louder and louder, and then blew whatever was in her hand into the wind. There was a loud screeching noise that made Samantha cover her ears and then silence once again.

"This is crazy," Samantha muttered.

Ophelia walked from one end of the tree line to the other. Each time she would stop, she would raise her hands and speak in the unidentified language, blow some substance into the air and then walk to the next section. She did it four times and after she was done she slowly walked towards the front yard, bypassing the house. Samantha ran to the front of the house and caught up to the woman just as she reached the front gate.

"Wait, is it gone?"

Samantha couldn't believe she was actually asking if a demon was gone but from what she'd seen she was willing to take a leap of faith. Ophelia stopped and turned to her. Her face was ashen and her eyes were dark and sunken in. Samantha exhaled a breath, wondering what exactly had happened to her when that wind circled her. Had the demon done this? Would she be okay?

"You are safe here," Ophelia finally said solemnly.

She turned back around and stepped outside the gate, walking across the street to slip into the front seat of an old Buick. As she drove off, Samantha felt a little worried.

Ophelia had said she was safe at her home but what about elsewhere? She swallowed thickly and hurried inside. While she believed what Ophelia said about her being safe at the house, she didn't want to take any chances.

Chapter Four

The next couple of days went by in a blur. Delilah seemed to be completely alright and was back to her old hyperactive self, aside from the fact that she didn't go near the wooded area any longer. At work, she was thankful that there were no real crises over the last few days because she wasn't sure she could handle that in her current mindset. She had also called Brody's grandmother yesterday to see how he was doing. She confirmed that Brody would make his scheduled appointment and told her that he was doing well. She supposed that was good news, maybe what happened on Monday was just a fluke, a weird reaction to the medication he was taking. She sincerely hoped that was the case. By the time Thursday came around she found herself very antsy and had difficulty concentrating. She wasn't sure why but she felt on edge.

"Hello?" she asked somewhat startled.

"Dr. Mathewson, your 4:00 is here."

"Thank you Carol, I'll be right up."

She took a calming breath and then headed up the flight of stairs at the end of the long hallway. When she reached the door to the waiting room she took one more cleansing breath before stepping through it. She glanced around the near empty space and saw Brody immediately. He had his head down and was mumbling and shaking his head. That was not a good sign. Samantha cleared her throat and smiled when Brody looked up at her.

"Hello, Brody. Come on down."

He rose and followed her, not making a sound which was definitely not his typical behavior. He was usually a chatterbox and wanted to tell her everything going on around him. She smiled once again at him as she got to her office and opened the door allowing him to step inside as she followed behind him. He took his usual seat except this time he sat straight up, watching as she sat down.

"How are you feeling today, Brody?"

"Are you a Christian, Dr. Mathewson?"

"I'm sorry, what?"

"Are you a Christian?"

"I was raised Lutheran but I don't really practice anymore, why?"

He was silent for a long moment as he contemplated her answer. He had never asked her about her spiritual preferences before and she generally didn't talk about things like that in session but she needed to know what was going on and if answering a few personal questions allowed him to open up then she would do it. Samantha continued to stare at him, paying close attention to his body language. He seemed uncharacteristically stiff in his chair.

"I can't talk to you anymore."

"And why's that, Brody."

"Because I was told that I can only talk to Christians."

"Well, I may not practice my faith as much as I used to but I don't remember reading anything in the bible that says only Christians can talk to Christians. I thought we were supposed to love one another as God loves us." At the mention of God she saw him visibly shake. "You know, I remember hearing in many of the bible stories that the devil would often disguise himself as an angel to trick people. Do you know any of these stories, Brody?"

His brows scrunched together again and he looked confused. Samantha wasn't sure what was bothering him but after her experience on Monday night and Ophelia telling her that there had been a demonic presence outside her house,

140

she knew something was going on. In fact she was witnessing something happening right before her eyes. The way Brody was acting and talking was unusual to say the least and he now appeared to be listening to someone.

"Brody, are you hearing something right now?"

He nodded.

"What are you hearing?"

His face paled for a moment. "He's saying that you're a bad person and that you're trying to stop me from doing God's work."

"I'm not a bad person Brody. You've known me for a long time. I care about you and your well-being. I want to help you."

His face altered and grew red with anger. "You don't want to help me. You want to lock me up. You want to ..." he stopped, his face shifting to look at something she couldn't see.

"Brody, do you see something?"

He nodded and pointed to the corner of the room. Samantha looked that way but there wasn't anything there. She turned back to him and moved forward, gently touching his hand. It was cold and clammy. He jumped slightly when she touched him and turned back to her. There was sadness in his eyes as he looked down at her hand on top of his.

"Brody, please let me help you."

He looked up at her, his expression hardening. "I need to go now."

He stood abruptly causing her to lean back. She pushed the chair backwards slightly and stood as well. She wasn't prepared to have him leave as she was extremely concerned for what he might do in his current state of mind. He reached his arms out to her as if he wanted to hug her which was something he had never done before. She didn't generally hug her clients but if they needed one she would always oblige them. She stepped towards him and he put his arms around her.

"You can't help him," he muttered in a voice that wasn't his own.

Her body stiffened and she suddenly felt cold. Her heart swelled with sadness and despair as if all the joy within her had been sucked out and all that was left was a hollow shell. She saw flashes of her father dying and her husband leaving her. She saw the verbal berating her stepfather would give her which often times had turned violent. She saw a lonely little girl with no friends cowering against the wall. Tears involuntarily slipped from her eyes as these images floated through her mind. There was a deep chuckle that emanated from Brody; that frightened her out of her wayward thoughts.

"I see what you try to hide, Samantha. You are mine now," the voice said cryptically.

Samantha pulled away from Brody and immediately felt the coldness wash away from her. Brody stood before her with an awkward expression and then a small smile crept onto his face. He turned slowly and stepped out of the door as if nothing had happened. Momentarily stunned she stood there in shock and confusion before she finally rushed to the doorway just in time to see Brody step outside the clinic door.

"Are you okay, Dr. Mathewson?" Veronica asked from the doorway across the hall.

Samantha blinked a few times and nodded. "Yes, just, umm, nothing."

She closed her door and immediately went to her desk. She started tapping furiously on her computer until Brody's chart appeared. She searched for his phone number and dialed. Mrs. Fisher answered on the first ring.

"Hello?"

"Mrs. Fisher, this is Dr. Mathewson."

"Is Brody alright?" she asked with concern.

"That's why I'm calling. He just left my office and informed me he wouldn't be seeing me again. Did you know anything about that?"

"Oh my goodness, no, I didn't. Why would he do that?"

"Mrs. Fisher, has he been taking his medication?"

"As far as I know he has."

Samantha ran her fingers through her hair. "I don't believe the medications are working. We need to look into changing them or possibly readmitting him to the hospital."

"Are you sure that's necessary? He's doing so well."

"I'm afraid he's not doing as well as you think, Mrs. Fisher. Is it possible for you to bring him into the clinic tomorrow morning to see me?"

"Yes, I can do that. I'll have him over there first thing."

"Thank you," Samantha said hanging up.

She laid her hand over her heart feeling it beat rapidly. She took a couple of deep breaths trying to settle down. Her soul felt heavy which bothered her. She had dealt with and managed all her old ghosts. In truth she hadn't thought about her past in a very long time. She tapped her fingers on her desk and sighed as she stared at her computer which was already logged into Brody Fisher's medical file.

"How the hell do I even chart this?" she wondered with another sigh.

She shook her head and thought for a moment how she would explain the encounter she had just had with Brody. After a moment she logged into the therapy note template and began writing. Once she had completed Brody's note she took care of the rest of her paperwork. She had all four clients show up after lunch and had a lot of charting to do before she left for the evening. By the time she was finished with everything and locking up her office the hallways were already dark and completely void of people. She shook her head and groaned.

"I hate when they do that. They know I'm still in here why do they need to shut all the dang lights off?"

She started to walk down the darkened corridor. Normally the dark hallway didn't bother her because she knew everything was locked up but today, well, after the day she'd had she was feeling a little freaked out by it all. She found herself pausing by every open door and then darting passed it, until she got to the exit. She breathed out deeply and chuckled at herself for getting so worked up.

"Dr. Mathewson," she heard as she stepped out in the cool night air.

"Brody, Jesus, you scared me. Is everything alright?"

"It will be."

Before she could contemplate this further he grabbed her. She didn't see the knife in his hand until he was wielding it at her chest. The sharp pain caused her to scream out but Brody pushed her to the ground, raising his arm once again. Samantha could hear shouting and screaming in the distance but inherently she knew that it was likely too late for her. As Brody raised his knife once more she saw it, the demon Ophelia had spoken of. His face was transposed over Brody's. It was a face of raw terror smiling down on her as Brody made the fatal blow. Samantha's body began to shut down. Her breathing slowed and all she could think was that now it was time for her to sleep. There was no more pain as her eyes closed for good.

"Dr. Mathewson, hold on."

People moved around Dr. Mathewson franticly trying to save her to no avail. The man who had done this was being held by two officers. He was screaming nonsense about a demon that made him do it. Officer Hudson who had just arrived on the scene kneeled down and inspected Dr. Mathewson's wounds. She never stood a chance.

"Take him away," Officer Hudson said sadly. He couldn't believe this could happen here, in Grieselton, a place where nothing bad happened.

~*~

Ophelia stood outside the front of her store and looked to the sky. She felt a sudden rush of sadness invade her and quickly brought out the root in her pocket, chewing on it until the sadness disappeared once again. She shook her head and walked back inside her store, only to exit out the back. She knew what she needed to do. She drove to 419 Sycamore Place in no big hurry as no one would be there. When she approached the house she walked around to the back and turned the knob on the door. The little dog barked fervently and then wagged its tail as she entered. Ophelia kneeled down picking up Delilah who immediately started licking her face, happy to see her.

"You must come with me, little one. We have to prepare."

T. M. Witko

Epilogue

Five Weeks Later...

Parker stared out her window as her previous life got further and further behind her. She hated this, hated that she would be starting a new school and that it was already October. The new school year had begun almost seven weeks ago. She would be the odd one out. Everyone would stare at her. She sighed as she thought about the friends she left behind in Lincoln, Nebraska. She had lived there almost her entire 16 years of life and couldn't imagine living anywhere else.

"Whatcha thinking about?"

"Nothing, mom," Parker said with a roll of her eyes. "Everything's just ... great!"

"Oh, come on, honey. This will be a new adventure for both of us."

Parker turned around and stared at her incredulously. "I didn't want an adventure mom. I wanted my old school and my old friends and ... Dad, there I said it. Dad lives in Lincoln."

Sage took a sharp intake of breath and shook her head slowly. "Well, 'Dad' doesn't want us, so there I said it."

"No, he doesn't want you," Parker mumbled.

"Yeah, that's probably more accurate," Sage replied, her eyes watering.

"Mom, I'm sorry. I didn't mean that."

Her mom smiled half-heartedly and kept her eyes on the road. "You did, but, it's okay. You're entitled to your feelings."

Parker turned back to the window frowning. She was so frustrated she wanted to spit nails. Her father, Samuel Joseph, had left the family a few years ago but they had all remained amicable. That is until her father started to bring his new woman around. She seemed nice enough and she made dad happy which was good, even her mom had said that. That all changed however when he decided to marry her. That's when her mom had difficulties. Parker had caught her crying many times until finally her mother had said enough. She wanted to move out of state, away from any reminders, she wanted to start fresh.

"Hey look, Georgia!"

Parker smiled and nodded. "Are we almost there?"

"Are we there yet? Are we there yet? Are we there yet?" her mother repeated in a sing song voice while bouncing in her seat and bobbing her head.

Parker laughed. "Mom, you're seriously nuts. You know that right?"

"Why yes, I do know that," she replied with a smile. She then reached for her daughter's hand. Parker smiled and took her hand in hers. "I know this is hard for you. Thank you for being such an understanding daughter. The creator really smiled down on me and Samuel when we had you. You were always such a perfect baby and now you have grown into such a beautiful young woman. You," she waved their joined hands. "Are gonna knock 'em dead when you start on Monday."

"I hope so mom."

"You will."

They continued to drive until they passed a sign that said 'Welcome to Grieselton'. Parker noticed that the whole area seemed to be surrounded by woods. Parker turned to look over the back seat. Her Australian Shepard was laying comfortably on the backseat. Sensing her owner's eyes on her, the dog lifted its head up, wagging her tale as she sat up and started licking Parker's hands and then her face. Parker laughed and hugged her.

"We're almost to our new home, Sunni."

Sunni waged her tail even more. She didn't know what she was talking about but liked the idea that the word home was used. Parker turned back around and Sunni sat up on the backseat, barking until the rear window was lowered. Parker glanced at her mom and laughed. They discovered early on that Sunni had somehow figured out that if she put her paws on the levers that the window would roll down. Once she learned that she did it every time she was in the car so now they had to keep the windows locked, much to Sunni's dismay. The crisp autumn air blew into the SUV with gusto as they slowed down.

"This must be downtown," Sage stated curiously.

"Not much to it," Parker replied, rolling down her window as well.

"Don't be a snob, Parker. I think it's quaint. Don't you?"

"Un huh."

Sage slowed the vehicle to a stop as she waited for a car to back out of its parking space. Parker felt eyes on her and turned to see an old woman standing outside a store, holding a black Chihuahua in her arms. The woman cocked her head to the side and placed her free hand over her heart as a smile crossed her lips. Parker shook her head as she and her mom started moving again.

"Creepy," she mumbled.

"What's that honey?"

"Nothing mom, just some old woman was staring at me."

"Well, small towns and all, there's bound to be a few looneys in the bin."

"Wonderful," Parker sighed uncomfortably.

Meanwhile, Ophelia watched as the vehicle drove away. She had felt something in the presence of the young girl in the SUV. She was never wrong when it came to sensing the energy around people. This girl had a strong gift. Ophelia would need to pray about it and consult her books but she suddenly felt that things were making a turn. She grinned down at Delilah who licked her on the nose repeatedly.

"This is very interesting, little one. That girl," she paused and looked in the direction of the retreating vehicle. "I believe she will be our salvation."

To be continued in
An Unexpected Gift
Book 1 in The Diakrisis Tales

ABOUT THE AUTHOR

Author T.M. Witko lives on the Standing Rock Indian Reservation with her children, Adam and Deanna. They are accompanied by their many animals, which includes an Australian Shepherd/Border Collie mix named Bella, a couple of ornery cats (Edward and Lil Bit) and their horses, Eagle Bear and Wild Spirit. She and her family enjoy attending wacipis, participating in tribal ceremonies, and living a quiet life without the hustle and bustle of the cities.

Ms. Witko is a licensed clinical psychologist, a full time writer/editor and one of the co-founders of Winyan Press, LLC, an independent publishing house geared at helping female writers find their voice. She is a multi-genre author who writes Young Adult Fiction, Crime/Suspense Stories, Adult Romances and Native American Fiction. In addition, she has put together a collection of short stories called SNAPSHOTS which are geared at giving readers a sample of her different writing styles. Look for it on Wattpad and as a FREE e-book, Fall 2016.

SOCIAL MEDIA CONTACTS
Facebook: https://www.facebook.com/TMWitko
Twitter: https://twitter.com/AuthorTawaWitko
Instagram: https://instagram.com/tawa823
Tumbler: https://www.tumbler.com/blog/tmwitko
Website: https://authortmwitko.com

T. M. Witko

Susan Burdorf
Text Copyright © 2016 Susan Burdorf

Gone Fishing

The body of a local gambler is pulled from a lake which sets in motion a series of mysteries for Sheriff Pete Malone to solve. When his troubled little sister, Belle, shows up unexpectedly he has to juggle the hurt feelings of his girlfriend, and keep his sister from running away, all while trying to solve the murder. When his sister takes a job at the local resort next to the lake, and discovers clues that could help solve the murder, the killer begins to stalk her pushing up the timeline to solving the killing before Belle becomes the next victim.

Gone Fishing

By

Susan Burdorf

Susan Burdorf

Acknowledgements

I would like to thank Laura Perez for creating this opportunity for all of us join together once again to thrill our readers with stories of mystery and suspense. I would also like to thank Kelly D. Abell for creating my wonderful cover, just wouldn't be a mystery story without you. Finally, I would like to thank the readers who take time out of busy schedules and lives to visit with us through our stories.

Susan Burdorf

Chapter One

"Hold it right there, Harry."

The tone in the voice of the other man held a certainty that he would be obeyed.

Harry stopped.

Peering into the darkness of the alley he noted a figure standing in shadow. His shoulders were broad and square. The large bulk of the man was outlined in a silvery shimmer from the sparse moonlight that filtered into the deserted cut through between the two buildings.

Harry nervously rubbed his hands together and flashed his million dollar smile, brilliant white in the dark night, and swaggered over toward the other man. Harry glanced behind him toward the boat he'd almost made it into and sighed.

He rubbed his jaw, already anticipating the beating he was about to receive, judging how much the repair dental work would cost him. But she was worth it. Blonde bombshell and built to please, she had been loads of fun, and even though he now had to pay the price for that illicit dalliance, he was okay with it.

Her husband wasn't supposed to arrive at the resort until the next day. A billionaire, the man had companies all over the world, surely one of them was in need of his assistance? But no, right in the middle of their rendezvous he'd shown up necessitating the need for Harry to dress in the closet, in the dark, while she'd lured her husband out for a skinny dip in the pool.

He thought he'd gotten away with it as he slipped out the front door... and right into the arms of the man's bodyguard. Talk about bad luck! That old adage about if it wasn't for bad luck he'd have no luck at all, rang through Harry's mind and he shook his head.

"Hey man," he said walking toward the shadow with his hands up as if in surrender, his tone light and conciliatory, "not sure what to tell you, but she wanted it…"

The figure stepped from the shadow into the moonlight, the barrel of the gun reflecting silver and Harry stopped moving, fear catching his breath.

"Whoa, wait a minute, you can't…" and then a twang sounded in the stillness of the night and he dropped soundlessly onto the ground.

The man unscrewed the silencer from the gun and gestured to the other two figures waiting in the shadows. "Put him on the boat. I think it is time to take him for his last ride."

"Yes, boss," said one of the men. He lifted Harry's legs and his partner lifted the prostrate man under the arms. The two men crab-walked Harry's body to the boat. They threw him on board as they reached the side of the bobbing vessel.

The boss got onto the boat and walked over the body heading toward the motor. He gestured to one of the men to remove the rope from the mooring point and shove the boat off. Starting the motor he headed out into the narrow inlet that separated the resort docking area from the rest of the lake.

A short while later he cut the motor. The boat drifted, gently rocking on the unsettled surface of the water. He gestured for the men to grab the chain holding the anchor to the side of the boat. They knew what to do, having done this a few times before. Wrapping the rope loosely, but securely around Harry's legs they threw both the body and the anchor overboard.

162

Gone Fishing

There was the sound of a splash, then a few bubbles, and the body disappeared below the surface of the water.

He watched it sink below the surface, weighted down with the anchor and smiled. The smile did not reach his eyes. The two men with him looked over at their boss and then back to the place the body had disappeared. The bubbles had stopped after a few minutes in, and they waited for further instructions. In the distance they could hear the putt-putt of another boat on the water as it drew closer to them.

"Make sure the boat is wiped clean of our presence, especially where you might have touched anything."

He handed them each an envelope which they slipped inside pockets immediately without looking inside. They began cleaning the boat as the boat they'd heard earlier grew closer.

In a few minutes the other boat drew alongside and the three men stepped into it. No care for the man who was now beneath the water.

He was no longer a problem. Their boss would be pleased. And to think the fool had thought anyone cared that he was sleeping with another man's wife. That had been the least of his problems.

Smiling, the large man chuckled as he nodded to the blonde at the helm of the other boat to go forward. He was still chuckling at Harry's misinterpretation of the reason for his death as they pulled to the dock. The poor sucker never knew when he'd been set up. And now he'd paid the price for his ignorance.

Susan Burdorf

Chapter Two

"Come on, Belle, get up, time to go."

"Mom," the teen in the bed said opening one eye and then closing it again. "I'm tired. Let me sleep." To give emphasis to her condition she rolled over and pulled the covers over her head, loudly pretend snoring.

"Nope, Belle, not this time. You agreed."

Her mom tugged the covers off the sleeping girl trying not to gasp at the fact that her youngest daughter preferred to sleep in the shortest shorts she'd ever seen and a tank top that was barely there.

Kids today, she thought as she left the room and went down the hall to her room where she found her husband packing their suitcases.

"Is she ready?" He asked. His tone, she noted, was not hopeful. He, of the two of them, seemed to understand their youngest child best. Belle had been their change of life baby. Just when they'd thought they were done with children she'd discovered she was 'in that way' again as women said when they found themselves pregnant at forty-three. Their oldest two had already flown the nest and the only child left at home was their twelve year old son, Peter. Peter had been so self-sufficient they'd gotten used to not being hands on parents, and here they were once again with babe in arms.

Perhaps it was true that a baby born to older parents is smarter than children born to younger parents, at least Belle proved that to be true. Reading at age three, she'd constantly blown the curve on any test she took. She was bright, but she was also difficult. Rebellious to a fault, she'd at least been under control when Peter lived at home, but by the time she was six, and he'd gone off to college, and then on to other things that took him far from home, she became impossible.

At their ages they'd been looking forward to retirement, and the fun that comes from travel and antique hunting and eating breakfast at out of the way bed and breakfast inns. Belle, however, hated all of that 'froo-froo' stuff, and in spite of the fact that she had a closet full of dresses and dresser drawers full of appropriate clothing, she seemed to enjoy wearing clothes that shocked and caused whispers at the country club or restaurants when they went out to dinner.

Her usual Goth garb had been replaced lately, thank heavens, with something a little less scandalous, but not much. She had a feeling Belle was just biding her time to whip out the next transformation and she could only hope it wouldn't be too hard to explain. The excuse that she was just a teen-ager was getting harder and harder to pass by their friends, most of whom were grandparents, not parents of teens any longer, and had no patience with them when they had to leave events to bail Belle out of trouble.

"Mom," said Belle through a yawn she covered with a hand sporting glittery black nail polish and a few temporary tattoos she drawn on her hand herself. "I talked to Peter yesterday, and he said that if it was okay with you, I could stay with him while you went on this cruise."

Her face remained carefully quiet and without expression, but her mom could see a tenseness in her daughter's posture that spoke to her nervousness.

"Bryan, what do you think?"

Belle glanced at her dad with a hopeful expression. He, in turn, glanced at both the women in his life and sighed. His wife appeared to be even more hopeful than his daughter that she would be allowed to stay with her brother.

"Pete said it was okay?" He sounded skeptical.

"Yes," said Belle, her tone way too casual alerting his parental radar that something was amiss.

"Hmmm... and how do you plan to get there?"

"Bus." Said Belle with confidence. "There's one that leaves in two hours and should arrive at his town later in the day. You can drop me at the bus station before you go."

"Maybe we should call him... just to confirm that he can pick you up when you get there..."

"No need." Belle said quickly. "I already confirmed it with him and he is out of town until later tonight so you can't reach him. I think his girlfriend is picking me up at the bus station."

"I would feel more comfortable if I talked to him," her mom said. She reached into her purse for her phone.

"Really mom, it's okay, but if you want to call him I'm sure he won't mind. He's just out with some of his buddies, I'm sure it won't be embarrassing or anything for him to get a call from his mother."

"I'm sure it's fine, Eleanor, let's just go. If we have to drop her off at the bus station we need to leave in fifteen minutes."

"Okay, okay."

Belle met her parents at the car and threw her small suitcase up on top of her parents' luggage. Settling in she waited for her parents to get in and get the car started. She could tell by the look her parent's shared that she was about to get 'the lecture' and so grabbed her headphones and turned her music up loud.

They got to the bus station and her parents walked inside with her even though she tried to convince them she was fine to do this on her own. She carried her suitcase in one hand, her purse in another, her expression sullen and anxious. Her dad left them for a few minutes and when he returned he handed her a ticket. Her dad slipped her some

167

money and her mom gave her another lecture, before her it was time to board the bus.

Her parents stood there watching her until the bus pulled out of the station before looking at each other with smug expressions.

"Do you think she knows that we know what she tried to pull?" Eleanor said to her husband.

"Not yet. But she will. Along with the money I slipped her a note letting her know we were on to her little game and that Pete would be prepared for her arrival with instructions to keep her until we return. And also that the bus driver was also alerted to her attempts to escape and that he was not to let her off the bus, no matter what she said."

"Can he do that?" Eleanor looked at her husband in confusion.

"I slipped him a hundred with a promise of more if she got there safely. I left an envelope for him at the front desk. He'll get it when he comes back."

"What if…?"

"Not to worry, there are no stops between here and there. I put her on the express bus." His smug grin was matched by the one on his wife's face. She grinned as she realized her daughter would be a little angry when she realized what her father had done and how her plans were spoiled now. She was sure Belle thought the next two weeks were going to be parent-free and that she could do what she wanted to, but not now. Now she was stuck with her brother for two weeks. She felt a momentary twinge of guilt for thrusting her daughter on her older brother Pete, but then she figured it would be a good chance for them to bond a little.

"I'll text Peter to let him know she is on the way." Eleanor said pulling her phone from her purse and starting to text her son a message.

Gone Fishing

Going on cruise with your father, she texted, *sister coming to visit be back in two weeks. Love, mom.*

"Not sure who will get the greater surprise today." Her husband chuckled as they got back in the car and pulled away from the station. They had a half hour to meet up with their friends, the Butlers, whom they were going on the cruise with. Once they arrived there they were taking a cab together to the airport to catch their flight to Miami and begin their vacation.

Bryan found himself whistling as he drove. He felt more lighthearted than he had in a long time. He reached over and grabbed his wife's hand, squeezing it. She squeezed back, a small sigh of contentment escaping her lips as she rested her head on his shoulder.

Yep, he thought, *this was shaping up to be a great vacation.*

Susan Burdorf

Chapter Three

On the bus Belle got the shock of her life when the bus driver made the announcement that the schedule had been changed slightly to accommodate a passenger.

"We had one scheduled stop in about an hour, but the bus is running behind schedule so we will not be stopping at that location. My apologies for the inconvenience."

Belle, texting on her phone jerked her head up at the announcement. "What?" she shouted before she realized she'd spoken aloud.

"Yes, miss?" the driver asked. She could see his eyes and the top of his balding head reflected in the mirror. He looked amused. Her eyes narrowed as she put two and two together and realized her parents had outfoxed her.

Great, she thought as she texted her friend on the phone. *Change in plans, meet me at the lake. I'll have gas money. Pick me up at the sheriff's office.*

Take that dad, she thought as she plugged the earphones in and turned her music up loud. She glanced down and gave a satisfied smile at the answer. *Two can play this game, dad.*

Susan Burdorf

Chapter Four

"What you got, Baxter?"

Reed Baxter, who doubled as the local Veterinarian and the county coroner, grunted.

Sheriff Pete Malone walked up to his side. Several campers and fishermen were standing around watching the coroner as he bent over the prone figure on the pavement of the parking lot.

A smear of glistening water and mud, signifying the body had been dragged to this spot, discolored the pavement. Malone carefully stepped around it. The body had not been removed too long before he got there, he noted, as the water was still quite fresh looking, and the mud hadn't yet dried in the early morning heat.

The body had the sickly sweet smell of decomposition mixed with a slight fishy scent overpowering the other odors. Malone covered his mouth and nose for a minute while he examined the scene.

Malone frowned. Looking back toward the dock and boat launch where the body had been retrieved from he cursed silently under his breath. His men knew better than to tamper with evidence. Why had they moved the body here and not left it near the water?

His deputies, Cramer and Bracey, were nearby interviewing some of the resort's guests and some locals he recognized. Most of them were typical Saturday afternoon fishermen. There were also a couple families, parents hugging children to their sides to keep the little ones from seeing the tragedy, even while they were staring with open curiosity at the scene. They had probably been swimming and picnicking at the beach a few hundred yards downstream from the boat launch area, never realizing until they returned to the resort, the drama that was unfolding around them.

One father in particular caught his eye and Pete nodded to him before scanning the rest of the curiosity seeking crowd. Another man, wearing dark sunglasses that hid his eyes and had pinched lips looked on without a trace of pity. He was wearing a polo shirt with one of those logos on it that read, 'Cabana Haven' and its sky blue color identified him as one of the resort staff.

Malone didn't recognize the man, but then, the resort had recently expanded so perhaps he was one of the new hires. The name badge he wore was silver with gold lettering, and hard to read as the sun was reflecting off the surface and Malone wondered if that was intentional, then quickly shook his head. He had to stop seeing suspects every where he looked, the man was probably just a curiosity seeker like the rest of the crowd gathered in solemn tribute to the victim.

hen the man turned his head to stare at Malone. The stern expression didn't change, but the man nodded at Malone as if acknowledging his authority, then swiftly walked back toward the private entrance to the resort area. In seconds he was gone. Malone pinched his lips and made a mental note to find that man later and question him.

He continued scanning the crowd. Standing in back of the taped off crowd, curious but aloof, were the true guests of the resort. They were easily identified by their expensive Sperry's brand of boat shoes or Gucci loafers that were popular with the upper echelon of America's 'rich and useless' as he liked to call them. They all looked on with the bored posture of people who were used to ignoring things that displeased them.

Mothers were shielding their children even while trying to get a glimpse of the man pulled from the lake. Men were watching with curious or annoyed expressions depending on their fishing schedule. Some of them looked red faced and sweaty, they must have just come in from the lake about the same time the coroner arrived, which meant they couldn't leave. Others were itching to get in the lake and start their fishing. They were easily identified as they were mostly standing around muttering and complaining, just loud enough he could hear them, but not so loud they were distracting the police from their work.

Malone studied their faces one by one while surveying the scene. No one seemed too interested in what was happening beyond the normal curiosity over viewing a dead body. There wasn't a single person who stood out as overly interested in the proceedings. Most of those he glanced at answered his look with a nod, or shake of the head, which he acknowledged whether he knew them or not.

"Dead body…" Baxter responded to Malone's question after a minute in his normal monotone.

Nothing ever rattled the old guy and that was one reason Malone loved working with him. He was like that old TV detective from the sixties, the one who always said, "Just the facts, ma'am," and then solved the case. At their disparate ages, Malone a young twenty-something, to doc's much older and wiser sixty something, the two were an odd couple, but their styles matched perfectly when it came to solving a case. It was like they were two halves of the same coin.

The two of us are a dying breed, Malone thought as he bent down to examine the body waiting to be zipped into the bag. Neither one of them willing to admit that modern day technology was what solved cases like these nowadays, both preferred old-fashioned police work. He and Doc

175

shared many a beer discussing modern day police work and its advantages and disadvantages.

"Hold on, don't close him off yet, doc," Malone said. Something about the body caught his eye. His glance traveled down the yellow polo shirt, the kind men wore out on the golf course. The victim was wearing khaki's and he noticed a large and shiny silver belt buckle, the kind usually worn by folks in western garb only instead of a steer head, or horse head on it, this one had a large leaping fish on it with some writing around the outside that was unreadable because of the seaweed covering it.

He took out a pen from his pants pocket and slowly lifted a corner of the bag further away from the body. "What's this?" he asked touching something spongy and gray that was matted to the man's skin at the side of his neck.

Doc Baxter bent down and, with a gloved hand, removed the item Malone pointed to.

"Looks like a leech, but it is an odd color..." reaching into his bag lying on the ground next to him, Baxter shook out a Ziploc bag and dropped the bloated and offending creature into it. "I'll check it out back at the office."

"You taking him back to your place?" Malone asked as he stood up and out of the way. Baxter finished zipping the bag and nodded.

"Yeah, I think so. Easier to do an exam there and quicker too. They're a bit backed up in Monroe with that mob hit a couple days ago, no room. I called and they said it would be at least a week before they could even schedule him. At least if he's here I can check him over and give you some x-rays and maybe figure out if it was a drowning."

"You think this is that guy reported missing a couple days ago?"

Malone was referring to a call they'd gotten from a distraught wife whose husband had come out to the resort this past weekend and was supposed to be home Sunday night, but hadn't made it back. It was now Tuesday. Malone, at first, thought the guy was probably just enjoying some time away and hadn't given it much thought, but now... well, now he wished he'd paid more attention.

"Got any ID on him?" Malone asked, walking back with the doc to get the body into the back of the doc's station wagon which doubled as the vet's work car and the coroner's car.

"Yeah, here you go." Doc reached inside his black bag and pulled out another Ziploc bag filled with a soggy wallet, a useless phone, and a key ring.

The key ring held five keys and a supermarket tab for the ShopSmart grocery store chain. Nothing remarkable or unique, except for the small sized new looking gold key that had the numbers 324 stamped on it.

A safety deposit key?

But to which bank?

"I assume everything was photographed? By the way, where is your nephew?"

Doc's nephew, Vernon, was the local news reporter and photographer. He usually

worked the country club scene, preferring to wear khakis and polo shirts when out taking photos so he could fit in with the crowd. Malone had not seen him when looking over the crowd earlier.

Vernon was annoying. He published a small newspaper in town called "The Resort Report" and most of the articles were related to social events in the nearby resort, or golfing events at the country club. Vernon referred to the folks who frequented those places as 'his people' which irritated Malone no end. He only tolerated the spoiled young man because of Baxter. The doc had raised the boy since Vernon's parents were killed in a car accident ten years ago.

"Got anything else for me?" Malone said.

Baxter looked at him with a straight face before speaking.

Doc grinned then said, "I know it's a male. About forty I would say. His face was pretty chewed up and bloated from being in the water." All things Malone already knew from his quick glance at the body.

Malone waited. He knew the doc was hesitating to give out too much information, but he also knew the doc was a cautious man by nature, so he wouldn't want to give anything concrete until he had time to examine the body.

"Anything else?"

"Like what?"

"Like maybe a guess for how long in the water? Cause of death?" Malone knew from past experience that just because something looked like an accident, it sometimes wasn't. He hoped that wasn't the case here. He was about a week shy of his first vacation in years, and he really wanted to take that time off. A murder would mess up those plans big time, and he wasn't sure his girlfriend, Savannah, would appreciate his mood if he didn't get away.

"Judging by the condition of the body, and how bloated he still is, I think it is probably just a couple days since he was walking around. As for the cause of death I would hazard a guess that it will turn out to be drowning, accidental or otherwise, but until I can check him over I hate to say for sure…" Doc took off his glasses and rubbed them on his shirt. A nervous habit Malone recognized.

"And?"

"I'm thinking he might be your missing fisherman you mentioned earlier today. But his wallet should have that information. I did notice a couple funny things, though…"

178

"Yes?" Malone prompted. Out of the corner of his eyes he saw one of his deputies gesturing to him. Raising a finger he motioned to Cramer that he would be there in a minute.

Cramer nodded and went back to questioning the grizzled older man in the khaki vest. Its many pockets were bulging with fishing lures, and small clippers and the usual fisherman necessities. Although Malone doubted the banana sticking up from a pocket in the front was typical fisherman equipment.

"The guy did not appear to have any underwear on."

"Oh? Maybe he likes to go commando," Malone smiled at his joke.

"Maybe," but Malone could tell by his tone that Doc didn't think so. "And his shirt's inside out too."

"Well now, *that* is interesting," Malone said. He pursed his lips and considered the implications of the body not being properly dressed.

Could the victim have been in a hurry? Maybe left his underwear someplace, or needed to get dressed before being found someplace he shouldn't be? Malone knew that people were people, and this resort, filled with the rich and famous, was a well-known retreat for those who wanted a discreet place for an affair.

Just last month a couple of married actors had been caught *in flagrante delicto* by their respective spouses. From what Savannah had said when the news broke, the resort was as infamous for its affairs as it was for its Salmon with Mint Sauce. But the staff of the exclusive resort usually handled those types of political time bombs with skill and silence, the only reason that story had broken at all was because one of the actors had slipped up on a national talk show and admitted to the affair.

179

But had that happened to this guy? He was so bloated that it was hard to tell if he was the type women would be drawn to or not. Malone studied the face and shook his head. No way could he tell anything just by looking at this disfigured body. He said a silent prayer for the poor soul and turned to Baxter.

"See you later, doc," Malone said. As he walked away Doc loaded the body into the back of the station wagon and slammed the door.

Malone walked toward Cramer, watching the crowd as he moved around the crime scene tape and motioned the crowd to disperse. When he got to Cramer's side he nodded to the deputy and his witness.

"What's up, Deputy?"

"Sir, this gentleman..." he flipped a couple pages until he found what he was looking for, "... Mr. Henderson, was out fishing pretty early this morning and found the body."

Malone raised an eyebrow and said, "How early were you out, sir?"

He kept his voice light and interested even while carefully observing the man's demeanor. He wouldn't be the first witness who turned out to be a murderer, *if this guy was even the victim of anything but an accidental drowning,* he reminded himself.

"I got here around 5am... wanted to get on the water before anyone else," he said. "I'm looking for the best spot to fish the Bass Competition..." he explained further.

Malone groaned inwardly. How could he have forgotten? The competition was set to start this weekend, and most of the local fishermen were going to be all over this lake for the next few days. The professionals would be coming in closer to the date of the event, probably in a day or two.

Gone Fishing

The resort, which leased part of its lake access for the event, often allowed guests to rent its outlying cottages for the duration of the competition. Malone wondered, as he glanced toward the private entrance the man in the ice blue polo had just left through, if this was why that man had been looking over the scene, protecting his assets as it were.

Probably checking to make sure it wasn't one of his guests. Hoping to prevent a public relations nightmare, and probably relieved to discover it wasn't a guest of the resort.

Malone's attention was brought back to the witness by the man's next comment.

"It was kind of funny the way he just floated up from underneath my boat. I thought at first it was a joke. That someone was pranking me, or something. I got some buddies who could pull something like that off," he said. He leaned toward Malone as he whispered the last.

"Floated up?" The Deputy asked.

"So the body wasn't there when you took the boat out?" Malone said. He knew he was interrupting Cramer, but something was tickling the back of his brain and he wondered what it was.

"Yep. He looked like he'd been stuck in the seaweed near the boat launch and my engine's propeller might have released him. He was covered in bits of seaweed when I pulled him up."

"Was he wrapped in anything else?" Malone was still struggling with something in the back of his mind. He knew he had a question, but he couldn't figure out what it was.

"Nope."

No ropes holding him down, nothing wrapped around him like he'd been hidden. Very interesting. Maybe it is an accidental drowning? Or maybe planned that way to appear to be an accidental drowning?

Malone paused before asking another question.

Finally he said, "Give the deputy your information. We'll be in contact if we need anything else. Oh and," he said as the man turned away, "don't discuss this with anyone. Not anyone. Not even your wife."

The man nodded. He gave Deputy Cramer his information and solemnly walked toward his boat. He'd pulled the banana out of his pocket and was eating it as he walked away.

"Sir?" Said Bracey walking up beside him. "The men want to know when they can get their boats out…"

"This is a crime scene. I'm not releasing it until I'm satisfied everything has been photographed. I want a diver brought in," Malone made that last comment as an idea occurred to him.

"This dock is closed for the day, folks. Sorry for the inconvenience." Malone announced as he walked up to the gathered fishermen.

"How long?" said one disgruntled man. He looked like he wanted to argue, but Malone smiled, deflating the man's anger.

"Hey guys, I know this is rough, what with the competition and all, but we gotta investigate. I'm sure you understand."

Grumbling, the crowd dispersed and Malone was left with the drying streaks of water and mud and the crime scene tape that circled the place the body had lain.

"Who were you?" he asked the pavement.

"Harry Bellows." The voice was behind him, causing Malone to spin and when he confronted the speaker he was not surprised to see the ice blue polo and khaki pants clothed man looking at him with a neutral expression. His sunglasses had been placed in the vee of his shirt which had the top button undone. A small tuft of ginger colored hair was revealed along with a bit of lightly tanned skin.

182

His arms, crossed in front of him, were muscular and also covered in a fine coating of the same ginger colored hair. Freckles dotted his arms and were lightly sprinkled on his face. His lips were pinched thinly giving his expression a disapproving air.

Malone raised an eyebrow in confusion.

"The man you just sent off to the vet's office was a guest of our resort. His name's Harry Bellows."

"How do you know that?" Malone took out a notepad from his pocket. "That's not the name on his driver's license."

"He uses Harry Bellows as his professional name."

"Professional name?"

The resort executive, Malone could read his name badge now which identified him as Winston Chambers, Resort General Manager, snorted. "He fancies himself a professional, anyway."

"What is his profession, then?" Malone tried to keep the impatience out of his voice, but he had the feeling this guy was enjoying dragging out the great reveal.

"He's a professional gambler. He comes here once a year for the big Poker Tournament we run during the Bass Fishing Competition."

"He's not a fisherman?" Malone suddenly flashed to the large belt buckle on the victim which had a huge leaping bass in the center of the buckle. Why would someone who gambles, wear a buckle like that?

"No." The man's tone was final. He waved behind him to the resort, "I have to get back to the office. Let me know if you need anything else. I would like to remind you…" hesitating, he pinched his lips and put a finger across his lips before finishing his thought, "we are very important to the economy of the town, it would be nice if this could be

183

kept quiet. It wouldn't do to blacken the name of the resort during the investigation."

Malone gazed at him speculatively. Of course, he would want to protect the reputation of his employer, but was that all that was behind his request for the investigation to be handled delicately and with the least amount of disruption to the guests?

"I will need to speak to the guests who are currently here, and also get a list of guests who may have left in the last few days." Malone said without apology.

The manager nodded, "What days are we looking at?"

"Probably from Friday to now," Malone answered, not taking his eyes from the manager's.

"That information will be available to you if you come back in two hours. Is that all?"

"The staff, too. Also any vendors who were onsite, maintenance crews... what day is your garbage picked up?"

"Friday mornings," the manager said. "It is hauled away to Springville to their dump."

Springville, Malone thought annoyed, *that was seventy miles away and that dump was huge as it supplied space to most of the towns in the area. Finding anything there would be almost impossible, worse than the proverbial needle in a haystack.*

"I will make sure you have information, at least as much as I can provide, of anyone who was here from Friday to now. Is there anything else?"

"Not right now," Malone said. His tone was tight and he groaned inwardly at the thought of the numbers of regular people who might have been in the area enjoying the lake during the time of the murder. Tracking down casual boaters on the lake, or swimmers, or families who had visited the area during the weekend would prove nearly impossible.

Malone took the card proffered by the manager and the two men nodded. The manager walked briskly back through the door to the resort. Malone watched him go, his face slack and blank as he considered the contradiction between what the manager had said about the victim and what he'd observed on the body.

It didn't add up. Nothing about this case appeared to be cut and dried. Was he a gambler? Was he here to see a woman, as might be implied by his lack of undergarments and a shirt that was hastily put on inside out?

He would have to follow the man's movements and see what turned up. He flicked the corner of the gold-edged card with his thumbnail as he pondered the possibilities and the next step.

Should he wait for doc to get him the results of the autopsy and finalize the cause of death, or should he start talking to people now? His phone rang, ending all thoughts of the indecision.

"Hey, Savannah, what's up?"

"Are you busy?" she asked. Judging by her frantic tone she didn't want him to be busy, so he wasn't.

"Nope, not busy at all. What do you need?"

Malone started to walk toward the parking lot, waving to his deputies who were finishing up the interviews with the last of the stragglers.

Both men nodded to him and turned back to the people they were chatting with before closing their notebooks and heading to their patrol cars. He watched them stop and chat with each other for a moment before they turned on their cars and headed toward the exit.

"Sorry, what did you say?" distracted by the lone straggler, also watching the deputies leave from his vantage point at the end of the boat launch area, Henderson was his name Malone remembered, he missed the last of what Savannah had said.

He thought he caught something about "sister" but the rest was a jumble of words all spoken quickly together.

"Whoa," he said. "What's going on?"

"Your sister, Belle, is here."

"My sister?" Malone stopped for a minute in confusion. What would his little sister, Belle, be doing here? She was with their parents on some cruise or holiday or something.

Savannah went on to say more that made no sense. Malone slipped inside the car and turned the key. Putting the car in gear he slowly turned it around, his eyes once again caught by the man Henderson who was now watching him. Although he was pretty far away by now, Malone shivered a bit at the intense expression on the man's face. His cop instinct on alert he almost turned back around and asked him what was wrong, but Savannah's tone told him he needed to get home as quick as possible.

Great, leave it to Belle to show up at the wrong time, as usual. He wondered what had precipitated her running away this time. Belle was a change of life baby for his parents who had pushed all their children out of the nest and were enjoying a very comfortable early retirement when his father won the lottery. His mother's pregnancy sixteen years ago with Belle had been quite a shock to them all. Probably more than picking six numbers at random had been.

He called the office and told them he'd be a little late getting back and parked the car in his driveway. Getting out a little slower than usual, hoping to delay the inevitable confrontation with his unapologetic and a bit cantankerous sixteen year old sister, he sighed.

Chapter Five

Putting his hat on the seat next to him he eased himself from the vehicle and walked toward the front door. Before he'd even reached the knob the door was flung open and Savannah stood there with a very annoyed expression on her face. Her arms were crossed and she nodded toward the living room. Her lips were pinched shut tightly as if she was holding back words best left unsaid.

"She's in there," she said in the same tone she used when Ginger, their Golden Retriever puppy, left a 'surprise' for them to clean up.

Stepping to the side she held open the door, exiting as he entered. He reached out to touch her arm, but Savannah shrugged it off. "See you later," was all she said as she stepped outside and walked briskly toward her house down the block.

Uh-oh, he thought, *what did Belle do now? I think I'd rather be fishing than walk into this mess.*

"Hello Belle," he said from the doorway of the living room. He leaned against the door jamb and looked at his sister. His tone was cautious, and soft. No sense setting her off before they had a chance to talk.

Belle was sprawled out on the couch, her long legs almost reaching the end of the large three cushioned couch. She hadn't taken off her shoes, and was wearing earplugs connected to her phone and seemed to be checking her phone for messages or maybe playing a game. She was silently mouthing the words to a song she was listening to.

When she didn't answer his comment he considered taking the cowardly way out and leaving the room, but then thought better of it. No sense delaying the inevitable any

187

longer. He needed to find out why she was here, and how she got here, and what her plans were.

Walking toward her he pulled one of the earplugs off one ear to get her attention. She jumped up, an annoyed expression on her face, opened her mouth as if to speak and then shut it when she realized he was standing there.

Lowering her eyes she frowned, fiddling with her phone and the earplugs, finally pulling both from her ears and staring at him with a sullen expression on her face.

He motioned for her to sit back on the couch and he took a chair across from her. Staring at her with his hands folded across his knee he studied her face for a sign of anything that might tell him what was going on.

She met his gaze without apology.

Finally, the silence getting to her, she said, "Hello brother. What's up?"

"You tell me," he said without rancor. No sense getting her angry at this point, not until he found out what was going on.

"What do you mean?" he could tell she was avoiding his question, and she could tell he knew it, but neither wanted to open the can of worms that would start a war of words. They were pretty good at arguing with each other, and nobody ever won.

"Okay, so…" Belle started to say. Biting her lip she looked up at her brother, her eyes pleading with him to understand. "They're so old…"

"Who? Mom and dad?"

"Yes," she said softly, "and I know they can't help it, but it is soooo boring to go anywhere with them."

"… and the thought of two weeks stuck on a ship with them and fifty of their old cronies was too much to bear?" he finished for her.

A small smile twitched at the corner of his lips. He knew exactly how she felt. Their parents were wonderful people, fun and active in their old age. But they were definitely old. And for Belle, at her tender young age of sixteen 'old' meant 'ancient', so he could see why she didn't want to go with them.

Seeing his smile she was quick to light up, hope written on her face that she wouldn't be in too much trouble for her rebellion. Their parents were probably relieved to be rid of her for their vacation as much as she was relieved to be gone.

The only one not too relieved was him. Belle and Savannah had never gotten along. Mostly, he felt because Belle was jealous more than Savannah didn't like the teen, but Belle went out of her way to embarrass or upset Savannah every chance she got.

Was he really prepared to deal with the two women in his life having issues while he was in the middle of a murder investigation? He sighed. This was turning into quite a day already.

"Belle, while I get that mom and dad are old, you cannot just show up at my house without warning? What if Savannah and I were gone? What would you do then?"

Belle threw her head back, flipping her hair off her face, and smiled her megawatt smile, the one she knew always got her what she wanted no matter how bad she'd been. "Mom said she was texting you and it all turned out all right in the end, right? I mean, you're here and so is… Savannah…" her frown at the mention of Savannah's name was quick and he almost missed it.

"Yes, we're here. But Belle, I'm pretty busy at work and I won't have a lot of time to spend with you, so you're going to have to promise me you'll behave, and not get into trouble."

189

Belle clapped her hands, her face lighting up again at the success of her plan. "I can always call a friend and have them come get me. That way I will totally be out of your way."

"No, I don't think so. You're here and you're stuck with me.

"Wait a minute, there's more. You're going to have to get a job for the time you're here if you want to spend time here. You can't just hang around and do nothing."

"What? Where will I find a job in this backwater place?" she sounded more than annoyed.

"It just so happens I have a connection at the resort down the road and can get you a job there. Probably as a maid, but at least it's something to keep you busy and out of trouble. I would hate for you to be bored."

"This is because of Savannah, isn't it?" she pouted, dropping onto the couch dramatically.

"Has nothing to do with Savannah," Malone started to say then stopped. Actually, this might be a way for Belle and Savannah to get some time away from each other. Maybe if Belle has a job she might appreciate how hard Savannah works and what having the responsibility of making money in order to spend it really means. One of Savannah's biggest beefs with Belle was that everything got handed to her on a silver platter since his parents were wealthy, and that meant, in Savannah's eyes anyway, that Belle didn't appreciate the value of money.

Pete stepped into the other room and called the manager at the resort and had a job for her in the morning.

"All set," he said coming back into the room. "You start tomorrow at 8. I'll take you over and introduce you to the manager who will get you situated. You will probably do something at the kids area, he said. I told him you were a

190

lifeguard at home, so he said they can use you at the pool. Hope you packed your swimsuit."

Belle groaned. Just so happened she remembered putting her suit in there, but she wasn't sure her skimpy swimsuit would work for the pool there. She hoped they would issue her one.

The rest of the night passed quickly. Belle texted her friend and told him that plans had changed and she was stuck here so he would probably need to leave. She would text him if she could get away.

His response wasn't a happy one, but she didn't really care. All of a sudden, and for some reason she couldn't explain, she wanted to stay.

After a quick dinner and some ice cream Belle left the room when her brother called his girlfriend. Sitting on the front porch with her ice cream she listened to him placating Savannah with promises of a dinner out after the case was solved and that Belle wouldn't be here that long.

He joined her on the porch after the call ended and leaned against the railing, arms crossed, watching her.

Finally Belle sighed and set the ice cream bowl and spoon on the small table next to her.

"Out with it," she said, "I know you're mad. I just…"

"You just didn't think," said Pete. His voice was soft, and he looked tired.

"Yeah," Belle drew her legs up and rested her chin on her knees. Wrapping her arms around her legs she looked up at her brother with pleading eyes. "But, seriously, mom and dad are so old and so boring…"

"I know," Pete said with a grin. He sat on the wicker loveseat next to her. "But Belle, I'm in the middle of a murder investigation and having you here is going to make it difficult for me to focus on the case so you have to promise me you will behave. No getting into trouble. I can't watch you and solve this case, too."

"I promise," she said raising her hand and crossing it over her heart, "cross my heart, and hope to die... oh, wait, that probably wouldn't be appropriate to say that."

She giggled, and after a minute he smiled. Leaning his head back onto the house he stretched his legs out and stared out into the night sky.

"Want to tell me about it?" Belle asked after a few minutes of silence between them.

"Can't. Confidentiality and all that..."

"Oh, come on, who am I going to tell?"

He just looked at her with a raised eyebrow like he suspected her of a trick.

"I might be able to help. I'm pretty good at solving puzzles..."

After a minute he said, "We found a body today in the lake. It was a local guy who is a gambler and a bass fishing champion. There's a competition every year at the resort, and according to the manager of the resort this guy won last year."

"The gambling or the bass thingie?"

"The bass championship, but he likes to gamble, too."

"So, does he owe anyone money?"

"Not... sure," Pete looked at her in surprise. "That is a great point. We need to check into that."

"And has he pissed anyone off lately?"

"Not sure, but he might have."

"What makes you say that?"

"He was found with no underwear on, and his shirt was on inside out."

"Oh!" said Belle after a minute. She started laughing. "So, he was probably in a hurry to get dressed? You think he

192

was involved with someone's wife or girlfriend and they killed him for it?"

"It's a possibility." Pete acknowledged.

"I would think he would get beat up for that. Not killed. I think if you are going to kill someone, you would kill them for something more than just sleeping with your woman."

"Maybe," Pete agreed after thinking about it.

"So, I think I would focus on the money angle. Nobody likes a thief."

Pete laughed. "I'll do that. Now, I gotta get to bed and so do you."

They walked inside and Pete turned off the lights. Belle stepped back outside to pick up the bowl she'd forgotten. As she turned to open the door she caught a shadow separating itself from the house. She shivered watching a shadowy figure move deeper into the shadows of the trees around the house and then shook her head.

Did I see someone, or was it my imagination? She thought.

Susan Burdorf

Chapter Six

The next day dawned with a slight mist that caused her to shiver. She dressed in black slacks and a white tank top with a button up shirt in a soft blue plaid. Pulling her hair into a ponytail she was waiting in the kitchen when Pete made his way into the room.

Belle looked at her older brother with concern. He looked exhausted. "You okay?" she asked.

Pete nodded. Reaching into the refrigerator he opened some juice and drank from the carton making Belle wince. Her mother would kill him if she saw him do that and then Belle shook her head. She was too young to be channeling her mother.

"Come on, I'm going to be late."

They got to the hotel and Belle was taken immediately into the office. As she suspected her suit was totally inappropriate and she was issued a red one with the resort logo on it. She was then taken to the pool by the other lifeguard, a totally adorable blonde and tan boy about her age who took one look at her and rolled his eyes.

"You can't have all those piercings on, and you have to hide that tattoo." He pointed to her ankle where a tiny butterfly danced.

He went to the first aid kit and pulled out a waterproof band-aid and made her put it on. Then he pointed to the lockers and told her she could change in there. "The locker will cost you a quarter, but you get it back when you come back at the end of your shift."

She nodded.

"There are flips in there for you to wear and I'll give you the whistle when you come out to the pool. We start our shift in twenty minutes so hurry up."

Belle hurried. As she changed she realized she didn't even know the boy's name.

When she came back outside he was standing by the concession area chatting with the tall blonde behind the counter. Belle felt a stab of jealousy and then quickly dismissed it. She didn't even know his name, what right did she have to be jealous?

"Hi," she said holding out her hand to the blonde girl, "my name's Belle."

"Allison," she said, "And this is my brother, Adam."

Brother? Cool, thought Belle. But instead of saying anything she just nodded at them both before turning to the pool. Adam had taken off his windbreaker and his tanned toned body was distracting to say the least.

At the end of the day Belle met with Adam and Allison to head to the locker room to change into her street clothes. The day had passed in a blur, between keeping an eye on the children at the pool and stopping them from running or horsing around she found she had not even had a minute to spare for looking at Adam. She'd caught glimpses of him as he walked around the pool, but her attention stayed focused on the kids.

"You did great today, Belle," said Allison with a wide grin.

"You were watching me?" She felt a sense of shock at how Allison's kind word lifted her spirits.

"Yep, it's my job to make sure things go smoothly here. Parents trust us to watch out for their kids so they can play in the resort without worrying about them."

Belle nodded, made sense. Happy parents would return and spend more money.

196

"So, what are you going to do now?" Allison asked walking next to Belle.

"Not sure, I think my brother is coming to get me, but I don't know for sure. He's working on a murder case right now."

"Oh yeah," said Adam enthusiastically. "I heard about that."

Allison looked puzzled. "What murder?"

"That Harry guy, you know the creep who's always hitting on you and every other woman in the place."

"Really?" Allison looked surprised. "When?"

"They think it was Friday nite, that's what I heard from that guy Henderson. He heard the cops talking about it."

Just then a guy holding a camera walked up to them and sidled up next to Allison who quickly put herself and Belle between them. "Hello Allison, Adam... who do we have here?"

Neither Adam nor Allison responded to him. He continued to stare at Belle. His eyes were dark and glittery, his expression kind of creepy. "I'm Belle," she finally answered not offering a hand or her last name.

"Oh, you're the sheriff's sister, right?"

"How'd you know that?" Belle asked, shocked.

"I'm a reporter, can't you tell?" he held up his camera and giggled, a sound that grated on Belle's nerves and made her wonder just how old this guy was. He looked old, at least ten years older than her, but he sounded like he was in high school and he didn't look much older with his pimply face and scrawny body.

"Um... yeah, I see the camera," Belle said walking a little quicker down the path to put some distance between them.

197

"Wait, I want a quote for the newspaper," he said hurrying to catch up to her. He grabbed her arm, and before she could yank it free Adam grabbed Vernon by the shoulder and pulled him away.

"Back off, Vernon. She has nothing to tell you. Leave her alone. Get lost."

Vernon started to say something but then looked behind Adam and his face paled. He mumbled something about 'see you later' and hurried away in the opposite direction.

Belle looked but couldn't tell what had spooked Vernon.

"Hey, Adam, I gotta go. I'll be back in a few minutes."

Allison hurried back toward the pool. Belle watched, confused about the abrupt departure of both of them. As Allison rounded the corner Belle saw a man step out and follow her.

"Who's that?" Belle asked, pointing.

"James. That's Allison's boyfriend. He works around here with one of the frequent guests as a bodyguard. The guy practically lives here."

Something about the way that man moved seemed familiar to Belle but she couldn't quite figure out why.

"You okay?" Adam asked her.

"Yeah, sure. Why?"

"You just looked like you saw a ghost. Sure you're okay?"

"Yeah, fine."

They stood there awkwardly, neither knowing what to say. Belle had the feeling that Adam was warming up to her, and she was fine with that.

198

"So, what are you going to do, now?" He asked her. His voice was casual, but she could tell he really wanted to know.

"I've no plans, but I have to talk to my brother and see what he's got going on. Why?"

"I thought we could grab a bit to eat. Since we work here we get free food."

"Really?" Belle hadn't known that.

"Yep, tell you what. Call your brother and let's grab a bite if he doesn't have plans."

"Great. Let me get changed and I will call him."

Pete was fine with it when she rang him, telling her he would meet her back at the house and that she could call him when she was ready to go home.

"I'm headed to the bank to check on something, so if you need me you can probably catch me there. I have a feeling I'll be there for a while."

"The murder?" Belle asked.

"Talk to you about it, later." Pete promised.

Skipping a little when she came out of the locker room she found Adam with Allison who was crying.

"What's up?"

"Nothing," Allison said drying her eyes.

"What did your brother say?"

"He said it was okay. Allison you want to join us for dinner?"

The three went to the dining room and out onto the patio overlooking the lake. They sat down and placed their order with the waitress who joked with Adam and Allison and nodded when introduced to Belle.

They ate in silence and then Belle, curiosity getting the best of her asked Allison what was the matter.

"I might get in trouble for taking a boat out the other night without permission. I was trying to get my boyfriend,

199

James, to agree to vouch for me, but he told me it was my problem."

Belle patted her on the arm. "Is it a big deal?"

"Yeah, I could get fired if my boss finds out. Right now all he knows is that someone took it out, and if he finds out it's me I will get fired."

Belle and Adam looked at each other and then back to their dessert. "I have eaten more ice cream in the last two days than I have in the last month," Belle said trying to distract everyone with inane chatter.

Allison gave her a weak smile and Adam squeezed her arm. She liked it when he touched her.

Chapter Seven

Adam gave Belle a ride home and she got there a little before Pete came home. She was in the kitchen pouring herself a soda when he came in.

"Any news on the murder?" she asked handing him the soda. He took it gratefully, then grimaced.

"Sorry," he said handing it back to her, "I thought it was a beer." He reached into the fridge and took out a beer. Popping the top he poured it into a glass and drank deeply.

Belle pointed to the table and they sat. "So tell me what's going on."

Pete hesitated, and then said, "Whatever I tell you is in confidence, right? You cannot repeat it."

Belle nodded, holding up a pinky she made a pinky-swear promise with her brother like she used to when she was little. He grinned, the smile relaxing the worry lines making Belle feel better.

"We figured out the way the murder happened, we just don't know who or why."

"Well, that's good, right?"

"Yeah. One of the boats from the resort was used to take the killer or killers from the scene where the body went into the lake. We found the boat belonging to the victim on the lake just drifting, the anchor was damaged."

Belle went cold. "What night was it?"

"We think Friday nite."

"I think you need to talk to someone." Belle said in a small voice.

She told Pete about the conversation she had with Allison earlier. Pete got up before she'd even finished speaking. He grabbed his phone and called his deputies to go to Allison's house and pick her up.

A few minutes later his phone rang as the deputies said Allison was not at home. Her brother said she'd gotten a call from her boyfriend and had left to meet him back at the resort.

"You stay here," Pete said as he rushed out of the house. He grabbed his gun as he ran out. Belle watched him leave, her blood running cold. Allison was in trouble.

Just then she saw someone walking quickly away from the house, something glinting in their hand as they hurried away. She rushed after the man, following him as he walked swiftly away. She recognized him when a light from the street light shone on his face. It was that reporter guy, Vernon, and he was hurrying toward the resort. Then he did a funny thing. He went to the boat dock area and got in one of the boats.

Just then Adam stepped in front of her. "Belle," he said. "What are you doing here?"

"That reporter guy, Vernon, is there. He was eavesdropping outside my window tonight. Then my brother called his office to have his men pick up your sister, Allison to ask her about the boat. I had to tell him what she said," Belle apologized.

"It's okay," Adam said, "I told her to go to the police anyway."

"But she's missing. I think he knows where she is."

"Who?"

"Vernon. I think he knows where she is. I don't know why, I just know he does."

"Okay, let's follow him."

"He's gone," I said pointing to the lake where he was driving off in a boat. He appeared to be in a huge hurry.

"I know where we can get a boat. Come on, hurry."

202

Belle and Adam raced off to get another boat. They got into it and he pulled off the mooring ropes, tossing them in, then jumping in and starting the motor. Belle watched, carefully scanning the lake for any sign of Vernon.

"There," she said pointing and looking back at Adam. "I see the boat over there at that dock."

They moored the boat and carefully made their way through the brush toward a small cabin set off the lake a bit into the trees.

Adam bent down to pick up something. Holding up a scarf he mouthed the word 'Allison' and pointed to the cabin. Belle nodded her understanding. Taking the scarf from him she tied it around her waist and followed him toward the cabin.

A few minutes later, walking carefully to avoid making any noise to alert whoever might be in the cabin that they were there they found themselves outside the structure. Belle pointed to the dirty window but Adam shook his head. Instead he gestured they should walk around the back of the building. They did and found a small cleared area near a door. Stepping carefully up the steps to the porch they ducked down.

Inside they heard muted voices. Then some that were raised. Belle listened carefully. She thought she heard at least three voices, but she couldn't be sure. She moved closer to the door, ignoring Adam's gestures to stay put.

Yes, three voices. One was Vernon's whine, the other a deeper male voice, and then a third that might be Allison, but she couldn't be sure. She needed to see who was in there. Standing up she tried to see into the room, but the windows were too dirty. The other side was better, less dirty, stepping she felt the floor under her feet give way as one of the old boards broke.

"What was that?" she heard from inside.

Panicking, Belle made as if to run, but her foot was stuck. Staring at Adam in a panic she didn't know what to do as she heard footsteps coming close to the door. Then she felt the scarf at her waist. Untying it quickly she tossed one end to Adam as the door opened. Out stepped Vernon and in a second they had twisted the scarf around him and used it to propel him off the porch. He hit his head on a tree and collapsed to the ground. Adam shut the door, and released her foot, but as the door closed Belle saw Allison tied to a chair. She saw Belle and her eyes widened in surprise and fear.

"What's going on out there?" The other voice shouted. "Vernon, where are you?"

Belle grabbed the board she'd broken and held it up, ready to swing when the next guy came out. A second later he stepped outside and she whacked him with it as he stepped out, heading toward the prone Vernon.

The guy fell and Adam looked at her in approval. "That was awesome."

"Come on, let's get Allison and get out of here before we are caught."

Untying Allison they quickly tied up Vernon and James and raced to the boat. They headed back to the dock and ran inside with Allison to find Pete.

Belle told him quickly what had transpired at the cabin and he sent his deputies to retrieve the two men.

A little later, over ice cream, Allison told her story.

"James told me he and the other two were out boating and that the boat had died and he needed me to come get them. So I took one of our boats out there to get him on Friday night. It was Harry's boat that I took them from. They said Harry had loaned it to them so they could do some night fishing. One of the guys that was on the boat with him was Vernon, the other guy I didn't know. I didn't know that they

204

had killed Harry." Tears formed in her eyes. Belle handed her a tissue and smiled encouragingly.

"So, what I don't understand," Belle said after a minute. "Why? Why kill Harry?"

"Two reasons," said Pete with a sigh, "both of them the oldest reasons in the world. Love and money. But mostly money."

Belle looked at her brother with a confused expression.

"Harry was with a woman when he was caught by her husband. We thought it was one of the gamblers, but it was actually the wife of the resort manager."

"Mr. Chambers?" Allison looked shock.

"Yep, but it was kind of weird. We thought he might have been poisoned, there was an odd colored leech on him, but it turns out that was nothing. But we also found a safety deposit key on him, and that was something. It was to a bank in town and in the box was a set of engraving plates, and counterfeit money. The manager was using the resort to launder counterfeit bills. Or rather, he was going to do it. Their trial run was brought to our attention just last week, and putting two and two together when we opened the box we realized what had happened."

"How did he find out about it?" Adam asked as he got his hand slapped by Belle for stealing a scoop of her ice cream.

"That was purely by accident. From what we gather he found the key in the bedroom when he met with Mrs. Chambers and thought it was just money so he went to the bank and found the money and the counterfeiting plates. From what James said when questioned he then tried to blackmail Mr. Chambers who refused to play ball and instead ordered the hit."

"Well, I'm glad that is solved," said Belle stealing a scoop from Adam's dish. "What happens now?"

"Now," said Pete, "I'm taking a few days off. Anyone asks where I am, I want you to tell them Savannah and I have gone fishing, and this time the only thing I want to take out of that lake is a huge Bass."

About the Author

Susan Burdorf is a mom and grandmother first, and a writer a very close second. If she isn't at the park with her grandchildren she will probably be found someplace quiet working on her next story. Primarily a YA author Susan currently has two novels in print. "A Cygnet's Tale" which is a modern retelling of the story of The Ugly Duckling and "Breaking Fences" which is a tale spun around a cattle rustling gang, rabid coyotes, an injured horse, and the love between two damaged teens who just want to be whole again are both found on Amazon along with several anthologies Susan has stories featured.

You can connect with her on
Facebook at www.facebook.com/susanburdorfauthor;
twitter at @sburdorf;
Pinterest at www.pinterest.com/sburdorf;
Amazon at https://www.amazon.com/Susan-Burdorf/e/B00LMGIAGM

Susan Burdorf

J. Nichole Parkins
Text Copyright © 2016 J. Nichole Parkins

What do you see when you look in the mirror?
Marigold Wilson sees regret.
A reflection of a life half-lived, a prison built with debt and depression.
Until one day her reflection looks back at her and doesn't like what it sees.

J. Nichole Parkins

Reflected

By

J. Nichole Parkins

J. Nichole Parkins

214

Reflected
Acknowledgements

Thank you to the Thrill of the Hunt team for another amazing project! Who knew when we all met at Indie Book Fest that we'd go on to release two collections together? Thank you for the comradery, feedback, and support throughout both endeavors.

Thank you to my fabulous beta readers who suffered through the hot mess of earlier drafts to help create the final satisfying story – Jaz, Megan, Jenn, and Jim. And my readers, who continue to amaze me with your wonderful comments and the fact that you plead for more. I am so very grateful.

As always, thank you to my family, without you my life would be nothing but a pale, flat reflection of what it is.

J. Nichole Parkins

216

CHAPTER ONE

The odor of sweat and oil clung to my clothes. I shed each piece as I walked through the house, my shoulders sagging as I spotted the dishes piled in the sink. The remains of food still stuck to the surface. Cans were peppered throughout the house, a collection growing on the counter that threatened to spill onto the floor. A small bump against the cabinets would cause an avalanche of aluminum and stale beer.

Turning, I ignored the mess. I hadn't spent the last twelve hours on my feet cleaning up after people to come home and do the same.

"Lather, rinse, and repeat," I said under my breath as I collapsed on the bed.

"What?" Sid grunted. His eyes never left the television, remote in one hand, beer in the other.

"Nothing." I breathed in, sinking further into the mattress. My aching muscles gave way to gravity.

Sid glanced over, a frown pulling at his eyebrows. "Tired?"

I didn't bother to answer, instead, I held his gaze in a death-stare. He chuckled, the movement shaking the bed.

"Stupid question." He turned back to the flickering television, the explosions on the screen more interesting. "You smell like grease, Marigold."

"Well, you smell like beer." I snapped before I could think better of it. The silence stretched between us, heavy and breathing like a living thing. I dragged my eyes to his face, wiped clean of any emotion except the pinched white line of his lips.

"I'm taking a shower." I walked to the dresser and yanked a tattered t-shirt and simple cotton underwear from the drawer. My days of wearing lacy thongs and clingy

217

dresses had passed years ago. Five years to be exact. Now it was function and comfort above fashion.

Another explosion flashed on the screen. The soot-covered hero ran into a burning building, while a barely dressed woman twenty years his junior screamed for him to save her.

I padded across the cold tile and shut the bathroom door with a measured force, careful not to slam it. The click was loud in the cocooning silence. I wrenched the knob of the shower, droplets of cold water hitting my skin as I ducked the spray. I waited for the water to warm, gooseflesh turned my skin into a tight, bumpy roadmap.

I glanced at my reflection. The dark bags under my eyes forced my gaze away before I could pick out any more flaws.

Steam rose in a cloud around the tiny bathroom as the water heated. I was grateful that it obscured my reflection. Frustration rose inside me and my throat tightened. I stuck out my tongue at the blurry image in the mirror, my pink tongue flashed in a formless blob. It didn't help.

Shoving the plastic curtain aside, I stepped under the hot spray, unable to hold back my moan as the steamy water beat against my skin. It turned pink under the heat, but the loosening of my tight, weary muscles was worth the sting.

The spray flattened my long brown hair. It ran over my face and down my body, washing out the dirt and stink that clung desperately to my skin. God, I hated fried foods.

Lathering a hot pink nylon poof, I replaced the lingering smell of the diner with that of the artificial strawberries from my body wash. After scrubbing every inch of skin, I sank against the back tile and let the water cascade down my body, gravity pulling the soapy swirls down the drain. I struggled to ignore the dots of green that grew on the cheap curtain. Later. Later I would catch up on the endless housework.

Tension replaced my earlier relief as the mildewed dots seemed to grow in front of me, spreading, their circumference widening every minute I stood under the spray. I pinched my lips in a tight line.

I couldn't even relax in the shower.

I twisted the shower knobs, cutting off the hot spray as I wiped the water from my face with the scratchy, bleach-stained towel that hung from the shower rod.

I sniffed as my throat tightened again and pretended the burning in my eyes was from the soap.

The steam dissipated, droplets of water clung to each surface, giving the room a slimy look. I wrinkled my nose as the lingering odor of mildew from the pile of forgotten laundry in the corner assaulted my senses.

I added laundry to the growing list.

The sigh hit me from nowhere, dragged out of me as the weight returned to my burdened shoulders. I stared into the mirror, my reflection nothing more than a blur of washed-out peach, the lines undecipherable in the clouded mirror and the soft vanity light. Leaning forward, balanced against the sink, I dragged my hand along the cool surface, revealing what I'd rather have left hidden, but driven by some desperate need to prod at old wounds.

I traced the angles and sharp edges of my body in the mirror. I was no hourglass.

"More like a stick," I mumbled into the empty air.

The past transposed onto the current image. In it I was more soft than sharp, my rounded belly glowing a soft pink. Filled with life, filled with—

My hand traced what was missing in the cool glass. The sound of dripping water bounced off the tile as it blended with my empty heartbeat.

J. Nichole Parkins

Looking down at the flat planes and pointed joints of my pale body, I poked my finger into the flesh of my side, running it along the hard ridges of my ribs. My lips pulled down into a frown. I was losing weight. Again.

I turned my head left, then right picking out the flaws for the umpteenth time. The dark circles under my eyes, the bags, the sagging skin, the deep wrinkles aging my mottled sun-thickened skin. Over forty years in the Florida sun and I'd regretted every moment left baking unprotected.

But it was too late to fix anything. My shoulders sagged. The rounding of my back more pronounced. I tilted to the side. One day I'd probably have a hump if I didn't do something about my posture. I sighed, the breath shuddering out of my defeated body. It was probably inevitable.

My eyes met those of my reflection, the weariness visible in the deepening lines in the surrounding skin. The shine had fled long before the end of the first year of working two jobs. Two disappointing, unforgiving jobs where I worked too many hours for little pay and had to deal with people who would rather spit in my face than treat me like a human being.

It was endless. I'd never be free. Free from the debt, free from the memories, free from the loss—

I stopped myself, knowing that was a road I couldn't travel down. The despair would be too much.

I pulled at the mirror. With a click, it revealed the shelf behind it. A line of deodorants, hair products, and other hygiene odds and ends filled the shelves. I grabbed the toothpaste, squeezing a thick line onto the brush. The minty odor wafted to me. It smelled cool and clean.

I pushed the mirror closed, my reflection sliding with the movement. I sucked in air, gasping in surprise. The scream tore through my throat loud and raw, echoing in the small space.

CHAPTER TWO

"What is it?" Sid's large body filled the door frame. His giant hand reached along the wall until he found the light switch. I blinked as the blinding overhead light filled the room.

I pressed against the bathroom wall, heart pounding as I struggled to figure out what I'd seen. "I thought I saw something." Heat infused my cheeks as I was engulfed in embarrassment.

"What?"

I shrugged, my naked shoulders lifted. The movement was reflected in the large mirror that spanned the bathroom wall. "In the mirror." I pointed, my index finger shaking in the rush of adrenaline. "I don't know. Something. I—I saw something move."

Sid rolled his eyes and turned. His feet beat against the tile as they retreated into the bedroom. I watched him leave, unable to resist another quick peek at the mirror.

Had I seen something?

I could have sworn there was something moving, something that wasn't right about the image reflected in the glass.

Or was it simply a fabrication of my exhausted mind?

I flicked off both lights and followed Sid. The lingering feeling of unease coiled between my shoulder blades as I turned my back on the mirror.

The cool sheets welcomed me. Exhaustion weighed heavily on my limbs but my mind wouldn't shut off, wouldn't stop replaying what I'd seen — or thought I'd seen.

Motion caught in the corner of my eye. Movement where there shouldn't have been any, where nothing was supposed to be. Empty blackness that was filled with *something*. A shadow within a shadow.

I shivered. My nana had always said that was a sign that someone was walking on my grave.

That thought didn't help my unease.

Darkness was heavy, my exhaustion bone deep, but I tossed and turned, unable to sleep. The uneasy feeling of something *wrong* never left me, it only got worse as the night went on.

****

I woke to a bone-deep weariness, an ache that spanned my entire body. I'd maybe slept an hour or two, imagining sounds and noises. Occasionally I was forced to check, my anxiety spinning tales made worse by my imagination. Every noise, every sound felt ominous.

I kept my head down as I crept into the bathroom. My reflection moved in my peripheral as I dressed for work. The lingering trepidation from the night before weighed me down. I didn't bother with makeup. The thought of seeing myself, even in pieces, was too much this morning.

"Are you ready?" Sid's deep voice called out from the living room. "I'm going to be late."

I slipped on my shoes and tossed the waves of brown hair behind my back. "I'm good to go." I forced cheer into my voice, failing as it fell flat.

Sid's mouth dipped and he pressed a quick kiss to my lips. "Trouble sleeping?"

"Yeah." I shrugged, wishing the tightness between my shoulder blades was that easy to shake off. "I kept having bad dreams."

"Only twelve hours and you'll be done." The keys rattled as he locked the door behind us.

"Fantastic," I mumbled, my frown deepening. He might as well have said an eternity.

"Sorry." He pushed the button on the remote, unlocking the rusted compact car in front of the house. The lights flashed in the low light. The sun barely peeked over the horizon. "I'll pick up dinner."

Warmth spread and a smile curved my lips. "Thanks." I slid my fingers between his after he started the car and drove me to work.

Sharing a car was difficult but necessary. Some mornings we got along and the commute was pleasant. But more frequently than not we rubbed against each other like a two porcupines in a trash bag.

We switched places at the factory, the scent of burnt plastic heavy in the air as I slid into the driver's seat and sped away. My fingers tapped a relentless beat on the steering wheel as I fought the traffic.

The resort appeared to rise from the trees, visible from the highway as I inched along. I hated the boxy structure. Hated everything that it stood for. It loomed tall and awkward, an attempt at beauty that crumbled in the difficult economy. The once pristine paint job was chipped, the expensive landscaping littered with weeds and garbage.

Throwing the car into park, I ran across the almost vacant parking lot, my heels clicking on the pavement. I couldn't be late. I couldn't lose this job.

I ignored the terrifying view as I hurried.

And miles to go before I sleep.

I threw myself into work, the only way I'd make it through the long shift. Retail was no joke: hours on my feet, constantly complaining customers, unreliable co-workers — it wasn't for everyone.

I'd been working there for a while, struggling to make ends meet on shit pay and an unsteady market. The

223

added job at the shop almost made our checkbook balance but was hell on my back.

Hours later, I walked through the door. I dumped my purse on the coffee table and sank into the couch. My face buried in a cushion.

"I got sausage and peppers," Sid said from the doorway of the dining room. I tilted my head and peeked at him. His eyes were tired, the skin around them folded and dipped in wrinkles that weren't there a couple of years ago.

What had happened to us?

Weren't we just kids the other day, sneaking around behind my parent's back? Forbidden love had always tasted sweeter, but we'd outlasted their criticism, their barbs. Thank God they were all dead now. I couldn't survive the judgement of what our life had become.

We were broke. The daily struggle to balance too little time and too many demands was wearing.

"You are awesome." My words were warped by the fabric.

"I know." He winked and disappeared, the lingering scent of hot cheese and spicy meat was too tempting for even my tired bones. I could have sworn they creaked as I walked across the room.

Lost in the routine of the day, in the motions repeated one after another until I was in an automatic daze, I'd completely forgotten about the night before. Until bedtime.

The light in the bathroom was bright, casting its glow across the room and banishing shadows. I scrubbed the day off my face and teeth and drew a brush through my hair, carefully working through tangles.

I smiled at my reflection, admiring my white teeth as they flashed in the mirror.

I wasn't so bad. My despair from the night before was replaced with a foreign optimism. I was almost forty. I turned in the mirror. My body showed the wear and tear of almost four decades, but it had held up. Not a hundred percent intact, the thought sneaked in. My good mood wavered but I pushed away the negative thought, desperate to hold on to the good feeling that wrapped me in comfort and borrowed energy. Moments like those were a rare and precious thing.

I rested my hands on my hips and pushed out my chest, my breasts bouncing gently with the movement. I cocked my hip and smiled at my reflection. I still looked good at forty, better than I'd expect at any rate. My smile spread as I lifted the hairbrush to my hair.

And my reflection winked.

But I didn't.

I gasped, my hand froze mid-movement. The brush slipped through my fingers, knocking and clattering as it hit the tile floor.

J. Nichole Parkins

CHAPTER THREE

"It was just your imagination." Sid rolled his eyes and return his attention to the television.

I hiccupped and wiped the tears from my face. "It looked real."

"You're just tired." He clicked through channels, brushing off my worry just as easily.

I frowned and picked at the threads in the bright green comforter. The bed was soft, luring me in with the promise of oblivion, of an escape into the world of dreams.

"Come to bed." He patted the space beside him, but never took his eyes from the flickering box.

Exhaustion pulled at me. Surely he was right. It was just my overactive imagination, fueled by too many sleepless nights tossing and turning with worry.

What other explanation was there?

I gave in and slipped between the covers. I pressed my body against Sid's. His warmth seeped into my skin. I fell into the blackness of sleep, thankfully empty of dreams – good or bad.

****

"They switched my shifts," Sid mumbled around a mouthful of food as we ate dinner the next evening.

"When?" I didn't want to go back to empty nights and endless stretches of silence.

"Tomorrow."

"Damn." My brain was flying with the logistics of functioning with one car.

"Trevor said he could give me a ride." Sid lifted his beer to his lips and emptied it. I watched the movement of

227

his throat wishing I had the energy to feel something other than a mixture of relief and exhaustion.

"Thank God. Otherwise, I'd have to take the bus."

"Not from the diner." He frowned. It wasn't in the best part of town.

I shrugged. "If that's what I have to do." I'd uttered that statement hundreds of times over the last few years.

Getting a second job.

Selling my car.

Moving into this shithole.

Cutting out a part of my body.

I flinched and stood fast from the table, knocking over my glass in the process. At least it was empty. Sweat broke out along my palms.

"What?" Sid asked, his tired eyes jerked to mine.

"Nothing." I picked up my half-empty plate.

My chest squeezed. We didn't talk about it.

It was better to avoid dredging up all those old feelings and memories. And the pain.

I closed my eyes against the onslaught, hardened my heart against the feeling. Even after all these years the pain was as fresh as the night I—

Stop.

I had to stop.

I walked into the kitchen. My eyes darted around the room, bouncing from the worn and chipped cabinets to the foil covered burners, of which only two worked. A new stove was on the growing list of things we needed, a list that never seemed to shrink, instead, it multiplied while we slept.

The pile of dishes in the sink grabbed my attention. I flipped the faucet on, filling one side with warm soapy water. My mind drifted, satisfied at the act of doing something, anything repetitive and familiar. It gave me peace from my dangerously wandering thoughts.

Reflected

****

I stared at my reflection in the glass. Faded and pale, it looked back with caution-filled eyes. Eyes that looked flat and empty, a void where a soul should be.

"Miss?"

Blinking, I pulled myself together and ripped my gaze from the window. "Yes? Sorry." I smoothed my hand on my apron and twisted my thin lips into a smile. Or so I hoped.

"What are the desserts tonight?" The young girl repeated. She looked about seventeen, fresh and filled with sunshine.

I listed them, struggling to remember the last time I felt as happy as she looked. My hand went to my stomach automatically and a chill worked its way along my spine. I jotted down her order and escaped to the back.

One minute, I just needed one to get myself back together. I leaned against the sticky wall in the hallway, a restless twisting static in my head. Sucking in a breath, I held it for the count of ten, fighting to slow my heart rate.

"Marigold, your table is waiting." Fran's raspy smoke-filled voice snapped me out of the void.

"Got it." I could get through today. Just like I got through the last. And the one before that. An endless stream of *getting through*, and not enough *living*.

I plated a banana cream pie, the sunny yellow blob a match for the girl's disposition. She was a shiny penny, unmarred. For now anyway. I'd be curious to see how shiny she was after life had its way with her for another seventeen years.

God, I was a downer. My shoulders sank. Is this what I had been reduced to?

229

I plastered a smile on my face and brought the sugar-ladened dessert to the girl. The boy she was with smiled and handed me a wad of cash with the bill.

"Keep the change." His eyes never left the sunshine girl.

I mumbled my thanks.

Watching the couple hurt. The pain was a jagged knife to the gut. That used to be us. Sid's eyes on mine instead of the television, his smile warm instead of laced with bitterness and contempt.

I slid into the bathroom, free from watchful eyes.

Or so I thought.

****

I stared at my hand, at my simple stainless steel wedding band. I'd had to hock my original set to afford the deposit on our shithole of a house.

I lifted my gaze to the reflection, watching as my movement was perfectly matched.

I reached out and brushed my fingers along the glass. So did my mirror image.

My shoulders sank as I dropped my arm, expelling a breath as my body relaxed.

"I guess I'm just crazy." I watched the mirror me repeat the words soundlessly. Feeling silly, I laughed, throwing my head back in a torrent of loose curls.

The mirror me didn't. Instead, she watched with slivered eyes.

The laughter stuck in my throat, trapped. I felt my eyes widen, felt the panic bubble up as my breath became ragged. But the woman in the mirror just stared, her eyes cold and calm.

Reflected

"You're not crazy." Her lips formed the words, but no sound accompanied them.

"Jesus," I managed to squeak between gasps.

"Not even close," mirror me retorted.

I slapped my hand across my mouth, holding back my scream. The beat of my heart was so loud, it drowned out the hum of the evening traffic outside.

My eyes wrenched closed. I pinched them tight. If I couldn't see her, she wasn't really there. Please let her go away, I pleaded to myself.

Please. Please. Please.

I waited, chanting in my head. Begging no one, terrified to open my eyes.

I focused on the sounds around me, anything other than my frantic heartbeat and my gasps as I struggled to breathe through the increasing panic. My hands were clammy with sweat. I wiped them on my pants, the fabric soft on my over-sensitive skin.

The cars. I focused on the sound of the tires on the pavement, of the engines and the horns and the other noises of the city. My heart slowed. I focused on the sound, the rhythmic beat soothed my frayed nerves. The air left my lungs with less force. The sweat evaporated and left me chilled.

But I still waited. Another minute passed and I peeked through one eye. The woman in the mirror did the same. I looked ridiculous.

My lips trembled into a smile. I rolled my eyes. Mirror me did too, only hers didn't stop. They fell out of her skull and rolled along the sink until they fell out of sight.

I jerked my gaze back to my reflection. The holes in the skull were once again filled with the missing orbs. They blinked.

"Boo." The lips formed.

231

I screamed.

CHAPTER FOUR

The house was silent as I walked in alone after fleeing the diner. The oppressive, heavy silence had its own presence, its own breath almost. I'd rushed to my boss, babbling something about leaving sick — or at least that's what I hoped I'd said. I didn't remember the drive home, but I was thankful to be away from the watchful eyes of others.

I wandered the house, avoiding the bathrooms, and tidied up despite my weariness. I had to keep busy, keep moving to fill the void, to keep the desperate panic at bay.

Eleven came faster than expected. I needed to go to bed or else I'd be a zombie tomorrow.

Who was I trying to kid, I already was a zombie — moving through life half-dead, drudging through each day like it was a chore. There was no more joy, only an endless stretch of work and bills and debt. And Sid.

I used to love him. Our love was young and bursting at the seams when we were teens. We grew together with time, not apart like most couples who married young.

Then I failed to give him the one thing he wanted, the one thing I wanted. Its absence ate at us and stretched the threads of love until they threatened to snap. A baby.

Then came the tests, the treatments, and the money we'd managed to save all our lives disappeared. But it all seemed worth it the moment the little pink plus sign appeared.

We had eighteen weeks of joy before—

I dug my knuckles into my eyes. The pain forced my focus back to the here. The now. And away from the dangerous past.

233

I stumbled into the bathroom, splashing cold water on my stark white face. My lips were bloodless and flat, like my reflection.

I looked away, refusing to see another hallucination. That was what it was, right?

My breath caught in my throat, lodged in place as icy fingers of fear danced up my spine.

Movement in my peripheral vision.

I swung my eyes to the left, picking apart the image in the mirror that stayed still and perfect except the motions of my heaving chest as I sucked in air like I was drowning.

Nothing. There was nothing.

I lifted a trembling hand to the cool flat surface, the movement slow as dread continued to fill me.

I had seen something. I did, I had to. It wasn't my imagination, wasn't the overactive action of a troubled mind.

There was something there.

But my hand met itself on the otherwise still surface. Nothing.

My shoulders dipped, shifting with gravity until my knees gave way and I landed with a thump on the lid of the toilet, my gaze trapped in that of my reflection.

Shouldn't I feel relief?

Shouldn't I feel happy that there was nothing there?

But all I felt was a gathering uncertainty, a static like the air was charged before a storm.

****

"Thank you," I chirped to the customer as she took the bag from my hand and strode out the door. The bell chimed on her way out, a sound I heard in my sleep.

Two hours left in a sixteen-hour shift. I'd snagged a double when one of the teens hadn't shown up.

Reflected

The ache in my feet pulsed through my body, reminding me why I hadn't worked a double at the store in the last few weeks. But with hours dwindling at the diner I needed the extra money.

It always came down to that: money.

We worked to live but never made it to the actual living part. I struggled to remember the last time I had fun, unable to come up with a memory that wasn't a decade old.

What was I doing? This wasn't a life.

It was. It was my life. It was a sentence I was living out, no parole in sight. The white envelopes with red warnings continued despite my exhaustive schedule. Each demanding money I didn't have, while I paid them just enough to keep them at bay. Interest and fees racked up, trapping us in a continual cycle of debt we'd never escape without a miracle.

The chime tinkled again and I watched the next customer stroll along the shelves, picking up and discarding each trinket as they went, finding nothing of interest. The souvenir shop catered to tourists, knickknacks and chachkies, t-shirts with funny slogans and cheap fabric, and a variety of travel needs for those that forgot something.

I wished I could forget.

I wished I could step outside of my life and into someone else's, someone's that wasn't an endless stretch of monotony and duties. Whose life wasn't being slowly suffocated under the weight of regret and debt.

"Do you have scarves and gloves?" The tourist with her bright eyes and flushed face called from the front. Her red nose and pink cheeks were windblown, stung by the biting cold that blew outside.

I pointed to the left. "There's also hats and coats if you need any."

Her face flushed even more and she scurried away as she called out her thanks.

The temperature had dropped last night. Locals were used to the sudden fluctuations in temperature. The store banked on the fact that tourists were not.

After several trips back to the dressing room, the woman walked to my counter and set several outfits in front of me.

"It got cold fast." She dug through her purse as she spoke and pulled out her wallet.

"The weather changes quickly here." I pressed the numbers into the ancient register, wishing again that the owner had invested in a newer system. The old register was clunky and loud, and the nine sometimes got stuck. I had to keep a close watch on the totals so I didn't under-charge. That mistake had come straight from my paycheck. Sid's red face flashed in my mind. He'd ignored me for weeks afterward, his anger simmering the whole time. His occasional forced words stung like wasps.

I made mistakes but I rarely repeated them.

"You live here?" The woman smiled through her question, imagining my life in ski lifts and fun whipping down the mountain. I'd seen it before a million times.

"Yup." I folded each item and bagged them, careful to keep the bags light. The cheap plastic tended to tear.

"Must be nice." She gazed outside at the falling snow as it drifted down, the darkness hiding the mountains beyond.

It sucks. "It is," I said, hating each word that escaped my lips.

"I'm from the coast of South Carolina." She handed me her credit card after I mumbled the total. "It's flat. I've never seen such a beautiful place. John's talking about

236

buying a cabin." Her wistful voice was laced with excitement.

"That's great." I passed her a receipt, smiling with stiff lips as I shifted from one aching foot to the other.

I cringed at the sound of the bell as she left.

The darkness beyond the glass seemed endless and heavy. I pulled off my shoes and stood against the cold surface. The wind beat against the window like it was fighting to get in.

Light reflected off the white ground, blinding in the daytime, eerie and bleak in the night. While the woman saw beauty outside the doors I only saw my prison. Even though I couldn't see them, the mountains loomed in the darkness, bars in my cage. If I looked long enough my throat would get tight and my heart would race.

I turned away, straightening the shelves and picking up fallen clothing as I prepared to close. The dressing room was a mess. The woman had tried on more clothing than I owned, leaving each piece where it fell, another mess for me to fix.

Clothes were piled in my arms, face barely visible in the mirrors that surrounded me. My eyes froze as they caught mine in the mirror. The beating heart in my chest, still alive despite not living, lurched and restarted at three times the pace. Blood surged through my veins.

Each silent heavy moment passed longer than the one before.

It was just me, just my reflection and nothing else. I was being ridiculous, like Sid had said, his words charged with contempt. The voice of reason in the void that was my life.

I laughed, although it came out in a choked whisper. I suddenly feared breaking the silence. Each breath hung suspended in the air. Goosebumps broke out along my skin.

My eyes widened as I realized I wasn't just looking at one reflection. Three mirrors faced me with three replicas of myself. Three times as much skin. Three times the blinking, dull eyes, dead with the things that never were.

More than three.

I shifted my feet, five reflections moved with me. It was all physics. I remembered learning something about it years ago in high school. I had been too busy paying attention to Sid and the next party than actual classwork.

I stepped closer and two of me disappeared. Evaporated into thin air.

If only it were that easy.

I stepped back and they reappeared.

Unease slipped along my spine, lifting the hairs at the base of my neck. A warning. A primitive reaction embedded deep within the brain where we know things that we haven't learned, where we feel things we can't see.

I swallowed the unease.

The wind howled outside, the winter storm intensifying.

The overhead lights flickered.

It's just the storm.

I was plunged into darkness. A darkness as complete and full as the one that lingered outside the valley, the endless drop over the side of the mountain.

I dropped the pile of clothing on the floor, my arms weak and shaking. My eyes darted around, pupils wide as they searched for the minute particles of light that would ease the racing of my heart.

I was alone, in a darkness so complete it had a presence. Thick and heavy like syrup it trailed over my skin, looking for a way in.

I was alone.

Reflected

My trembling legs collapsed under me. My hands reached for purchase and found the side table along the wall, no barrier to my weight and the draw of gravity as I crashed to the floor.

The pile of clothes softened the blow of my knees on the hard tile floor, the fabric gathered beneath me, the textures bled onto my starved skin. The different fabrics and materials were soothing, my lack of sight replaced with touch.

I leaned forward as the adrenaline seeped out of me and onto tile of the dressing room floor. My head rested against the smooth cold glass of the mirror. It reminded me of the storefront window as the cold beat to get inside.

What was trying to get inside of me?

The numbness that resided inside refused to be awakened. I refused to feel. It hurt too much. My life was an endless loop of trying to keep up, running on a treadmill with an endless supply of electricity.

Panic crawled in my gut as I crouched on the floor half buried in clothes. I felt the presence in the darkness. There was someone there.

But the bell above the door never sounded. The store was empty.

My brain fought the panic, supplying rational arguments that had no impact on my racing heart and shaking hands.

Light pressure on my face, a finger trailed down my cheek, tracing the bone that created a shadow on my skin.

You've lost weight. They'd say as my cheekbones became more prominent, their voices tinged with reproach and jealousy.

A hand cupped my chin. I wasn't imagining it.

There is no one here.

But there was.

239

I felt it on my skin. I felt it in the tightness along my back, the undeniable feeling of being watched. A heaviness that lingered as eyes searched the dark corners but saw nothing.

The lights flickered.

On.

Off.

On.

Off.

On.

My eyes darted around the room. It was empty. As empty and barren as my body.

Nothing.

I was alone. Alone in the light as I was alone in the dark.

I was imagining things.

I fought my racing heart, fought to calm my ragged breath. My face hot even though there was no one to witness my embarrassment. The coolness from the mirror a blessing.

I laughed. The sound empty in the room, it bounced off the walls. A mismatched echo that would have convinced me there was another presence had I still been trapped in the dark. In the light it made me feel even more ridiculous.

Standing, I picked up the pieces of the side table that didn't survive my fall, the splintered wood rough and jagged against my palms. My shoulders sank along with my heart when I realized its cost would probably be taken out of today's meager pay.

Would there be anything left?

My ears echoed with the shouts of Sid's would-be response when I admitted my mistake.

I frowned, clenching my hands around the rough wood.

Reflected

But my reflection did not. She stood, arms at her sides, brandishing the broken wood like a weapon. Eyes more alive than mine looked back, a grin split her lips.

J. Nichole Parkins

CHAPTER FIVE

"You got fired?" Sid's bellow rang in my ears as I failed to hold back the tears that slid over my cheeks like rain on a window.

"I broke a table and a shattered a mirror." Or three. "It was an accident. The lights went out."

"The lights went out." He mocked, his voice raising in pitch as his lips twisted into a sneer. The disgust on his face tied a rope around my heart, squeezing the organ until I worried it would burst from the pressure.

Would that be less painful?

"Jesus, Mari. You know we need the money." He dragged his fingers through his hair. The ends stuck up in all directions, the disarray matching the frantic look blazing in his eyes. "How could you do something so stupid?"

I sucked in a breath.

I wanted to say tell him the truth, what had really happened. I urged my lips to form the words, prayed that my voice would take flight and release the festering worry that was growing like a tumor in my chest.

Fear had taken over any rational thought. I'd thrown the broken table at the glass, shattering all three mirrors in the time it took to blink. I didn't tell anyone that part, though.

I blamed my clumsiness and the darkness from the storm.

I was fired anyway, the cost of replacing the table and dressing room mirrors more than I could cover in one paycheck. I was out two weeks work and a job.

Was I seeing things? Was there really a woman in the mirror, one that took pleasure in tormenting me? Or was it all in my head?

I didn't know which answer frightened me more.

243

I pinched my lips together and kept the words trapped inside.

He'd say I was seeing things, that I was being ridiculous, that I need to see someone.

How? With the insurance and money we don't have? Maybe I could barter for therapy – if I had something of value to bargain with.

Loud footsteps stalked to the fridge as my head fell. My eyes traced the web-like pattern in the broken kitchen tile. The hiss of a beer opening hit my ears.

Would it sound the same if the pressure in my heart was released?

"I'll get a new job."

"Damn right you will." His throat bobbed as he swallowed, draining the whole can in seconds. He reached back into the fridge.

Lather, rinse, repeat.

"What was that?" he growled, narrowed eyes searching out the patterns on my face.

I must have accidentally said that out loud.

"I'll start looking tomorrow," I tried to soothe. He stomped off, grumbling as he flicked on the television and sped by channels so fast I knew he saw nothing.

I turned on the water and gripped a dirty glass, making a list of places to apply.

****

I'd driven up and down the tourist section of town, stopping at shops and restaurants that were likely to be hiring.

They weren't. Tourist season was in full swing, they were already fully staffed.

I returned home feeling defeated.

244

Reflected

I needed to find something — and fast. The bills would pile up and we'd be back in collections before the season was over.

Walking into the bedroom I stripped off the skirt and button-down top I'd sweated through. It might be freezing outside, but my nervousness made me a sticky mess. I needed a shower, but I wasn't ready to force myself into the bathroom.

I took a cue from Sid and grabbed a beer.

The hiss of the can did nothing to settle my nerves, neither did the watered-down taste of the cheap beer. I poured it down the drain after choking down half the can, knowing Sid would lose it if he found out I'd wasted the other half.

The scent of beer lingered, melded with the odor of sweat and disappointment and I couldn't take it anymore. I crept into the bathroom but avoided looking at the mirror. It was impossible, it took up almost the whole wall.

Hands shaking, I turned on the spray and jumped in without letting it warm. The freezing water made me gasp, my eyes widening with pain as the water beat against my skin like needles.

After it warmed I sank into the spray, washing away the bitter day.

Marginally better after the shower, I dried myself and reached for my toothbrush. My hand froze as my reflection waved at me, a gentle motion of her fingers.

I gasped, terror wrapping its hand around my heart in an icy grip.

"Don't go." The words were spoken without sound, a movement of lips only. It had no voice to speak with.

"Wh-wh-why?" I stumbled over the word, dragging it out between trembling lips.

"I'm sorry." Her brown eyes, exact replicas of my own, were sad. They begged me to stay, to listen.

"Why do you torment me?" My heart pounded. I screamed the words at her. Weeks of frustration exploding from my lips.

"I didn't mean to," she frowned, "I was just playing and it got out of hand."

"That wasn't playing. That was cruel." I backed away a step, hovering over the threshold.

"I'm sorry." She waved both her hands, pleading. "Don't go. I won't do it again."

"Promise?"

She blinked. Her brown eyes were framed by lashes so thick they left a shadow. "I promise."

On wobbly legs I stepped closer to the mirror, gripping the towel still wrapped around my body. "What do you want?"

"A friend."

"A friend?" I frowned, drawing my brows low. My reflection stared back at me with hopeful eyes, no frown in sight. It was unnerving.

"I'm lonely." Her head dipped, shoulder slumping. "So lonely."

My chest tightened. I understood loneliness, the ache that had you pushing people away as much as you wanted to pull them closer and never let go.

"I know what you've been through." She mouthed words that burrowed into the empty places in my soul. "I was there with you when your sadness was so strong, so all-encompassing that all your friends left you."

"Why didn't you appear then?"

"You weren't ready."

"Ready for what?"

246

"Ready for me." She tilted her head, brown curls tumbled over her shoulder. Curls that were shiny, bouncy, and healthy. I glanced at my own only to be greeted with split ends and a cut that was uneven. My salon days were long gone.

I wasn't sure what she meant, but I was afraid to ask.

"I'm here now."

I snorted. "So I see."

"I didn't mean to get you fired." She bit her lip, a move so similar to mine a chill moved up my spine. "I am sorry for that."

She was me. She looked like me, acted like me, had the same gestures. The tilt of her head, the way she held herself, the way she moved — they were all reminders of a younger me, a me from *before*.

I ached to remember this version of me. Ached to remember what is was like to be Marigold Wilson before the dominoes in my life started falling.

I could use a friend.

So I sat, wrapped in a towel and perched on the toilet lid and tried to make friends — with myself.

J. Nichole Parkins

CHAPTER SIX

With Sid working the night shift, my empty evenings were filled with her — the me reflected in the mirror. The loneliness that had permeated every moment of my life the last few years began to fade.

Three weeks after losing my job at the shop, I sat on the bathroom counter, smoothing paint on my toenails. The light green color was almost identical to the spring green that I'd picked out for her nursery. I don't know what possessed me to pick it up. I'd walked into the pharmacy section of the superstore to buy soap, but the green caught my attention. I walked by the tiny bottles, lined up neatly in rows on the shelves twice before I picked it up. Compelled, I slipped it into my pocket, my heart pounding. I rushed to where Sid was waiting in the aisle with the razors and cloying scents of men's deodorant. The tiny bottle weighed heavily against my side. I was convinced it would fall out and expose my larcenous act at any moment. I kept my elbows pulled tight to my side the rest of the trip, my heart racing the entire time.

I don't know why I did it. It was only five dollars, but those five dollars were a lot on our tight budget. I had to have it, had to wear some sort of external reminder. I wanted to show the world the pain that sat tightly coiled inside me, even though no one would understand the significance.

It was an empty gesture.

"I understand," my reflection mouthed. The understanding in her eyes filled my heart.

She would.

I returned my focus to my task, struggling to stay within the lines of my nails.

"I know he hasn't forgotten her." I dug my teeth into my bottom lip as I squinted my eyes. "Sid's just very practical. He focuses on what is right in front of him." I blew out a breath from the bottom of my lungs. "He's great at fixing things, and accepting things for what they are."

"But you miss what was," She said silently.

"What should have been," I whispered. Pain cut through my chest. I turned my head and looked into her eyes. "I wanted a little girl." I tried to swallow the tears but they overflowed and dripped down my face. I watched as they fell down hers.

"I had her for such a brief time."

The sounds of the beeping machinery from the hospital echoed around me, magnified by the tiny space. I looked around the room, blinking through the tears, but nothing had changed. I was still in my bathroom, not the hospital. I sniffed the air, the smell of antiseptic singed my nose.

I dropped the polish applicator. It bounced against the counter, droplets of color falling in its wake.

"Want to know a secret?" Her lips formed the question as my breath came in pants. I wouldn't have been able to hear her through the rushing in my ears anyway.

This whole thing was weird enough. I was sitting in my bathroom, basically having a conversation with myself. Only the woman in the mirror was a million times more at peace than I was.

"Maybe." I wiped up the spilled polish with the hand towel. The biting scent of acetone replaced the haunting odor of antiseptic.

She rolled her eyes at me. "Yes or no? Decisions shouldn't be based on maybes."

I stared into her eyes. Their brown color was deeper, warmer than my own. If I really looked I could see the differences. If Sid were here I'd show him. Maybe it would convince him I wasn't crazy.

"Yes."

She understood what I was going through – what I had gone through. My reflection gestured me closer and I did what she asked, leaning in. My nose almost touched the glass.

"Do you trust me?" I watched her lips form the words. I lowered my brow and considered the answer.

Did I?

"I don't know." The honesty rolled off my tongue without my permission.

She frowned, her eyes flashed with anger.

I jerked back. My hand grasped air as I lost my balance and slid backward off the sink counter.

My hand smacked the wall, jarring my arm. I pushed and swung my other arm out, catching myself on the back of the toilet. I dragged in a trembling breath as I returned to my awkward spot on the edge of the sink.

"That would have hurt." My laugh fell flat as flames engulfed my face.

"Nothing hurts here." My reflection retorted.

I blinked, but couldn't tear my eyes from hers. No pain. What I wouldn't give for a reprieve. "Nothing?"

She placed her palm against the glass but held my gaze. "Nothing."

The temptation coiled inside me and flowed out through my fingertips. My palms were sweaty, darkening the fabric of my pink yoga pants as I wiped them off.

It could be like a vacation.

"A break would be nice." I bit my lip. "A vacation."

"Yeah, exactly." Her teeth flashed in a smile.

My heartbeat was loud in my ears. I leaned forward, palm out, inches from the glass. Each breath beat against the mirror, leaving a cloudy trail that obscured my face. Her face.

Her eyes were visible. Eyes like mine, but not. Eyes shining with life, with purpose. I couldn't remember the last time I felt like I had a purpose.

"Just a break, right?"

"Sure." Her face softened. It was soaked in kindness, warmth radiated from her skin.

I leaned closer, wanting to feel a fraction of her excitement.

Just a break. A vacation from this life that wasn't one. I'd return refreshed and alive, with purpose — once I figured out what it was.

"Okay." The glass was cool beneath my palm as ours met.

"Close your eyes." Her lips formed the words.

I followed her instructions. A gentle pull dragged my body forward, a sense of vertigo made my stomach spin but I kept my eyes shut. A sudden stillness and calm washed over me.

I opened my eyes and met eyes so brown they almost glowed. A smile, wide and bursting, lifted my lips. Laughter lit my eyes. She was filled with life, alive. More alive than I'd been in years.

She flexed my fingers, rolled her neck, and looked right at me.

"How are you feeling?" Her voice was like mine but slicker, smoother. Filled with smoke and warm coffee.

"Calm." My voice was a flat reflection of hers.

I was a flat reflection.

My calm began to dissipate, evaporating on the stale, tepid air. I was surrounded by darkness, by nothing.

She opened a drawer and rifled through tubes and bags until her hands wrapped around a small black bag covered in red poppies. My makeup.

Leaning forward, she drew the eyeliner along her lids, the motion smooth and practiced. She rubbed along the line with her finger, giving it a smoky look.

The lifeless organ in my chest beat, a rhythm that increased by the second as fear wrapped itself around my throat like a noose.

"Wait," I called out to her. She continued pulling makeup from the bag, applying each with an ease and expertise that made my breath shake from my lungs.

"What is it?" She snapped after rubbing her lipstick slickened lips together. The dark red color a slash across her face, the whites of her teeth flashed between them.

Unease coiled in my stomach.

"I change my mind."

She threw her head back, the cackle shattering the remains of my control. Panic wrapped its arms around me in the empty dark.

"Too late."

"You said—"

"I lied." She flattened her hands on the counter and leaned forward, eyes sharp with malice were inches from mine.

My breath exploded from my lips and I fought to think, to find a way to fix this, to fix what I'd done.

"You were given a life that you wasted." Her words were barbs that stuck to my skin. "I've watched you for years, trapped in that hell of nothing, while you've squandered what you were given."

She dragged her fingers through her hair, twisting and lifting it into an up-do I'd never be able to accomplish without help.

253

J. Nichole Parkins

"Well, I won't waste it." She blew me a kiss and stalked out the bathroom door.

I beat my hands against the glass. The effort wasted as it did nothing except solidify my panic.

I was stupid.

I caught glimpses of her as she walked back and forth in the bedroom. She'd found an old dress hidden in the depths of my closet. The clingy red fabric gave the illusion of curves, her legs endless in a pair of strappy heels I'd forgotten I owned.

She didn't look back as she left, walking like she owned the world.

I'd give anything to take it back.

Anything.

About the Author

J. Nichole Parkins writes Urban Fantasy, Suspense, Horror, and New Adult. She is currently working on the next book in the Burned series and a New Adult stand alone. Wife, mother of three, and constant daydreamer, she is never without a story floating around in her head or a book or two in her purse. A Florida transplant, she can often be found writing poolside with a cup of Chai or reading her Kindle way after bedtime.

Visit her on the sites below – especially Facebook – because she's there way too often.

Facebook: www.facebook.com/JNicholeParkins
Twitter: www.twitter.com/JNicholeParkins
Wattpad: www.wattpad.com/JNicholeParkins
Website: http://jnicholeparkins.wordpress.com

J. Nichole Parkins

Escape

The beginning of the end.

When a virus destroys the Earth's plant life, colonizing other planets is the human race's last hope. Countries band together and create seven Advanced Relocation Colonies, sending them to habitable worlds. Between massive extinctions, bureaucracy, malfunctions, and anti-colonization terrorists, can humanity survive?

Laura Stapleton

Escape

BY

Laura Stapleton

Laura Stapleton

Acknowledgements

Who knew that the phrase, "I have another friend who writes," could lead to such a rich friendship with L.E. Perez? She puts together killer anthologies and I'm proud to call her my friend. I have to give huge thanks to Kelly Abell. It's easier to list what she can't do than what she can, and everything she does is with grace and charm. Finally, tremendous thanks to Miranda Nading for doing my math and being a fantastic editor. She is why my science is accurate.

Laura Stapleton

Chapter One

"You have got to be kidding me!" Doctor Frank Adams stood, his legs bumping the chair behind him into a fast roll.

A soft ding from his computer chimed before his personal artificial assistant Channi, said, "I'm sorry, Doctor Adams. I didn't quite understand your request."

"Ignore." He scanned the text again and sure enough, Bob Harper, the head guy for the North American Coalition's Project Escape, had budgeted for ten thousand people. Each Advanced Relocation Colony, or ARC, required four times that to succeed. "Not enough. Not nearly enough. The short-sighted asshole knows that." He pushed the chair back under the desk, his hand on the backrest. "Channi?"

"Yes?"

"Reply to Harper."

A new pop-up appeared, to and from fields filled in and an underscore blinked, waiting on the first line of the message text box. Adams growled, "If you think I'm signing off on one-quarter of the people we need for adequate genetic diversity, you're insane. Also, you're an idiot who has destroyed the human race by dicking around with money. To hell with you and anyone who looks like you." The words appeared on the screen as he spoke them. Each profanity felt good as he reread the reply. Almost better than sex.

After a couple of minutes, Channi asked, "Shall I send?"

He stared at the cursor for a moment, tranced out on the damage his tirade would do to his career. Oh, and the human race, and replied, "No. Delete message text."

"All message text?"

"Yes." He sat and waited until the field cleared before speaking. "Channi, message text. Harper, I realize you have a budget to meet. I respect that. However, money won't matter in another fifty years when no one is left to spend whatever you've saved by sending an inadequate number of people to the new colonies." Adams paused for a moment. "Forty thousand is the absolute minimum per colony, remember? There is a particular, scientific reason why we need that number. Channi?" The typing stopped when he said the AI's name.

"Yes, Doctor?"

"Clean up the grammar, sentences, all that. Attach Simplified Genetic Justification document." He put his elbows on the desk, head in his hands. "Add signature and send."

"Done." A few moments ticked by before she asked, "Shall I order dinner for you?"

Frank went through his choices. He was old enough to remember when food tasted good. People younger than sixty didn't know what they had missed. Shellfish of all kinds, tender, buttery fish, fresh fruits, and vegetables back when the flavor was still grown into them. He wanted all of it for dinner tonight. Not the super hybrids designed to survive today's world. "No. Not now."

An incoming message chime distracted him from further mourning the sterilized food chain. Channi opened the missive from Harper per his prior default instructions, and Frank read his reply.

He supposed he should be glad the administrator had increased the number at all. Still, thirty thousand wasn't enough. "Reply. I agree about terraforming here first. Bottom line is if you want the colonies to succeed, send the necessary amount of people. End message, send."

"Done."

"Thank you, Channi. Offline." The screen went dark except for the time, date, and outside temperature in dark characters on the left side of the screen. A grim reminder of Earth's massive warming. Dust clouds cooled small areas. Only, the wind sandblasted dirt to pain unbearable for too long. The invention of self-driving cars helped at a time like this. With GPS, no one needed visibility to get from work to home.....

He turned away from the wall. Frank didn't blame Harper wanting to save a buck, or thousand. People here in Des Moines needed every resource possible. All across the world, air conditioning morphed from chilling the air to de-humidifying it first. The new aerospace offices had San Antonio beat in comfortable temperatures. Easy to do when the southern branch of the North American Coalition ARC Project averaged 120F to the northern branch's 95F in the winter.

He went to his sleeping quarters, sensors switching the environmental resources from one room to the other. Fans pulled in and removed air moisture to help keep him cool. A wall screen lit up with the display from his previous computer. Nice, but Frank enjoyed his new neural implants.

The implant projected the same thing as his wall, but only in his mind. This latest upgrade to the old school devices amazed Frank every time he thought to use it. Instant information access at all hours and worth the hacking risk. As he walked to the bathroom, his apartment added his space to the electrical zone without taking away his bedroom power.

The geo-chilled water he splashed on his face revitalized him. He remembered how tap water hadn't tasted salty, but crisp and fresh every time. Frank missed those days. Today's youth had no idea what they'd lost by growing up on partially desalinated water.

He settled into bed. A soft ding sounded, and he glanced at the wall screen out of habit. His inner display overlaid his wall, seeming as if he had double vision. Bob had conceded and gave him 35K personnel? An improvement, but not enough. Frank said, "Channi, note. Get numbers from other continents to rub in Harper's face." The chime sounded again, and he snuggled in deeper.

Only his group, the North American Coalition, NAC for short, kept to a strict budget. Other leaders knew the race here was doomed if the virus continued its destructive course. The imaginatively named Foliage Virus, FV, mutated every second generation, rarely showing more than a couple similarities to previous genetic samples.

He remembered the fear from his parents when the news broke, and he'd never tasted an emotion before then. The three of them watched the broadcasts as leaders admitted FV was impossible to control, impossible to reverse. Terror hovered in the back of his throat with a metallic tang. The virus was supposed to keep predatory plants away from the vital food crops. Around the world, humanity reacted with shock, horror, and despair, with a few hundred fighting efforts in between. So much death. Flora, fauna, human.

He sighed, missing green above all else. Flowers had been beautiful, but the chlorophyll giving almost every plant its hue meant life. He'd learned to treasure that color. The pompous administrator was too young to remember the mass extinctions, too young to remember far more than a couple of billion people on Earth. Frank wasn't sure if the man didn't appreciate human life or just didn't care.

He rubbed his eyes and tried to get comfortable in the steamy room. He had to convince Harper to give the First Nations and United North a fighting chance at a new colony tomorrow. "Channi, cool a degree and sleep program three." The artificial replay of frogs and a rushing creek added to a rush of air that relaxed him. Sounds that few under thirty years old had ever heard lulled Frank to sleep.

The next morning, Frank went to his boss's work area. The man, or someone like him, moved in the enclosed office behind a light and sound barrier. The unfocused shield blocked visual distractions while the white noise muted voices and other odd sounds. He took a deep breath as if the obstruction didn't hold air before stepping through. When Bob glanced over at him, Frank said, "Ready for our meeting?"

Harper stepped down from his treadmill. "We couldn't just conference?"

"No. This is too important." He mirrored Bob's actions by settling into a chair opposite him. "I need to know you see the ramifications of following a budget instead of following survival."

He waved his hand, staring at the screen embedded in his desk. "Fine. Get on with it."

Frank yearned to hit the man over the head with anything strong enough to withstand that concrete cranium of his. Instead, he pulled up the facts. "Computer, access Adams, Colony, Survival, Genetics, DNA odds of contemporaries doc." The wallscreen lit up with the graphs he'd been working on for months to prove the new colonies required variety. "I updated the figures this morning. Russia is sending sixty thousand people. They randomly chose citizens from one side of their country to the other."

269

Bob gave a snort, glancing at Frank's presentation before going back to his desk screen. "They have always sacrificed their domestic economy for the country." He shrugged. "That's not what we do."

"True. If you look, even countries not sharing Russia's pragmatic and communistic tendencies are sending more than our minimum." He shifted in his seat before standing. "Computer, motion control." Frank scrolled down the document, going past the text to bring up the colorful pie charts he had created especially for Bob and his contemporaries. "Spanish America is sending seventy thousand, Australia-Europe sixty, and Africa?" He moved down to the mortality and population graph. "Even with massive losses on their continent, they're sending fifty thousand. In another year, that'll be a tenth of their entire population below the Sahara."

"That's what, half a million Africans left on Earth? Damn."

Exactly. We're sending, what? A fraction of a percent of the North Americans available? Even worse, we're not very diverse in our selection. We can save money and send thirty thousand, sure, but would have to go back hundreds of generations to make sure they don't share ancestors."

His attention still captured by the flashy colors on the screen, Bob said, "Come on, Adams. There's enough doomsday here without you adding to it. Plenty of human colonies were started here on Earth just fine with few people."

"Name one," Frank countered before holding up a hand. "No, wait. You can't. And if you start with the Native Americans and Australian Aboriginals? They all had waves of migrations over thousands of year, far more than forty thousand total genetic donors."

"What about the smaller populations like Hawaii?" Bob asked, leaning back in his chair, hands behind his head.

Frank stared at him for a moment or two while easing into his own seat. How to further condense down all the decades of genetics and human migration studies into simple concepts for a person barely aware of either subject? He liked a challenge as much as the next guy, but this? Shaking his head, he started with, "Places like Hawaii began with a few explorers hopping from island to island, picking up other populations along the way."

"How did those people get there? I bet they didn't have forty thousand on those islands."

Frank clenched and then unclenched his fists. "Probably not. They had hundreds of generations to do what we need to accomplish in one or two." Harper's mulish face pushed him to add, "Here, let me show you South and East Asia."

He stood, scrolling down to the chart. "Like us, they had explosive growth at the end of the twenty-one hundreds followed by the disaster. We were lucky to only lose half our populations. I'm continually surprised at how Africa has held on." Frank tapped the pie chart to highlight the section. "Unlike us, SE Asia a half billion people to pick among. Double our quarter billion."

"Are they as genetically diverse?"

"As much if not more so." Even the numbers guys like Bob recognized violence had spread when the Middle Eastern peoples moved out of their lands and into less friendly countries. With no water, and then no oil money to buy water, they had two choices. Move, or turn to dust like their plants and animals. "You won't believe this. They're sending a hundred thousand people total."

His jaw dropped before he recovered enough to say, "No, seriously?"

"Yes. Their Chinese benefactor wanted more from his country on board. The final twenty thousand were on their way to the Moon last week."

"Sneaky bastards. They told us ten a month ago." He sat forward, staring at his desk screen, tapping on it. "Sure. I'll make sure you get forty thousand, but I can warn you right now, it'll be a fight for every penny."

Frank let out the breath he'd been holding. "It's worth it, Bob. Now isn't the time to cut corners. Delete something the team and I recommends, no matter how small you think it is, and our colony is doomed." He made a closing gesture with his hand, and the wall blanked to an automatic display. "You can either pay full price now or start saving for a second go around when the first fails."

"I know." Bob stood and went back to his treadmill. "People will approve the funds once they realize other continents are succeeding where we are failing. No one wants to let their way of life go extinct. The NAC will make it happen."

"Right. Good luck in presenting the request," Frank said. At Bob's dismissive wave, he headed back to his own little haven.

Despite the evidence and all the disasters happening day in and day out, broadcasted into their mental uplinks, no one seemed to understand. People like Bob only saw their own side. Losing three billion people to famine and disease didn't slow the SE Asian's plans. Even Antarctica was sending as many people as their ships would hold. Refugees to the melting continent were still arriving, claiming asylum to get on an ARC. The young country would board anyone to hit their forty thousand colonist goal.

He walked through a once bustling complex. He paused, looking out of the large windows. Brown dominated the view. He wandered over, closer to the sun tint covered glass. They were lucky here in the north, he supposed. Their southern annex's district had been burned off two years ago. Nothing grew in the blackened landscape there. A friend of his had sent images of the devastation via mental uplink as it happened. He shuddered, remembering the fire tornadoes. The same would happen here, in due time.

Frank didn't want to preserve a lifestyle. He wanted to preserve life itself.

Laura Stapleton

Chapter Two

Three months later, to the day, Frank paced the floor of the conference room. As his colleagues checked in, their view bubbles appeared on the holo-screen to his side. This waiting for the NAC's virtual ARC tour killed his blood pressure. The health band he wore buzzed relax warnings so he took a deep breath and tried to biofeedback the numbers lowers.

He rechecked the time and checked to make sure his name badge faced out. The ID was a relic, like him, and Frank felt his age today. He and Channi had planned this to the second and across all the planetary and satellite time zones. Everyone attending had watched their own little portion of their ARC and maybe more of the others. But now? They'd be able to see every area as their guide went through the entire ship. He tried to relax. There had been virtual tours of Australia-Europe Alliance's ARC, or AEARC, and South-Asia Alliance's ARC, aka SEAARC, but this was his ARC. All right, his country's vessel and yes, it was special even if only to him. He checked the time again. A minute since the last time he looked.

True to human nature, the beeps from his health band grew in intensity as more people checked in for the tour. He pitied anyone who missed out on this as it happened. Sure, the historic event was being broadcasted and recorded. Various blueprints to planned monuments waited. The first humans to leave the solar system were the Earth's latest pioneers. But to see the interior of the intra-solar vessel with the rest of humanity was a once in a *species* experience.

Channi hummed his wristband. He knew. It was time. He took a deep breath and began. "Good afternoon, everyone. Thank you for attending this event." People quieted as he spoke. "Welcome to the North American Coalition's official tour of our Advanced Relocation Colony." He waved and the massive display lit up with a field of stars. "We started with nothing. Our world was dying, and nothing we did could save it." Per him and Chani's plans, the camera angle swept down to show their Earth. Burnt and dying plant life where it used to be green and a sick greenish where it used to be blue. He swallowed, wondering if he'd ever get used to seeing his planet dead under his feet.

Gathering himself, Frank turned to his audience. "As most of you know, we've had to make plans when our efforts to corral FV failed." He waved his hand, and the outside of the NAC's ARC filled the screen. Her beauty took his breath every time. ARC design was blocky, not aerodynamic in the least, but acceptable for cruising through a void between solar systems. The scene changed with the camera moving in until it seemed as if they'd fly into a porthole. He and Channi had planned this result. When one image stopped at the window, another camera picked up from there and would show the interior.

The effect went as planned, the crowd was transfixed. Frank gave a silent cheer to Channi via his uplink. She buzzed his wrist with simulated happiness. He grinned at the audience. "We'll take a look at the sleeping quarters, first." A three sixty sweep of the area showed nothing but blackness. "As you can tell, the lights are lowered to save energy. The vessel is nuclear, of course, with solar capabilities for emergencies." He sent a signal to Channi for better illumination. "We're doing everything possible to keep within budget. The last one out always turns off the lights."

Escape

He waited for three seconds for the command to hit the moon's orbit and come back. Four seconds. "Damn it," he muttered. They'd planned this, hadn't they? "Channi, interior lights for the UACARC."

"One moment, please."

Her usually calm tone didn't help him. "The people here will be asleep for the journey, so the comforts available en route are minimal." Light from the camera clicked on and cast a beam through the interior. Dust from the construction floated through the weightless vacuum. He smiled. "Excellent. This is where the crew sleeps until reaching the planet surface." A schematic of the current ARC flashed in his mind. This vessel didn't equal the plans. He sent a command to pan around the quarters. "Channi, is this room built to specs?"

"No, Dr. Adams. It is one fifth of the size smaller."

"Excuse me?"

"It is one-fifth—"

"Stop." He saw Bob in the audience. "Mr. Harper, why don't you come up here and help me with the tour."

"Sure." He went up onto the stage and waved to the crowd. "We made several post planning changes to the blueprint. These modifications are minor and will ensure a successful colonization."

Frank stared at the plump bureaucrat. No. *He* had gone over every spec of what an ARC would need. Nothing could be left out. "Modifications? Why don't you lead us to them, showcase what you've done for us."

"Well, first, we cut the overall size by a third. Less is more, am I right?" People clapped, and he waited until they stopped. "The lighting system was too extensive as designed. Our colonists will be sleeping for hundreds of years. I don't think any of them will be scared of the dark."

277

Frank watched as the camera hovered, showing the hibernation units. In this light, and hearing Bob go on, the units seemed more like morgue drawers. "What happens if there's a system failure and they're awakened too early? How will they see?"

He crossed his arms. "That won't happen."

The bureaucrat's mulish face told him everything. He and his cronies had never discussed contingencies. Frank rubbed his neck, suddenly hating his job. "What if it does? What if something goes wrong because you cut a cost, and these people wake up light years from their destination? We might hear about it in a couple of hundred decades, and I say we, meaning our decedents if any survive that long."

Bob's chin trembled, and he shoved his hands into his pockets. "Okay, let's add in a few lights, a dim one or two."

Frank turned back to the screen, searching. The other man seemed rattled. Good, but he suspected there was more to the story. "What else have you eliminated?"

"Not much. All the redundant systems."

He gritted his teeth at the unintended insult. "Nothing in the design was superfluous. What did you cut?"

Bob looked from him to the audience and back to him. "Just the filtering system for the ARC."

That narrowed it down a little. "Water or air?"

"Both."

He blinked hard, literally seeing red. Losing his temper wouldn't help. He snapped off the crazy buzzing health band and set it on the podium. "Seriously? No wonder the idea of them waking early upset you. What the hell happens if something malfunctions, then? What do you expect them to do for air? What if the planet is uninhabitable after all and they need to go to their next option?" He took a step forward, nose to nose with Bob. "I'll tell you what they do, Mr. Harper. They die. They all die."

"Now look here, I've had enough of you." He stood nose to nose with Frank as if feeding off of his anger. "This is not a pleasure cruise. They either get there, or they don't."

Frank put the back of a hand to his mouth in a mental effort to keep from swearing at him. The man was an idiot. He examined the audience for confirmation he wasn't off the mark. Not everyone had to be as myopic and cheap as Bob. Spotting a few rattled faces, he relaxed, knowing he wasn't the only one scared by the changes. He had to get through to him. "Everything you've taken away reduces their already slim odds of survival. You know that, don't you?"

"I hardly think the death of our colonists will doom the human race." He ignored the audience's gasp and turned to the screen. "Let's see what else this little baby has. Move the camera around the room, find the door."

Frank stared at him, at the little toad of a man who happened to be too young to even remember that such creatures once existed. He shook his head, unable to form a decent argument. Bob had never known a time when there weren't massive die-offs in one form or another. Losing a few thousand people at a time didn't crush his soul like it did Frank's. If it did, Bob kept the pain well hidden.

He shouldn't have been surprised at how much Bob relied too heavily on the other ARCs' potential successes. When Frank turned back to the screen, the camera floated through a door. The scene reminded him of old videos. They could easily have been exploring the wreckage of the Titanic. The weightlessness mimicked sea water. Especially now, with all the die off.

"And so, with fewer square meters, we're looking at serious savings. This surplus will be funneled back into FV

279

R and D. We'll beat this thing, yet, and not have to leave home to do it."

Everyone began clapping, and then standing. When the applause died down, one of the attendees stood and said, "Dr. Adams does have a point about an early wake up for the colonists. Would we provide them each an emergency pack of rations? Also, would we want them to have a way to get a message back to Earth of their condition?"

"Good point. It's worth looking into," Bob replied.

Frank shook his head. Too little too late. He blamed himself, having been focused on an adequate genetic population while overlooking the deleted logistics. Other scientists worked on the ship, true, but everything went through him before implementation. His stomach heaved. He'd failed the colonists before they had even stepped on board.

Chapter Three

Back from the bathroom, Frank sat in the seat Bob had vacated and stared at the screen in a trance. The man yammered on about the state of the art technology installed, money they'd saved, how fast the ARC would go. Sure, all of that mattered. Until something horrific happened. A meteor, a power malfunction, or an event no one even suspected? Anything was possible out there. The only hope he clung to was how close the others were to leaving the solar system.

His mind link chimed in his head, and he glanced up. Even Bob stopped mid-word, his mouth still open. Frank saw his vibrating wristband still on the stage. The chime stopped.

"Security is now red. Please take precautions. Security is now red. Please take precautions."

The message played over and over in his mind until he recovered enough to send an acknowledgment. He checked everyone else's reactions. Like him, they sat still, or in Bob's case, stood still. Each stared ahead of them as if daydreaming. That always creeped him out, but he did the same, accessing the news feed with his mind.

"Mass casualties as several explosions rock the Earth, Moon, and Mars. Judeo-Islamic Alliance claims responsibility." Images of the carnage flowed in with the words. "Details are not known at this time. Focus was on the ARC Project."

He recognized their South office's security post only by the building behind it. Or rather, the gaping sinkhole where security used to be. He never wished brain hacking on

281

people, but the Judeo-Islamic Alliance? They could rot in hell.

Bob recovered as each person caught up and resumed watching him. He looked to Frank, who nodded. "Well, that was a surprise. A very ugly surprise." He rubbed his forehead with a noticeably shaking hand. "Let's get back to our tour."

Updates continued in his mind, like background noise or an old style television left on in another room. Frank relaxed a little in the auditorium chair. They'd made their point. Time for JIA to move on.

"And here is the nuclear power supply." Bob beamed as if he'd assembled it with his own manufacturing robot. "It's small, isn't it? You probably expected much larger. We came in on time and under budget, thanks to my modifications."

The screen exploded to blinding, then black. Frank exhaled as if punched in the gut. His uplink began, "This just in, a massive fireball appeared over the United America Corporation moon base." He called to Channi through the link, asking her to show the tour's outside camera.

Fire erupted from the vessel like a supernova. Frank closed his eyes as the uplink displayed the receding view. Shock waves propelled the camera backward. A piece of the hull raced up to him, crashing into his mind. Everyone in the room gasped, some cried out before quietly sobbing. Frank realized others must be on the same frequency and getting the news as well.

"Our budget...." Bob whispered.

For once, Frank agreed with him and his obsession with money. His chin trembled. He'd succeeded and failed. Now, the North American Coalition was doomed. He stood, swaying on his feet for just a moment. "If you'll excuse me? I need some time alone."

He walked out, not waiting for permission. After sending a message to turn off what might be left of their tour, he leaned against a wall. Huge sobs burst from him. He could no more stop the sorrow than he could Earth's death. Frank had cried in great gulps of air before the keening wails from the bottom of his soul drowned out Channi's chiming in his mind about his blood pressure.

When the pain subsided a bit, Frank stood up, determined to get a grip and recover his mission. Six ARCs remained, one already close to the edge of their solar system. Humanity would go on, even if only one vessel succeeded. Stress and exhaustion. They are what led him to overreact to the disaster, that's all. He sniffed, wiping his face with his sleeve. Others needed his help. Security had to be examined, the JIA punished. He didn't have time to be cowed by his emotions. He cleared his throat to address the soft chime in his head. "I know, Channi."

He didn't want to go back in and face Bob's apologies for disallowing funds for a backup ARC. Better to just discard his attachment to his youth and rely on his neural implant. "Switch wrist controls to internal. Disable wristband."

"Yes, Doctor. Done."

Frank wiped his eyes. It would take the signal sixteen hours to reach them from the edges of the solar system. Not a good time to get distracted or oversleep. "Set alarm for AEARC exiting the heliosphere, plus fifteen hours, thirty minutes."

"Yes, Doctor. Done."

Time until alarm, he thought. Twenty-four hours displayed in a small box in front of him. Frank marveled hover the hallucinatory effect of the neural link. He wrung his shaking hands to calm them. Anxiety about the event almost overrode today's tragedy. He'd be too keyed up to sleep tonight. The first humans would be outside of the Sun's influence. He smiled, taking comfort in the knowledge they would succeed where he'd failed. A few hours' worth of messages, condolences, and new plans lay ahead. Work might help to slow his mind down later when he needed rest.

"Priority message override. Please respond," Channi's voice sounded in his head.

Frank stopped just outside of his office door. "Continue."

"The South-East Asia Advanced Relocation Colony launch has been rescheduled due to security. SEAARC personnel will remain in quarantine until launch. The AEARC Heliosphere Event will continue as planned."

He shook his head, shutting off the feed. Like the old time network news broadcasts, his uplink scrolled other news below the announcement. Frank went in and stepped on his treadmill. The words wouldn't leave his mind. The Judaeo-Islamic Alliance's chant, *One God, One Earth-He put us here, not there* might as well be embedded in everything.

Frank, Bob, and everyone else on the project knew their slogan and logo all too well. Removing spray paint from the walls, ARC factories, employees' homes and cars had been factored into the budget. Security had been added from the first day. Even without the One Earth people, he and his higher ups planned for the random loony. The JIA just happened to be the first group to volunteer.

His parents had told him horrific stories of what the religions used to do to themselves and others. It was too irrational to be believable. It felt a lot like fiction until Frank was old enough to watch the videos. The friend of my enemy is my friend, indeed.

The AEARC, nicknamed One by nearly everyone, was almost in interstellar space. He had to focus on AEARC being successful. SEAARC, or Two, would be swept for explosives again. The S-E Asians would leave Mars. They'd be cranky, thanks to quarantine, but they'd soon be headed toward Kapteyn's planetary system. By then, Three and Five, from Antarctica and Russia, would be finished and out of the Moon's factory. Meanwhile, back at the ranch with him and the NAC... He paused with an idea, carried back a foot or so by his treadmill before continuing his walk. They might be on their way to replacing the destroyed NACARC with the SAARC if South America approved.

"Doctor?" Channi said.

"Yes?" Frank thought back.

"You have fifty, more than fifty priority messages accumulated. Turn off the alarm?"

He sighed. "How many from my level or higher?"

"Seventeen. Twenty-two. Thirty...."

The numbers didn't surprise him. He said aloud, "Stop counting, stop alarm, sort messages by level and priority."

"Doctor Adams?"

A different voice from Channi's surprised him. He stopped walking, stepping from the belt. "Hello, Nahla."

Dr. Nahla Buhari came in with a tentative smile. "I stopped by to offer my condolences."

"Thank you." He grinned back at her, already enjoying the company. "It's been a while. How are you doing?"

"I'm good." She came up and gave him a hug.

285

He enjoyed looking at her. Frank had always thought her perfect dark skin was beautiful. Shyness hit him when their eyes met and their gazes lingered. He'd almost like a direct mental link with her, eliminate speaking aloud altogether. "How is the African ARC coming along?"

"Slow. Horribly slow. The people are fighting over skin color, and how many of each shade represents who." She rubbed her nose. "We're trying to sort it out by percentages."

She was one of the few pure dark people left on the continent. Not that he thought the last pure white person should have any advantages in being a colonist. "There are so many shades of every skin color. How does anyone but the middle brown dominate?"

"Exactly." She reached out and straightened his lab coat. "Have you heard about Seven?" He shook his head. "They've spent their budget, trained their colonists, but don't have a working vessel."

His smile at her casual reference to the South American ARC turned into dismay at the countries' lack of preparation. "Bribes, I assume?"

She nods. "All bribes."

Her news didn't surprise him. Every group had their people siphon funds off of the top. Stealing from their projects for what? Prolonged life on a dead planet? He didn't share their motivation to live on a former Eden turned hell hole. "The South America people should have been proactive like the South-Asian accountants were."

"Budget for the bribes? They were too busy fighting over who controlled what to notice the skimming from the top."

He snorted. "Yeah, skimming from top, bottom, and middle, you mean." Frank hesitated, aware he might sound like a gossip, but this was Nahla. "They have spent the most so far but have next to nothing built. Have you seen it? They've had to enhance the publicity images. "

"No! They're enhanced?" She shook her head. "How horrible. What did the original ship look like?"

"Let me find them." He searched his memory and sent them over. The virgin images showed the bare bones frame of an ARC. The next picture he showed, the altered one, had a hull, and engines added. Her expression changed when she received the message. "Amazing, hmm? It almost looks real," he said.

"Those poor people."

"I suspect they're keeping the colony candidates far away from the real thing."

"They have to be." She patted his shoulder before leaning against him. "I could have looked all this up myself or asked you over the link, I know. I just wanted to see how you were doing. In person." She stretched to kiss his cheek before taking him in her arms. "I'm broken hearted for you and can't even imagine how I'd feel in your place."

He swallowed down the lump in his throat and relaxed into her arms. "Let me know if your African ARC needs a chief operations officer. I'll cut my salary for you, even."

Laughing, she gave him a squeeze before letting him go. "You're on. If NACARC isn't rebuilt, I'll add you to my team."

Frank's smile froze, and he looked away. His ARC was gone. Where would they get the money for NACARC 2.0?

Laura Stapleton

Chapter Four

"Doctor? The EAARC is minus 30 minutes from interstellar space."

Frank opened his eyes and wiped the drool from his chin. He'd fallen asleep at his desk again. He wiped the display screen on his desk with a sleeve. Channi began broadcasting the festivities straight to his link. Sometimes, he wanted the pleasure of actually watching a program. "Channi, view screen."

She switched the display to the external link. The television-like screen took up one entire wall. He slipped out of his lab coat and tossed it into the laundry chute. Next to the laundry was the food and drink dispenser and he always questioned the logic behind the design. Didn't matter, not when humankind hovered so close to the biggest event of their existence. He got a drink and settled into his chair, facing the screen.

Parties all over the world had sprung up. People wore headbands with galaxy shaped antenna. He smiled despite the gaping hole in his heart where Four's success would have been. Bob had been kind this afternoon, leaving him alone as requested. The bureaucrat had promised to find funds for a second vessel, but Frank knew neither one of them had hope. He smiled as someone walked past the camera with sunglasses, #1 had been painted across the lenses.

He took a drink, proud of the Australia-Europe group. They'd earned their number one status. Despite the arguments over whom among them to send, despite the cost, and despite the JIA, they pulled together and met the minimum. A-E had completed the first step, or would do so today when they left their solar system.

289

Low priority messages popped up along the bottom of the screen. Well wishes, condolences, greetings from Frank's colleagues working on One's mission, scrolled across. This would be all right. Four might not be a go, but there were several more chances to reach the few habitable planets they'd discovered. The Americas could cooperate and create a new ARC together. It could happen. The two continents had compromised in policy before now.

Seeing a message from Nahla, he smiled. Maybe he'd give up and just let the JIA have their way and keep humanity in this solar system. Live on to help her before FV's effects killed them all. He'd have a great life with her until then.

A shudder went through the crowd on the screen. The lapse in the broadcast affected him as well. His heart skipped a beat, and he sat up straight. It passed, and everyone relaxed. Every human in the solar system stood transfixed with him. He couldn't wait, even if interstellar space was the Great Void. Mars would see it first and then four minutes later, the Earth and Moon would receive the signal. Everyone onscreen relaxed. Just a hiccup. Certainly not a distress message from AEARC.

He stood and refilled his glass, glad all the bases had lined up so well for this. If the planets had been in opposition, the Earth might have lined up first or at worst the Earth would receive the signal twenty-four minutes after Mars. Again, a ripple ran through the crowd. He leaned forward as if that would help steady the transmission, allowing audio input.

"....traveling sixteen hours to where we are now. Sadly, you Earthlings and Lunans will have to wait for another four to five minutes after we get to experience humanity's greatest feat." The reporter went to a random

290

person. "Are you ready for the next step in preserving the human race?"

"Sure! I mean, we've had enough death. Time to populations the universe, man. Earthlings rule, Martians drool." The kid held up both hands in a victory sign and ran off through the crowds.

She smiled, apparently picking up on the party atmosphere. "And there you have it, a general air of excitement, optimism, and probably intoxication."

Frank rubbed his forehead, remembering now why he kept the news on mute. Populations the universe, indeed. Still, their excitement was contagious, and he smiled. A small square in the lower left of the screen, a camera tracking the ARC's progress, flared blinding bright and went back to its prior black.

The flash sickened Frank. Just like his NACARC's explosion, but couldn't be. He hurried back to his chair, putting his glass on the desk. Channi began chiming in his ear.

"Priority message override. Permission to display?"

"Yes," he croaked and stumbled back into his chair.

"Connection with the Australia-Europe Advanced Relocation Colony has been lost. Several attempts to contact the vessel have failed. Later transmissions indicate a massive explosion destroyed the colony. The ARC program for all continents has been suspended until further notice."

The halo screen caught up to the announcement. Some people were motionless, stunned into silence. The devout was easy to spot, cheering and chanting "One God, one Earth," in the background. The reporter, like Frank, was tranced out, probably getting more information than the general populace. After a moment, she said, "I have catastrophic news for Australia and Europe. Their ARC was lost before entering interstellar space. All aboard are presumed lost. Please pray for these sixty thousand souls. The Judeo-Islamic Alliance claims responsibility as do several other organizations determined to keep mankind in its own solar system. More later on what this means for our planet and its people."

Frank leaned back in his chair, his heart hammering. He'd thought NACARC was a tragedy. He'd been wrong. His was nothing compared to Australia-Europe's loss.

Four ARC's remained.

For now.

His uplink burned with a priority message and he answered, "Yes, Nahla. I'll do whatever it takes to help AARC succeed."

About the Author

With an overactive imagination and a love for writing, Laura Stapleton decided to type out her daydreams and what-ifs to share her lovable characters and their worlds with readers. She currently lives in Kansas City with her husband, daughter, dog, and a few cats. When not at the computer, you'll find her in the park for a jog or at the yarn store's clearance section.

Social Links
 If you enjoyed this story, leave a review. To find out more about the next story in this series, follow Laura
https://twitter.com/LauraLStapleton,
https://www.facebook.com/LLStapleton, or at
http://lauralstapleton.com.
Subscribe to Laura's newsletter and keep up on the latest updates and new releases.

Laura Stapleton

11:34

295

L. Marshall James
Text Copyright © 2016 L. Marshall James

Eleven thirty-four.

There is nothing particularly special about the numbers, nothing unique about the time. To most people, it is a 60-second period that happens once before lunch and again when they're are asleep.

It is something altogether different for me.

In the darkness of night, in the empty space of my door frame, in a flicker of time too quick to discern, an old woman appears. I don't know who she is, I don't know where she comes from, and I don't know what she wants.

All I know is that when she appears, the time is eleven thirty-four.

L. Marshall James

11:34

BY

L. Marshall James

L. Marshall James

300

11:34
Acknowledgements

My heartfelt thanks to my family and friends for their love, encouragement, and support in the past, present, and future.

L. Marshall James

I first learned about the woman on the day I turned six.

We had just moved into town a few weeks or so prior, so I didn't expect much for my birthday. I had my hopes set for a few presents and an ice cream cake. My mother had hinted about having friends over, but I only knew a few kids at school and I wasn't comfortable inviting them, being the shy girl that I was. Without much to work with, my parents pretended to let the matter rest, then gave me a surprise party when I came home from school. I stepped into a house festooned with bright paper streamers and a celebratory banner, where the guests—neighborhood families I had met briefly, if at all—sang me "Happy Birthday" as my parents presented the cake.

Once the song was done and cake slices were distributed, my parents encouraged me to mingle. It was the sort of awkward event you cringe at in hindsight, but I was too young and sincere to know any better. I tried to talk with everyone at the party at least once, including the adults, but I naturally fell in with some of the younger crowd. Some of the other kids seemed as unfamiliar with each other as they were with me, so I didn't feel entirely alien, at least at first. Inevitably, though, the group dynamic changed and two cliques coalesced. Being younger than most of the others, I fell into the lesser of the two cliques: those that are toyed with, rather than those that do the toying. In time, the focus turned entirely toward me, the new girl in town.

One of the older kids, a dark haired boy with a smirk and squinty eyes, leveled his gaze at me. "You know, your house is haunted."

It was a statement of fact. I didn't buy it.

"Ghosts aren't real," I said, making a face. "Everybody knows that."

303

"It's not a ghost," came the reply. "It's an old woman."

That first mention of the old woman riveted my attention. "Who?" I asked.

"The woman who used to live here."

"*Used* to live here?" I said, and scrunched my face. "Where does she live now?"

The smirk grew, but he said nothing.

In the silence, another boy stepped forward. He was obviously the dark-haired boy's twin, but with lighter hair and face that was devoid of emotion. "She still lives in your house, dummy," he said.

"*Where* in my house, *idiot*?" I said indignantly. "I've seen the whole inside, even the attic. And the garage."

The smirking child spoke again. "It's not yet time."

I blinked. "What does that mean?"

He pointed across the room and I followed the direction of his finger, through the gaggles of chatting adults, to my parents' grandfather clock.

"You have to summon her," the smirking boy said as I returned my focus to him.

"Summon?" I asked, my skepticism faltering. "What's that?"

The empty-faced boy spoke again. "Hate," he said. "That's what."

"*What's* hate?" I said. "What's a summon?"

The smirking boy chuckled. "She's a dunce," he said, then turned and walked away. His twin followed after him.

The group dispersed as I stood dumbstruck, and the twins sauntered toward the front door as the rest of the kids scattered toward the chatting adults. The empty-faced boy looked over his shoulder as he pulled the door open, and he smiled with a mouthful of jagged lines and sharp points as he stopped outside. Then, the door closed and they were gone.

The vague concept of the woman haunted me for the rest of the party. I smiled through the opening of presents and the rest of social time, but even as all the guests migrated back to their homes, she stood in the back of my mind, nebulous and nightmarish. I eyed every nook and cranny with a suspicion that I carried all the way to bed. My dreams were neither good nor a bad, and their contents evaporated when I opened my eyes, but they left a residue of fear and disquiet. The dreams came again the next night.

And the next. And the next.

For the first many nights that I woke from the dreams, I laid perfectly still and stared at the ceiling, too scared to move or make a sound, even to breathe. On those nights, I waited for something to reach over the edge of the bed and pull me under, for something to fling open the closet door and run shrieking toward me. But after each uneventful eternity lying in the darkness, my fear and tension would gradually fade and I would slip back into sleep. In the morning, I would wake up just as tired as the night before.

My parents might have suspected that something was off, but I wasn't the sort of girl to tattle and I was too proud to say I was scared, especially of something as silly as some old woman. I weathered the nights as best I could. Gradually, my dreams and waking fears gave way to anger and resentment toward the buttheads that thought they could scare me with dumb stories. Those stinking boys would regret their stupid game if I ever saw them again. I began to look for them with the same intensity that I watched for the woman. When I was alone, I sometimes spoke aloud as I relived our brief conversation and imagined new ones wherein I emerged triumphant. As all-consuming as my anger was, it inevitably gave way to a bitter hatred. My young mind grew crowded with awful things that I wished would happen to those boys. Then, one night, I rolled onto one side and peered over the contours of the bed toward the shadowy silhouette of a woman in my bedroom doorway.

Most of my childhood memories are dreamlike snapshots or vague snippets of truncated video, but this memory—and almost every memory I have of the woman— is as vivid as red on white.

She stood with her back to me, and even in the darkness it was clear she was naked. This by itself didn't disturb me. I had seen my mom naked many times by that point in my life, either when dressing or in the shower, and while this woman looked different, she was still similar enough to my mom that her nakedness was no more strange than the fact that she was there in the first place. I remained as still as I possibly could, and tried not to breathe as I watched her.

A twisted mess of hair hung from the woman's head and well past her bare butt, a black and reddish hue that formed a scraggly pile on the floor behind her. Her face was hidden from view, and aside from pale patches of skin visible only through gaps in her mane, her neck and the middle of her backside were hidden as well. Her shoulders slumped away from the dark stripe of hair, and withered hands hung beside lumpy sides that led down to bony legs and bare feet. As terrified as I initially was, she seemed harmless. Frail, even. With the way she hunched over, she looked kind of like my nanna had before she died. But it *wasn't* Nanna or anyone I knew. She was definitely a stranger.

Though there wasn't anything about her that seemed scary, I knew enough to be scared. Whether or not she was a ghost, she didn't belong in my bedroom. In hindsight, I think I remained quiet on the desperate premise that as long as I didn't disturb her, she wouldn't do anything bad to me. I watched her in perfect stillness and silence, deep into the night and beyond the threshold of my fatigue. I woke several times that night in flashes of muted terror to see her standing there, unmoved and silent, facing away from me. Finally, I woke and she was gone. Morning had arrived.

I was more exhausted than usual the following morning, but if my parents noticed they didn't mention it. In my tired little mind, I felt something bordering on excitement. The dread of anticipation seemed to have died when the woman finally made her appearance. I had finally seen her, and she hadn't hurt me. She wasn't as terrible as those stupid kids made her out to be.

The woman appeared again on the following night. Despite having had a glass of water too close to bedtime, I remained quiet beneath the covers. I waited a long time for her to go away so I could use the bathroom, but in the end, I peed the bed. Since I was too scared to move, I had little choice but to sleep in the dampness. On the following night and every night thereafter, I made sure to never drink anything close to bedtime. It's a good thing, too, because the woman came back every night.

I woke up sporadically through the nights to see her in the doorway, and for a long time, I lied awake to watch her. Several weeks passed before I was able to sleep through an entire night, and although my vivid watchfulness gradually decreased, I always tried to be awake when she appeared. On one side of a second, the doorway was empty; on the other side, the woman was there.

After I'd become a little more comfortable, I tried talking to her. "Hello," I would say. "What's your name? Where are you from? Why are you standing there? Are you cold? Do you want a Goldfish cracker?" My hope for a response might have lasted a few weeks. In time, I talked to

307

her in much the same way as one would speak to a pet or write in a diary. I told her about my days, my hopes and dreams, my frustrations and pains, everything a young girl could express. I never knew if she ever heard me or understood, though, because she never so much as grunted or shrugged in response. She always stood with her back to me, perfectly still and silent.

It was three years before that changed.

I had just finished telling her about math class and the stupid boy—Bradley—who wouldn't leave me alone, when something moved elsewhere in the house. It sounded like a blow of air from one of the vents, but louder and longer. I was nine years old by that time, old enough to know about cat burglars, but I didn't think much of the sound until the woman turned her head toward it. It was only a slight movement, barely enough that I could see the pale blot of her cheek in the dark, but it captured my total attention. I didn't know *why* the sound attracted her attention and I was too shocked to wonder. After so many nights of inaction, that subtle movement of her head was like a bombshell. Then, the woman stepped away from the doorway and disappeared down the hall.

I wasn't scared as much as intensely fascinated. The woman's presence was old news by then, but now... now, she had moved! Maybe this meant she *could* hear and understand me. Maybe she could talk. My mind raced with speculation about what would happen when she came back. Maybe I would finally see her face. Maybe she would notice me. I only realized something was really wrong when I heard a voice from the kitchen. It was a man's voice, throaty and mean like the bad guys in movies I wasn't allowed to watch. His words were punctuated by an explosion.

The sound was so frighteningly loud that at first I thought it was a bomb. I only realized what it was after four more explosions in succession. For a few seconds, I was afraid for the woman. Guns killed *people*, but could they kill the woman? Would she come back if she was injured? What if my parents found her body? The ensuing screams answered most of my questions, and the scene in the kitchen answered the rest. He was everywhere in that room, splashed on the walls and the ceilings, strewn about the floor and the table, and lying halfway out the window, where he choked on his own shredded tongue until he slipped limply to the floor.

My parents burst screaming from their room and ran, first to my bedroom and then to the kitchen, where they held me and tried to shield me from harm or the trauma of witnessing the horrific scene. They were too late. The harm had already been committed on someone else, and I would never forget what I saw that night. Police and medics stormed the house a few minutes later, but they were too late, too. There wasn't enough left of the intruder to arrest or save, and the woman was gone.

I asked everyone what happened, partly to hide my knowledge but mostly to see if anyone else knew about the woman, but no one—not my parents, the counselor, or even the police—offered a likely explanation. Mostly, they told me that something bad happened and it was all over now. Those who tried to answer offered a few possibilities or vague explanations, but I knew they were all guesses because I knew the truth.

Soon after, we moved to a new house in a different neighborhood, where my parents hoped to distance ourselves from the horror of what had happened. The woman followed. She appeared in my bedroom door every night, like always. The only differences were the exit wounds that seeped black blood onto her pale skin.

My relationship with the woman was different after that. I didn't know anything about her, but I knew that if someone came into my house, she would kill them. It was no stretch of the imagination to think that she could easily kill me, but she hadn't. The uncertainty and vague fear that permeated her presence was partly replaced with a sense of safety and protection. She became something like a member of the family or a guard dog. But she was never quite either.

I never came up with a name for her. It didn't seem right, and I had no reason to name her, anyway. If I couldn't talk to anyone about her before, I definitely couldn't mention her after what had happened. It would have to remain our little secret. But I was okay with that. In my own way, I was comfortable with her.

I still never drank water before bedtime or left my bed while she was there, but I felt content with the knowledge that she wouldn't hurt me as long as I didn't break the rules. I could only guess what the rules were, though, and after countless hours of asking unanswered questions, the only thing I ever learned about her was that as long as no one else was around, the woman always arrived at 11:34.

The ambiguities of her presence haunted me. For a long time, I was scared that one of my parents would go to the bathroom in the middle of the night and the woman would kill them. Sometimes I woke to the sound of my parents' bedroom door opening, followed by the bathroom door closing, and I would watch the woman in stark terror, waiting for that subtle turn of the head. She stood as still as ever, though, and when one of my parents shuffled closer, she blinked out of existence as if she had never been there. When they walked away, the woman reappeared. She never hurt my parents or seemed like she might. For whatever reason, her protection extended over them as well.

11:34

Due to my unusual bedroom buddy and the effects of what she had done, my personality and childhood were flawed, to say the least. I was an average student at best, I shied from playing sports of any kind, and while my school was oddly devoid of cliques, I found myself on the fringe of anything resembling a social group. In short, I was one of the weird kids. My parents encouraged me to make friends and they did their best to help me adjust to the new neighborhood well beyond the point that it could have been considered "new," but their efforts found no purchase. I hated that they worried about me, but I knew I could never let anyone see the woman, and my terror of what could happen hindered the development with any real friendships. Still, I was torn between my parents' encouragement and my ever-present dread.

When I was twelve years old, I struck what felt like a safe compromise. Tammy was the sort of girl who might have passed for normal if she were only strange *or* sociopathic *or* was inclined to carry a many-bladed multi-tool, but she was all three. I befriended her in the same way one might befriend a feral badger, and I chose her specifically because I knew that neither my parents, nor I, would ever grow close to her.

Tammy was my only "friend" and I was hers, so we spent a lot of time together, either in our several shared classes, at the mall, or around the neighborhood. In much the same way that I adapted to the woman, I adapted to the badger. I learned the telltale signs of when Tammy was more likely to veer from merely strange to sociopathic—when she might unfold one of the many sharp instruments of her multi-tool with at least the ostensible intent to use it. I figured her out, or so I thought.

On the last day I spent with her, we went on a bike ride. We rode for hours that day, well beyond the distance I

311

normally felt comfortable with her, but she kept peddling and I had been given no cause for worry, so I followed. She seemed to be in a particularly good mood, though I had no idea why, and when I saw abandoned building in the distance, I felt a pang of adrenaline. She steered over to the back door and ditched her bike as she took off running. By the time I made it inside, she had already disappeared. The building only had six rooms so there wasn't much guesswork as to where she was, but I still flinched when she lunged at me from around a corner. The flinch was purely reflexive. I only felt a hint of fear when the blade pressed against my belly. I eyed the knife attachment of Tammy's multi-tool, then lifted my gaze to hers. Her face was blank, and I matched it with my expression and my response.

"What's in this building, anyway?" I asked.

She held the blade firmly against me. "I could have gutted you," she said, then lowered the multi-tool and looked around. "There's nothing much here," she said as she folded the knife away. "Just trash."

She flashed a grin and took off running. Wary of another ambush, I followed at half speed, winding through the clutter and shadows until we came to a windowless room in the middle of the building. There, she stood with her back to me and stared at something on the floor in front of her. I stepped up beside her. It was a cat, hog tied and half-dissected, lying dead in a pool of half-dried blood.

It was obvious that Tammy was responsible, and I knew immediately that our "friendship" would not continue. Still, I wasn't about to cut ties in an abandoned building in front of the cat she had mutilated.

I kept my voice level and glossed over the obvious. "You think it was alive when that happened to it?"

"Maybe," came her response. Then, a few seconds later, "Look at all the blood."

"It's a lot," I said.

I couldn't think of anything more to say. We stared at it a while longer, our faces blank but my stomach churning. It felt like forever before she finally turned and beckoned for me to follow, and I did my best to hide my relief as we remounted our bikes and headed home.

We returned to the neighborhood relatively late, around seven thirty. I had never brought Tammy to my home before, but that night she insisted and wouldn't accept any other answer. My house was closer and she said she was tired. What, did I want her to ride home alone *and* tired?

I kept as quiet as I realistically could as we approached my house so my parents wouldn't hear us, and when we reached my front lawn, I tried to stall at the edge. Tammy ignored me and rode to the front stoop, then waited for me. I rode the last thirty feet and set my bike on the grass as quietly as I could, then made a show of sitting hard on the stoop. Much to my relief and then to my horror, Tammy sat quietly beside me and the front door opened behind us to reveal my mother's smiling face.

My mother knew I had a "friend" and I'd managed to leave it at that. She had asked about meeting Tammy, of course, but I'd been able to put it off with any number of excuses: she had to go home, her parents said no, she felt sick, anything I could think of. Now that my mother finally had a chance to meet my only "friend," she could barely contain herself. She peppered Tammy with questions and I watched with wide-eyed unease as the badger wore the skin of a human girl. My mother made us snacks I was powerless to deny and kept us in the kitchen with small talk I couldn't weasel us out of, edging the time later and later until I knew we'd have to give her a ride home because it was too late to ride her bike alone. Instead, my mother asked if Tammy wanted to spend the night. The badger agreed, and a quick phone call cemented the deal. I might have feigned sickness or made something up, but my mother would have seen through it. There was almost nothing I could do. My first sleepover had begun.

All things considered, it seemed to go pretty well. Tammy and I played games and ate pizza—stuffed crust, my favorite—then ate popcorn while we watched a girly movie that Tammy made a good show of enjoying. As the credits rolled, my mother laid out some blankets and pillows in the living room. After brushing our teeth, we took our respective places on the floor, then wrapped ourselves in blankets and laid in the dimness. She fell quiet and eventually started snoring, but I stayed awake, watching and wondering. Would the woman appear if I was in the living room instead of my bedroom? Were the rules different for visitors? What would happen if Tammy woke up? I had no way of knowing. There was no clock in the room and I was too scared to get up to look, so I waited in the gloom for her to come until I was sure she wouldn't. The time of the woman had passed. Whatever the rules were, I had discovered an exception. Everything was going to be okay.

Then, the woman appeared.

I blinked. When I opened my eyes, the woman was standing in the archway between the living room and the kitchen, with her back to me. When I looked at the archway that separated the living room from the hallway, she was standing there, too. When I focused between the entrances and didn't quite look at either, she seemed to stand in both of them, flickering in and out like a candle.

The rules were not what I had hoped. I didn't know how to make the woman go away, and I couldn't even try without the risk of waking Tammy. All I could do was close my eyes and hope that when I woke in the morning, she would be gone and everything would be okay. It was a

314

struggle to keep my eyes closed and even more difficult to fall asleep, but I eventually managed. When I woke again, the darkness of night was replaced by the dim light of dawn, and silence was filled by shrieks of agony. The woman emptied Tammy's veins and covered the floors with her viscera. A sea of gore was scorched into my mind a second time. Again, police and EMTs marched through our home. Again, the woman was nowhere to be seen.

I maintained that I never saw anything, and it was true. As soon as I heard the first screams, I knew Tammy was dead. I had learned that much from what the woman did to the burglar. Instead of watching or trying to interfere, I cowered beneath my blankets and cried as quietly as I could. It was my fault. I could have found a way to keep Tammy from staying over. I could have gone to the bathroom and made myself puke, I could have screamed, I could have told my mother the terrible truth about my "friend." I could have done any number of things, but I hadn't, so she was dead. Not just dead, but torn to pieces and spread across half our house, her open multi-tool lying in a pool of her blood. She may have been a terrible person, but she didn't deserve that.

It was worse that time, not just because I had known Tammy, but because it was too much of a coincidence for such an atrocity to happen to the same family in two different locations. My greatest fears at that time revolved around the police deciding that someone in my family was responsible. Either they would seize on the obvious fact that only my father had the sheer strength necessary to do what had been done to Tammy and the intruder, or they would rule out both my parents and focus on me, the twelve-year-old with a secret so big I could barely hold it. A few well-meaning questions brought me to the edge of revealing the truth; a few more might have finished me.

In the end, the police thought the evidence pointed to someone else, an entity they could not identify or even begin to trace. My family was safe, at least for now. We moved again, this time to another state with a new school for me and new jobs for my parents. To prevent what happened from ever happening again—to keep the killer or killers from finding us again—we even got new names.

The woman followed.

Life was different after that, not just because of our new lives but because to some extent we were all living in states of heightened fear. At first, only my father bought a gun. My mother abhorred firearms and initially preferred pepper spray, but she eventually changed her mind. Their pistols lay atop their respective bedside tables as they slept, and they woke frequently to check on me as they walked through the house, weapon in hand. They even installed cameras on the outside of the house, plus a security system that would call the police at the first hint of a threat.

Our lives took on a strict regimen. During the course of our days, none of us were ever alone or unobserved, aside from the unavoidable instances of bathroom breaks or me sleeping alone in my room. In the mornings, we woke at the same time and had breakfast together before I walked to the bus under their nervous collective gaze. Then, they would drive to work together—they found jobs in the same company—and I would ride to school. My parents made sure to always leave work together so they could never be caught alone in the parking lot, and they adjusted their schedule to get home before I did. On snow days or other days when I was off from school while they worked, they would drop me off somewhere in town with the understanding that no matter what I did, I would surround myself with people at all times. Weekends were much the same. I don't know if they expected the enhanced security measures to prevent another incident, but I suppose they figured that if something *did* happen, at least we would know who was responsible.

My greatest fear then was that someone would ignore the bright blue security stickers on every door and window, and make the fatal mistake of breaking in. The woman would descend the stairway just outside my door and someone would die—disemboweled in the entryway or beheaded in my father's office—and the whole circus would happen again, except worse. This time, there would be more questions, more analysis, and more people wondering out loud how this could possibly happen a third time despite so many precautions. There would be no acceptable explanation. Equally disturbing was the awful realization that even if I revealed what I knew, the truth would only be interpreted as nonsensical ramblings because everyone knew that things like ghosts—or whatever the woman was—did not exist. If another person died, there was nothing I could say or do to prevent the inevitable: security would grow tighter, and our lives would be further restricted.

My parents went out of their way to give me as normal a life as was possible under the circumstances. They provided me with a huge allowance and were willing to drive me almost anywhere or drastically alter their schedules if I so much as asked, but even by the time I was fifteen, our security regimen hadn't relaxed. I did my best to make friends, but it was difficult. Overnighters were forbidden, so outings with friends were limited to afternoons and evenings. We never had visitors of any kind, such was our fear of a third incident.

When people asked why I never did much outside of school, I told them my parents were super religious. Most people shied away at that point, though some spoke in conspiratorial tones about sneaking out or running away. Sometimes, I was tempted. I didn't know if the woman

317

would follow me or remain with my parents if I ran away, but either my parents would be free of her, or I would. Eventually, I decided to stay because I couldn't bear to let my parents worry that I was dead somewhere, spread through a room or littered across a field like an IED victim. I had to stay even though it meant I could never have a night out with friends, I could never go on a vacation without my parents, and I could never fall in love or let someone fall in love with me. My parents wanted those things for me. They wanted me to have friends, to have fun, to find someone special. But as much as they supported me and as hard as we tried, my life would never be anything close to normal. And even if they offered to scale back our precautions, I would have declined because I knew the truth and I knew the consequences. It wasn't my parents' fault, and I never blamed them. It was the woman's fault. I blamed *her*.

The woman dominated my past, present, and future. My life was already on full lockdown as a teenager; what would happen when I became an adult? Could my parents bear the fear of my moving out and living on my own? Could I? Beyond mere independence, was it possible for me to live anything resembling a normal adult life? Could I have visitors? Could I *ever* fall in love? The more I dwelled on these questions, the closer I came to the conclusion that my only chance at a real life was to rid myself of the woman.

I lived a heavily sheltered life, both socially and culturally. If there was a chance of excessive violence, blood, or gore in a movie or show, I couldn't watch it for fear it would send me into an emotional breakdown. Reading held no such danger, and during my generally introverted youth, I developed a voracious appetite for books of every kind: comedy, adventure, mystery, nonfiction, even horror. However, while it had occurred to me that a supernatural creature like the woman would require a supernatural solution, I had read almost nothing of the occult. I suppose I was scared, really, that I'd find out there was no way to get rid of her. I don't know precisely when it happened, but I reached the point where my fear of the status quo overwhelmed my fear that I could never rid myself of the woman or that I would face terrible consequences for pushing my unknowable boundaries. A life with the woman would be a lonely and broken one, and that, in my mind, was the worst possible future. I decided that the potential risks were worth the potential reward.

I began my search on the Internet, but the stories and accounts I found were blatantly conspiratorial or obviously fictional, crafted for entertainment rather than education. I quickly abandoned the Web in favor of more believable and tangible sources. I moved on to the town library, where I felt stymied in much the same way. The non-fiction books were either irrelevant or were obviously fiction, and the dream interpretation books made no mention of real-life evisceration. I wandered to the fiction section with little hope, and although I was pleasantly surprised, the woman might have been the subject of any one of a thousand stories: a soulless phantom or a widower's curse, a she-devil from the bowels of hell, or a shadow's shadow. Nothing matched the vague existence of a woman who stood in silent watch, prepared to unleash a fatal fury on the hair-trigger of her own arbitrary whims. She was too strange for fiction.

Desperate, I convinced my parents to take me to the oldest church in the tri-county area. There, I was eventually permitted under direct supervision to peruse manuscripts that were ancient, at least by American standards. Some were too fragile for me to touch, but the priest was kind enough to assist me as much as he was able. I never told him about the woman or what she had done, but I hinted enough at the truth that it was obvious my need was both earnest and dire. He came to trust me, and he eventually referred me to greater archives elsewhere.

Not wanting to limit myself to one religion, I scoured what I could in the local Jewish synagogue. Beginning a few towns away and going as far as a few cities away, I searched two Muslim mosques, a Hindu temple, and a Church of Satan. I could never tell any of them the whole truth. Whatever strange stories *they* believed, I knew they'd think I was crazy. Still, my quiet and sincere persistence earned me access to at least some of their archives. Documents were imported in a few special cases, just for me. I scrutinized every relevant verse, spell, and incantation that even hinted at the truth of the woman. My research continued for over two years.

When I found all I thought I could find, I consolidated my notes and committed the most relevant bits to memory as best I could. Eventually, I decided there was nothing left for me to learn or memorize. All what remained was to steel myself for my first—and hopefully last— genuine confrontation with the woman. Every time I pointed myself toward home, I tried to prepare myself, tried to feel *ready*. Every day, I felt a little closer.

It was an unbelievable oversight that I had never investigated historical documents in the library. When our history teacher taught us how to access newspaper archives for an assignment, it was only on a whim that instead of researching the town I lived in, I looked into the town where the woman first appeared to me, in that haunted house.

I started by discovering the date the house had been built: August 1th, 1910. However, I had nothing else to go on, no search parameters to work with aside from that date. I knew nothing about the woman, and her nudity gave no clue as to the era in which she had lived. She might have lived and died in 1910 or any of the intervening years, and could be hidden anywhere in over a century of several daily newspapers, if she was there at all. I was no quitter, though. I decided that I would read every single newspaper if that was what it took.

With nervous glances over my shoulder so the teacher didn't catch me, I scoured every article in every newspaper for the first week of 1910 before the bell rang. On the ride home, I obsessed over my new and daunting task. It would take months, maybe years, to scan every day of every intervening year in the newspapers. There was no telling if or when I might find something. Even I found nothing, I would always wonder if I had only overlooked the truth. The final piece of the puzzle came to me like a vision as the bus slowed to a stop in front of my house, and I struggled to act normal as I walked inside under my parents' watchful gaze.

It felt almost impossible to get through after-school chores. I felt like I could have screamed the roof off the house, but I kept a damper on my emotions, partly so my parents wouldn't suspect anything, and partly so I didn't get my hopes up. Once I finally finished, I took my laptop and casually retreated to my bedroom. It wasn't long before I found a website that allowed me—with a trial membership—to continue my newspaper search, and I input the only search criteria I could, the only thing I ever I knew about the woman: the time she always appeared. 11:34.

I searched the year of 1910 and moved forward with a growing sense that I was on the right trail. I found her almost immediately. Tucked away on the back page of what seemed more like a newsletter than a newspaper, the time of her nightly appearance stood out as the time of her death. The time she was murdered.

The article didn't list her name, but I didn't need it, nor did I need a picture to know for sure that the woman in the article was the woman in my doorway. She was well-known around town, appearing in ragged clothing and bare feet. At the market, she scurried between carts and spoke little, if at all. She used only gestures or furtive nods to communicate, generally choosing the cheapest and least appetizing items: bruised cabbage, moldy bread, soft onions, and the like. She bartered so stubbornly that marketers dreaded her approach. At the butcher, however, she carefully scrutinized every gizzard, cow's tongue, or pig's foot, and selected only the very best.

She shunned other wares, never once purchasing an item of clothing, a book, a newspaper, or the like, and she was never seen in town aside from her fleeting visits for the bare essentials. Still, there were oft-repeated stories about her, sometimes offered tongue-in-cheek and sometimes offered with wide-eyed sincerity, but known to everyone in town. Stories of commotion near the chicken coop and missing eggs or chickens, with only a woman's bare footprints left behind; a woman's silhouette on the porch during evening meals; a woman in a distant field who fled upon being noticed, leaving behind only a butchered cow carcass and a bloody trail into the nearby forest. Perhaps most disturbing of all was the story told by travelers from out of town, who happened upon the woman as she walked naked along the side of the road, covered in marks and bruises, where she stood silent and unresponsive before walking into the forest and vanishing without a trace. These stories hinted at some dark horrors in the woman's life.

When she was found dead, many townspeople wondered at what sort of dark magic she might have brought upon herself. The article claimed, however, that the details surrounding her death were a lesson in humility and the evils of cynical faultfinding, for in truth, all horrors were to the woman's infinite detriment.

When her corpse was found hanging by the neck from the branch of a large oak, initial reports indicated that she had been there for some time. However, the town coroner reported that she was quite recently deceased, and what first appeared to be signs of decay were severe bruising and scarring. He was unable to find a single unbroken bone in her body. The rest of the article was written with a Tarantino flourish, replete with details the author couldn't possibly have known but which I knew were true.

Peculiar and inscrutable in public, the truth of the woman's private life was one of unthinkable abuse. She slept on a bed of rags beneath her home, and was often attacked by rats at night. Several of her toes had been taken by frostbite. These indignities were the least of her pain.

She woke before sunrise and tended to the chores throughout the day, caring for the animals, cleaning the house, and preparing food, but when her husband returned from the fields and sank into his whisky, her role was to absorb the terrible abuse that he and their two sons inflicted upon her. They beat her. They burned her. They cut and stabbed her. They forced her to eat rubbish. They raped her. No act was too wicked or depraved for her tormentors, and their abominable deeds pushed her well beyond the bounds of sanity on more than one occasion. Still, she carried on, alone in the world, until her husband and young boys finally committed the act for which they would be hanged. When she lost her life beneath their withering assaults, their final terrible act against her was to hang her in the woods near their home.

It was almost everything I had ever wanted to know about the woman. I could still only speculate as to why my hatred had summoned her, why she followed me, and why she had never spoken, but it seemed obvious. In death, the woman was determined to defend the defenseless from those who would do them harm. Ever since I first summoned her, the women had protected me, first from the armed intruder, and then from Tammy and her multi-tool. While I was still uncertain of her reasons, I now had what I never had before, despite all my wondering and searching. Finally, I knew at least some part of the woman's life story. Nothing would surpass that knowledge. Armed with the archives and what I had just learned, I decided that the time had come. I was ready to confront the woman.

I floated through the rest of the evening with anxious anticipation and tried to act as normal as I could. At dinner, I exaggerated the highlights of my day and made a show of being exhausted. After helping to clean up dishes, I went to bed early and stared from my pillow at the empty doorway, all the while silently reciting everything I'd learned and memorized. When my parents finally went to bed, I rose and scoured my notebooks—thousands of hours of research—for anything I might have forgotten. When the clock struck 11:34, I sat on the edge of my bed and prepared myself. For the first time since I was a little girl, I spoke to the woman with the hope that she would respond.

In hushed whispers, I sang hymns and charmed songs to comfort her ravaged soul. I chanted spells crafted to repel evil and make peace with malicious demons. I recited forgotten verses gleaned from crumbling manuscripts that summoned the full strength of almighty God for protection. I recited Latin across the room. The texts of ancients flowed from my tongue, everything I ever thought could sway her, arsenals of words slung like arrows through the dark. When I had exhausted myself, I fell silent and waited patiently for the woman's reply.

She didn't respond. She didn't say a word. She didn't so much as grunt or turn her head. Disappointment and frustration descended on me, and I fought them off. I had planned my recitations for months, well before I had any hint of who the woman was or what she had gone through in life. Now that I had *her* story, I could tell her mine. For the first time since I'd seen the woman, I braved the space between us. Barefoot and terrified, I crossed the room and stood behind her. I spoke to her, woman to woman.

I was almost eighteen, perched on the cusp of adulthood and what could be a future of independence and accomplishment. I wanted to become someone. I wanted my life to mean something. I wanted love. But that dream was impossible with her in my life. She had saved me, I knew that. The protection she had provided was honorable and noble, but at the same time, her presence kept me from living anything resembling the normal life I wanted. I could no longer live with her in my doorway. Whatever she wanted in return for her help, I would try to give her, but not that. I loved her for what she'd done for me, but I needed to live my own life. I needed her to leave.

Even as I revealed the pain of what she'd done and my dread of her continued presence, even as I bared my soul to her, the woman faced away from me and said nothing. She remained still and silent as if in mockery of all my efforts to understand her and everything I had gone through because of her.

I never asked for her protection. I never wanted her in my home. I never did anything to deserve the life she wrought for me, and I would rather have died than live through such a caged life. I stood behind her with thousands of hours of ancient texts in the forefront of my mind and my heart bleeding on my sleeve, and in a way I never felt before, rage and hatred bloomed within me. I could have settled for an explanation of her rules so I could try to work around them. I could have worked with a few words. Even gibberish would have meant something to me after all those years, but

325

she wouldn't even give me that. I had lived for too long saturated by fear and secrecy, hermitage and loneliness, and wishing she would go away. All at once, those many years came to a head within me and exploded outward. I lunged with all my strength and shoved the woman as hard as I could.

She made no effort to catch herself as she fell forward. Her head struck the corner of the top banister post, then twisted as she disappeared from view and tumbled down the stairs. Every thud of flesh against wood, every crack of baluster and bone rang out like gunshots in the night. When she came to a rest at the bottom, I heard a silence more complete than every word the woman never said. I tiptoed to the edge of the stairs, half-expecting to see her standing with her back to me, but she lay sprawled across on the bottom few stairs with her head on the floor of the foyer, face down and motionless. After all my wondering, fearing, and searching, all it took was a moment of violence to move the woman from my door. I left her lying where she was as I returned to bed. Though I woke many times throughout the night expecting to see her there, a black smudge on the top banister remained as proof of what I had finally done.

The next morning, no trace remained of the woman. I watched my parents closely during breakfast and the ride to school, but it was clear they hadn't seen or heard anything. I breezed through the day with a sense of freedom that felt utterly foreign. I was entirely liberated, unencumbered by the weight of the woman's presence and the terror she imposed on me and my family. My future was finally unobstructed. For the first time since I was a child, I chatted with friends and boys without the fear of growing too close. I was ready for my new life, for anything that might come my way.

For love.

If my parents had been oblivious in the morning, they knew something was different when I got home from school. I would never tell them about the woman or what had happened, but I would never again restrain my enthusiasms. I smiled in body and soul through dinner, through homework, through relaxing with my parents, and through surfing the Internet for fun instead of life-changing research. Even as I laid down in bed, my smile continued. I reveled in the novel feeling of true solitude and took a deep breath, ready for the next beautiful day. Then, the clock struck 11:34 and the woman appeared, bringing all my fear and dread with her.

Bright white bone protruded from one leg as she stood slanted in the doorway. A sharp dent in the side of her head seeped black blood that joined the discharges of her other injuries and dripped to the floor. Aside from a tremor in one hand, she was as placid as always. But now, unlike every other night, the woman had turned her back on the rest of the house. Now, she stood facing my room.

Beneath smeared blood and filth, her old and unfamiliar face appeared as gentle as my nanna's, and equally marked with what might have been demented confusion as she stared into the far corner of my room. Her presence made it clear that all my efforts to get rid of her were for naught, and when I opened my mouth to speak, the turn of her head said the rest.

With that subtle movement, everything changed. Her eyes settled on me, and the words died in my throat. As slowly and quietly as I could, I pulled the covers over my eyes and tried to sleep.

I know my mistake, now. I thought that by reading about the woman's life and death, I understood her purpose in the afterlife. I was wrong. She hadn't come to protect me.

L. Marshall James

It wasn't love that resurrected her, or honor that gave her purpose. It was hatred that brought her back. It was violence that compelled her. In my indignant rage, I aimed my hatred at her and unleashed my violence upon her. Now, her gaze is fixed upon me, and I know she will never leave.

Not for as long as I'm alive.

About the Author

L. Marshall James hails from northwest rural Pennsylvania, where he ran around barefoot and played 8-bit Nintendo when he wasn't playing with tar in the middle of the road. After a subpar high school performance, he obtained an associate's degree in information technology. He then worked in the IT field for over six years before calling it quits and joining his girlfriend in Southeast Asia for a traveling foray that lasted almost two years. He returned home just in time for Thanksgiving. Surprisingly enough, his family still loved him. L currently works in the blistering Floridian heat, where he tries not to die of heat stroke.

L. Marshall James

Kristin Durfee

Revenge From Within

A parolee is gunned down in the streets of Seattle on his walk home from work. A woman accused, but acquitted, of murder is killed in her backyard. A vigilante is on the loose and seeking justice for those who've escaped it. Detective Stef Jackson and her coworkers are on a race to track down who the killer is, but what happens when the revenge comes, not from outside forces, but within?

Kristin Durfee

Revenge from Within

BY

Kristin Durfee

Kristin Durfee

336

Acknowledgements

First and foremost, thanks go to Laura Perez for organizing a fantastic anthology filled with authors I am so excited to be partnering with. My deepest appreciation go to Tawa Witko and Miranda Nading for giving my story an early read and edit and to the incomparable Racquel Henry at Writer's Atelier for polishing up my work and giving great suggestions (and forcing me to remove an adverb or two).

My beautiful cover is courtesy of Kelly Abell at Select-O-Grafix. You took the vision in my head and put it to fruition.

As always, thanks to my friends and family, especially my husband who put up with my long nights of writing and editing. You help me be able to do what I love and I am forever grateful to you for that.

Kristin Durfee

One

My heart raced as I heard my shoes click on the sidewalk. I cursed myself for the fact that I forgotten my sneakers. I hadn't expected the street to be so empty. Of course, part of me hoped they would be to eliminate any potential eye-witnesses, but I also wanted to blend in. To sneak through without notice. Few people ever seemed to notice me. Maybe the deserted block was a blessing.

The street was glazed with a thin film of rain. It had been like this all week, a steady drizzle. Must be that time of year. The time that makes me question all over again why I made this move. Why we packed up our lives and trekked across the country to a place known for its crap weather. It kept people away tonight, though, and for once, I wasn't too upset as the dark clouds rumbled above.

He stood about twenty yards ahead of me. Far enough away that people wouldn't think we were together, but close enough that I could keep tabs on him. I'd followed him for hours. It was as if this guy never planned to go home. I knew his routine, or at least I thought I did. He worked uptown and walked to the bus which he took to the twenty-four-hour grocer on the corner. He picked up some items, five, ten minutes tops, and made the short walk to his apartment. I found it odd though that he never went through the front door, and always opted to cut through the alley. Maybe he wasn't authorized to live there. Maybe it was a violation of his parole.

His parole.

The notion made my skin crawl. How could you kill someone and walk the streets five years later? Hell, not even five years. Fifty-seven months. Okay, so he was drunk. He didn't see the girl in the cross walk. Even more reason to keep him away from the rest of society. To never let his negligence take another life.

It was late. From what I could gather he cleaned the building uptown, probably some work-release program or some bullshit like that. I checked my watch as my hand bumped against the butt of the gun tucked in my belt loop: 1:35 AM. About an hour later than normal. I considered going home, doing this another night. If I was caught, caught not at home, not in bed...

But no. No one would know. I had plenty of time.

After an eternity where we must have walked half the blocks in his neighborhood, he headed home. I turned down the alley after and tried to walk on the balls of my feet and not allow the heel of my shoe to contribute to the noise. Even that felt too loud. I was sure he was going to turn around, spot me and confront me. Would he recognize me? It was years ago, but I sat in that courtroom. Would he remember?

He turned so I could just see the side of his face and my body froze. I held my breath and considered running the other way, but the street light hit him just right and I could see white objects in his ears. Headphones. I thanked the heavens above and took it as a sign that this mission was blessed. That I was about to right a wrong that needed to be fixed.

I took a deep breath to steady myself and slipped the gun out. It was a little small for my hand, a Glock 27, but it was reliable and available. I'd already put a cartridge in the chamber, I didn't want the noise to attract suspicion, but as I crept closer to him I could hear the beat of his music as clear as if I had the buds in my ears instead. I bet I could have shot the gun off and he wouldn't have heard it. But he wasn't the one I was worried about. I looked behind me. No one. The windows of the apartment building were all dark. I placed the bottle over the muzzle as I raised my hand and pointed it at the back of his head.

At the last moment against my better judgment—I just couldn't help myself—I reached my hand forward and plucked out one of the ear buds. He startled and whirled around. His look turned from confusion to anger to fear in such quick succession, I felt a smile pull on my face.

"This is for her," I said, and pulled the trigger.

Kristin Durfee

Two

Stef Jackson felt a dull thrum in her joints and muscles. It was much too late when she arrived home. Or was it too early? She knew her absence would be noted, but hoped she wouldn't get too much shit for it. He always gave her shit for it. Though, for the first time in recent memory, the house was still quiet when she put the key in the lock and walked in. Thank God for small miracles. The second one that day. She shouldn't press her luck and ask her captain about that vacation until next week. Don't want to push it.

The sun had just woken up and stretched over the horizon as well. She liked when she could get home and greet the morning from her kitchen. It felt normal, like something people did, though usually it was at the start of their day, not at the end.

She looked forward to the week being over so she could switch back from the night shift and go back on days. It was nice not having a never-ending schedule of evenings, but the six weeks on, six weeks off flip flop of day and night shifts taxed her. Jeremy hated it. Not that she liked it, but what could she do? She was a homicide detective. If she only worked days, she'd probably never catch a case, and if she only worked nights, holy hell. She'd quit if she only worked nights.

It was going to be temporary though. In two years her captain would retire and she'd busted her butt these last few years to put herself in the prime position to take his place. Along with the pay bump came more normal hours. It was the carrot that dangled and kept her going. That and, well...

No. No she couldn't think about that. Shouldn't let her mind wander to *that*. Stay focused. One thing at a time.

She'd just placed her keys on the counter when Jeremy walked in. His eyes were red with sleep, though he looked like he'd gotten little of it.

She rolled her eyes. "Up late watching the History Channel again?" she asked.

He yawned, as if on cue. "They are running a bunch of nine-eleven specials. I don't know what it is, but I can't not watch them. They suck me in every year."

"I don't know why you do that to yourself."

He shrugged and started to put water in the coffee pot. He gestured toward her, but she shook her head.

"Nope, I'm trying to wind down, that's the last thing I need."

His eyes snapped to her and he looked at her, hard. What was the expression on his face? She was exhausted and really didn't want to get into a fight. Not now. They'd had a pretty good week. *Please don't ruin it*, she begged. He stepped forward, the half-filled coffee pot still in one hand. She shrank back half a step, not sure why she flinched at his approach.

"What?" she asked, trying to keep the waver out of her voice and doing a marginal job.

"On your face, along your hair line, is that…" His eyebrows pinched together in concentration. He reached a hand out, and then pulled it back suddenly as realization hit him.

Adrenaline and fear rushed over her and left a metallic taste in her mouth. *Shit.* She instinctively rubbed her fingers along her temple. Red flakes dusted her fingers. Images of the night before pushed into her mind even as she fought to stave them off.

"Shit, shit I'm sorry." She ducked and rushed around him, flicked on the sink, and rubbed her head with a wet paper towel.

"What happened?" He pinched his brows together in concern, but there was a layer of frustration under the question.

She sighed and turned the sink off as water dripped into her eye. "Nothing. Just that something went down with a perp last night. It was fine. I'm not hurt, must have gotten a little on me. Thought I got it all." She turned to him. "Better?"

He nodded.

She reached out to touch his chest, but he backed away. He poured the water in the maker and scooped out the powdered coffee. She took a deep breath. Fine. It was all fine and was going to be fine.

"What's on your agenda for the day?" she asked. It took effort to make her voice sound light and airy. Her heart took its time as it returned to its normal speed.

"Same old boring work stuff," he said.

"Any interesting cases?"

"Not really. Guy fell down in a store and is suing the owners. Nice older couple. He tried to go through their insurance but they denied him. They think he's faking the injuries, so now he's going after the owners."

"And is he faking the injuries?" She hopped up on the counter next to where he worked. He didn't take his eyes off his task.

"That's what I have to find out. Meeting today with a private detective the owners hired. You know, there's good money in that work. And the hours are a bit steadier."

She knew he was trying to be subtle, but the hint felt like a punch in the gut. She put her hand on her scar just below her belly button and rubbed it for a moment before she realized what she was doing and dropped her hand.

"Takes the right kind of person," she said, again with forced casualness. "Plus, you have to be good at tailing

345

people. I think that's why I'm good at homicide. I make too much racket." As if to really make the point, she hopped off the counter and her shoes made a loud clunk as she crashed down.

He laughed and turned to her. His face relaxed into a soft expression. It made him look five years younger. "You know it's not about the money, right?"

"I know." She looked into his eyes, her heels brought her up to his height.

"I'm trying, it's just…" his voice trailed off.

She reached out and held his free hand, the other one held the cup of sweet-smelling coffee. "I am, too. It will be OK, though. I know it will."

He smiled and kissed her forehead, one of her favorite things. She dropped his hand as he pulled away. Moments later she heard his feet on the stairs and the shower start. She walked to the small half-bath under the stairs and turned on the light to inspect herself in the mirror. Her hair was still matted and wet, but she combed through it and made sure she got all the blood. She felt her heart pound again, but told it to quiet down. He doesn't know. He doesn't have to know what happened.

Three

She was already foggy with sleep when he kissed her goodbye. His lips were warm on her cool cheek and she wanted to pull him into bed, to beg him to stay and hold her for just for a minute. When she was able to mustered up the strength to wrench herself from the edges of her dream, her hand met thin air. He was already gone.

She groaned and rolled over. The light peaked through in a small slivered gap in the blackout curtains. Should she get up and shut them all the way and risk not being able to fall back asleep? Or try to shut her eyes and ignore the color she saw through her closed lids? She tossed the other way. Maybe if she didn't face the window directly she'd be plunged back into darkness, but the light was still there. It thwarted her plans to sleep during unnatural times of the day.

She'd had varying luck over the years with the shift changes. Sometimes they hit her hard and left her confused as to what day it was. Other times she floated between them without effort, like she led a double life. But didn't she?

No. Clear your mind, she told herself. The therapist's words reverberated in her head. She squeezed her eyelids shut and counted to ten.

"Screw it," she said out loud and threw the covers off. Maybe a warm shower would help. She rinsed off at the precinct, but hadn't done a good enough job or Jeremy never would have seen the blood on her. She was sure it was all gone, but she still felt like there was an invisible film on her. Images of the night before flashed through her memory.

No. Don't think about that. The past is the past. More quack garbage. She imagined herself physically pushing the picture out of her head and it worked well enough. Whether it was lack of sleep or she'd finally mastered the task, she

347

didn't care. She didn't flick the switch as she turned the shower on. Enough light came through the closed slats of the blinds that it mocked her attempt to push the sun out of her life.

The small room filled with steam as she pulled her clothes off. She caught her reflection in the mirror as it fogged. She didn't have a terrible body. Long hours and too many coffee and fast food runs had turned her once firm frame a little soft, but she still fit into her size six pants, albeit a little tighter than a year ago. Although, if she thought about it, she hadn't even worn pants a year ago.

Her hands fingered the scar that ran just above her pubic bone to her belly button. In the mirror it looked like a fun house image. Like she could pretend it was made-up or someone else's body. She could look at it clinically now. Jeremy could barely look at it at all.

It was almost silly how it happened. Was silly the right word? Maybe it was ironic, tragic even?

She'd been walking home from her day shift. It was bright freaking daylight out. She hummed along and made lists in her head of what to bring to the potluck that night. Greg and Jennie were hosting game night and she agreed to make dip. Should she do the artichoke? Or the buffalo chicken? Maybe she'd just do both. She'd asked Jeremy what his thoughts were.

She'd just passed the park when the branch snapped next to her. Her body didn't even react at first. You'd think with all the training she'd had and the classes in the academy she'd be prepared for it, but instead she was caught unguarded.

He'd grabbed her by the strap of her gym bag, the strong nylon cut into her shoulder as he yanked her off her feet. For some reason, for some stupid reason, she tugged back. A voice in her head reasoned that it wasn't his. He

348

couldn't take it from her. He had about a hundred pounds on her. As they struggled she locked on to his eyes. The rest of his face melted into a million faces, but his eyes. Those would stay with her forever.

He pulled her into the bushes and she realized too late that she'd lost the upper hand. She reached for her gun, but he grabbed her wrist. The pain that shot through her was shocking. Worse than that time, in the crappy apartment she rented right after college, she burned herself on a frying pan as she tried to make eggs. She'd thought that was the most unbearable pain, being burned. But this, as her insides twisted and cracked, was at a whole other level.

The moment she realized she should scream, he punched her in the stomach. The air whooshed out of her in a rush and tears sprang to her eyes. For the first time in her life, the realization that one day she would die crashed into her. Was this it? Was she going to be murdered on the side of a busy road? Would she be the homicide detective killed in broad daylight as passer-by's did nothing?

These thoughts fought for her attention along with the fear. Then her instincts kicked in. She bucked, arching her back into him. It was at that moment she realized she was on the ground and he was on top of her, using the knife to saw her bag off. She wondered why he didn't just take it off and run, but then remembered it was draped cross-body on her. He worked one-handed, his knee holding her one arm down as his other hand still held her throbbing wrist. She didn't know it yet, but it would require three pins and six weeks in a cast to heal.

Her wits finally about her, she began to fight. She jostled him off her just enough that she was able to raise her knee into him. She wasn't sure what she came into contact with, but he let out a moan and released the arm held by his knee. She swung up and hit him across the face, but it was her less dominate hand, which didn't have as much oomph. In a last, desperate attempt, he slashed at her bag. The knife cut through the strap, and her, in one movement.

He tugged it from her and ran, one hand on the bag as the other held his pants up as he cut through the park. She rolled over and watched him disappear behind a tree.

What happened next was relayed to her from eye-witnesses as she had no memory. She had gotten up, stepped through the bushes, and promptly walked into traffic to flag down a car. The poor woman whose minivan she stepped in front of screeched to a halt, which caused the taxi behind her to swerve and crash into the Civic next to him. The drivers were fine, but got out and started to yell at one another until they saw her.

In a calm, clear voice, she informed them that someone stole her bag and her cell phone had broken in her pocket. She asked them to please call the police, she identified herself and even gave her badge number. Then she sat on the sidewalk and waited for the ambulance, hands pressed into her bleeding abdomen.

That was a little over a year ago. Jeremy had been sick with worry. Wanted her to quit the force or, at the very least, stay on the temporary desk job they'd saddled her with until the stitches and cast came off. She tried to reason with him. It wasn't even her work that got her hurt. If anything, her training had saved her, but he was convinced that the man knew she was a cop. That he targeted her.

The fact that they never found him didn't make it any better.

She stepped into the water and let it wash away the bad memories along with any traces of last night.

Four

"The police confirmed today that the body discovered behind the Whispering Oaks Condominiums is that of Juan Rodriquez, thirty-four. Mr. Rodriquez was recently paroled after his hit-and-run involvement with a case six years ago that resulted in the death of five-year-old Becca Alberta. Rodriquez was sentenced for twelve years, but served only five after his parole was granted earlier this month. Police are asking that anyone who may have seen or heard anything to please call 1-800-COP-TIPS. They state they are unsure if it is gang related. Stay turned to News 6 for any further details. Coming up next, find out what in your pantry could be deadly to your cat or dog this holiday season."

I turned off the news. The fact that the police had no leads was encouraging. It had only been a few days, sure, but if they didn't know anything by now, the chances of new information was slim. Ineptitude was going to work in my favor for once.

The gang aspect was also an nice twist. I assumed people would think it was in response to his release, but maybe he was busy in the three weeks since he walked away from that cell. No matter. He got what he deserved in the end.

My eyes glanced to the gun on the night stand. It looked innocent as it quietly kept our secret. I'd debated on if I should throw it into the river or bury it in the woods, but what if I needed it again? And I'm sure it would be noticed if it went missing. No, it would stay. I'd let it rest up.

I'd felt a strange itch in my fingers and stretched them to dissipate it. It had been *easy*. Too easy. Point, shoot, drop, and just like that the world was rid of one more useless body that took up space. I'd give it another week before the news didn't even mention it anymore. Maybe less if something else trumped the story. But my work, my work I'd have to space out.

The kill wasn't my last. Not with how good it felt. Not with the righteousness that coursed through my veins. Maybe I'd find the one I really wanted.

A buzz ran through me and I thought about how it would be to look into those eyes and watch life leave them. I'm sure there were more just like them. More people who got away with terrible crimes and who paid little back to the society they'd robbed. The system failed to keep us safe.

I'd pick up where it left off.

Five

"Morning, Jackson."

"You know, that joke never gets funny." She put her bag on her desk, careful not to tip what little remained in her thermos.

"Oh come on, it's totally funny," Gibson said.

"It's five. O. Clock. PM." She annunciated each word as if he may or may not understand the language she spoke.

"I thought you'd be happy this morning."

She groaned. She knew what he was doing. They all tried to do it, to keep some normalcy in their lives. If he said good morning to her every day, whether true or not, for a short period of time they could pretend like they were normal people starting their day. Like they didn't have folders with pictures of dead people scattered over their desks.

She and Gibson had been partners for four years. He had a terrible sense of humor and made a crap pot of coffee, but he had her back, was sharp, and kept her on her game. Even when *it* happened, he didn't treat her any different. The other guys in the division adverted their eyes or mumbled some sort of apology—what they were apologizing for, she didn't know—but not Gibson. He told her the cast made her look like RoboCop and that she wasn't getting out of paperwork because she had a little cut. She could have hugged him if she hadn't hurt so bad.

"And why would I be so happy this *evening*?" she emphasized.

"Rodriquez!"

She shook her head and pulled some things from her bag before she stowed it in her desk.

"Do you seriously have that much of a shit memory? The hit-and-run guy that got released a few weeks back."

353

"What about him?" She tried to keep her face void of emotion.

"Someone off'd him. Dunno who, probably some dude he owed money to that could finally collect. And, the best part, it happened downtown, so it's Pasel and Ankley that have to deal with it, poor SOB's." Satisfaction pulled the corner of his lip up.

"One less person to have to keep track of."

"That's it? One less person?" his voice rose in mock imitation of hers.

She narrowed her eyes. "Look, people die every day. He was a bad one, so good he's off the street, and luckily he isn't our problem. There. You happy?"

He beamed. "Why yes, yes I am."

"Why don't you take your happy ass down to the fax machine and see if the ME's office sent us anything." His smile still plastered to his face, he wiggled his butt as he walked. She couldn't help but laugh.

As soon as he rounded the corner and was out of her view, she rushed to turn on her monitor and pulled up the news website. She scanned the details the reporters knew, which was pretty little. Just a short blurb about what happened. She was sure more details would come in the next few days. Maybe she'd eavesdrop on Ankley during one of his breaks. That man could be hired by any gossip mag in the country for how much he liked to spread rumors. She blinked the image of Becca's small, lifeless body out of her vision.

"Nothing."

She didn't hear Gibson return and jumped at the sound of his voice. "They still backed up?"

"I called yesterday and they said the holiday rush is already starting." He sat at his desk across from her and sorted through the ever-growing stack of folders. "Luckily, we have plenty to tide us over." His smile was dark, as if they shared a deep-rooted secret.

Kristin Durfee

Six

I should have waited. I even told myself I would, but as I watched the news to see if there was any new information about the Rodriquez case, another familiar name popped across the screen.

> *"In a dramatic turn of events, Alma Evans was released today into the custody of her parents. The seventeen-year-old was suspected in the drowning death of her seven-month-old daughter in May. The State Attorney's office was forced to drop charges when the one alleged eye-witness in the case, a Rob Parker, was unable to be located. A representative for the office stated that while they regret that justice for Lexus may not be forthcoming, they are confident that more information in the future may allow them to continue with a trial at that time. A spokesperson for the family said they are relieved and look forward to putting this behind them."*

Putting it behind them? As if the murder of a child is something that could be brushed aside. I knew where she lived. I knew how to find her.

I expected the place to be surrounded by cops and media, but for some reason no one seemed to give a damn that this monster was free. Her little girl was dead and buried in the ground and here she was, able to walk around her backyard like nothing ever happened. That wouldn't do.

Kristin Durfee

I'd taken the gun with me. I knew I shouldn't, but it practically begged me to come along.

I watched as the station wagon pulled out of the garage and down the long, narrow dirt drive. This was a shit part of town. Took me almost an hour to get out here with all the transfers and the walking, but it was worth it. Tucked away, no neighbors for miles, people shot all the time out here. I should know, I grew up right around this area where the fact that guns went off in the middle of the night was a way of life.

"Don't worry," my mother would say when I would run into her room, heaving with fear like a startled rabbit. "Just Old Man Cox shooting at squirrels."

And that was it. Just brushed off, shrugged away. No one called the cops. No one asked around to make sure everything was okay.

I unloaded three shots just to make it seem more believable. Make the neighbors think, oh, maybe they missed the first time. Hope they got whatever they were after.

Did I ever.

Seven

"Combed those damn woods for nearly two hours. Nothing. Going to head back out there later with the metal detector, see if it comes up with something."

Ankley was sitting on Gibson's desk when she arrived. He held a stack of papers in his hand, waving them in the air as he spoke.

"Why didn't you do that in the first place?" Gibson asked.

Ankley pointed the stack, now jutting in each direction, at him like an elongated finger. "Didn't think it would be that much of a pain in the ass. She was shot in the backyard, figured the cartridge cases would be right there. But maybe they shot from the woods. Crime scene is still out there, but I needed to run back here to get some papers for court, then the guy pled at the last minute. Doesn't that just figure?"

"Pasel still out there?"

"Oh yeah, and I know he'll have my head for not rushing right back, but I needed to grab a snack and was going to try to find that good detector. Crime scene's battery was dead in theirs. Guess they don't use it that much!" He barked with laughter.

"What's up?" Stef asked when she got to her desk and tugged her suit jacket off. She'd spent the last three hours in court. Three hours that she should have spent home asleep. If only her guy had pled.

"How was court?" Gibson ignored her question.

"Same old. So what happened?"

"Someone shot Alma Evans this morning," Ankley said.

Her eyes widened. "The mom who killed her daughter?"

"Allegedly," Gibson and Ankley said in unison.

"But yes," Ankley continued, "sunbathing in the backyard. Parents went out to run an errand. When they got back a few hours later, she was dead. Damndest thing, too, can't find any cartridge cases but she had three holes in her."

"Revolver maybe?" she offered.

"Eh, maybe. I'll know more when the lab gives me some details. A bit strange though," he paused.

"Strange, how?" Gibson asked.

"Well, we got two perps. People who have walked away from their crimes in the period of a few days get killed. Probably just a coincidence, but seems a bit strange."

"Maybe Seattle's got their very own Batman," Gibson joked.

She tried to force out a laugh, but it caught in her throat.

"Alright, I better get back. Pasel probably already has his panties in a bunch over there." He raised his shoulders in a half-apology of his off-colored remark, but she waved him off.

"Really though," Gibson asked. "How was court?"

"They must have hired a bunch of new attorneys out of high school. They were all young and lost," she said and sat with a satisfying thump into her chair. She closed her eyes and took a deep breath and regretted it right away. The smell of old papers and unwashed bodies flooded her nose. She opened her eyes and looked at him. "It was fine, really. I just had to help the kid out a bunch, but I think the jury got the gist."

"That's all we can do."

"Any word back on anything?"

They both chuckled at the vagueness of her question. "Sad that we have so many cases, they start to get lumped in together. We need that Batman to give us a hand," he said.

Revenge From Within
This time when he laughed, he did it alone.

Kristin Durfee

Eight

Screw waiting. There was too much bad out there. Too much and no one was doing anything about it. I tried. I seriously tried. I was in court for what felt like all day today, but what good did it do? Nothing. Guy walked on a technicality.

How can we compete with that? How, as a society, can we possibly rid the world of evil if bureaucracy just gets in the way? There's no way we can keep our citizens safe if we don't get those people off the streets.

The system tries. Hell, I'll even give it that. It does, it gives a valiant effort and when it fails, it won't admit it. It hides behind procedure, and calls it the law working. That the law is to protect everyone, but they count the scum as people, too. They're wrong.

It tries and it comes up short. There are gaps. I know now that my purpose is to fill them.

I scanned the newspapers and TV for updates on the cases.

I eavesdropped on my coworkers when they discussed what they're working on. It's hard not to devote all my time to my new calling, but I must be patient. I've seen what happens when people rush, they make mistakes. My work was too important to risk being caught.

I hoped that having a front seat to other's mess-ups would help me avoid them. The stakes were too high. I had to do everything in my power to ensure I succeeded. Too many people's lives depended on it.

Kristin Durfee

Nine

"In the sixth attack in as many weeks, Seattle residents are fearful who will be next. Seemingly random, the only connection the police can find between the victims is that they were all once convicted or suspected in crimes themselves. The mayor is urging residents to be vigilant and to report any suspicious activity. The State Attorney's office also released an official statement condemning the attacks. Assistant State Attorney Bethany Goodman is quoted as saying, "While we understand that the criminal justice system can, at times, be frustrating, we ask people to remember that justice is best served through the law, not through vigilantes." The Seattle Chief of Police is also asking residents to allow law enforcement to do their jobs. The agency said they are working with the state crime lab, but they still have no suspect or leads in the case. We turn now to Dr. Richard Marson, Director of Clinical Psychology at Baxter University. Doctor, thank you for speaking with us."

"Shit," Pasel said as he turned off the TV. They stood around it in the break room. Since the fourth death, a suspected pedophile whose computer evidence got thrown out because there was an issue with the search warrant, it was all hands on deck.

"What time is it even?" Gibson asked. "Jackson, you got a watch on? My battery died."

"Nine-thirty," she said.

"AM or PM?"

"Oh hell, you need to go to bed. Any word from the lab yet?"

"Yes and no," Ankley said. His eyes had purple rings under them. "Prelim results show all bullets have the same characteristics."

"Encouraging," she said.

"Sorta, only they're marked like crap. Lab's been at it for days and they don't know if they'll be able to give me anything definitive, other than we're looking for a 40 or 10mm caliber, possibly Glock or H&K, maybe something else."

"Damn, and still no cartridge cases?"

"Scenes are clear each time. Whoever is doing this is picking up after themselves," Pasel said, frustration heavy his voice.

"But," she continued, wanting to get as much information as possible. "They don't think they can ID?"

"Not looking like it. Can't wait for that press release," Ankley said.

"Luckily, we won't be the ones having to give it," Pasel said. "I think for the first time in a long time, I'm glad I'm just a peon."

"Cheers," Gibson said as he raised an imaginary glass.

Ten

It was so easy now, it made me feel invincible. The cops practically shouted from the rooftops that I was going to get away with it. I mean, not that I ever thought I'd get caught, I wouldn't have done this if I thought I would, but it still thrilled me to hear someone else say it.

When the lady on the news stated how the lab was having trouble, that they were only able to narrow down to possible types but couldn't confirm a single source for the projectiles, I knew I was in the clear. They'd never suspect me. They'd have no reason to. I was close enough to all the action not to raise suspicion, yet far enough away to still do my work. And what important work it was.

There was even a fan page on Facebook set up for me, or at least there was before the administrators took it down. People were glad. I thought that there would be some attention from it, but I never expected the outpouring of support. They were happy that their streets were a little safer. Sure, there were groups who condemned what I had done, but there always were. I could open up a rescue for cute fluffy kittens and someone would be upset that I excluded puppies. You can't please everyone.

When the page was up, there were even requests. Request! People posted other cases where the suspects didn't get the full justice the user thought they deserved. One in particular caught my attention. A mother lamented how the rapist of her daughter had gone free. The girl had pointed him out, described him and the sexual assault kit even confirmed his involvement, but he swore up and down it was consensual.

How the jury could have believed that, I would never know. The guy had even pulled her off a trail at a park and assaulted her in the bushes. *The bushes.*

I looked up his information and it turned out he resided right here in Seattle. I think I had my plans for the weekend.

Eleven

"I just don't understand."

She rubbed her eyes. Exhaustion permeated through her. "Jeremy, you know that it's all hands on deck right now."

"But you were supposed to ask weeks ago." He talked through clenched teeth.

"I asked, but they revoked all leave," she lied. Well, sort of lied. They had revoked leave, she'd just never actually asked for the dates like she'd promised. She meant to, honestly she had, but the last few weeks had been so crazy it slipped her mind.

"It may be too late to cancel."

"You should see if your brother wants to go with you," she suggested, trying to act excited at the prospect. It would be nice to have him out of the house for a few days, she could get a lot of work done. She was sure she'd get more accomplished if she didn't have to worry about sneaking around him. The hours she kept made it difficult to juggle all of her responsibilities.

"My brother? On a romantic cruise?" he asked with an expression like he'd just smelled sour milk.

"It's not a couple's cruise or anything. Look, I'll talk to my chief. If he's really firm about it, I'll see what the department can do, maybe they can call the travel agent and get a refund or re-schedule for us, how about that?" She moved toward him and placed a hand on his arm. Her fingers rubbed something and she looked down. A large bandage was covering a portion of his forearm. "What's this?"

"Klutzy me. Banged it on the edge of a counter at work just right and cut myself. Not a big deal, but I kept knocking it, so it's more a protector than anything."

Kristin Durfee

She leaned forward and kissed it lightly. He ran his fingers through her hair, pulling her lips to his. A soft groan released from the back of her throat as she pulled away.

"I have to go to work," she said in a whisper.

"Weren't you just there?" His eyes narrowed.

"Not really, I was at court earlier, but nights start back up. Though I feel like the shift changes are just a formality, we're basically working around the clock."

"I hear the dealership is hiring."

She looked at him, already weary from what was sure to be a fight, but there was no malice in his expression. He winked at her and she allowed a short laugh. "Don't tempt me," she said. He enveloped her in a hug.

"I'm just worried about you."

"I know." She breathed in deeply, inhaling fabric softener, aftershave, and something she couldn't quite put her finger on. It was vaguely familiar, yet sharp in her nose. "I gotta go."

He kissed her one more time. Confusion swam in her head. What was she doing? She wanted to tell him, to confide in him, but knew it wasn't time yet. There would be a perfect moment and when that came, he'd understand. He'd get why she disappeared sometimes and then they could start over. Things would be as they should and they could move forward, together.

Twelve

I tried to stop. I did. I thought after the rapist that it would be out of my system. Maybe one day, when I was close to death, I'd tell the nurse who took care of me what I did. How I tried to do my part to save the world, to save people from evil. Who knew what my legacy would be then. Maybe I'd be a hero, maybe no one would even remember, but I'd say it. Say their names as I passed into the next life, peace on my soul.

But each one that got taken away was replaced by two more. Three. Hundreds. I opened the paper and there was another. I sat in court and heard two attorneys as they lamented about their cases not going well. I turned on the radio, another person released. Another not-guilty verdict. It was too much. I couldn't just stay away, I had an obligation.

I'd gotten careless. I'll admit it. I was so used to being able to hide in the autonomy of the position, the black pistol by my side, as the masses cheered me on, I bought into the notion that I was invincible. I should have noticed that a person trailed me. They were probably there to keep an eye out on my target. He'd just been released and it was all over the news. I should have known that it would have been best to lay low for a little bit, let people think nothing was going to happen to him, but like I said, I felt unstoppable.

I messed up.

I was able to get in and get out in my usual quick manner. I was still able to accomplish my goal, but I noticed the man and left in a rush. It was messy and I hated to leave a mess. It wasn't until later that night, after my heart and breath resumed their normal patterns, that I realized my mistake. My stomach dropped like I had descended a hill on a roller coaster.

I'd left the cartridge case at the scene.

Kristin Durfee

Thirteen

The knock at the door wrenched her awake. She sat straight up, her chest tight. The memory of some dream floated over her. There was running, yelling, but she couldn't remember the details. A gun was raised and bang. Bang. Bang.

She groaned, stretched, and jumped when she hit something. Jeremy was asleep beside her. When did he get here? She couldn't remember what time he was supposed to get home, but it was a shock to have him in bed with her.

She felt groggy, almost drunk with tiredness. She picked up her phone and noticed a slew of missed calls and messages from Gibson. Confused, she noticed the silent toggle was on. The knocks continued, more urgent now.

"Coming," she called.

Jeremy opened a lazy eye. "What's up?" The words came out in a single syllable.

"Shh, go back to bed. It's the door. Probably something with the case."

He sat upright. "What case?"

"Shh," she repeated. "Don't worry about it. I'll be right back."

She threw on a bra and grabbed her robe from behind the bathroom door. She stuffed her feet into her slippers and padded down the stairs. Several dark forms were visible behind the frosted glass of the front door. Her skin prickled as she pulled the door open.

Gibson was flanked by three uniformed officers. They stood erect, failing as they tried to look casual. She nodded and they nodded back.

"Can we come in?" Gibson asked. It didn't make sense. Her instincts told her no, told her to deny them and run. She stepped aside and they entered.

She heard the bed shift above her head as her pulse quickened.

"Where's your firearm?" Gibson asked.

She nodded her head in the direction of the small console table by the front door. Gibson gestured to one of the deputies who walked over and slide open one of the drawers.

"SIG," the deputy with a sandpaper voice said as he held the weapon with a gloved hand.

"Where's your backup?" Gibson asked.

"In there, too."

"Ruger LCP," the deputy said after he pulled the second firearm out from the back of the drawer.

"Thought you had a Glock?" Gibson asked.

"I used to carry that, but the Ruger is a bit lighter. I switched a few months back." She tried to keep her voice calm and even.

"Where's the other weapon?"

Her eyes flitted upstairs on reflex, answering the question before her words did. Jeremy was halfway down the stairs, eyes wide and frozen at the scene below him. He moved to the side when two of the officers went past him and into their room. They came back down, the Glock enclosed in a clear, plastic evidence bag.

"I don't understand," she said.

"I'm going to need you to come with us," Gibson said.

Jeremy shrunk back. "What?"

Gibson stood in front of her and addressed her full in the face. "We are going to need to ask you some questions.

A union rep will be there, you know the drill, but you might be better off answering their questions."

"Their questions? What about you?" she asked.

"I had to beg the other officers just so I could come with them to bring you in. There's no way they are going to let me interrogate you."

"Interrogate?" The fear rose in her, the taste of vomit pressed at the back of her throat.

He lowered his voice and stepped toward her. "I don't know what to tell you, if you should keep your mouth shut or explain everything, but Jackson, we made a hit on prints left on the cartridge case at the scene. They're yours." He took a long breath before he continued. "Then they ran it through the database and your gun popped up."

She knew he could lose his job if someone found out that he gave her details about an open investigation which involved her, but it didn't make sense. It was impossible. What were they tying to her?

"I, I—" she stammered.

"I need you to come with us. If we walk out casual, I don't see any reason to cuff you or alert your neighbors that anything out of the ordinary is going on. Jeremy." He turned to address her husband for the first time. "I'm not sure how long we will keep her, I can call you when we're wrapping up."

"Can he come now? Can he follow and wait until you're done?" She didn't try to hide the panic and fear from her voice. Maybe it would help her. Maybe if Gibson had to testify he'd recall how terrified she sounded.

Jeremy fidgeted, but Gibson nodded and waited for him to get his keys.

"You can follow us," Gibson said. "No lights, so don't worry about losing us."

Kristin Durfee

Jeremy nodded and she stepped forward. One of the officers reached out a hand to stop her then hesitated. He allowed her to wrap her arms around her husband. Her body trembled. Was it her or him that was shook so bad?

She pulled away and looked at him, his eyes dilated with fear as Gibson laid a soft hand on her arm and pulled her away and out of her house as the pistol followed close behind.

Fourteen

Seventeen.

They were going to charge her with seventeen murders. There had to be a mistake. Had there really been seventeen? There were so many she'd lost track, but it still felt like an unreasonable number.

The lab had her gun now, but she doubted it would make a difference. It was just a formality, the computer system rarely made a hit when there wasn't one. She'd forgotten she'd given them standards from her weapon when she catalogued it as her backup and of course they had her prints on file.

She spent hours in the room. They brought her coffee and treated her well, she had to admit that, but her body ached with lack of movement. They came back with a typed-up statement and had her sign the bottom. Her hand shook so bad, it made the signature appear like she'd written it with the wrong hand.

"Can I go now?" she asked with hope in her voice.

The left side of the officer's lips tugged up for an instant. He looked like he didn't want to give the answer he had to. "I don't know ma'am. I'm still waiting to hear."

"Is my husband here? Can I see him?"

"I've gotta clear it first, but I'll see if he can come in."

She wasn't sure how long the officer was gone, but when the door re-opened, Gibson's large frame obscured most of Jeremy as stood steps behind her partner. Jeremy's color had paled about three shades and he was covered in a film of sweat.

"Let's keep this visit short, just a couple minutes," Gibson said as he looked back and forth down the hall. "Shit Jackson, I'm sorry, but we're going to have to keep you a little while longer. You'll go to processing next, and..." his words trailed off but she knew. And he knew that she knew.

"Thank you, Gibson."

He nodded and shut the door He'd give her this one last thing. Allow husband and wife a moment alone before their world would be changed forever.

Tears burned her eyes and flowed down her cheeks. She was proud that she'd held them back this long, but when she saw him there, she couldn't hold it anymore. He lifted her in a hug.

"I just don't understand," she said. She knew, out of respect, Gibson would have kept everyone away from the viewing window. This may be the last time they would be alone together for some time.

"Understand what?" he asked, his mouth hung slack and his brows raised in a question as he pulled away.

"How they think I did it. They say they have a cartridge case, that it was found at one of the scenes along with a partial thumb print. It just doesn't make any sense."

"All of the murders?" He sat down and she joined him across the metal table.

"They're probably going to try. Lab wasn't able to ID the bullets they had so far, so it's debatable if they will be able to tie them to a gun, but the cartridge case, maybe. But does it matter? One murder or a hundred? Just depends on how many life sentences."

"They don't suspect anyone else?"

"Why would they? They think they've caught the person, why keep looking?"

"How do they think you did it?" he asked as he leaned forward.

She frowned. "They think I followed these people. I wasn't at work. My alibi—Oh Jeremy, I don't know how reliable it will be." She buried her head in her hands. It was time. Time to tell him what she'd been doing in the voids between work and home. "I was trying to fix it, fix it all."

"I don't understand?"

"I was seeing a healer. I thought you'd make fun of me, call it gibberish."

"A healer?"

"To fix, to fix what went wrong from the attack. I thought it could remove my scar and maybe help us have a family."

They sat for a long time, the only noise in the room the buzz of the fluorescent lights that glared above them.

"And why is this a bad alibi?" he finally asked.

"I paid in cash. I didn't want you to see. I wanted it to be a surprise. A miracle. It's a little shop in Chinatown. I don't know if they ever took down my name and I saw a couple different employees there. What they did, it's not regulated, so they may not want to talk to authorities and vouch for what I'm saying. Hopefully they will, but," her voice trailed as the words hung in the air between them.

A soft knock at the door made them each jump. Gibson popped his head in. His shoulders were rounded and his head hung like a scolded dog. "One minute, then we gotta go," he said

She reached both of her hands forward and grabbed Jeremy's. It was like she was falling. Like she was about to plunge off an edge and needed him to hang on to. Like he would save her. He pulled her to her feet and brushed his lips against her ear.

"You know," Jeremy whispered, so soft it was barely audible to her. "Next time, you should get a bigger gun,

379

something other than a sub-compact. It's like holding a toothpick."

He pulled the breath out of her as he walked away. The words and truth swirled in her head as the officers entered the room. Jeremy threaded passed them, nodded at Gibson, and disappeared around the corner as she felt metal cuffs tighten around her wrists.

Fifteen

I walked out of the precinct and closed my eyes as the sun warmed my face. Seventeen. That was my final number. And she'd go down for all of them. Part of me felt bad, the old me. The new me knew it was a price that sometimes had to be paid for justice.

I loved her once. We had such promise. Both of us young, poised for successful careers. We'd talked about starting a family, then that man jumped out of the bushes and wrecked it all. Wrecked our dreams along with her body. I tried to be supportive, but things had changed. *We* had changed.

I felt alive again when I killed Rodriguez. It was like I had purpose after feeling lost for so long. This would be my legacy. I'd felt damned after I knew I'd never have children with her. What had destroyed her had done the same to us. I'd thought we would have to get used to the idea of growing old together, just the two of us.

Guess it didn't turn out that way, but she saved me in her own way.

We had such dreams. I thought I was going to change the world and save lives by being a lawyer. She'd get them off the streets and I'd put them away. It would be perfect, only it wasn't a perfect system. It was maddening and heartbreaking. Case after case pled or got thrown out. Sentences went half-served at best. When I heard about that drunk driver, that child killer, going free, I snapped. It was too much. But I gave her justice. Gave them all justice. I did what I never could do professionally.

And now I could move on with my life.

I walked down the street and wondered where I'd end up. No one could blame me if I left my serial killer wife.

They'd sympathize. Maybe I'd go on a show or two, talk about how I had no idea. How she seemed like the perfect spouse. Or maybe I'd just fade away, allow people to forget us.

I got in my car and turned on the radio.

"Breaking news. An arrest has been made in the vigilante killings. Reports from an insider are saying that the police have a suspect in custody and, let me reiterate this is unconfirmed, but the reports say that it may be a fellow officer. We will keep our listeners updated as soon as we have further information. In other news, jurors in San Francisco have acquitted Derrick Wilson in the brutal murder of his estranged wife. One of the members of the jury that agreed to speak with us said that the evidence from the experts was confusing and circumstantial and they felt there wasn't a preponderance to have a guilty verdict. Mr. Wilson has been released where he will be reunited with his two small daughters."

San Francisco. I heard that was a nice place to live. Warm, sunny, and, as the skies opened and I pulled up the information on my phone, I noted not a drop of rain in the forecast.

382

About the Author

Kristin Durfee lives and writes in Apopka, Florida. Her first book, **Four Corners**, is a Young Adult fantasy novel published by Black Opal Books.

Four Corners is *"a fun, magical adventure that is beautifully written...This story has a nice balance of adventure, action, and relatable friendship that is just perfect."*
—*Janella Fila for Reader's Favorite, 5-Star Review*

*"I devoured [**Four Corners**]! I could not put it down. I give Four Corners 4 out of 4 stars. While it is geared towards young adults, any adult looking for a fun and fast read would enjoy this book."*
—*Official Review from Onlinebookclub.org*

Two Worlds, the second book in the Four Corners Trilogy is set for release by Black Opal Books in the fall of 2016.

She also has a short story entitled *Project Bright Star* that has been included in the *Return to Earth* science-fiction anthology available now on Amazon.

Visit Kristin at www.kristindurfee.com for updates on all of her work.

Kristin Durfee

Miranda Nading

Book Cover by Select-O-Grafix, LLC
www.selectografix.com

Game Night

A group of retired women in small town America get together once a week to play poker. When Ruth discovers one of their own murdered, a chess piece left behind by the killer, she knows something more sinister than a random act of violence has touched their lives. With her own chess piece in hand, Ruth is pulled into a game where the winner truly does take all, and the loser pays the price

Miranda Nading

Game Night

By

Miranda Nading

Miranda Nading

Game Night
Acknowledgements

A very special thanks to those readers who have continued to support and encourage my misbehaving brain, and by doing so, have helped us raise money for a great cause.
Keep Reaching~

Miranda Nading

Chapter One

Ruth Moore wasn't sure when it happened. One day she's admiring herself in the mirror and the next, she's avoiding it; as if the old child's legend, Bloody Mary, was waiting just behind the glass, ready – hungry even – to snatch her up. It had become a habit to turn her head away every time she walked by one of the blasted things. Trying to tell herself, and her friends, that they'd earned every gray hair, every wrinkle, and that they should be honored – smelled a lot like bull biscuits when she was alone and looking into that darned glass.

"When did you get *so* old?" she asked the woman staring back at her.

Frustrated with the weight of this new life pulling her down, as surely as if at the exact moment of retirement gravity itself had conspired against her, she pushed back from her dressing table and grabbed her purse.

Tom the Toad was in the living room. With his wife-beater t-shirt and saggy boxers, he was the poster boy for the life of ease and decadence that everyone strove for, from the time they punched their first timecard, cashed their first payroll check. That time in their lives when they left the age of reason behind and entered the age of uselessness. Even the cold beer sitting close to his left hand should have been replaced with a glass of orange-flavored fiber.

In fact, the only thing missing from this picture was his hand down his shorts, scratching his crotch with the absentmindedness of a lifelong lays-about. He'd achieved his six o'clock perch on the couch to watch a rerun of the same old game show. His retirement had come six months before hers and it was a wonder his place on the couch hadn't already achieved a permanent butt-divot, to match his spreading hind end.

"Dinner's in the oven," she muttered walking across to her recliner on the other side of the room. It was just a bit too early to leave for her Friday night game. "Why don't you try eating it, instead of that junk food?"

"You know," he answered without turning to look at her, his eyes distant, almost bored as he continued to watch his game show, "your ma was an old nag, too. Didn't much like her, neither."

Ruth sat a little longer, watching The Toad watch his darned game show. Part of her waited for him to pick his nose and flick it across the room. No, that was unkind. The Toad had become a fixture in this stagnant pond, but he'd never been vulgar like Brother Bob.

The game show host put his arm around a pretty young contestant, gave her a big kiss on the cheek, and with a flourish worthy of every five and dime magician she'd ever seen, whipped out a card with the question. *Where would you find oil?*

Tom answered. "In the car."

"Do you remember when we used to go down and skip rocks at Dewer's Pond? Back when we were still in high school, before we got married?"

"Skip rocks?" Tom laughed, but it was a bored, disinterested laugh. "Is that what they call it nowadays?"

"We did too skip rocks."

"You also got knocked up with Lilly. Course, that was before what the good Lord gave you started sagging." He finally glanced over at her, one eyebrow arched, before returning his attention to the TV. "What brought this on?"

"Nothing."

Except, it wasn't nothing. These days, the more distant memories seemed to be the most vivid. She just didn't want to face another disheartening side effect of growing up, growing out and growing old. Those brilliant days and nights were the best times, the golden times. Everything was good and nobody wanted anything more than what they had. The only thing Ruth was really sure of was that The Toad didn't remember those golden days with the same loss that she felt.

And that stung.

"And now look at us," she muttered, picking herself up out of her easy chair. The knee she'd had replaced right before retirement was singing a ditty. "Heading over to Phyllis's."

"You know Lilly doesn't like you going over there anymore. You're getting too darned old to be traipsing around town after dark." It was an old lecture, one she'd heard from their daughter more times than she could count. Especially after she'd twisted her knee on the way home one night after a game and spent the next six months in physical therapy, learning how to use the new one. "Don't see the hoopla over playing Bridge anyway."

The irritation that surged to the surface over being told what she should and shouldn't be doing was trumped by the fact that her daughter and husband still thought she and the girls had been playing Bridge all these years. Ruth bit down on her lip to stifle the laughter that boiled up. If they thought Bridge was too much for this old lady, they would be in for quite a shock if they knew the truth. "Don't wait up."

"Never do," he answered, right before he answered the game show host. "In the Alps."

On the porch, she stopped and took a deep breath of evening air redolent with the scent of oleander and hyacinth. The moon, an early riser for a change, hung heavy and fat just above the rooftops across the street. For the moment, it brightened all but the deepest shadows, bleaching the color out of everything it fell upon, creating a negative still life of their small town. Past experience, however, said if she didn't turn on the porch light, the moon would be on the other side of the sky when game night was over and she'd certainly step wrong coming up the stairs and lose her other knee.

She reached back inside, hit the light and dug through her heavy, 'Friday Night' purse to make sure she had her keys, before locking the door and closing it behind her. As she turned to leave, light caught a small black fob sitting at the head of the steps and danced across its surface; a starburst, there for only a moment before the single step she'd taken made the angle wrong and the reflection of light passed.

The grandkids hadn't been over yet this week, and if they'd left something there she would have seen it before now. Using her new knee to bear her weight instead of the old, she squatted down and picked it up. Heavier than she thought such a little thing ought to be, cool to the touch despite the warm evening, she turned toward the light to get a better look.

A piece from a chess set, the queen, but not a cheap children's set. The small piece in her hand had been carefully shaped out of black glass. The set which that beautiful piece called home must have cost a pretty penny and she couldn't remember ever seeing one quite like it.

Beautiful though it was, holding it in her hand sent a chill dancing along Ruth's spine until it grew into a full-blown shiver.

II

Ruth made it to Phyllis's house, two blocks away, right on time, and walked in without knocking. A chorus of 'hello's' drifted around the dining room, but she went straight for the bar. It was Tina's night to play banker and bartender and in front of her on the bar, only two sets of chips and two glasses of wine remained.

Ruth plopped her heavy purse onto a stool and pulled out four rolls of quarters. They wanted to have fun, not gamble away their social security checks. You had to start with a hundred bucks, but no one could lose more than a hundred in a night. Because Myrna was such a bad poker player – she'd lose her head if it wasn't tucked safely up her can – they'd started Poverty Poker Rules. After the hundred was gone, she could run through two more banks for free to keep playing.

Tina finished filling out Ruth's slip and grinned. "Your name was drawn."

"Ha, finally got a break with you sharks." Ruth nodded her head towards the other bank. "Who're we missing?"

Phyllis, the youngest of their group and the Hostess with the Mostess, put her arm around Ruth's shoulders in her signature one-armed hug. "Debbie. I was thinking her trip to her daughter's wasn't until next month."

"I saw her boy and his family over earlier this afternoon," Myrna said, as she and her twin sister Myra stepped up to refill their glasses. "They might have taken the old girl for the night. I know they've been worried about her."

"Me too, for that matter," Myra chimed in.

As the oldest member of their group, pushing seventy-five now, everyone worried about Debbie. The ice she was skating on wasn't as thick as it used to be and none of them bounced as well as they used to, or healed, for that matter. Ruth flexed the titanium joint in her knee and sighed. "Should we wait?"

Phyllis shook her head. "I tried to call a few minutes ago. No answer. Myrna's probably right and we'd spend half the night staring at each other's ugly mugs for nothing."

Grabbing her wine and chips, Ruth settled in at the table and started shuffling the cards. Between the rhythm and the routine, she slowly pulled herself out of her funk enough to enjoy herself. She tossed her ante in the pot and started dealing out the cards, two face-down and three face-up in front of each player, then another three face down in the middle of the table. "The Good, The Bad, and The Ugly. Sky's the limit."

Myrna cast a suspicious eye over her cards as if knowing their only goal was to betray her, and asked, "How long, do you think? Before they put Debbie in Rutherford Home?"

"Probably not much longer," Tina offered, adding her first bet to the pot. "Did you see the bruises after that fall she took in the shower?"

Everyone cringed, Ruth tossed in her bet and flipped the good card over for everyone to see. "Treys are wild. I was thinking about old Aril this morning. The way he went. Sometimes I think dying too young is tragic, but times like that, I think it's somehow worse to live too long."

A somber nodding of heads followed around the table as they threw in their next bets. Ruth threw hers in and flipped the bad card. "Get rid of those jacks, ladies."

Two jacks hit the discard pile and the betting started again. Myrna frowned down at a jack she obviously needed to get rid of. "The way my Frank has been in and out of hospital this past year, I can see it. But – and I hate to be this way – I'd rather he stays with me as long as he can. Even if things get bad for him."

"It's because you love him, dear," Myra patted her twin sister on the hand and threw in her bet. "Raise," she called and threw in a blue chip. Everyone followed her lead.

"It's selfish," Tina answered as she matched the raise.

Phyllis knocked on the table. "Call."

Tina continued, a little more gently than before. "Would you want him to suffer, dear? Just to keep from being lonely?"

"She wouldn't be lonely," Myra insisted. "She's got me."

Ruth reached for the ugly and everyone held their breath. A king. Myra and Tina both had to fold and Myrna and Phyllis threw in their bets and raised the stakes. With the possibility of a small straight staring at her, Ruth couldn't quit just yet, so she matched the pot and dealt the last card. "Sometimes I think I'd rather be in Rutherford Home. The Toad feels more like a roommate than a husband, and I can't turn around and say boo without Lilly jumping on me and telling me where to go and what to do and how to sit... making me feel old."

"What's going on with you, two?" Myra asked. "You used to be so close."

Ruth sighed and dealt out the last card to the remaining players. "Final bet. I don't know. Seems like if he's not sleeping or eating, he's watching one stupid game show or another. It's like he doesn't care about anything anymore. And snarky. Always has to be snarky."

Tina laughed. "Well, you did go from both working to being stuck together twenty-four hours a day. Get the man a hobby, something to get him doing again. Some people just can't handle retirement. Old Albert said he felt like he was just sitting around, waiting to die."

Phyllis threw her bet into the pot and gave Ruth a sharp look. "I'm sure calling him Tom the Toad can't help matters."

"I've called him that for years, he's never minded before."

"Still, he's your husband. Try treating him like one. And be thankful you have a family. One that cares enough to worry about you."

Ruth glanced up at Tina and Myra – both widowed – their faces flushed with more than wine as they, too, felt the sting of Phyllis's remarks, though for different reasons. Of their small group of six, Ruth was the only member whose small nuclear family was still intact, untouched by death and abandonment.

Phyllis took the first pot with three of a kind and Tina began the next deal. "Let's start this night off with a bang, folks. Russian Roulette, pull the trigger."

Chapter Two

After the bank had been divvied out and the kitty had
been fed, Ruth stood on Phyllis's front porch with a heavier
purse than she started with, and waved goodbye to the others.
Concern for Debbie still tugged at her mind; the sweet little
woman had been struggling lately and Ruth was sure that her
kids weren't taking her to the airport for another three weeks.
She'd thought about asking Myrna to look in on her as they
were practically neighbors, but they had played 'til almost
eleven and Myrna and Myra both looked tuckered out.

"Do you need a ride home?" Phyllis asked as Ruth
continued to stand on her porch and stare down the road.

"No," she hesitated and then came right out with it.
"I'm sorry if what I said tonight hurt your feelings."

Phyllis laughed and shook her head. "I love my life,
Ruth. I've never been married or had kids, never had the
urge, either. But sometimes, I look ahead and wonder if that
will change as the years start drawing in around me as they
have Debbie. But you, you've always had Tom and the kids
around. I think you're problem isn't them, it's you."

"What do you mean?"

"You're feeling the sunset and you can't stand it.
You're growing old about as gracefully as a three-legged,
bobbed-tailed dog on ice skates. Get over yourself. We all
have to grow old and you're wasting the precious little time
you have left by feeling sorry for yourself."

Ruth clamped down hard on the retort that surfaced.
She was too tired to stand there half the night arguing. They
were practically the same age, but Phyllis was still in great
shape from decades of teaching P.E. She rarely got sick, and
as far as Ruth knew, she'd never been under the knife to

replace the parts that had grown rusty and weak with time. She sure as dickens didn't have a limp to show for it.

"Have a good night, Phyllis," she responded instead, and stepped carefully down the stairs. She followed the cobblestone path and was almost to the sidewalk before she finally heard the door shut behind her.

The walk home was no different than it had been over the years they'd been meeting for poker night. She'd been right about the moon, it had long since drifted to the other side of the city and though it was full, most of the neighborhood was huddled in shadows. Porches, jaundiced by the yellow bug lights the area favored, did little to relieve the darkness and by the time she stood on the porch of her own home-sweet-home, the depression she'd been dealing with had become heavy with dread and foreboding.

"Dammit, Debs," she sighed, convinced that the concern blossoming in her chest like some sick and ailing flower must come from that quarter of her little world. *Should have had the girls check on you.*

There was nothing for it. If she hoped to get a minute of sleep, she'd have to make sure Debbie had, in fact, gone off for a night of protective custody under the watchful eye of her well-meaning children. With this goal in mind, she set her feet to the sidewalk with a purpose and made quick work of the few short blocks that stood between them.

Half a block from her destination, she could see that the small Dutch cottage was dark except for one small square of light on the north side, just behind the garden gate which led to the backyard. That window, Ruth knew, was the little one above the kitchen sink. Instead of going to the front door, she stepped through the little picket fence and stood on tiptoe to look inside.

There was no sign of the eldest member of their gang in that immaculate kitchen, but the back door stood ajar.

"Debbie?" Ruth called quietly as she pushed the back door open a little further. "Debs? Are you home?"

No answer, save for the tick-tic-ticking of the ladybug clock above the stove.

Something tugged at the back recesses of her mind and she took a step inside, trying to figure out what seemed to be amiss. She called a little louder this time. "Debbie?"

The butcher-block island stood sentry in the middle of the room, with its odds and ends assortment of daily essentials. As she looked at it, she realized what was missing. Everything Debbie touched succumbed to the ladybug itch. A set of fine cutlery, knives of all sizes and uses, had stood for years at the corner of the island, little red and black ladybugs crawling up the handles, which had always sat near a small ladybug carving board. Its customary place now sat vacant.

"Debbie!" she called again and moved around the island. She saw Deb's legs a moment before she tripped on them and went sprawling. A scream locked itself in her throat, cutting off her air as she landed – pain raced up her knees and into her hips – palms down in a pool of cold, sticky blood. *"No no no nononono!"* she whimpered as she crawled forward, trying to cradle her old friend in her arms.

The six knives missing from the butcher's block stuck out from Debbie's frail chest like a twisted game of points. Her faded blue eyes were open but unseeing, clouded over by death. Though Ruth knew her friend had been gone long before she stumbled across her, she cradled Debbie's face and called to her, tears streaming down her own cheeks.

One tiny hand was clenched into a fist on Deb's stomach. Ruth took this in her own hand and held it to her cheek while she cried. Though Debbie was beyond need, Ruth muttered around her tears, "I have to call someone, Debs. I gotta get help."

403

As she went to lay the delicate hand back on her lost friend's chest to reach for the phone, Ruth realized something was clenched in those frail, ashen fingers. With some effort, and more than a little shame, Ruth managed to get her pinky finger pulled back enough to see a small black edge catch the light and dance with it. Before she could stop herself, she pulled the piece out.

A pawn.

Her stomach dropped and though she didn't faint, the world grayed at the edges as she remembered the small black queen resting in her pocket. She pushed herself away from her friend. Reaching for the phone and calling help, forgotten. She had never seen a chess set so elaborate or elegant, and to see two pieces that looked as if they had come out of the very same box, first on her own porch and then in her dead friend's hand – it was too much.

II

Outside, the cool night air dried the tears on her cheeks, Ruth forced herself to stand still, forced herself to breathe, to think. Her eyes roamed the night-bleached back yard, looking for only God knew what, and seeing only the birdhouses and ceramic ladybugs that Deb had loved so much. None of this could stop the emotional turmoil threatening to split her at the seams, none of it anchored her against the storm, and nothing helped to get the old gray cells going. She might as well have been beating her head against the wall of the cottage for all the good it was doing.

The only thing she knew for sure was that she needed help.

When her eyes fell across the open gate in the back fence, they locked onto it like a target and she finally put one foot in front of the other, getting herself moving. Myrna's house had a similar gate that led into her back yard from the alley. Her husband would be asleep, but Myrna would still be licking her wounds from the poker game with a cup of hot tea and a sink full of dishes.

It occurred to her, as she stepped out of the back porch light and into the gloom of the alley, the killer could have come this way. Could even be waiting around some dark hedge, watching. Her steps faltered only a moment before she forced them back into action.

It would be too easy by far to allow those thoughts to freeze her up, leaving her standing there like an idiot until the sun came up and cops arrived. Almost hidden behind the blaring announcement her mind was casting out, '*DEB IS DEAD DEB IS DEAD* ', some little alarm warned that having the chess piece in her pocket when the cops arrived would not end well for her.

In moments, she was standing at the gate to Myrna's house and looking at yet another kitchen light, a small, lonely sign that someone was still awake. How closely this scene resembled the one she'd walked up on only a short while ago chilled her, sending cold fingers up her spine that turned into a wracking shiver.

Afraid that stopping now would leave her standing in the dark, vulnerable, when the tide of loss and fear finally overwhelmed her and she dropped to her knees again, helpless – she forced herself to move yet again.

At the window, separated by only a thin pane of glass and a planter overflowing with petunias, the dam holding back the panic that boiled inside of her finally let go. A scream, carrying the full breadth and depth of her terror, locked tight in her throat and she watched, through a shimmering veil of tears, as Myrna's limp hand was opened and a small dark object placed in her palm.

405

The hateful thing that stood over her was wearing faded denim jeans. An oversized dark hoodie covered its head, hiding its every feature. Whoever it was, they were doing something to Myrna's body, but she couldn't make her mind register what it was. A sob escaped Ruth's lips, no more than a whisper, but the thing with Myrna tensed. As it began to turn her way, Ruth dropped to her knees and pressed her body against the wall under the fragrant fall of petunias.

The light above her faded, as if a cloud had passed before the sun and Ruth knelt, with her hands clamped tightly over her treacherous mouth. It felt like an eternity before the light from the kitchen fell through the window again, letting her know the foul thing had moved away. Part of her, that hysterical, screaming woman locked inside a prison of fear, insisted that if Ruth stood up and turned, she would see who it was, who had killed her dear friends and placed that darned chess piece in Myrna's hand, as if it were some twisted weirding stone in a sick lottery, where all were black and none were white, all were death and none were light.

A floorboard creaked within and her paralysis broke. Ruth crawled through the dirt, kicking until she could get her feet under her to get away. Running – her gait broken by her strained knee – down the center of the street, she tried to scream, tried to call out, but reason seemed to have been trumped by madness, thought replaced by blind terror. A cry broke the night, chasing after her like the wailing of angry banshees.

III

Rather than feeling safe once she was on her own porch, the bug light seemed more like a yellow spotlight,

406

highlighting her position. She felt exposed, vulnerable… watched. She struggled with the doorknob but it wouldn't yield beneath her quaking hands. Ruth was just about to beat on the door, a racket that would wake even Tom from his impervious slumber, before she remembered the key in her purse. It took too long, a lifetime it seemed, to ferret it out from among the quarters, pens and tissues that filled the bottom of the bag, to dislodge it from the sewing thread and ribbons.

The rising sounds of the banshees outside were diminished by the closing of the heavy oak, and Ruth locked the door behind her before running to the kitchen to ensure the back door was barred against an intruder. Flipping on the light over the sink, she grabbed the phone from the wall and hit only the first digit of nine-one-one, before the stark reality of the blood on the phone's white plastic surface seized her. She looked up, her field of view taking in the window over the sink, which looked over the back yard. A reverse image, resembling the negative of a photograph of what she'd seen at both Deb's and Myrna's homes, rocked her.

She eased the phone back down and turned the light off. Standing in the dim light of the kitchen, Ruth looked down and realized she was covered, pretty much from head to toe, in Deb's blood. The wine and chips she'd eaten during the game rebelled and she bent over the sink, violently emptying her stomach. When she was done, Ruth turned the hot water all the way up and scrubbed the blood from her hands.

As she turned off the water, the distant wailing abruptly stopped, as if someone had flipped a switch and she realized only too late what her panicked brain hadn't registered. A siren. Somehow, someone had realized the dark things which had been done this night and had called for help. That, or they had seen her running down the road like a lunatic, covered in blood. That, or someone's cat was up a tree and it had nothing whatsoever to do with Ruth and her friends.

She had to know. One way or the other. And she needed help.

Standing just inside the bedroom – the hulk under the covers rattling the rooftop with his snoring – she realized something else that she'd missed. Frank. She'd been so terrified; she hadn't thought to check to see if the old man was alive or… had joined his wife in the ever after.

Instead of waking up Tom as she was wont to do – what on earth was she going to tell him, what was she going to tell anyone – she grabbed a change of clothes from the bureau and slipped into the bathroom. Leaving her ruined clothes on the floor, she left the bedroom without waking her husband and after a moment's hesitation locked the bedroom door behind her. If whoever was doing this came for them, they would have to wake Tom up before they could get close to him.

With all evidence of Deb's horrible death removed from the phone, she picked it up and dialed Phyllis. After the fourth ring, it went to voice mail. "Phyllis…" she couldn't think for the life of her what to say. What if she was already like Deb and Myrna, dead and growing cold on the floor of her kitchen? As the digital spool continued to reel, she simply said, "Something terrible has happened. There are sirens down by Myrna and Deb's, I'm heading over there. Please come. I need to talk to you."

Using one trembling finger to hit the hang-up button, she dialed Tina. This time, the ringing was uninterrupted by a greeting, mechanical or otherwise. After the thirtieth ring, Ruth realized she could sit there and count rings all night long. She was terrified, so she was procrastinating. She felt like a coward. Forcing herself to hang up the phone, she left her purse where it lay on the table but shoved her key into her pocket along with the malicious chess piece, and rechecked all the locks.

Miranda Nading

Chapter Three

A goodish crowd of rubberneckers and gawkers had already gathered on Colorado Street, and they were not watching some hapless fireman pull a kitten out of a tree in the middle of the night. Susurrations of whispered horror and confusion drifted through the crowd as they waited to discover what tragedy had come so close to them. Though Deb's house was largely ignored, the front door of Myrna's was open, every light in the house lit against the evil that had paid a visit.

She looked for Tina and Phyllis until a commotion at Myrna's front door pulled her attention. Tears, hot and unnoticed, fell as Myra's sobbing, a world of pain in that sound, drifted through the night air. The crowd fell silent as Frank and Myra stood together, holding each other up against a storm only they could feel.

"It was Myrna." A voice spoke over her shoulder and Ruth jumped, issuing a tiny little squeal before turning to find Tina and Phyllis, their arms around each other. Tina wiped the tears from her eyes and continued. "They haven't said how yet, maybe a heart attack or stroke."

Phyllis, her mouth still trembling with imprisoned emotion, tears falling freely, held out her free arm and Ruth went to them. They stood in the middle of the street, off to one side of the small sea of lookie-loos, and held each other as their grief washed over them. When they were able to pull apart, Ruth whispered. "I need to talk to you, privately."

"I just want to go home," Tina shook her head. "I'm wrung out, exhausted."

"It wasn't a heart attack, or a brainstorm, either," Ruth finally admitted. "She was murdered, just like Debbie."

What she registered in their eyes – shock and confusion – brought out a sigh of relief. She hadn't even realized she harbored thoughts of either of them as suspects until she didn't. "Have either of you found anything, today or tonight? A small black chess piece? Not the Five-N-Dime kind, but a real nice one, made of glass?"

Each dropped a hand toward their pocket and Ruth grabbed them, stilling them. "Not here. Not now. Phyllis, how about your house? It's the farthest from here."

"Yeah," Phyllis breathed, fear settling into her faded blue eyes.

"Tina?"

"What's going on, Ruth?" Tina sounded as if she'd been running a marathon and couldn't catch her breath. "What happened to Myrna and Deb?"

"I'll tell you everything I know, hon. But not here. Come with us."

Fresh tears fell, but Tina nodded her head and Phyllis led them to her Olds, just down the block, as Myra and Myrna's devastated husband were shuttled into a sheriff's car.

At least they were safe, for the night anyway. Yet, now that Ruth had her friends – what was left of them – around her, the steam engine that was her old gray cells, began to cycle, trying desperately to put the pieces together. She suspected Frank had never been in danger, not really. If he had walked into the room while the murderer was still there, he would have been just as dead as his wife.

Whatever was going on, it was about the six of them.

II

The green felt still lay over Phyllis's dining room table, the glasses and poker accouterments still on the

412

counter. When the other two stood around the table with Ruth, she reached into her pocket and pulled out the black queen. She sat it down on the table without a word.

One by one, hands shaking as hard as her own, her friends followed suit. In front her own place at the table, Tina sat down a rook. Phyllis, a king. "Deb," Ruth swallowed, forcing the words around her grief, "had a pawn in her hand, but I didn't see Myrna's."

She told them all she knew, everything she had seen and done as they listened in rapt silence. When the telling was over, the women tried to wrap their minds around a murderer in their own neighborhood, one that had arrived like a thief in the night and ripped their small world apart.

"The only three two left would be the knight and the bishop," Ruth said at last.

"But why these pieces; why us?" Phyllis asked. It was the question that had been hammering around in Ruth's head from the moment she set eyes on Deb's little omen.

"Deb was the oldest of our lot," Tina offered. "What was she? Seventy-five?"

Ruth was nodding her head, "Myra and Myrna were pushing seventy. Would be in two months."

"I just turned sixty-seven." A tentative smile touched Tina's lips.

How well they all remembered that birthday poker night, and the hangovers that followed. Ruth turned toward Phyllis and found her scribbling rapid-fire on a small notepad, listing their names, ages and the pieces they all held to this dark puzzle. "Ruth? You're sixty-five, aren't you?"

"Yep."

"I'm sixty-four." Phyllis drew a bracket around Myra and Myrna, sharing knight and bishop between them. She shoved the pad to the middle of the table and asked, "Tina, you're our chess player, what are the values of the pieces?"

Tina looked at the notepad only a moment before nodding her head. "That's about it. The pawn has the lowest sacrificial value…"

She trailed off, catching the word she'd just used, and a visible shiver rattled her. Ruth felt a goose walk up her spine and looked at Phyllis, to see that she had also caught the word *sacrificial*. "Go on," Ruth whispered, "tell us what you know."

"That's, um, how they're valued." Tina tried to shake off the shiver but didn't look like she'd been all that successful. She swallowed hard. "It means which pieces you're okay with your opponent taking, opposed to another. "The pawn is the lowest value, the knight and the bishop are sort of interchangeable, depending on strategy, then the rook, the queen, and of course the king has the greatest value. You spend the entire game protecting it."

"I need a drink." Phyllis pushed away from the table hard enough to knock over their pieces and went to the wet bar.

"Count me in," Tina and Ruth answered and moved to join her.

Ruth hesitated, then snatched up the chess pieces and brought them to the bar. The other two women stood motionless, watching her do it, and she offered an awkward shrug. "I know the pieces aren't doing the killing, but I don't like having the little bastards at my back."

Phyllis reached under the counter and brought out the good stuff. She knocked the dust off the bottle of Patron Silver and poured a round. After she shot hers back, she shuddered and said, "We have to call the police."

"Are you crazy?" Tina threw hers back, her eyes wide over the rim. After the initial warmth rushed through her, she echoed Phyllis shiver and said, "And tell them what?

414

Game Night

That a bunch of old geriatric poker players are being targeted by a mad chess player?"

Ruth shivered, rolling the little glass between her palms to warm it, and herself. "My fingerprints are all over the place at Deb's, and I don't know that our county boys are the brightest bulbs in the box, but I'm sure they could match my shoes to the flower bed under Myrna's window."

"Even if we tried to tell them the truth," Tina rubbed at her face with her hands, "I don't think they'd believe us. And it might be your prints in the blood and bushes, but I'm the only chess player in our little group. Never mind that I don't have a fancy board with glass pieces—"

"I think they're obsidian," Phyllis offered, holding the little king up to the light.

"—they'll rake me over the coals before they take the time to figure it out," Tina finished, glaring at Phyllis. "If we come forward, they're going to rake us all over the coals because our fingerprints are all over everything in their homes and we were the last people to see Myrna alive."

"What about Tom," Phyllis asked, looking at Ruth with something akin to hope shining in her eyes. "Can he help us?"

"I don't see how," she sighed and finally drank down the contents of her glass. "If he believed anything I said, and that's a big if… he'll want to go to the police. Interrupting the status quo, interfering with the nice little routine he's bogged down in won't be easily swallowed, no matter what's going on."

"So where does that leave us?" Phyllis asked.

No one had an answer. The dark pieces sat on the counter, glistening under the light as if they were mocking them.

415

"Deb must have been gone before the game," Tina mused out loud. "Laying there the whole time we were playing."

"What does that have to do with anything?" Phyllis snapped. "The only thing I care about right now, is not ending up just like her."

"Hear me out, Phyllis. As far as I can see," she held up the rook, "I'm next and as far as I know, the killer could be waiting in my house right now."

Tina glanced at the clock. Ruth followed her gaze and found it was already one in the morning. *How time flies when you're having...* She had to bite back a hysterical giggle that threatened to slip loose.

"I talked to Deb earlier in the day, so she probably passed between three o'clock and six yesterday evening. We left here at what? Eleven, or just after?"

"I don't think a timeline matters here," Ruth said and shook her head. "If we hadn't been together for so long tonight, this might already be over. Checkmate."

Phyllis nodded her head thoughtfully. "I agree. I think what matters is our *sacrificial* value. Ruth? Do you think the guy saw you? Beneath Myrna's window?"

"I don't know... I don't think so. I think if he saw me, he wouldn't have wanted me to get away. Too risky. I might have gone home and called the police, just like I almost did."

"Why didn't you?" This was Tina.

Ruth bit her lip, thinking, feeling almost ashamed of her cowardice. "It was the blood on my hands. On the phone. I think, subconsciously, I was afraid they would think I did it."

"They still might," Phyllis covered Ruth's hand with one of her own and gave her a gentle squeeze. "But I think we need to bring a stop to this, tonight. One way or the other.

416

Before the boys in brown have time to run prints or forensics, or whatever it is they do."

"What are you suggesting?" Tina asked, a look of horror bringing her brows together over eyes too big for her face.

"I think we're on our own, and I think we have the edge. As far as this freak knows, we don't know anything. I found a chess piece and left it, forgotten, in the bottom of my purse. We've lost a friend, that's all. And I don't think he'll want to wait until tomorrow to finish. We might all be together again, mourning the loss of our friends. And by then, Deb's kids will most likely realize something's wrong and the cops will start questioning all of us."

"And the prints, they might have them back by then." Ruth was nodding her head. "I think you're right. He either takes us out tonight, or he's lost the game."

"And that's exactly what this is, a game." Tina began to catch what they were saying. "And we're the real pieces, aren't we? The real pawns."

Phyllis nodded her head, meeting their eyes with a calculating gleam shining in her own. "I think it's time we set the board up the way *we* want it."

Miranda Nading

Chapter Four

If the street side of the homes in their neighborhood was shrouded, the alley between the back fences and the trees was the dark side of the moon. Ruth walked slowly, yet with a purpose. After the time spent sitting at Phyllis's, her knee had stiffened and made her limp worse. Careful not to trip on a stray surface root or carelessly tossed child's toy, she made her way behind the yards toward Tina's house. If the man responsible for this night of horror was still playing the game, he'd go for the rook. Could even be there waiting in her kitchen at that very moment.

Tina, trailed by Phyllis on the other side of the neat little row of houses, would be five minutes behind her. Just enough time to scout out the back yard and try to determine if their opponent was there, waiting. Enough time to send out a warning as they had in younger days when the parents – of one or the other – left the house and they had mischief on their minds.

If the stakes of this grim game had not been so high, if this had been any other night, the memories that surfaced might have been a pleasure. As it was, even the moon seemed to conspire against them, hiding its face behind a scrim of clouds and casting a dark pall over the world around Ruth that seemed deeper, more ominous, than it ever had before.

At the corner, where Tina's yard met her neighbors, Ruth stepped up on a stump to sneak a peek. The back of Tina's house was dark, including the small black eye that was the window over the sink. The gate leading into the backyard, latched. Though it was a pool of shadows nestled in even deeper shadows, the back yard was quiet, seemingly undisturbed by their game night rival.

419

Yet, peering over the fence into the darkness, she found herself thinking about Tom. He'd changed over the past few years, diminished somehow by retirement – and his sense of humor, along with his tongue, had sharpened into a painful edge, but he was still her Tom. After the years that had passed, everything they had been through together, she wanted him next to her now. The need to talk to him, tell him what was happening, was a potent, almost physical requisite pressing down on her.

"How'd we come to this, Tom?" she asked the night and jumped at the sound of her own voice.

Listening for furtive sounds, she lifted a little higher over the fence and scanned the shadows for the slightest sign of movement.

Nothing.

She let out a little squeal of surprise as the light over the kitchen sink flared to life and almost fell from her perch on the stump. Tina's face, drawn and pale in the harsh light of the kitchen, peered out into the darkness before moving away.

With Tina inside and Phyllis standing watch in a corner of the front yard, Ruth slipped through the gate and took up a place in the darkest corner of the yard. Unless the fiend was already in Tina's house, hiding, they would see him no matter which direction he chose to strike from. If she had followed the plan, Tina had left both entrances unlocked and started a pot of coffee. She would also have armed herself with one of the very tools the game master seemed to favor.

They had the upper hand; it was his move and they had but to wait him out.

So why did she feel like a fish in a barrel, just waiting for that silent hook to enter the water and rip her from her world? Ruth tried to shake the feeling off, but as time slipped by and the shadows in the yard shifted, the feeling that the game master had made a move that she hadn't seen coming became a certainty.

From where she hunkered down, she could see only a small patch of the kitchen through the lit window, framed by its sunflower curtains. As her unease began to grow into an echo of the panic she'd felt earlier, she eased herself into a slinking, standing position. Flinching and watching the shadows as her joints popped, loud as gunfire in the stillness of the night, she eased closer to the house.

The small patch of wall framed in the window widened until she could see one delicately carved chair sitting at the table and part of the hutch behind it. Closer still, she could see the full length of the table and hutch, and as she got even closer, she could see the countertop and oven, yet there was no sign of Tina.

Hoping Tina had simply gone to the bathroom – a need that had begun to grow in Ruth with maddening urgency – yet expecting to find her prone body near the table, her singular rook cupped in her palm, Ruth felt herself drawn closer to the window. A breath locked in her chest as she raised herself up on the sill and prepared herself for the loss of yet another friend.

The floor was empty. Not a single dust ball or speck of blood could be found, yet Tina had still not come back into the kitchen. She should have been relieved. *Should have been.* Instead, the dread continued to grow. The panicky little flight of the butterflies in her chest transformed into the flutter of birds wings.

When Tina failed to come back after several minutes, Ruth moved to the corner of the fence that bordered the front yard, hooked her toes on the brace and hoisted herself up. "Phyllis, I—"

Phyllis wasn't there.

Ruth's eyes searched the looming shadows, but there was no sign of her. Easing back down to the ground, casting a suspicious eye on the gathering pre-dawn darkness, Ruth's mind raced in time with her anxious heartbeat. Was it possible that both women had been caught off guard and she'd heard nothing of the struggle? Never in her life. At least one of them would have gotten a cry out and there would be some sign, blood or otherwise. Phyllis was no slacker, still trim, fit and in great shape from years of teaching P.E. There would have been a fight, and a good one... unless...

Ruth raced back to the window and looked in one more time before running to the back gate. If one of her dear friends had been the game master this entire time, the other would have been caught completely unaware. Casting her mind back as she hit the alley behind the houses and ran for her own, she realized there had been no evidence of a struggle in the lonely kitchens of her other two friends. Not a single overturned chair or canister. From all appearances, Frank had slept through the entire thing. Who else would Myrna have been so comfortable with in her kitchen than a dear friend?

She hesitated at the corner, searching the deeper darkness around the intersection for any sign of her friends before limping across the road toward home. Replaying the last meeting with the two, sitting at the bar in Phyllis's home, she struggled to wrap her mind around which one could do such a horrible thing.

Had it been Tina who first renounced calling the police? No, of course not. Ruth herself had been unable to make the call, for fear of being singled out. Likewise, it had been Ruth who had felt as if the value of her life had fallen like autumn leaves as she grew older, not Phyllis. And then there was the blue hoodie. Now that her mind was twisting and turning, feeding on itself and second guessing everything, a low voice in her head asked, *Was it not familiar to you?*

It was, but her frantic thoughts couldn't pinpoint why. It had been just a simple blue, hoodie, several sizes too big for the frame that wore it. As to the other questions, the answer was neither. She'd known both women since childhood, played poker with them every Friday night, and had gotten into plenty of mischief with her friends over the years. Neither of them seemed capable of such brutal duplicity. On the news when a serial killer was finally identified and caught, everyone said they would never have suspected, such a quiet neighbor, they were a good friend… all that blather that you never believe because there should have been some sign of the animal within. Yet she couldn't match either face to the horror that had torn her little world apart.

II

Slowing as she drew near her back gate, the hair on the back of her neck stood at attention, as if she'd been standing in the sun and a drifting cloud had cast a shadow over her. As she fumbled the key from her pocket, determined not to drop it, her eyes were in constant motion, searching the gloom for any sign she was walking right into the hands of the game master.

Her brain screamed to slow down, be stealthy and quiet, but she could feel herself hanging over the abyss of hysteria. The closer she drew to her back door and her dear Tom, the closer she slipped toward the edge. When at least she mated the key to the lock, the soft laughter behind her pulled a sob loose and tears fell, the first since finding the bodies of her friends.

She pulled the key free, tempted to hurl it at the woman standing behind her.

As if reading this thought, Phyllis laughed again. "No, you don't. Open the door and let's go in and have a chat."

"What if I don't?" Ruth asked. "What if I don't want you anywhere near Tom?"

"Ah, the sudden concern about Tom after all the years you've spent complaining about him. I couldn't care less about Tom. Didn't I leave Frank sleeping, oblivious in the next room?" Phyllis laughed again and moved up behind her, digging something sharp into Ruth's back. "Besides, what's to stop me from killing you out here and then using the spare key under your begonias to go and kill Tom?"

"Why are you doing this?" Ruth sobbed. "What have we done to you?"

"You said it yourself, Ruth. Sometimes it's better to die too young than suffer being too old. Now open the door or I *will* invite Tom to play the game."

Ruth slid the key back into the lock and after a deep breath turned the knob.

"And if you scream or try to wake him up, I'll kill you both."

Of this, Ruth had no doubt. When the door opened, Ruth moved to the far side of the kitchen and turned to look at her friend in the dim light from the microwave nightlight, before hitting the switch and letting the fluorescents chase away the shadows. "I don't understand."

"Are you really so thick it isn't obvious by now?" Phyllis moved to Ruth's side of the kitchen and Ruth backed into the corner, as far away as she could get. "You of all people should get it. Didn't you tell me just last night that you wished they'd just put you in a home and get it over with? Your husband has grown tired of you. Your daughter smothers you, giving up her valuable time with her husband and kids because she has to take care of you. Your life has no value anymore. You're a burden, a heavy stone hanging around the necks of the people you're supposed to love, but all you do is whine about poor little you."

Ruth was shocked to hear herself say, "That's crap. Yeah, I've been whining and feeling sorry for myself, but Deb didn't whine, and Myrna loved her life. What is it about them that you hated so much? Why did you feel the need to end their suffering?"

"What do they contribute to the world now?" Phyllis hissed and took a step forward, forcing Ruth to press her back harder into the corner. "What good are they now that society doesn't want them anymore?"

"You're all of three years younger than me, Phyllis! Tina was only five years older than you! What are you going to do with that king? Finish us off and then kill yourself? I think you're full of crap!"

"Shut up!" Phyllis yelled and lunged, the knife cutting through the fabric of Ruth's shirt, but missing the skin as Ruth jerked left, putting the table between them.

"You're jealous!" Ruth nearly yelled in her surprise and edged around the table, trying to keep it between them. "Oh my God, you're jealous! Deb might have one foot in the grave, but she has a family. Myrna and Myra had each other, and Frank. I have Tom and Lilly, and my grandkids. Tina has her grandkids. Who do you have?"

"Shut up!"

"You have nobody! You're alone and you're scared! And whose fault is that? Whose choice was that?"

Phyllis yelled again, feinting left and shoving a chair out of her way to go right. She cornered Ruth at the far end of the table, the knife raised high as the bedroom door crashed open.

Tom stood there, still in his boxers, holding Ruth's bloody clothes in one hand and his pistol in the other. His sleep-shrouded eyes were wide with confusion and fear as he yelled out. "What the hell?"

As soon as Phyllis looked toward the banging door, Ruth grabbed the largest toadstool canister from the bench and slammed it against her head. Phyllis, already on the move, was only clipped by it, as a cloud of fine white powder filled the air. She spun, stumbled, and then regained her footing, putting the table between them again as she turned to Tom. "Tom, she killed them! She killed all of them and she's trying to kill me! She's going to kill you, too… then Lilly and the grandbabies! *Shoot* her!"

Enraged further by the look of dull shock in Tom's eyes, Phyllis roared and lunged at Ruth. The gunshot was deafening in the small kitchen. Ruth cried out as Phyllis was spun around and thrown against the counter. The spray of blood hit the spilled flour in bright points, sending little poofs of the white powder into the air. Ruth's mind sent up a frenzied image of the Red Queen in *Alice in Wonderland* before the world grayed at the edges and she slid down the cabinets.

III

In the end, it was Tom who made the call. The sheriff's deputies had been gentle as they questioned her and loaded her into the back of a deputy's car. Ruth knew most of them, had tried to teach them to love the works of such writers as T.S. Eliot and Emily Dickenson in bygone years. Most had been more interested in football, or the cheerleaders, than good literature, but they'd been good kids back then and were good kids still as they fingerprinted her, gave her warm coffee, and questioned her in a little room at the Sheriff's Department for more than four hours.

Exhaustion had taken hold on the ride to the county seat, but it did not begin to pull her down until she, at last, received the news that Tina's injuries had been critical, but they'd gotten to her in time. She would heal, at least physically. It seemed that in her rush to finish the game with the one player she had left to her, Phyllis had stabbed Tina only once.

Ruth sat with her head resting on the table, half dozing, when the door opened and Tom walked in, carrying another helping of coffee. He sat across from her for several long moments before arching one bushy eyebrow. "Poker, huh? All these years?"

Ruth offered a sad laugh and shook her head. "I'm so sorry I hid it from you, Tom. Sorrier still that I wasn't a good wife, calling you Tom the Toad."

"Sorry?" Tom laughed, his eyes dancing as he reached across the table and took her hands in his. "Do you remember the field trip in the third grade? Went down to the wetlands?"

"Oh my, yes," Ruth laughed with him.

"The way you chased those little frogs around, I used to think if she could love me like she loved those stupid toads, that'll be enough. And you did. Calling me a toad was never an insult, Ruthie. Never think it."

He moved to her side of the table and wrapped his arms around her shoulders. She leaned her head against him and cried softly. "As far as not being a good wife, I can't imagine anyone else I'd rather spend my life with. Old woman, you're my best friend, always have been. And I've been too comfortable, too... satisfied. I've not been paying attention to the way you've been feeling. For that, my love, it's me who owes *you* an apology. I can't promise to turn into some Don Juan, but I'll try not to take you for granted."

"If I ever get out of here…" She wiped her tears from her cheeks and leaned back. "Do you think they're going to arrest me?"

Tom laughed. "I tried to get them to keep you, but they've already told me I have to take you home. Shoot, Lilly's already got the kitchen cleaned up."

"Oh, no…"

"Cut it out, woman." Tom snapped, then gently lifted her chin up so she'd meet his eyes. "I heard what Phyllis said and you ought'a know better. How many years and tears do we have invested in our Lilly Pad? Far as I can tell, she owes us."

Ruth stood up and hugged him before letting him lead her to the door. He stopped with his hand on the knob and gave her a wink. "Maybe, in a few weeks, when you feel up to it… maybe we'll have us a little picnic down at Dewer's Pond."

"Is it even still there?" Ruth asked, surprised.

"Yup." He looked sheepishly at his Dockers, then back up before kissing her on the tip of her nose. "I drive by once in a while to check the place out. Good times, those were. Good memories."

"I guess I've been so focused on growing old and useless—,"

"Speak for yourself." He laughed. "I'm a long way from old yet."

"I wasn't paying attention to anything but how I was feeling."

"You and me, both. But we see it now, and if we see it, we can fix it."

About the Author

Miranda Nading is a southern Nevada transplant from Wyoming. She currently lives and works in the Lake Mead National Recreation Area. When not writing or working, she can be found reading, scuba diving, exploring, or getting up to mischief. Her published works include Echoes of Harmony, Caliban, Canyon Echoes, and the emergent Extinction Series.

A. L. Awtrey

Text Copyright © 2016 A. L. Awtrey

Tomas Salazar sailed into Key West on his charter boat, only intending to stay for a week or two. Then he met the beautiful and talented Kyla singing at the Parrot Dice Bar and Grill and stayed for five years, taking charters to make ends meet and hoping Kyla would eventually return his affection.

Kyla appears to be a woman in her mid-twenties, but is actually an eternal elemental water spirit called an Ondine. Her kind were the truth behind legends like mermaids and the Sirens of Greek myth, which makes playing music in a beach side bar the perfect cover.

When Veto Quesada comes into the bar, Tomas immediately recognizes the danger he represents. To earn the money to buy his boat, Tomas smuggled for the cartels and only ever feared the dead-eyed enforcers who killed for money.

Tomas warns Kyla off when she becomes fascinated with a human seemingly immune to the power of her voice. Her fascination draws Veto's attention and Tomas must risk everything to keep her safe.

A. L. Awtrey

When The Water Burns

By

A. L. Awtrey

A. L. Awtrey

Acknowledgements

For my own muse, Hala, who keeps me singing.

A. L. Awtrey

Chapter One: Tomas

Tomas felt a shiver up his spine the instant the guy walked in the bar. He was dressed like the other tourists in a guayabera shirt, khaki shorts, and brown leather sandals, but there was an awareness in his unblinking expression that tugged at Tomas' memory.

As he paused the doorway, the guy scanned the bar, glancing behind the door before walking in. Spotting a free table in the corner, he glided through the crowded bar like a shark splitting the surf and sat with his back against the old red brick wall.

Tomas turned away before his scrutiny drew unwanted attention. He'd had to do some sketchy work in the past to pay for the freedom his fifty foot charter boat gave him. Back when he still felt young and invulnerable, the only people who ever scared him were the dead-eyed enforcers for the drug cartels he smuggled for. That guy in the corner looked like an enforcer and Tomas hoped he wasn't working because if he was someone was going to die.

He considered going back to the boat where he lived to avoid getting involved, but just then Kyla came into the bar carrying her guitar. She had gorgeous auburn hair framing her face, deep blue eyes, and always exuded a kind of crackling, elemental energy. She smiled when she saw him sitting at his usual table and he smiled back despite himself.

The first night Tomas came to the Parrot Dice Bar and Grill was to meet a potential charter. Kyla had been playing quietly next to the main bar for most of the night, but when she started singing the raucous atmosphere stilled. Her voice had a rich, sensual quality that reached deep inside and hooked him through his heart like a fish on a line. Instead of moving on after a few jobs like he'd done for years, he'd stayed in Key West, always promising himself he'd leave soon.

Tomas signalled the old bartender by raising his empty bottle and tipping it at Kyla who was just sitting down across from him.

"Thanks, Tomas." After sitting her deep blue Ovation guitar to lean against her chair, she put her elbows on the table to study his face. "How was the fishing today?" she asked in her soft, lyrical brogue.

"Good. Caught a marlin. The guy just took a picture with it and then released it." Tomas knew Kyla was a little hippy-dippy and didn't like when people mounted trophy fish for display.

"Evenin', y'all." The old bartender slid a couple of bottles of Honey Bottomed Blonde on their table.

"Thanks, Mitch," Tomas said, then sipped the cold, sweet beer.

"We got fresh grouper tonight. If y'all want some, lemme know." Old Mitch gave Kyla a pat on the shoulder, then headed back to the bar with a smile on his face.

As soon as he was out of earshot, Tomas leaned towards Kyla. "Don't be obvious, but do you see that tough looking guy with the buzz cut in the corner?"

Kyla's eyes flickered that way. "Yeah. So?"

"He's trouble. Stay away from him."

Kyla grinned and said, "Don't be jealous. It doesn't suit you."

"I'm serious." Tomas tried to hide it, but he was always jealous when Kyla picked up some tourist for a fling.

She claimed to have a rule about not dating locals, but he had just arrived in Key West when she told him that. It turned out she knew him better than he did himself because he was still hanging around her five years later. "I think he's a heavy hitter. Real bad news."

440

"I'm a big girl," Kyla said with an amused smirk. When she sipped her beer, her eyes flickered the guy's direction again.

Tomas mentally kicked himself for pointing the guy out. There was no telling Kyla anything she didn't want to hear. "Just be careful."

"I always am." She pulled her pile of wild curls through her hands and put a scrunchy around it to make a loose ponytail. "I gotta go play."

"That's why I'm here," Tomas sighed as she laughed and grabbed the neck of her guitar.

She swayed over to the stool near the end of the main bar. Mitch flipped on the spotlight as she sat down. The bright light brought out the colors in her sparkly blue spaghetti strap top. The cream colored peasant skirt swirled around her calves as she sat the guitar on her lap. After checking the tuning, she picked an upbeat arpeggio and smiled out at the crowd.

Kyla played what she wanted and rarely took requests. The songs spanned a wide range of years and styles, anything from folk to classical to modern. Judging from her youthful appearance, he had initially assumed she would play more modern pop, but she seemed to favor the kinds of jigs and reels her Irish ancestors probably danced to.

The song she started singing was unfamiliar to him, but the effect it had on the crowd was immediate. Even without amplification, her voice cut through the noise and left smiling silence in its wake. The lilting gaelic lyrics were incomprehensible, but still seemed to paint pictures of love and home. People nodded and tapped along with the rhythm and a few brave souls got up to dance in front of her. She smiled broadly, turning her attention to the room and seemed to glow in the warm spotlight.

441

Tomas risked a glance at the dangerous guy in the corner. He was rapt, but his expression was closer to a predatory hunger than the open smiles she created in others. This was exactly what Tomas had been worried about when he pointed the guy out to Kyla. There was blood in the water now and he was circling for the kill.

Rubbing his face with his palms, Tomas tried to still his racing heart. Kyla was in more danger than she would admit. In the past, when he knew she was going to take someone upstairs to her apartment or back to a resort, he'd leave so he wouldn't have to watch it happen. He could admit he loved her to himself, but was never brave enough to risk their friendship over his desire for more.

Sometimes he would find an auburn haired tourist looking for a vacation fling and closed his eyes to pretend it was Kyla. It rarely helped, but it was all he could do to keep from going crazy sometimes. That wouldn't work tonight. She was going to go with that guy, he could feel it, and he was going to hurt her somehow. A premonition washed over him and rang his heart like a ship's claxon.

"Damn it, Kyla," he muttered and settled in for a long night.

Chapter Two: Kyla

The bright spotlight made it hard to see clearly, but Kyla couldn't miss the fact her voice didn't seem to charm the man Tomas had pointed out earlier. The puzzle intrigued her more than the man did himself. He was attractive enough, but nondescript. She probably wouldn't have noticed him for his looks alone.

He had short hair, like the men in the military always seemed to favor. Too short to grab, but long enough to pad a helmet or keep the sun from burning their scalp. The image of a Roman Centurion she'd once known flashed through her mind, but she couldn't recall any details about him other than his short brown hair. He was just one of thousands of people she'd known over her long existence.

Kyla only remembered the most recent past clearly, but it never bothered her. She lived in an eternal *now* that had no beginning or end. Her most distant memories was of a time when only plants covered the land and the sea had been filled with life. After that she could recall awesome creatures that dominated the land and sea until a bright light came from the sky and ushered in decades of darkness.

But that was all long before humans came to be. They were just another kind of animal until she noticed them making interesting things. That drew her away from her watery home to take their form so she could pass among them unnoticed. This allowed her to learn their languages and songs. And that was when she discovered she could charm them into doing anything he wanted. Life became much more interesting after that.

She focused her attention on the man in the corner as she sang the love song, but he remained a blank spot in her mind. It was like he wasn't there at all to her deeper senses and that puzzled her. She may have encountered others like him in the past, but couldn't recall them now. It didn't matter, he was right over there and he fascinated her.

After singing a few more songs, she got up and smiled warmly at the loud praise of the crowd around her. On the whole, she enjoyed spending time with humans. They provided an endless diversion for her.

Although she didn't need to eat, she loved the flavors and scents of their food. And while she couldn't reproduce like they did, she enjoyed being intimate with them. The ones who fascinated her the most were the hardest ones to understand. When they gave her their water, even through a simple kiss, it opened them to her understanding and, ultimately, her control.

She felt compelled to solve the puzzle of the man in the corner and hoped that his water would provide the answer. But since she couldn't compel him, she would have to entice him into giving her a taste. The man watched her walking up with a wide grin and a shark's eye, but she feared no predator because she could not die.

"Join me?" he asked as she walked up.

"I'm Kyla," she said as she sat down opposite him and leaned her guitar against the table.

"I'm Veto." He kept his eyes on hers rather than examining her form the way most men would. "May I buy you a beer?"

"Yes, please." Kyla was close enough to catch his scent. It was redolent of oil and smoke, reminding her of the machines they all used. Beneath that was the salty tang of blood, but it was not his own.

Veto waved over the old bartender who frowned at Kyla as he approached, likely for her poor choice of company. "Two more, please," he said.

Kyla gave her old friend a reassuring smile and nodded for him to bring the beers. When he went back to the bar, she returned her attention to the man at the table. He exuded confidence and control, not fidgeting under her cool scrutiny. She noticed he never seemed to blink, holding her gaze without looking away.

"You have a lovely voice." His own voice was carefully modulated. Usually humans provided a vocal subtext that she could read better than a lie detector. Veto gave nothing away of his true feelings.

"Thank you," she said. "Are you in town for business or pleasure?"

"Why not both?" Again, his voice gave her no clue. It was maddening.

Old Mitch sat the beers down and walked away without a word. Kyla could feel Mitch's unease like a bubbling spring pushing through otherwise solid earth.

"Why not," Kyla agreed and raised her bottle. "To pleasure."

"And business." Veto said as he tapped the neck of his bottle to hers.

"So what is your business?" Kyla asked, pushing hard on his impenetrable shell with her mind. If she could find an opening somewhere, she could get him talking and figure him out.

"Contract services," he said without blinking. Kyla felt something quiver in him. Something moved in his darkness, like a writhing ball of eels, then it was gone. "And you play in a bar?"

"I do," she said and took another sip of her beer.

The water in the beer carried memories of boiling heat. She could also taste the lives of the tiny creatures who were suspended in it. Beer wasn't very interesting. The process to make it destroyed its long memory.

"Is that all you do?"

Kyla amused herself by imagining what would

445

happen if she told him the truth. *I'm an eternal water spirit that guards these waters and any creature who lives in or around them. If you're a threat to those I protect, I'll kill you.*

Perhaps she should eliminate him just to be careful, but the need to understand his nature held her back. He could be some other kind of spirit, but he certainly wasn't another elemental spirit. The Gnomes of the earth, Sylphs of the air, and Salamanders of the fire all felt different than her fellow Ondines, but none of them were so blank as this human.

"I'm also interested in protecting the environment," she said.

He nodded. Relying on his expressions alone made her feel what she imagined a blind human would feel.

"An environmentalist, of course. You look the type."

"The type?" she asked.

"I met a few hippies in the rain forests in South America. They were committed to their cause to their very end."

"As am I," she said. She finished her beer and grabbed her guitar by the neck. "Thanks for the beer and the company."

"If you'd like some more company later, I'll stick around," he said with the same unwavering gaze and predatory smile.

Maybe if she could get him alone, she could tease out his secret. "I'd like that."

Chapter Three: Tomas

Watching Kyla chatting with that killer made his chest ache. Tomas couldn't resist glancing at them across the room, but he only began breathing normally when she stood and picked up her guitar to resume playing. Fear ate him hollow. There was nothing he could do to change her collision course.

Old Mitch came over with a plate of grouper and slid it onto his table. "That guy's trouble with a capital T."

"She thinks she knows better than me," Tomas answered. Kyla had already been playing at Mitch's bar for years so he knew her just as well. "I told her to stay away."

Old Mitch gave him a watery, blue-eyed stare. "You don't know much about women, do you?"

Tomas sat up fast at his sharp comment, immediately offended, but then slowly slumped back to rest his elbows on the table when he realized it was true. "No."

"I've known Kyla a long time. I don't like that guy, but she's gonna do what she's gonna do."

"I think that guy works for the cartels," Tomas leaned in to whisper.

Old Mitch's sarcastic reply was, "No shit.

"We gotta do something!"

"Dude, you really don't know women," Old Mitch sighed as he walked back to the bar.

Tomas ate the spicy grouper despite his lack of appetite. And like a cool breeze on a hot day, Kyla's voice soothed him as she sang her last set. She played a soul stirring ballad that kept his attention so focused that he didn't notice when the killer sat down at his table.

"You love her," the man stated matter-of-factly and Tomas jumped like he'd been speared.

447

The killer's brown eyes were so dark they looked black as they bore into him. It stole his voice.

"I saw you watching us talk." Though his voice was low and steady like a friendly conversation, the threatening undercurrent dried Tomas' mouth. "She isn't yours."

"She's not yours, either," Tomas whispered at last through his tight throat.

"Not yet," he said with a toothy grin. "But she will be."

Applause drew his attention away from the intense stare as Kyla walked up and joined them at the table.

"Tomas, this is Veto. He's in contract services," Kyla said as she leaned the guitar against the table and stole Tomas' beer to take a sip. "Veto, Tomas is a local charter captain."

"We were just discussing you," Veto said with his pleasant mask firmly in place.

"I'm flattered," she said and caught Tomas' eyes. "Relax. It's okay."

Tomas suddenly felt like he'd just taken a huge bong hit. Her words filled him like warm smoke, soothing the places his fear had eaten away. Stunned to silence, he sat there trying to focus his thoughts when Kyla turned to stare at Veto.

"My set's over. You still interested in some company tonight?" she asked.

"I don't want to intrude if you had plans with Tomas."

"Oh, he's just a good friend. Besides, I don't date locals." Kyla stood and picked up her guitar. "Let me go put this away and I'll meet you out front in five minutes."

Once Kyla left the bar, Veto turned to study Tomas with a puzzled frown. "Where did your fear go?"

Tomas pushed at the fog in his mind, but still

448

couldn't focus his thoughts. He knew he should be concerned about Kyla leaving with Veto, but it was like trying to light wet driftwood on fire. "I don't know."

"It doesn't matter." Veto let his mask slip to show the shark lurking beneath. "I'm going to enjoy your *friend*. You can have whatever's left over when I'm done with her."

The fog lifted slightly as he clung to his love for Kyla like flotsam in a storm. "Don't hurt her."

"Pain and pleasure are two sides of the same coin, and I spend freely. Which side faces up in the end isn't my concern. I enjoy them both."

"Please," Tomas begged as Veto got up and strode from the bar without a backward glance.

Fighting the lethargy that still lingered, Tomas leaned on the table as he forced himself to stand. Kyla had no idea what she was getting into. He had to keep her safe somehow, but could barely walk. He'd only had a couple of beers, but it felt like he was at the bottom of a long bender. Had Veto slipped him something?

Walking carefully into the night, Tomas saw Kyla and Veto heading towards the waterfront resort just up the beach from the bar. He kept them in view, but couldn't catch up fast enough to follow them inside. Collapsing on a bench near the entrance to the resort, Tomas bent over and tried not to retch.

His imagination painted horrific pictures of what might happen, but at least his mind was beginning to work again. Focusing on the crushing pain of Kyla being with a man like Veto pushed the fog back even more. Why would she want to be with someone like that?

Tomas was a fool. He should go to his boat and just sail away. There were thousands of other ports in the Caribbean where a charter boat could earn his living. It had been easy before he came to Key West and walked into that bar. Before he'd seen her and heard her sing.

His life had been an uncomplicated series of transactions. He loved the sea. Loved fishing and seeing new places. Now his anchor was stuck and he couldn't go anywhere. His only option was to cut and run, but Kyla had chains around his heart he couldn't break without breaking himself.

Sitting up as the nausea passed, Tomas stared up at the lighted windows towering above him. She needed him even if she wouldn't acknowledge it. And since he couldn't do anything else, he waited in the hope that when Neptune's price came due, it wouldn't include losing her.

Chapter Four: Kyla

Veto remained a puzzle. Most men desired her because her form was pleasing. Others she influenced with the power of her voice. She was used to seeing that attraction communicated in some way. At the very least she should have been able to read subtle cues in his voice, no matter what words he said. Veto was polite, glib, and utterly unreadable, leaving her to guess at what his intentions truly were.

One regret nagged at her as they waited for the elevator in the lobby of the resort. She had used her power to influence Tomas for the first time. She wanted to keep him from worrying until she could solve this mystery, but now she worried things would change between them.

Unlike almost all the men she'd known over the years, Tomas opened his heart to her from the beginning. Kyla could force anyone to love and obey her eventually, but it was a rare man who would give himself to her as a friend and companion of his own will. Eternity had become lonely and making humans into puppets offered no surcease. Worse, if she joined with him the way he wanted, the act would ultimately destroy the quality she valued most about him—his freedom.

Tomas always told good stories and cared deeply for her as a being, wanting nothing from her but friendship. She could read that as clearly as the ocean waves. It was comfortable to be with him. She dreaded the day he moved on or grew feeble and died, as they always did eventually. Feeling his memory fading away would be the closest thing to pain she could experience. Kyla pushed the uncomfortable thoughts away and returned her attention to Veto.

"Here we go," Veto said as he guided her into the

451

open elevator. She'd been to the resort with attractive and interesting tourists before for the pleasure they provided. The lobby was an open floorplan with large windows that showed the marina. Soft colors accented the decor in the comfortable suites that overlooked the water.

Kyla nodded and stepped into the closed metal box. She had never known fear, but elevators, cars, and other enclosed spaces made her yearn for open water. Veto entered and pressed the button for the top floor. When the elevator doors opened, Kyla felt relieved. She followed him out of the elevator towards his penthouse suite.

"Thank you," she said as he held the door to the suite open for her.

The room was lit by the glowing moon shining through the floor to ceiling windows. The large bed was covered with bright white covers that seemed to glow in the moonlight. A kitchen area near the door had fresh tropical flowers in a tall glass vase on the table. She walked towards the overstuffed sofa that faced the open sliding glass door to the balcony and sat down at one end.

"Would you care for a drink?" Veto asked as he turned on the light in the kitchen area. "I have water, white wine, or beer."

"Water is fine." Kyla smiled as she studied him. His movements were efficient as he took a glass from the cabinet, filled it with ice from the freezer, then filled it with water. He popped the top off of a beer and carried the bottle and glass to the couch.

Sitting down close to her, he handed her the glass. She sipped it, ignoring the bitter taste of the minerals in it. Earth might be her complimentary element, but that didn't mean she enjoyed it contaminating the water she drank.

Veto studied her in turn with a faint look of confusion. It was the first genuine emotion she'd seen on his face all night. "Who are you, Kyla?"

"A guitarist in a bar on the beach." She knew what he was really asking, but feigned ignorance. "And who are you, Veto?"

He pursed his lips and didn't answer her question. "You're not afraid of me."

"Should I be?" She didn't hide the amusement that bubbled up in her tone. It was absurd that a human would cause her fear. His apparent confusion shifted to a shuttered rage at her question.

"If you knew who I really was, then yes, you should be."

"And who are you, Veto?" she repeated and sipped from her glass of water again.

"I'm a killer," he said as he watched her carefully.

His bald statement made her chuckle. Why would she be afraid of a killer?

"You think I'm kidding? I've killed dozens of people—men, women, it didn't matter to me. It's my job and I love my work."

Kyla had killed thousands in her long life and smirked at his arrogance. Men who thought to take what she would not give them drowned when she forced her living water into their lungs. Others tried to take her possessions or abuse those under her protection and met similar fates. She could not be injured. She could not die. And this mere human thought she should fear him?

She felt his rage boiling to the surface giving her another unexpected glimpse into the inky darkness deep inside him. Again, the image of a writhing ball of black eels came to her mind. She was used to seeing the perverse nature of men in their thoughts, but his darkness was alien to her experience.

"I could kill you now before you could cry out for

453

help."

"No, I don't think so," she said evenly.

His rage was gone in a blink, replaced again with confusion. "You truly do not fear me," he whispered as if to himself. "You are a treasure. I think I'll keep you."

He stood and gripped her arm. Kyla allowed him to pull her to her feet and drag her across the suite towards the bathroom. She wasn't physically strong, but it hardly mattered since there was nothing he could do to harm her. When he pushed her into the bathroom and blocked the doorway with his body, his expression was finally open to her.

"You will stay here until I pack my car, then I will take you somewhere so I can explore how far your lack of fear goes."

"Kiss me before you leave," she whispered, feigning desire.

He stepped close and pressed his lips against hers. She opened her mouth against his and drank him in. Images flashed in her mind as she pierced his walls. Veto dealt out death, cruelty, and pain, but his only emotion was a detached curiosity. She saw he was clearly human, but broken in some fundamental way.

Where humans were a balance of both thoughts and emotions, Veto was coldly logical. Instead of a smooth palette of desires and feelings, Kyla only saw that he possessed the primary drives of lust and rage. And while he wasn't capable of experiencing love or fear, he understood them well enough to use against others.

Kyla now understood why she couldn't manipulate him and it made her uneasy. He was dangerous to those she protected and was immune to her influence. The decision to end his life was a simple one to make at that point.

Before she could act, Veto shoved Kyla back to fall

on the floor and wiped his mouth with the back of his hand. His walls were up again and she could no longer read his intentions, but she did see an odd expression on his face, almost like he knew what she had done to him.

He slammed the bathroom door before she could get up. When Kyla stood to open the door, she saw Veto had reversed the knob so the privacy lock was on the outside leaving her locked inside the small room.

Rather than panic, Kyla raged as she stepped into the shower and turned on the water. As the water flowed around her and wet her clothes, she willed her body to dissolve into its natural state. Joining her form with the water spray, she left her clothes soaking in the tub and flowed down the shower drain. Once she was free, she would return and take his life.

A. L. Awtrey

456

Chapter Five: Tomas

It was a long, miserable night for Tomas sitting on the cold cement bench outside the resort. The fog in his head had finally lifted, leaving his thoughts all too clear as he imagined what Veto might be doing to Kyla upstairs. It wasn't just jealousy. Kyla had always made it clear she didn't want to be more than friends.

Despite her personal strength and character, she'd always had a certain naivete that brought out Tomas' protective nature. Other women her age seemed to be fixated on fashion and social media. They were mercurial and eternally attached to phones or tablets, taking selfies everywhere to bring the world's attention to their little lives.

Kyla had an old soul. She didn't own any electronics that Tomas had seen. Her conversations were often light, but never shallow or distracted. She always appeared to be exactly where she wanted to be, and Tomas was grateful it was so often with him. Except now he was afraid he might lose her forever.

As soon as the sun lightened the sky, he rubbed his face and felt the rough growth of his beard. He needed coffee. Tomas decided to sneak into the resort's hotel for a cup but before he could, Veto emerged from the automatic doors pulling a red rolling suitcase and carrying an aluminum attaché case. Tomas stepped behind a pillar to avoid being seen.

Veto walked to a large black sedan and put his bags in the back seat. He appeared energized and happy as he walked back to the resort. Tomas watched him go through the sliding doors then sprinted to his car.

Veto had locked the car doors, so Tomas moved to hide near the trunk. If Kyla didn't appear before Veto tried to leave, Tomas intended to question him. If she were injured or dead, Tomas intended to make Veto pay, no matter the danger to himself.

He waited for what seemed like forever. Ants crawled around his sandals. The ocean breeze swept his hair into a tangle. Eventually, rapid footsteps and an angry mutter announced Veto's return. Tomas controlled his fear and stood to confront the man who had taken Kyla away.

"You," Veto growled and veered towards Tomas at the rear of the car.

"Where is she?" they both said at the same moment. Then Veto smiled and Tomas felt his stomach roll over.

"How did she escape a locked bathroom if you didn't help her?" Veto slowed until he stood still.

"I…" Tomas felt a thrill that interrupted his response. *Kyla escaped!* "I don't know."

Veto squinted as he studied Tomas' face. "Tell me what you know about her now or I will make you suffer." He gripped Tomas by the shirt and dragged him to the rear car door.

"I don't know anything." The blow to his jaw felt numb at first, but when his head knocked back against the car, pain exploded through his skull.

"You must know something useful about her. Tell me and I'll stop."

The second blow against his lips was hard enough to fill his mouth with blood. Tomas held his tongue. Then a third blow against his left eye knocked his head back hard enough to shatter the car's side window.

Tomas rocked back to give Veto a bloody smile despite his fear and pain. "I've known Kyla for five years," he muttered through bruised lips. "And I hardly know anything about her at all. She loves nature. She plays guitar and sings in that old bar she lives above—" He stopped talking the second he saw Veto's eyes light up in victory. *Shit, shit, shit*, Tomas thought.

"Good enough," Veto smiled and slammed Tomas' forehead against the trunk of the car, and Tomas knew no more.

A. L. Awtrey

Chapter Six: Kyla

Kyla reformed her body from the water of the surf as she stepped onto the beach. Fists clenched in rage, she walked naked toward the Parrot Dice Bar and Grill on the other side of the road. It had taken hours for her to flow through the pipes and sewers of Key West. Hours spent learning more about the people of the city than she ever wanted to know. Hours that delayed her revenge on the human who thought to possess her.

A few early risers were on the the beach as the sun boiled just below the horizon. Seeing a nude woman walking across the beach wasn't such an odd occurrence, but people still stared at her. Kyla ignored them all as she passed around the side of the bar to the stairs that led up to her tiny apartment.

The hidden key above the door let her into her one room apartment, then she slammed the door shut behind her. Veto would have a long time to think before she let him die. She would teach him the very lesson he sought to teach her. Perhaps she could force him to understand as she filled his lungs with her living water. She would choke the life out of him slowly, giving him just enough breath to remain conscious until the very end.

She dressed in shorts and an old t-shirt before slipping on some sandals. The trappings of humanity would be necessary to blend in so she could take him by surprise. He might be able to overpower her physically, but Kyla wasn't limited to her physical strength. No one could grasp water long enough to escape its relentless power. She was like the tide in that way—never tiring, never stopping, wearing down hard rocks until even the mountains crumbled before her.

And Veto would crumble. She pulled her loose

auburn hair back in a tie and glared at her reflection. She would make him beg before she let him die.

A sudden explosion of sound startled her before her apartment door burst open. Tomas fell to the floor in the doorway. His face was bruised, his lips torn, and his left eye swollen shut as he groaned on the floor. In the doorway stood Veto with a smoking gun pointing at Tomas.

"You may not fear what I plan to do to you, but do you fear for Tomas?" he asked as his unblinking eyes scanned her face.

In all her years, Kyla had never been overly concerned about individual humans. Years passed quickly for her and all the people around her seemed to age unto death overnight. They were fragile creatures, often dying from small cuts or coughs. And yet, here was Tomas who was suffering only because he knew her.

"I'm sorry," he wept as he rolled on his back. "I'm so sorry."

Kyla knelt beside him and touched his wounded face. She had never known him intimately, not even a kiss, but now her fingertips wiped away tears from his eyes. A *knowing* stronger than any she'd felt before ripped through her.

He had offered her friendship without reservation when they met, and now she felt him offering her something even more precious. It felt like a bright sun melting the fog at dawn and suddenly she *knew* his love. It suffused her being and filled her with a longing she could not name. His offering hung there, but nothing about it was forceful or intrusive. She could choose to accept it or not.

She looked up at Veto and for the first time in her life she knew fear. Not for herself, he was right about that. For Tomas. Veto could forever take him away and she would never know what this new thing she felt meant.

"Fine," she whispered. "I'll go with you if you leave Tomas here."

"Ah, but that will never do," Veto said as he relaxed at her acceptance. "Why would you stay with me if I don't possess him as well?"

Tomas leapt to his feet and rushed Veto. He knocked the gun out of his hand and pushed him down the stairs. He reached for Kyla's hand and yelled, "Come on!"

She ran with him, not knowing what else to do. Killing Veto was no longer as important as keeping Tomas safe. They rounded the edge of the bar and Tomas faltered, so Kyla put her arm around his back to keep them moving.

"Hurry," Tomas gasped. "I can get us away if we can make it to my boat.

They made it down the road to the entrance to the marina before she heard the first gunshot ring out. As they reached the key-coded gate the the docks, Kyla moved her body to shield Tomas from other potential shots. He quickly punched in the code and pulled her through. The gate slammed behind them, shutting Veto out.

Just as they reached his boat, another gunshot fired and Tomas stumbled. Kyla glanced back to see Veto aiming his gun through the chainlink fence, and she pushed Tomas into the boat. She'd gone out with him often enough to know how to cast off while he stumbled up to his pilot chair and started the engines.

Moments later, the boat was powering out of the marina and into the open water. Until that moment, Kyla hadn't noticed the blood cascading out of Tomas' upper back.

"Tomas!" She ran to him slumped over the wheel. "Tomas, we have to get you help."

"It's too late," he whispered, barely audible over the engines and the wind. He turned his head to give her a weak smile. "At least you're safe. When I'm gone, take the boat and go far away. It's yours."

"Stop it! I don't even know how to drive this stupid thing," she said as unfamiliar feelings battered her heart.

Tomas had no way of knowing she was never in danger. Glancing around the horizon, she extended her senses into the water to find anyone who might help them. There were other ships nearby. She had to go get him help!

"I've loved you since the first time I saw you." The sincerity of his words struck her like a blow. "My only regret is that I was never brave enough to tell you until it was too late."

"I've known all along," she whispered and kissed his bruised lips. The rush of knowing came again as she tasted his tears and blood. He wasn't just offering his boat; she knew he was offering her his soul, just as openly as he had given his friendship. She could taste the intensity of his life. This moment made her own long existence pale by comparison. She'd never truly known her own life until she kissed his tears.

The magnitude of what he was offering filled her with terror for the first time in her life. If he should die, part of her would die with him. This memory of him dying would never fade like the rest of her memories and these new memories would torment her for eternity. She had to save him.

"I forbid you to die," she shouted at him and turned to leap off the boat. Her clothes fell to the deck as she transformed into her natural state. Like living quicksilver, she splashed into the ocean and raced towards a large boat miles in the distance. She could only tell it's size, and she hoped it would have someone who could help Tomas.

When she reached the white and red vessel, she transformed back into her human form to call out to the men on deck.

"Help! Help me! My friend has been shot and is bleeding to death!" She waved her hands and continued to shout until the engines cut and men lined up along the deck to throw her a life ring on a line. Ignoring their open stares at her nudity, she climbed aboard the boat.

"Someone's been shot, ya say?" one of the men asked.

Kyla pointed unerringly towards Tomas. She could feel him like he was part of her. "His name is Tomas and he's over there in a charter boat."

"I don't even see a boat," the man said as they brought her a blanket to wrap up in. "You'd have to be a really strong swimmer to get all the way over here."

"You have to trust me," she begged. "He's going to die if we don't reach him soon."

"Take her up to the wheel house and see if she can lead us there."

When the large vessel came within sight of Tomas' boat, Kyla was completely overwhelmed. She'd never had emotions batter her like this before. She'd watched humans try to handle these feelings for much of her existence, but it gave her no help in how to deal with them herself. She wept openly as their boat came alongside Tomas', and she continued weeping as the men boarded his boat to help stop his bleeding.

Knowing he was still alive and that someone would look after him, Kyla turned her new emotions to the man who threatened her and nearly killed Tomas. She would make Veto pay a price that no man had ever suffered before. Slipping away from the sailors who were focused on Tomas, she dropped her towel on the deck and leapt into the ocean.

Racing through the water back to the bar, the sea boiled around her. Kyla had never been so consumed with rage before, causing the water to swirl and froth around her. Focused on revenge, she burst from the surf with steam echoing her fury. She realized the raw energy pouring out of her was making the water burn white flames as she stalked onto the beach.

She ignored the gasps of humans around her as she walked across the sand leaving glass footprints in her wake. She didn't bother going to her room because she knew where Veto would be waiting. The bar wasn't busy at breakfast and Veto sat alone at the table he'd used the night before. He had a pleased smile on his face when he recognized her.

"I knew you'd come back to me," he said. "Fate brought us together."

Focusing her rage, she prepared to shift her form to drown the smug look off his face. His eyes followed her but his smile slipped as she approached. A worried expression escaped his control and he lifted a pistol from beneath the table.

"Stop," he commanded, but she ignored him. She was invulnerable and eternal. And Veto was going to die.

The loud gunshot filled the bar with an acrid smoke. Kyla felt like someone had shoved her and looked down to see a bubbling red hole in her chest. Puzzled, she lifted a finger to the wound as she paused. Confusion shuttered her thoughts as a harsh feeling grew out of that ugly hole that marred her breast.

"What?" she whispered to herself.

"Hey, what's going on here?" Old Mitch yelled as he came out of the back with a large shotgun.

He took one look at Kyla bleeding and immediately blew a chunk out of the brick wall by Veto's head. Veto ran for the door while Kyla struggled to understand the horrible sensation she felt in her chest.

"Mitch?" she gasped, her hands shaking as he ran to

466

her. "What happened to me?"

"That sonovabitch shot you," he announced and immediately pulled out his cell phone. "Lemme call for an ambulance. You sit down right here. Why are you naked?"

"Tomas," she said as her connection drew them together again. He wasn't breathing so she reached out to breathe for them both. "I need Tomas."

"And won't he be glad to hear *that*," Old Mitch muttered as he put the phone to his ear to call for help.

467

A. L. Awtrey

Chapter Seven: Tomas

"You should be dead," the doctor said. He had been saying a bunch of medical stuff that Tomas didn't understand, but he knew that last sentence was the absolute truth.

Tomas looked over at Kyla. She hadn't completely woken up from the surgery that had saved her life from Veto's gunshot, but she had refused to calm down until the staff moved her into the same room with him.

"I know," he whispered.

It hurt to take deep breaths and his shoulder blade was throbbing. Luckily his gunshot wound came from a small caliber pistol bullet or he would have died on his boat. He knew some cartel assassins favored small caliber pistols because they were quiet and easy to conceal. The bullets usually only had enough energy to penetrate once, leaving no exit wound and nasty bullet fragments bouncing all around.

"She's gonna be okay," the doctor said, seeing the direction of his stare. "The bullet didn't hit anything important and came out in one piece, unlike yours. So is she your girlfriend?"

Tomas shook his head, but didn't answer out loud.

"Yes," Kyla murmured with her eyes closed. "I'm his and he's *mine*."

The possessive way she said it warmed his heart.

The doctor chuckled. "Both of you need rest, but press the call button if you need anything else." He left the room and shut the door most of the way.

Kyla sighed and turned her head, opening her eyes to give Tomas a weak smile. "Hey."

"Hey," he replied as he drank in her face like a thirst-starved man.

His last clear memory was her jumping out of the boat and turning into something that looked like a splash of mercury. Nothing would convince him he had been hallucinating, but he also hadn't mentioned what he'd seen to anyone else. Especially the Coast Guard investigators who were confused by how she beat their cutter back to shore to get shot in a bar.

"So are you a superhero or something?" he asked.

"Well, I'm obviously not bulletproof," she sighed. "Not anymore, anyway."

"But you can change into water. That was how you got out of Veto's bathroom, wasn't it?"

She weighed him with her eyes. "Yes."

"Anything else?" he asked.

She nodded. "I used to be invulnerable, but something changed. I don't know what happened, but I think it has everything to do with you."

"Are you sure you're not a superhero?" he asked with a playful smile, trying to lighten the mood.

"I'm an Ondine. A water spirit." She looked down to pick at her fingernail. "This is all so confusing and overwhelming."

Tomas sat up carefully, pulling himself up with his left arm. After getting his feet on the floor, he leaned on the IV stand to shuffle across the room to her bed. Sitting down, he reached over to touch her face and moved a few strands of her auburn hair.

A connection between them zapped like a static shock. He could feel her confusion inside his head and wrapped it in the love he felt for her. She gasped and looked with wide-eyed wonder at him.

"How did you do that?" she whispered.

"Do what?" he chuckled.

"I can feel you," she whispered.

He leaned down and touched his lips to hers. The connection came again, stronger this time, and for Tomas it felt like coming home.

A. L. Awtrey

Chapter Eight: Veto

Veto was almost back to Miami after his business trip to Key West. He regretted killing the beautiful Kyla. He should have killed the old bartender for interfering, like he had Tomas, but things had gotten too complicated in the end to risk another murder. Besides, the old man didn't really know anything.

His job had been to deal with the person who'd stolen from his employer. Killing the guy and recovering the money had been the easy part, as it turned out. He'd stopped at a bar near his resort to have a beer and relax when everything had gone to hell.

The woman had been a mystery he felt compelled to solve. Everyone feared Veto Quesada, but in one afternoon she had sought him out and driven him crazy until he had to possess her. He was certain she was the special one he'd been waiting for his whole life. So many women over the years, so many disappointments, but Kyla had a potential that none of the others showed.

After locking her in the bathroom, he'd taken a short nap and then prepared to take her back to Miami with him. There had been no way out of the bathroom, not even through air vents or the plumbing access panel, but she was gone just the same when he opened the door.

It was the little mysteries that bugged him the most. Why was the shower running? Why had she left her wet clothes in the bathtub? It drove him crazy trying to figure it out, especially when she later appeared at the bar, *naked*, looking like an avenging angel out of a movie.

He had overreacted at her refusal to stop. He should have just knocked her out, but some deep instinct made him shoot her instead. In the end it didn't matter. She was just another dead woman now. Another disappointment. Nothing

473

to fixate over anymore.

He turned up the radio and stuck his elbow out the driver's side window of the car as he approached his beachside condominium. When the song ended, a news story caught his attention.

"This is radio Miami bringing the latin beat despite the heat. Breaking news out of Key West right now. A charter boat captain and a popular local musician have been shot by the same gunman. Both are currently in stable condition at the Keys Medical Center. Both the Coast Guard and local police are asking the public to be on the lookout for a Veto Quesada, a short-haired man of Hispanic descent, approximately five-foot ten. A sketch is available on our website. A reward has been offered for any information that leads to his capture."

Veto pursed his lips as he slowed down to make a u-turn on US 1. It would take him some time to get back to Key West. His employer would be most upset; he hated loose ends.

About the Author

Anthony has been writing novels for fun and profit since 2012. He's a member of the Central Florida Chapter of the Romance Writers of America and Florida Writers Association. When he's not writing, he's the CTO for a technology consultancy and a professional singer.

A. L. Awtrey

Thank You

On behalf of all the authors in this anthology, we would like to thank you for taking the time to read our stories. We hope you had as much fun reading them as we did writing them.

The best compliment you could give us would be to take the time to grant us a review. They are so appreciated by authors.

If you would like to meet the authors on Facebook, follow our Facebook page:
https://www.facebook.com/TOTHanthology

Thank you Kelly Abell at Select-O-Grafix for cover work on most of the stories and for formatting this wonderful endeavor

www.selectografix.com

Laura E. Perez, Publisher
Palmas Publishing
www.palmaspress.com

Thrill of the Hunt: A Collection of Suspenseful Tales

THRILL OF THE HUNT

A Collection of Suspenseful Tales

Foreword by Jana Oliver

L.E. Perez + Kelly Abell + TM Witko
Susan Burdorf + J. Nichole Parkins
Laura Stapleton + L. Marshall James

If you enjoyed this book be sure to check out the first Thrill of the Hunt Anthology.

In this Collection of Suspenseful Tales take a ride on the wild side with us as we explore the paranormal, psychological and frightening turns your life can take.
With a Foreword by Award Winning author Jana Oliver, open your minds and enjoy the ride.

L.E.Perez ~ Devil's Cut
Katerina 'Kat' DelaVida is faced with a dark destiny when an old sword slices open a future filled with death. The darkness of the blade threatens to overwhelm her at every turn, as does the mysterious man who wants to take possession of it.

Kelly Abell ~ Sweet Revenge
Destiny Dove is really in it deep this time. In trying to help a Shade discover his killer, she becomes trapped in his desperate need for Sweet Revenge.

TM Witko ~ Shattered Glass
For Eileen Marshall, life was simple enough. Teach, come home to her husband, wake up and do it again. But when new student Marcy Daniels enters her classroom her life is turned upside down. The events that follow prove just how dangerous the girl is, but is it real or only in her mind? The truth may very well destroy her like a piece of shattered glass.

Susan Burdorf ~ Eye of the Beholder
Dive into The Pet Stoppe, where Shelley has returned home to help her mother run the popular pet shop. When a strange and exciting woman with two poodles enters the shop,

Shelley changes her mind about life and love forever. The woman's murder has Shelley being stalked by two men, one who loves her and one who wants to kill her. Who is who is the question. Missing diamonds, a supposed haunted house, and a couple of dogs who save the day remind Shelley that life is meant to be lived.

LEAK ~ J. Nichole Parkins
All of her coworkers were dead - or so Lydia claimed. A simple coin toss had spared her life. On the run, she's fleeing across the country, trying to keep her family safe in a race against time and nature. Will their luck hold, or is it too late for them all?

Imposter ~ Laura Stapleton
A fake doctor played the medical hero with Dr. Aaron Nicholson's credentials. No one died, but what about the next patient the identity thief treats? Afraid of the next time this guy impersonates him, Aaron must find out who his imposter is before someone dies.

Follow ~ L. Marshall James
Jil's beautiful son is dead. Despite counseling and the passage of time, her unbearable sorrow persists. Desperate to find a way to let go, she visits a medium with the hope of contacting her son. She says she is willing to give anything for her son. Soon, she may find that anything is not enough

Buy Your Copy Today on Amazon

Thrill of the Hunt: A Collection of Suspenseful Tales

www.ingramcontent.com/pod-product-compliance
Lightning Source LLC
Chambersburg PA
CBHW071217250626
47163CB00001B/17